COLD DAWN

CARLA NEGGERS

COLD DAWN

ISBN-13: 978-1-61664-892-3

COLD DAWN

Printed in U.S.A.

To Margaret Marbury and Adam Wilson—
many thanks!

One

Black Falls, Vermont—late February

Nick Martini rolled out of the four-poster bed in his spacious room in an older part of Black Falls Lodge and turned on a light on his bedside table. He glanced at the clock radio.

Four-thirty.

"Hell," he said, tempted to crawl back under the down comforter.

Instead he stood up on a thick, brightly colored carpet—yellow sunflowers against a blue background—on the pine-board floor and walked over to the double windows, their cream-colored drapes pulled tightly shut against the Vermont cold.

He'd arrived after dark last night. It'd still be dark out now.

He opened the drapes, anyway.

Yep. Dark.

He felt the below-freezing outside air seep through the windows but left the drapes open. In Southern California, he'd be asleep. Even in northern New England, with the three-hour time difference, he should be asleep. After his long flight yesterday and his drive from a small airport an hour north of the lodge, he'd almost turned around and found somewhere else to spend the night.

He'd always expected he'd check out Black Falls, Vermont, at some point, but it wasn't his ten-year friendship with Sean Cameron, his business partner and fellow smoke jumper in California, that had finally brought him East to the Green Mountains and Cameron country.

It was a serial arsonist. A killer.

And it was Sean's sister, Rose.

Nick looked over at the bed with its posts and pictured Rose in his bed in Beverly Hills eight months ago, her skin glowing in the aftermath of their lovemaking. She'd caught him staring at her and had pulled the sheet over her nakedness, as if only realizing just then what a huge mistake she'd made.

He raked a hand through his hair and bolted for the bathroom, with its gleaming porcelain and chrome and its soft, ultrawhite towels. He turned on the shower and tore open a bar of Vermont-made goat's milk soap while he waited for the water to heat up. He climbed in, stood under the stream of water as hot as he could stand and told himself he still could turn back.

He didn't have to see anyone else in Black Falls.

He didn't have to see Rose.

For ten years he'd fought wildfires, and for six years he'd served on a navy submarine. He'd faced dangers and hardships, and he'd seen people die—he'd come close to death himself. He'd always done his best and acted honorably, even when he'd screwed up.

Until Rose Cameron.

As he shut off the shower and reached for a towel, he could taste her mouth, feel her breasts under his palms, hear her soft cries as she'd climaxed under him, clawing at him, sobbing his name.

They'd known exactly what they were doing that night.

Exactly.

Nick toweled off and got dressed in the warmest clothes he'd packed. He doubted he'd pass for a Vermont mountain man, but he didn't care. He headed out to the hall, shutting his door quietly behind him and taking the stairs down to the lobby. The lodge, long owned and operated by the Cameron family, hadn't seemed crowded when he'd arrived at nine o'clock last night. From what he'd learned from Sean over the years, it drew its biggest crowds in the warm-weather months.

Just as well, considering the spate of violence the town had experienced since the fall.

Since last spring, really.

A brochure tacked open on a bulletin board in the lobby listed daily winter activities. Nick could take his pick of such diversions as snowshoeing, cross-country skiing, arts and crafts, yoga, nature walks and dance lessons. He wouldn't lack for things to do, except he wasn't at the lodge for fun.

A fire was already crackling in the stone fireplace just down from the front desk, where A. J. Cameron, the flinty eldest of the four Cameron siblings, stood, still in his canvas jacket. His blue eyes and the hard set of his jaw reminded Nick of Rose. She'd said Sean was the charmer of the family.

It definitely wasn't A.J.

Or her, for that matter.

"Coffee's available," A.J. said. "Breakfast doesn't start until six."

"That's fine. I thought I'd head over to the Whittaker estate. Sean mentioned Rose has been training her search-and-rescue dog out there one or two mornings a week." Nick tried to sound matter-of-fact instead of like a man who'd impulsively slept with the Cameron brothers' baby sister at a vulnerable moment in her life. "He says she's an early bird."

A.J. unzipped his jacket. Unlike his two younger brothers, he'd lived in Vermont his entire life. So had Rose, but as a search management consultant and member of an expert disaster search-and-rescue team, she traveled frequently.

Her eldest brother frowned. "I suppose you want to see for yourself where Sean nearly got himself killed last month."

"Yes," Nick said carefully, settling on an incomplete answer. "I'm up. Might as well get moving."

A.J. didn't relax, but he didn't look suspicious, either. "I take it you know Rose from her trips out to California."

"We've run into each other a few times when she's stopped in to see Sean."

That was Nick's rehearsed answer, and he thought he delivered it reasonably well.

The Cameron blue eyes narrowed. Nick understood A.J.'s scrutiny. For eighteen months, quiet, cerebral Lowell Whittaker had run a network of paid killers, putting people who wanted someone killed together with people willing to do the killing. During that time, he and his wife, Vivian, had bought a country home in Black Falls.

Now they both were under arrest—Lowell on serious, multiple charges for his role as a murderous mastermind; Vivian, for attempted murder. She was cooperating with authorities to get the charges reduced. Her husband wasn't cooperating with anyone, including, apparently, his own lawyers, who were urging him to turn over any information he had on his killers, his clients and their victims and potential victims.

Among Lowell Whittaker's past victims was Drew Cameron, the seventy-seven-year-old father of A.J., Elijah, Sean and Rose Cameron, killed last April after he'd come too close to figuring out the Black Falls newcomer wasn't the gentleman farmer he pretended to be.

At first, Drew Cameron's death in an early-spring snowstorm had appeared to be accidental. By November, everyone knew better. He'd been murdered—deliberately left to die of exposure—by two of Lowell Whittaker's assassins, both now dead themselves.

In between April and November, Rose Cameron had turned up in Los Angeles to lead a training session.

And now here I am, Nick thought.

A.J. tilted his head back. "You want to tell me what you're doing in Vermont?"

"Curiosity," Nick said with a smile.

A.J. didn't press him further and gave Nick directions. And why not? Why shouldn't any of the Camerons trust him with their sister?

No reason. None at all.

"I have no regrets about last night," Rose had told him that morning in June. "I just want to go home to Vermont and pretend it never happened. I won't say anything to anyone. I hope you won't, either."

Nick had promised her he'd keep his mouth shut.

He thanked A.J. for the directions and went out into the frigid mountain air. His jacket, boots and gloves weren't rated for temperatures in the low teens, but they'd have to do. The sky was lightening, Cameron Mountain looming across the quiet road that ran along a ridge above the village of Black Falls. The Camerons' mountain resort consisted of the main lodge, cottages, a shop, a recreational building and several hundred acres of picturesque meadows and woods that hooked up with public land, offering guests an extensive network of trails for hiking, mountain biking and backcountry skiing.

Another time, Nick thought.

His rented car started on the first try. Given the winter conditions and mountain roads, he'd gone with all-wheel drive. He followed the ridge past a line of bare maple trees to an intersection that A.J. had described as Harper Four Corners. A former early nineteenth-century tavern Sean owned was on one corner. Across from it was an old cemetery, its rectangular slabs of granite tombstones etched against the predawn sky. A white-steepled church occupied the corner across from the cemetery. On the fourth corner was a crumbling barn.

Sean had tried to explain his hometown of Black Falls, but Nick could see for himself as he turned up past the tavern and old barn, onto Cameron Mountain Road. He knew Rose's house was up here somewhere.

She lived a totally different life from his in Southern California.

Eventually the road wound its way to a shallow, rock-strewn river, frozen and snow-covered in the Vermont winter cold. He came to a sprawling, boarded-up farmhouse on an open hilltop above the river. It had partially burned in January when Lowell Whittaker had set off a bomb, hoping to kill his wife and a local stonemason he was trying to frame. His wife had figured out what was going on, saved herself and left Bowie O'Rourke, the stonemason, to die in the fire. Sean had saved O'Rourke. Vivian Whittaker now insisted she'd been in shock. The truth was, she'd wanted her husband to get away with murder.

Just not *her* murder.

Nick had seen pictures of the Whittakers. They looked like an ordinary, upper-class couple.

He pulled into an icy but plowed turnaround and parked next to a black Volvo sedan. It wasn't Rose's. He didn't know as much about her as he should, given their brief, intense love affair—never mind that she was Sean's sister—but he did know she drove a Jeep.

So who owned the Volvo?

He grimaced as he got out of his car. What if she were

meeting some guy here and just didn't want her brothers to know? The prying eyes of a small town and all that. He hadn't seen or even been in touch with Rose in eight months. He couldn't expect her to keep her life on hold, especially since she was pretending their night together had never happened.

He wasn't. He hadn't spoken of it and wouldn't, but he wasn't about to pretend it had never happened. He wanted to remember every second of making love to her, even if it had been a mistake.

A big one.

Nick hunched his shoulders against a cold breeze and headed onto a shoveled walk that led to a small stone house that he knew, from Sean's descriptions, was the Whittakers' guesthouse. He noticed footprints in the blanket of white on the slope up to the main farmhouse. He didn't much feel like a trek through knee-deep snow. All he needed was to trip and end up having Rose Cameron and her search-and-rescue dog come find him.

He stepped into one of the prints, a clump of wet snow falling into his boot. Served him right, he thought, and followed the prints, which looked relatively fresh, to the edge of the woods above the river. He figured he could always forget this whole thing, backtrack to his car and go have pancakes at the lodge, but he continued up toward the farmhouse.

The breeze stirred again as he crested the hill.

He smelled smoke in the air and went still.

The smell was distinct, unmistakable and recent. Nick was positive it wasn't the residue of the January fire that had almost killed two people and burned down the place.

He dipped past a white pine and squinted up at the gray clapboard farmhouse. The sunrise glowed on the horizon, its deep pink color spreading across the sky.

Something was wrong. Badly wrong.

Rose.

Nick moved faster through the snow.

Two

Rose Cameron paused on the shoveled walk up to the farmhouse that had been built in the 1920s by a New Yorker with a romantic view of Vermont. Too expensive for Black Falls residents, it had always been owned by out-of-staters, but none, she thought, quite like the despicable Lowell and Vivian Whittaker.

But Rose didn't want to think about them and shifted her attention to Ranger, her eight-year-old golden retriever, as he ran into the snow along the edge of the walk. He looked good, she thought. Healthy and agile, not as stiff as earlier in the winter. Taking the time to concentrate on training was paying off. She'd parked her Jeep in the main driveway, and he'd jumped out, as eager as a puppy.

She smiled as she watched the vibrant fuchsia and purples of dawn melt into the early-morning sky. The cold weather didn't faze her. She was dressed for it. She appreciated the solitude and quiet beauty of the riverside estate, with its stone walls, mature maples and oaks and rich landscaping. She wanted to believe that the classic, picturesque setting would help everyone—including a future buyer—forget its last owners.

State and federal investigators had finished their work over a month ago, covering every inch of the place in search of evidence. Nowadays only the occasional local cruiser would swing by. Rose had never seen one this early in the weeks she'd been coming out here.

Ranger gave a short bark, getting her attention. She turned from the sunrise and saw that he was looking at her, expectantly, from his position near a shed behind the boarded-up farmhouse. He was clearly confused, but she couldn't figure out why.

A light breeze blew up from the river, bringing with it the faint but distinct smell of smoke. It was jarring, unexpected.

Now she understood what was bothering her dog.

Rose signaled for him to wait and moved toward him. The smell didn't dissipate. It was strong, persistent, unnatural in the clean winter environment. The farmhouse had sustained extensive fire, smoke and water damage in January. Could someone have removed the plywood from one of the windows and somehow let out fresh smells of the fire?

"Ranger, come."

He obeyed, pushing his way through the heavy, wet snow back out to the walk. She instructed him to heel to her left—her nondominant side—and continued with him around to the back of the house, stopping in front of the shed. She peered down the wide, open slope toward the stone guesthouse of Lowell Whittaker's dream-come-true gentleman's farm. The early-morning light created undulating shadows in the undisturbed drifts of snow. There was no sign of anyone else there. No smoke from the guesthouse chimney, no footprints in the snow.

The breeze stopped, the stillness and silence almost complete. The river was frozen, no sound of its steady flow east to the Connecticut River. That would come later, with the spring thaw.

She could hear only Ranger panting next to her, awaiting her next command. He was an experienced search dog, but she hadn't told him what to do. She hadn't expected the smell of smoke and had to decide whether to check for its source or go ahead and call it in.

The sun rose over the horizon and sparkled on the snow, the sky turning to a clear, cold blue. She'd dressed in layers and was warm in her windproof and insulated outdoor clothing, but she'd left her ready pack in her Jeep. She and Ranger weren't here on a mission. She patted him on his broad head. He was patient but paying close attention to the situation. They had encountered charred conditions in their work together, although not since last summer in Southern California.

Now wasn't the time to think about that experience.

Rose noticed the door to the shed was padlocked. Lowell Whittaker had stacked cordwood out front, playing the congenial new neighbor while inside the shed he'd assembled at least three different crude pipe bombs.

She stood back from the door. The unoccupied buildings, the fire damage and the mix of open space, woods and river provided a challenging environment for keeping her high-energy search-and-rescue dog exercised and on top of his game. For the past six weeks, every Wednesday at dawn, and sometimes more often, they'd headed out whatever the weather—rain, snow, sleet, freezing rain, fog, frigid temperatures. Except for the occasional passing car or truck, they'd never encountered a soul.

Could someone have camped out here, or stopped to check out where a wealthy killer mastermind had lived—where two homemade bombs had gone off?

The doors to the house were covered up with plywood. Getting in would require a crowbar or ax. The temperature was just in the upper teens now, but Rose wondered if the wet, warmer conditions over the past few days had brought out the smells of smoke and burnt wood.

Ranger raised his head, nose in the air as he sniffed, alerting to a fresh scent. She gave him a signal to follow the scent. He moved quickly, leading her onto a narrow, icy path that circled around to an ell off the back of the shed, facing the woods above the river.

Her normally playful, inquisitive golden barked fiercely, stopping at the solid wood door to the ell. Rose saw that it was ajar, its padlock broken in half.

The scent of smoke was sharp, nauseating.

She got Ranger back to her left side and signaled for him to stay. He sat on the path, panting but quiet, and she tapped the door, opening it farther. If any part of the shed had burned in January, she'd have heard about it.

She peered inside. The sun didn't reach the solitary eyebrow window high up on the back wall, and her eyes weren't adjusted to the dim light inside.

She kicked the door open wider, letting in more light

and gagged at the overpowering odor of burnt flesh, burnt hair, burnt clothing.

With a gloved hand over her mouth, Rose stepped onto the threshold. A sleeping bag and a backpack lay on the rough wood floor to the right of the door, as if someone had just popped in and dumped them off. The ell was small, used primarily to store old furniture and seldom-used yard equipment.

She steeled herself against what she knew she would see and, remembering her training, focused on the task at hand.

Someone was dead in here, possibly someone she knew.

Her eyes adjusted to the dim light. In the back corner, the body of a man lay sprawled facedown on the floor. He was clearly dead, badly burned from his waist up, unrecognizable. Bits of glass and metal were embedded in his neck, head and upper torso. Something—a kerosene lamp, perhaps—must have exploded, and he'd taken the full brunt of the ensuing flames and shrapnel.

The fire appeared to be out. Rose suspected he'd extinguished any flames when he'd hit the floor, either from the impact of the blast or from trying to save himself. He'd almost certainly been dead hours before she and Ranger had left her house in the predawn darkness.

She could make out strands of dark blond hair that hadn't burned. He appeared to be about six feet tall and had on insulated pants, thick socks and good boots that were untouched by the flames. Rose noticed he wasn't wearing a coat and glanced to the side wall, where an expensive parka hung on the back of an old wooden chair.

Why camp out here, in the cold? How had he gotten here? Had he been hiking in the woods along the river? Had he been lost, unaware of who owned the property, and seized on a dry spot to spend the night?

Was his death just bad luck?

Had Lowell left behind a clever little bomb that the victim happened to trigger?

Rose shook off her questions. A basic tenet of her work was to stick to the facts and not leap ahead. Nothing indicated the man he was, but she knew she needed to let the police check his backpack and coat pockets for identification.

She stepped back outside, where Ranger was still in position, waiting for her. "Oh, Ranger," she said quietly. "It's not a pretty scene in there."

She pulled off a glove and dug her cell phone out of a jacket pocket. As part of a regional wilderness search team, she and Ranger generally dealt with lost or injured hikers, Alzheimer's patients who'd become disoriented, runaways in over their heads in the woods. Shock and hypothermia were usually the biggest concern, but they'd encountered scrapes, bruises, broken bones, head injuries and heart attacks.

And death, she thought.

Their disaster work was often intense, but this was different. She'd been caught off guard, and she and Ranger weren't with a team. They were alone.

She couldn't get a cell signal and motioned for Ranger to go with her around to the front of the shed.

Lowell Whittaker had used a cell phone to detonate two bombs on his property. There had to be a signal out here somewhere.

She heard a movement in the woods just as Ranger stiffened and barked once. She quieted him with a hand command and steadied her footing, prepared to run or defend herself. She could grab a hunk of cordwood, a shovel. She wasn't entirely sure how Ranger would react if she were attacked. He wasn't trained in apprehension and his work in search and rescue, as well as his temperament, made him comfortable around strangers.

A shadow fell on the snow and a man walked out from behind a spruce tree.

Rose took in the short-cropped gray hair, the dark eyes, the strong jaw and lean, fit body and motioned to her golden retriever to remain at her side.

Sexy, rugged Nick Martini was in Vermont, less than ten yards from a dead man.

Less than five yards from her.

"Hello, Rose."

His voice was tight, controlled, his gaze narrowed on her. She closed her fingers around her cell phone.

Eight months ago, they'd fallen into each other's arms after another fire, another death.

"Nick," she said, her own voice tight. "There's been a fire. A man's dead."

"I know. I saw."

"I have to call the police." She noticed she had a signal and hit 911. "Why are you here?"

"I was looking for you. I stayed at the lodge last night. A.J. gave me directions here."

"A.J.?"

"Your brother."

"I know who he is. In Vermont—why are you in Vermont?"

"Later."

"Is Sean with you?"

"Sean's in California."

Her call went through and the dispatcher came on. Rose gave him the details, her voice crisp, professional, even as her mind raced with the possibilities of who the victim could be—of why she was standing in Nick Martini's shadow on a cold, bright Vermont morning.

"The police are on the way," she said as she disconnected. She debated calling A.J. but dropped her phone back into her pocket. She'd wait for the police and the firefighters, get through their questions, before she tried to talk to her brother. "Do you know who the victim is?"

Nick shook his head, his eyes still on her, as if he were taking in every movement she made, every breath she took. "What about you? Any idea who it is?"

"No, none." She slipped her gloves back on. "He had a sleeping bag and backpack. He must have planned to camp out in the shed. It looks as if he didn't have much time to get settled before the fire."

"The fire's been out for a while," Nick said, not casually but not with a lot of emotion. "It looks as if a kerosene lamp exploded."

"That's what I thought, too, but kerosene wouldn't just explode like that."

"Maybe the lamp wasn't filled with kerosene."

Rose blinked against the bright sun and tried to accustom herself to Nick's presence. He was dressed warmly, but not for an extended period in cold winter conditions. As if to remind her of the weather, a gust of wind struck her full in the face, numbing her cheeks. Nick had his back to it and seemed not to notice.

"When did you get here?" she asked him.

"Just before you did. I parked at the guesthouse. Another car's parked there. A black Volvo. It has Vermont tags and a several alpine skiing bumper stickers."

Rose's stomach lurched, and she could feel her legs buckling under her.

A Volvo. Ski stickers.

Derek.

"Rose?" Nick's arm shot out, and he grabbed her by the shoulder, hard, steadying her. "Who does the car belong to?"

"I can't say for sure."

"Who, Rose?"

Her jaw ached from tension. "A private ski instructor named Derek Cutshaw."

Nick's intense dark eyes narrowed even more.

She eased herself from his grasp. "I don't know it's Derek. He could have loaned his car to someone. It could be stolen. We can't jump to conclusions."

"If it is this Derek?"

"We're not friends, if that's what you're asking."

Nick made no response. He kept his gaze pinned on her, assessing, probing. He was a skilled firefighter and a highly successful businessman in a very tough, competitive world. He was used to scrutinizing people, seeing through them—gauging what was in their minds, if not, Rose thought, in their hearts.

"He's not local," she added in a half whisper. "He's not from Vermont."

Rose didn't tell Nick that if she'd seen Derek's car, she'd have turned around and gone home without stopping.

"Where's he from?"

She looked down past the main driveway to the quiet road, avoiding eye contact with Nick. "Colorado, I think."

"What else?"

"Nothing," she said. "There's nothing else."

"Did he know you train Ranger out here?"

His tone edged close to inquisitorial but she ignored it and gave him a straightforward answer. "It's not a secret. Ranger's very familiar with my house and the surrounding area. There are good challenges for him here—the river, the woods, ledges, open ground and, frankly, the fire damage." She shifted back to Nick and added, keeping her own tone neutral, "And it's quiet. No disruptions."

"Until today."

The wind gusted again, blowing through his short hair. His skin was California-tanned. Rose imagined her own was red from the cold. She knew the basics about him, mostly from Sean. Nick's father was a retired navy captain. His mother was a geology professor. They lived in San Diego. He had one sister, a navy officer. Nick had served on a submarine for six years. After the navy, he'd trained and then worked full-time as a smoke jumper.

He and Sean had pooled their resources, bought a run-down building in L.A., renovated it, sold it and turned a profit, thus launching Cameron & Martini. They both continued to fight wildland fires.

That was how Rose had seen Nick last June: as a fire-fighter. Only when she'd entered his condo in Beverly Hills had she remembered that he was also a multimillionaire…and her brother's best friend.

At least at first. Once Nick had kissed her, she'd forgotten everything else.

Ranger rubbed against her leg, as if he knew she needed to get her head back in the game.

Nick touched her chin with a gloved finger, moving her head gently so that she was facing him and couldn't avert her eyes. "You're not in good shape, Rose. No BS, okay? Were you meeting this guy, Derek Cutshaw, here?"

"No."

"Were you seeing him?"

"No, Nick, I wasn't seeing him." Not now, she thought. She wished she could say not ever, but it wasn't true. "Ranger and I have been coming out here at the same time, on the same day, for the past six weeks." She pulled back from Nick, and he lowered his hand, although his intensity didn't lessen. "That doesn't mean Derek—or whoever is back there in the shed—was here to meet me."

"When's the last time you saw him?"

"A few weeks ago. In town. We didn't talk. I hadn't realized until then he was even in Vermont."

A town cruiser barreled around a curve and turned into the main driveway, closely followed by a fire truck and ambulance. Rose felt her mouth and throat go dry as she watched Zack Harper, a firefighter she'd grown up with, jump down from his truck and glance in her direction, as if to say *not again.*

A state cruiser pulled in behind the town cruiser. Rose was surprised to see Scott Thorne behind the wheel.

She glanced at Nick. "I thought Scott was in California with Beth Harper."

"He came home early."

"When?"

"Monday night. He only stayed the weekend."

Rose frowned. Why hadn't Beth told her? But that was her friend Beth, a paramedic who was closemouthed about her love life if about nothing else.

Then again, Rose thought, she was standing next to a man she'd made love to on one wild night, and another man who hadn't wanted to take no for an answer was likely dead a few yards from her—and almost no one knew about her association with either of them.

She watched Scott walk up the driveway, grim and ramrod straight in his trooper's uniform. He was a fair, strongly built man with little sense of humor. Rose hated to see him and Beth go their separate ways, but the violence of the past months had been hard on everyone.

She wondered if the FBI and the ATF would be next to descend on the scene, perhaps even the Secret Service. Vice President Preston Neal and his wife and five children had visited Black Falls in early February and planned to come for the winter festival at the lodge in a couple of weeks. It was meant to celebrate the last days of winter and to put the violence of the past months behind them.

Everyone believed Lowell Whittaker's arrest had put his killer network out of business.

Rose felt Nick standing close to her. Did *he* believe it? She remembered him sweeping her into his arms last June, holding her tight as he pushed back the memories of a friend who'd died earlier that day in a wildland fire.

The friend, Jasper Vanderhorn, had been an arson investigator obsessed with a serial arsonist.

She turned, facing Nick. "Are you in Vermont because of Jasper? Do you think his serial arsonist followed you and killed Derek?"

Scott Thorne was within a few yards of reaching them. More police cars and fire trucks arrived. Nick's expression didn't change. "Not now," he said.

"We're not done yet, Nick."

He fixed his gaze on her. "That's right. We're not."

Three

Rose welcomed the cold air as she let Ranger out of the back of her Jeep. She'd parked in front of Three Sisters Café on Main Street, across from the common in the middle of the village of Black Falls. She wondered if Sean had ever tried to explain their hometown to Nick over mojitos by the pool, or looking out at the view of Beverly Hills from their Wilshire Boulevard offices.

She'd left Nick with two state detectives.

She snapped a leash on Ranger and, bypassing the café's main entrance, went into the 1835 brick house through its center-hall door. Sean owned the building. Three of Rose's friends—"sisters" in spirit—had converted the corner rooms into a breakfast-and-lunch enterprise that few in town had believed would survive six months. Almost two years later, it was thriving.

Without waiting to be told, Ranger lay down in the hall. He looked tired. Rose had given him a treat and water in the Jeep, but he wasn't as resilient as he'd been even just a year ago. She suspected he was reacting to her stress as much as his own at the unexpected scene on the river. A body burned beyond recognition. The likelihood that the victim was a man she knew and had hoped was long out of her life.

Nick's presence.

She took off Ranger's leash, hung it on a peg on the wall and entered the café. The early-morning rush was over, the only customers three middle-aged women fresh from their yoga class up the street. They'd leaned their rolled-up mats against the wall and were enjoying house-made yogurt, fresh fruit and muffins at a table overlooking Elm Street.

Dominique Belair, one of the café's three owners, was behind the glass case, her fine dark hair pulled back neatly but her face pale, her brown eyes wide, shining with worry. "I heard about the fire," she said as she reached for a mug in the café's evergreen signature color. "Is it true the man who died is Derek Cutshaw?"

"There hasn't been a positive ID," Rose said, pulling off her coat. She'd left her hat and gloves in her Jeep. "His car's at the guesthouse and footprints lead to the shed where the body was found."

"So yes, it's Derek. I can't imagine what it must have been like for you to go out there expecting a beautiful morning with Ranger and finding..." Dominique shuddered and pointed the mug at the glass case. "You should eat something. Coffee and a scone?"

Rose had brought a breakfast bar with her to the Whittaker place but hadn't touched it. Now it was almost lunchtime. She couldn't imagine eating and yet knew she had to. She nodded and attempted a smile. "That'd be great."

Dominique filled the mug from a coffee urn on a counter behind her, then pulled a cinnamon scone off a stack on a tray and set it on a small plate. She handed both the mug and plate to Rose. "Anything else I can get you?"

"No, thanks," Rose said. "This is perfect."

Dominique started to say something, but another customer entered the café and Rose took her coffee and scone to a table overlooking the river that ran behind the café. She wasn't sure why she'd come here. To have a few moments to herself, or to be among friends? Or just to avoid being alone at her house, or going up to the lodge and talking to her brother A.J. about what had happened—about Nick Martini and Derek Cutshaw?

She noticed Myrtle Smith come through the kitchen door behind the glass case. At fifty-four, Myrtle was tiny, with dyed black hair, lavender eyes and bright red nails. She'd been helping out at the café since January, when Hannah Shay, another of the three "sisters," had departed for Southern California with her two younger brothers, not to mention, Rose thought, one Sean Cameron. He and Hannah, a recent law school graduate, had exposed Lowell Whittaker as a killer.

Myrtle was an experienced Washington reporter who'd been touched by Lowell's violence herself when he'd arranged for the poisoning murder of a Russian diplomat she'd been involved with. Her investigation into his death ultimately had led her to Black Falls.

She headed straight for Rose's riverside table. "I hate

to speak ill of the dead," Myrtle said, dropping into a chair across from Rose, "but Derek Cutshaw could be one unpleasant human being."

Rose didn't comment. "When did you see him last?"

"About two weeks ago. I haven't seen him since. Dom, either. I don't know about Beth."

Beth Harper was the third "sister" who co-owned the café. She was in Beverly Hills visiting Sean and Hannah. Beth, her brother and Scott Thorne had flown back to California with them last Friday. Zack had always planned to stay just through the weekend. Not Scott.

"What about Hannah?" Rose asked. "Have you or Dom been in touch with her?"

"Dom said she'd call both Beth and Hannah when she knew more. They're supposed to be having fun—swimming in Sean's pool, shopping on Rodeo Drive, watching for Hollywood stars."

"Scott Thorne's back. Did you know that?"

"I'd heard," Myrtle said but didn't elaborate.

Rose decided not to try to figure out Beth's love life. Her own was complicated enough, or at least had been. Nowadays it was downright simple: no love life.

"What about your brothers?" Myrtle asked. "Have you talked to them?"

"No, not yet."

A.J. would be at the lodge. Elijah, her middle brother, a Special Forces soldier, was in Washington, D.C., with Jo Harper, Zack and Beth's older sister, a Secret Service agent. Sean, the youngest of the three Cameron brothers, was home in Beverly Hills with Hannah, who was still figuring out her life. Rose had no doubt they were as in love as they had been in January. Their feelings weren't rooted in the adrenaline of their encounter with the Whittakers. They'd been destined for each other since high school.

They were soul mates, if one believed in such things.

The yoga group departed, and the café was quiet. Rose stared down at the ice jams on the river, vaguely aware of Dominique setting a plate of quiche and fresh fruit in front of her.

She thanked Dominique before realizing her friend had already gone.

She felt Myrtle observing her as she tried a bit of her cinnamon scone. Only recently had she decided that what her family and friends didn't know about the past twelve months of her life wasn't anything she was hiding from them so much as letting be. She'd moved on, or had tried to.

Except now Derek Cutshaw was almost certainly dead, and Nick Martini was in Black Falls.

And walking into the café, Rose thought with a grimace, watching out of the corner of her eye as he glanced in her direction and headed to the glass case. His jacket was open, and he moved as if he didn't have anything more momentous on his mind than figuring out what kind of coffee to order.

Myrtle raised her thin, penciled eyebrows. "You know him?"

Rose realized her expression must have given her away. She tried to appear more neutral. "That's Nick Martini. He's—"

"The Martini of Cameron & Martini and another smoke jumper," Myrtle said with interest. "When did he get here?"

"Last night. He was at the fire this morning."

"You're friends?"

"I don't know him that well," Rose said truthfully.

Nick came over to their table, and, coffee in hand, pulled out a chair and sat down without waiting to be invited. "Nice spot," he said, nodding to the frozen river. "Same river we were just on?"

"Yes," Rose said, her voice almost inaudible. She picked up her fork and tried the quiche. Spinach, cheese, mushroom. She had no appetite for it, but it was warm and tasted good—and she knew she needed something more substantial than a scone.

Nick's dark eyes settled on Myrtle. "You must be Myrtle Smith. I'm Nick Martini. Sean's told me about you."

"I'm sorry," Rose said. "I should have introduced you."

"It's all right," Myrtle said, obviously already taken in by Nick's good looks and compelling presence.

Nick glanced out the window again. "I saw Beth and Hannah at Sean's pool yesterday before I headed East." He shifted back to Myrtle. "You're filling in for Hannah. Who's filling in for Beth?"

"Dominique hired a new part-timer," Myrtle said, "but there's no way to replace either Hannah or Beth."

Nick grinned. "That's diplomatic."

"I'm not staying in Vermont."

Myrtle seemed to be trying to convince herself as

much as anyone else. She'd arrived in Black Falls in November, after surviving a suspicious fire at her house that had destroyed her office and all the materials she'd methodically compiled detailing a network of paid assassins. She'd stayed at the lodge at first but two weeks had ago moved into Hannah's apartment above the café.

Whenever Rose saw her, Myrtle insisted she'd be back in Washington soon.

She got to her feet, retying her evergreen canvas apron. "I should get busy. I've been showing Dominique the art of making a four-layer fresh coconut cake like my mother used to make."

Rose gave her a distracted smile. "Can't go wrong with coconut cake."

"You can if you haven't made one in twenty years. Vermont seems to have brought out my Southern roots." Myrtle sighed heavily, obviously distracted herself. "People can't resist a good coconut cake. It looks like springtime itself."

Nick shrugged. "I think it looks like snow."

"We don't get much snow in South Carolina where I'm from. We have a real spring there."

"It's still February," Rose said, relaxing a little. "Spring's not for another month."

Myrtle grunted. "It won't be spring here even then. You all can get snow well into April." She winced, looking stricken. "I can't believe I just said that. I'm sorry. I don't mean to be cavalier."

Nick's eyes were half-closed, but he said nothing. Rose wondered where he'd been last April when her father had died on Cameron Mountain. Fighting a wildland fire? Making a deal for Cameron & Martini? Flying off somewhere in his private plane with a woman?

After all, what did she know about Nick Martini?

She and Ranger had searched for her father after he'd been caught in an fierce April snowstorm on the remote north side of Cameron Mountain, but it was Devin Shay, Hannah's younger brother, who'd found him.

The storm hadn't killed him. Lowell Whittaker's paid assassins had, on Lowell's orders.

"It's okay," Rose said quietly. "We're all ready to make our peace with the past. Pop wouldn't want us to be miserable. He'd want us to be happy." She smiled. "Coconut cake is happy."

Myrtle glanced out at the bright, snowy landscape, as if she couldn't quite believe she was there, working in a Vermont café. "It's made with egg whites. My mother would use the leftover egg yolks for boiled custard."

Rose raised her eyebrows in an exaggerated manner. "Boiled custard, Myrtle?"

"Best stuff in the world. It's like a cross between eggnog and pudding."

"Sounds wonderful. How much longer can you hang in here?"

She turned from the window and gave a short laugh. "When you see me digging a pit out back to roast a pig for pulled pork, do an intervention, will you?"

Rose laughed, surprising herself. Myrtle seemed relieved, which told Rose just how pale she had to be. Definitely a welcome distraction, she thought, to talk about coconut cake and pulled pork instead of Nick Martini and the tragic scene out on the river.

Of course, Myrtle was no more focused on food than Rose was and fixed her lavender eyes on Nick. "Do the police suspect the fire this morning was deliberate?"

"Too early to say," Nick said.

She shifted to Rose. "What do you think?"

Rose reminded herself that the woman scrutinizing her was a veteran journalist accustomed to rooting out lies, deception and simple stonewalling. "It looks as if a kerosene lamp or something similar blcw up. Derek— the victim's upper body was badly burned."

Myrtle shuddered, turning ashen, her lips thinning as she swallowed visibly.

"It could have been an accident," Rose added.

"I've been in this town for three months. None of the untimely deaths and near-deaths here so far have been accidents." Myrtle turned back to Nick. "Sean was out here with Hannah last week for a few days. Why didn't you come with him then?"

"Work commitments," Nick said.

She obviously wasn't satisfied. "What are you doing here now?"

"Visiting."

Instead of stomping back to the kitchen, Myrtle didn't seem bothered by Nick's light sarcasm. "You and Rose know each other through Sean?"

Nick drank more of his coffee. "That we do."

"He told you she'd be out there this morning?"

"Sean did." Nick leaned over and helped himself to a chunk of Rose's scone. "What do you know about Derek Cutshaw?"

Myrtle's eyes darkened slightly. "I only met him a

couple times when he stopped in on his way to different ski areas. He was well aware he wasn't a favorite around here. What was he doing out at the Whittaker place, do you know?"

"No idea," Nick said.

"Rose?"

"No, none," she said, feeling Nick's gaze burning into her. She smiled faintly at Myrtle. "Your reporter's habits die hard."

She adjusted her apron. "They've been buried in frosting and salad fixings and frozen in the snow. Apparently Derek was sharing a ski house in Killington with some of his friends."

"How do you know?" Rose asked, surprised.

"Dominique. She knows everything. I imagine the police are up there by now." Myrtle pushed strands of black hair out of her face. "They still don't have the SOB who set fire to my house. They think it was one of Whittaker's killers, probably the same one who taught him how to make a pipe bomb. He won't say. I think he's more afraid of this guy than he is of anything the FBI can do to him."

Nick set his coffee, barely touched, back on the table. "I'm sure if there's even the remotest possibility of a connection between your fire and the one this morning, the police are all over it."

"This pyro, whoever it is, is still out there." Myrtle moved back from the window and gave Nick an unflinching look. "You're a firefighter. You must hate arson."

"Most people hate arson," he said.

"I don't own a kerosene lamp. My granny did. I

remember. What a great woman she was." Myrtle seemed to give herself a mental shake. "I'll be in the kitchen. My self-imposed northern New England exile continues. At home in South Carolina," she said, obviously attempting to lighten her mood as she headed back to the glass case, "I'd be setting out pansies."

Once Myrtle was through the swinging door to the kitchen, Rose jumped to her feet. "Dom's quiche is amazing—help yourself," she said quickly to Nick. In a few strides, she was in the center hall, fighting tears.

It would all come out. Her and Derek, her and Nick. There'd be no more secrets. No discretion. Everyone in town would know her private business.

Ranger was asleep on his back, paws in the air. She didn't want to wake him, but he rolled over on his own and got stiffly up onto all fours. She grabbed his leash and snapped it back on. For the past eight years, he'd been her constant companion. They'd done so much together. He'd been tireless, solid and reliable, but he was slowing down.

She couldn't bear to think about that now and headed outside with him. Across the street on the common, kids and teachers from a local nursery school were building snowmen. Rose could hear their laughter and hoped what she'd seen that morning had been a terrible accident.

She crossed Elm Street and continued up Main, passing the only flower shop in town, cyclamen and pots of ferns in its window, but her mind was back at the Whittaker estate. She could smell the smoke and see the pieces of glass embedded in what she knew, in her gut, was Derek Cutshaw's burned body.

There was no question in her mind. The fire hadn't been an accident.

Derek had been murdered, and his killer could still be in Black Falls.

By the time she and Ranger reached O'Rourke's, a bar and restaurant whose owner, Liam O'Rourke, was a longtime friend of all three of her brothers, Rose was aware of Nick ambling behind her. He caught up with her as she started up the stone steps to O'Rourke's front door, a couple of big green shamrocks already stuck on the glass ahead of St. Patrick's Day.

"Pretty town," Nick said as he eased in on her right side. He'd zipped up his coat, his only apparent concession to the cold walk up Main Street. "Did you ever build a snowman on the town common when you were a tot?"

"Not that I recall, no." Rose cast him a sideways glance. "I've participated in a few snowball fights, though."

"My fair warning." He glanced out at the quiet street. "A lot of questions were raised back at the café."

She pulled her hand from the door. Ranger sat quietly, expectantly, next to her.

"Rose, last March, Derek Cutshaw and two of his ski-bum friends got into a fight here at O'Rourke's with the owner's cousin, a local stonemason."

"Bowie O'Rourke," Nick said.

"Sean told you the story?"

"That's right. He, A.J. and Elijah were all in town that night. Derek insulted Hannah and wouldn't leave her alone. His friends joined in, but he was the ringleader.

Sean hauled Hannah out of here before she could rip out a few eyeballs. Bowie stayed and ended up getting arrested."

"He's still on probation," Rose said. "No charges were filed against Derek and his two friends. He hurled most of the insults. He cut close to the bone, even bringing up Hannah's mother, who used to work here before she died, and implying Hannah—well, it doesn't matter now."

"You weren't here that night."

Her mouth was dry, her heart beating rapidly. "No, I wasn't."

She yanked open the door and bolted inside ahead of Nick. Ranger flopped down in a corner. O'Rourke's only did a light lunch business, and she knew Liam wouldn't mind. She climbed onto a high stool at the dark wood bar. Nick stayed on his feet, taking in the scattering of empty tables, the deep red walls and the black-and-white framed photographs of old Black Falls. Tall, broad-shouldered Liam was behind the bar, polishing a glass with a white cloth and regarding Rose with open suspicion, as if she'd brought bad luck.

She couldn't pretend not to know Nick, and introduced him. "Liam, this is Nick Martini of Cameron & Martini."

"Yeah, I know," Liam said. "He was with you this morning. I heard. This town's too small for something like that not to get around fast. The dead man's Derek Cutshaw, isn't it?"

Rose nodded. "I'm almost positive, yes."

Liam filled the glass he'd been polishing with water

from a small stainless-steel sink, then set it in front of her. "He was in here last night."

"Alone?"

"Yeah. I haven't seen much of him this winter but I knew he was back in Vermont. He had coffee and a sandwich and left. No alcohol. He's a mean bastard when he drinks." Liam sighed. "Or was, anyway."

Rose contained any reaction. "Have you seen Bowie yet today?"

"He's working out at the lake. He'll stop in later."

If Nick knew what "out at the lake" meant, he kept it to himself. Bowie O'Rourke and Hannah Shay had grown up together in an isolated hollow a few miles past the Whittaker place. Bowie still lived there.

Rose drank some of the water Liam had placed in front of her. "Given Bowie's history with Derek and where he lives—"

"The police will want to talk to him if they haven't already," Liam said heavily. "I've had my issues with Bowie, but he had nothing to do with Cutshaw's death. You know that, don't you?"

"Of course," she said, resisting the temptation to look at Nick for his reaction.

Liam grabbed his cloth and another glass. "What about you, Rose? Have you had much to do with Cutshaw lately?"

"I barely knew him."

"Then what was he doing out at the Whittaker place?"

She drank more of her water, just to give herself something to do and repeated what she'd told the police and then Myrtle Smith. "I have no idea." She slid off the stool and stood up straight, turning to Nick, who hadn't said a word since entering O'Rourke's. "I'm sure I'll see you back at the lodge at some point."

Ranger jumped up and followed her outside. Rose grabbed his leash in one hand and broke into a run. He matched her stride, his tongue wagging, as if he thought they were finally playing—finally having the fun he'd anticipated at dawn.

The wind and cold whipped tears out of her eyes, and when she reached her Jeep, she choked back a sob and got Ranger into the back, patting him, hugging him. He was so damn soft, so warm and reliable.

"I can tell you anything, can't I, buddy?" She sniffled and stood up straight, laughing at his eager expression as he panted at her. "Good dog, Ranger. Good dog."

She shut him in and climbed into the front seat. She checked her rearview mirror but didn't see Nick on Main Street. She wouldn't be surprised if he was having a beer with Liam, getting what he could out of him about her, Derek Cutshaw and life in Black Falls.

In his place, Rose thought, she'd probably do the same.

She started the Jeep, picturing the backpack and sleeping bag in the shed. Had Derek planned to camp there, waiting for her? He wouldn't have come to her house. He'd have known she wouldn't have let him in. Out at the boarded-up farmhouse on the river, he'd have been able to catch her by surprise, force her to talk to him. But why now? Why after a year?

Nick.

Had Derek found out Nick was in town and would come to see her?

But how would he know, and why would he care?

I still care about you, Rose.

She knew better. Derek had never cared about her in any of the ways that mattered.

She pushed back her questions and circled around the common—the children and their teachers still hard at work on their snowmen—and drove out toward the lake and Bowie O'Rourke, hoping this time Nick Martini wouldn't follow her.

Four

Rose navigated the dirt road—now covered in snow and ice—along the shore of a spring-fed glacial lake a few miles outside the village and pulled in behind Bowie O'Rourke's mud-and-salt-encrusted van. He'd parked in front of the dozen small, run-down cabins on twenty acres that her father had left to Jo Harper, a shock to everyone in Black Falls, including Rose. She sometimes wondered if he'd suspected, at least intuitively, that his end was near and had deliberately put Jo into close proximity to Elijah, his second-born son, who had built a house just through the woods while on visits home from the army.

Leaving Ranger cozy in the back of her Jeep, Rose picked her way along an icy path to the cabin where Jo and Elijah had holed up when they ran off together as teenagers. An angry, frustrated Drew Cameron had discovered them. Jo, the daughter of the Black Falls police chief, had just graduated from high school. Elijah, a year older, had been knocking around town, aimless. After their three days on the lake had been disrupted, Elijah left Black Falls for boot camp and a career in the Special Forces, Jo for college and the Secret Service.

The cabin door was open, and Rose found Bowie inside, wearing his usual bright orange sweatshirt, complete with stains and tears, and baggy work pants. His black lab, Poe, was curled up on the sagging floor. Bowie was as tall and broad-shouldered as his cousin Liam, although their similarities ended there. Bowie had grown up in tougher circumstances, and his ready fists and impatience with bullies had put him on the wrong side of the law, as recently as last March when he'd stood up for Hannah in his cousin's bar.

And for me, Rose thought.

Another of her secrets.

"Hey, Rose," Bowie said, standing up from an open metal toolbox. "Where's Ranger?"

"Asleep in my Jeep."

"Afraid Poe would corrupt him?"

She reached down and rubbed the lab's stomach, then stood up straight again. "Poe's a great dog. He misbehaves from time to time, but that's not his fault."

"It's because I haven't trained him."

She smiled. "Exactly. You haven't trained him because you don't care if he misbehaves."

"True, provided he doesn't bite small children, which he doesn't." Bowie shook his head, taking in the one-room cabin and its old, musty furnishings. "Jo's crazy. She should bulldoze all these cabins and sell the land to you Camerons. The lodge could use some lakefront."

Black Falls Lodge was straight up the wooded hill behind the cabins. "Maybe she's nostalgic."

"Nostalgic? Jo?"

Rose ran her fingertips over the red-and-white-checked vinyl cloth that covered a rickety square table under the front window. "You know why I'm here, Bowie."

"Yeah. Yeah, I do. A couple of state troopers just left. They can't say for sure it was Cutshaw you found, but they know." He shrugged his big shoulders. "I answered their questions. I have nothing to hide. I'm not going to pretend I like Cutshaw any better now than I did this morning before I knew he was dead."

"When did you see him last?"

"The fight at Liam's place last year, at least as far as I know." Bowie placed a measuring tape encased in yellow plastic in his toolbox. "I'm on probation. I'm supposed to avoid alcohol, trouble and troublemakers."

Rose looked out at the lake, still and frozen in the winter sun. She could feel Bowie's eyes on her and turned to him.

"You have to back off and let the police do their job," he said, shutting his toolbox with the toe of his boot. "I have to check the rest of the cabins. Jo wants an idea of what she's up against. She knows. She just needs to hear it from someone else. Then Elijah's got some stonework for me to look at over at his place."

"Do you think Jo and Elijah will come back to Black Falls to live?"

"Eventually." He lifted his toolbox as if it weighed nothing. "Rose—"

"I'm okay, Bowie. I have some work I can do at home,

and Lauren and I are planning winter fest weekend at the lodge. Have you heard from Hannah lately?"

"Emails once in a while. None today." He jerked at thumb at Poe, who eagerly jumped up next to him. "Does she know about the fire yet?"

"I haven't talked to her."

Nick could have called Sean by now and he could have told Hannah. Rose was aware of Bowie watching her in silence. He knew about her brief, troubled relationship last winter with Derek Cutshaw but nothing about Nick.

"Rose?"

"I'm on my way to the lodge," she said. "A.J. will have heard about the fire and likely have told Sean and Elijah. I don't need those three worrying about me."

"Not much you can do to stop them. Why's it so bad to have your big brothers worry about you?"

"I can take care of myself."

"Who said you couldn't?" With his free hand, Bowie scratched Poe's head. "How'd Ranger do with the fire?"

"He was confused at first, but he figured it out. He wasn't expecting to find a body. Neither was I."

"You two make a good team."

"I think so."

"But he's a dog," Bowie said with just the slightest hint of a smile.

Rose forced herself to smile back at him. "A dog is the best friend a woman could have, short of a stonemason willing to go to prison to save her reputation—"

"I wasn't willing. It just worked out that way. I didn't have to take the fight with Cutshaw as far as I did."

"You kept him from blurting out about my past with him." She watched a small clump of snow fall off the toe of her right boot and melt onto the cabin's worn floor. "Derek was a huge mistake on my part, but he also exaggerated and outright made things up about us. You stopped him from telling lies about me that I'd never have lived down—that would have hurt me professionally."

"It's okay, Rose," Bowie said gently. "I don't need to know the details. I didn't last year, and I don't now."

She looked up at him. He'd been Hannah's friend and defender since childhood, and now he was hers. He'd seen her and Derek together at Killington and had warned her to steer clear of him. By then, she'd already broken off with him. Derek had been volatile, possessive and verbally abusive, turning a few dates into far more than they'd ever been. Embarrassed by her bad judgment, determined to get on with her life, she hadn't wanted anyone to know. Bowie had kept her secret.

Then came the fight at O'Rourke's and Bowie's arrest, and her father's death a few weeks later. She'd retreated into silence and solitude, focusing on her work.

Except for that night last June in Beverly Hills with Nick Martini.

"I would have told the police about Derek and me after your arrest last year," she said.

Bowie shrugged. "It wouldn't have made any difference."

"You don't have to hide anything on my account."

"I know that, Rose. Go on. Go see A.J. Better he hears

the full story about this morning from you than from someone else."

She grinned suddenly. "Just what I need, another big-brother type trying to boss me around."

"Like anyone can boss you around. And I'm no Cameron. Not a chance. Call me if you need me." He opened the cabin door, the sunlight catching the ends of his dark curly hair as he gave her a serious look. "I didn't have anything to do with Cutshaw's death. I'm sorry it happened. I really am. I didn't like him and didn't want anything to do with him, but he should have had a chance to mellow."

Rose placed a hand on Bowie's muscular upper arm. "We don't know what happened today. Be careful, okay?"

"Yeah. You, too."

He headed outside, and she glanced at the old iron bed, the oak veneer dresser and mismatched chairs, the crooked door to the bathroom. In the months after she'd inherited the cabins, Jo Harper had let friends, mostly in law enforcement, borrow them for a week or long weekend here and there. In November, after Charlie Neal, the vice president's genius sixteen-year-old son, played a prank on her and she ran into trouble with the Secret Service, she retreated to the best of the lot until things in Washington could cool down.

Elijah had been home from war, a hundred yards up the lake. Now Jo was wearing the diamond ring he'd bought for her fifteen years ago, when he was nineteen and she was eighteen.

Rose shut the door tight behind her, barely noticing the cold on her walk back to her Jeep. Ranger sat up and yawned as she got behind the wheel. "Funny how things work out sometimes, isn't it, buddy?"

He slumped back down, and she turned the Jeep around and headed back to the main road.

Next stop, Black Falls Lodge and her brother A.J.

With any luck, Nick wouldn't be there.

When Rose arrived at the lodge, she didn't see Nick's rented car in the parking lot. She gave Ranger a quick walk, again not bothering with her hat and gloves. She paused and squinted out at the white-covered mountains in the distance. Up closer, she noticed a few cross-country skiers on the groomed trails in the meadow behind the lodge. If she'd brought Ranger here this morning instead of to the Whittaker place, who would have discovered Derek's body? Would he even have gone out there?

Would he be alive now?

She shivered in the cold and headed inside with Ranger.

She was surprised to find Brett Griffin, one of Derek's two friends who'd been in the fight at O'Rourke's last year, standing in front of the stone fireplace in the lobby. Ranger flopped down next to him.

"It definitely was Derek," Brett said, his voice quavering as he stared at the fire, flames rising from logs cut from managed woodlots on lodge property. He didn't seem to notice the heat. His light brown hair curled below the line of his jaw, and he wore a heavy wool sweater and wind pants that were baggy on his lanky frame. "The police found me at Harper Four Corners and told me. I was taking pictures for a photography project I'm working on…." He trailed off, his anguish obvious.

"I'm sorry, Brett," Rose said, suppressing her own emotions. "I know Derek was a friend."

Ranger placed his head on Brett's boot. Brett smiled, as if forcing himself to focus. "I guess I'm still in shock. I've only been back in Black Falls a few weeks. I'm house-sitting up the road for one of my ski students. It's perfect, or so I thought."

"Have you seen much of Derek since you've been back?"

"No, not really. I haven't had much to do with him since last winter. I thought he was going to stay in Colorado, but he had established contacts in Vermont. I ran into him at Okemo last week. He seemed good." Brett faltered, glancing back at the fire. "I know we weren't favorites around here."

Rose placed a hand on the back of one the comfortable, overstuffed chairs arranged in front of the fire. "People know you weren't a big part of the fight last year. You didn't harass Hannah."

"I didn't stop Derek."

"When you saw him, did he mention he wanted to talk to me or that he planned to go out to the Whittaker place?"

"No, nothing like that. We just talked about skiing. Damn. This is awful." Brett eased his foot out from under Ranger's head. "Just what you all need."

"Never mind us. We'll get through it."

"Finding him this morning must have been hard on you."

"It was," she said softly.

Brett didn't speak for a moment. The fire crackled, glowing chunks of a log shifting as it burned. "Derek liked you, Rose. He never got into whatever went on between you two last winter, but I know he felt bad about it."

Suddenly feeling warm, she unzipped her jacket. "None of that matters now."

"I guess it doesn't. It's hard to belicvc he's dead." Brett pointed to the lobby door. "I should go."

"I can run you up the road if you'd like."

He gave a faint smile. "The exercise will do me good." He lifted a down vest off the back of a chair and shrugged it on, then snapped it up, his hands steady but his movements slow, as if every snap were a struggle. When he finished, he looked at Rose, tears shining in his pale gray eyes. "I know that fight at O'Rourke's last year wasn't Derek's first or his last. He could be a real bastard. What if someone had it in for him?"

"Who would?" Rose asked. "Just because some people didn't like him doesn't mean anyone wanted him dead."

Brett pulled a knitted hat from his vest pocket but didn't put it on, just held it bunched up in one hand. "Rose...do you think there's any chance Derek killed himself? I don't mean to be so blunt, but if his death wasn't an accident, then maybe it was suicide and not murder."

"I don't know what happened to Derek."

"Of course you don't. Sorry. Damn, this isn't what I expected when I got up this morning. I'll be around. Let me know if there's anything I can do." His cheeks reddened with embarrassment. "As if there would be. You Camerons can take care of yourselves, that's for sure. I'll see you later."

He left quickly, mumbling hello as he passed A.J. coming in.

Rose watched her older brother walk stiffly to the stone fireplace. He patted Ranger, then grabbed a log from a copper box, pulled back the screen in front of the fire and set the log on the red-hot coals. "It's quiet around here," he said, replacing the screen. "Midweek, not that many guests. Most everyone's out enjoying the good weather."

"A.J.—"

He held up a hand and turned to her, his back to the fire. "I should have stopped you from going out to the Whittaker place from the beginning. I didn't understand why you wanted to, but I wasn't going to come between you and your work—you and Ranger."

"I appreciate that."

She could see the pain in A.J.'s blue eyes, which so reminded her of their father. "You must be beat. Have you had lunch?"

"I had something at the café. I just wanted to stop by before I head home."

"You shouldn't be alone, Rose. Why don't you stay here tonight? Your favorite room's available. Or you can stay with us at the house." He seemed to make an effort to smile. "The kids love their aunt Rose."

"Thanks, but I'll be fine at home. I'll have Ranger—"

"Ranger's great, but he's still a dog."

Normally she'd have come back with a retort, but she didn't have one.

A.J. sighed and unzipped his canvas coat. "I talked to Elijah. He's debating whether to head back up here. He says he's not getting much done in D.C., anyway."

"What about Sean?" Rose asked.

"Nick Martini had already called him." A.J.'s gaze narrowed slightly. "I assume you know Nick's staying here."

"I do, yes," she said, keeping her tone neutral.

"He was just here. He grabbed a sandwich and took off again. He didn't say where he was going. He drove. That's all I know."

Rose glanced down at Ranger, settled in comfortably on the hearth. She could hear the suspicion and curiosity in her brother's voice, but he wouldn't ask her outright if there was anything personal between her and Nick. She'd wondered last week when Sean was in town if he had begun to suspect, but he hadn't said anything. Of her three brothers, Elijah was the most likely to flat-out interrogate her about her love life, but they all kept a watchful eye on her, especially since their father's death. Now Nick would be facing her brothers' scrutiny.

Would he even care?

Probably not, Rose thought.

She couldn't imagine where he'd gone. To confer with the firefighters on the scene that morning? To pry information about her from people in town?

She could hear the squeals and laughter of small children down the hall and knew they were from Jim and Baylee, her four-year-old nephew and two-year-old niece.

A.J. took in a shallow breath. "Lauren's having a hard time with this," he said, referring to his wife of five years.

"I'm sorry, A.J."

"Never mind. We'll get through it. Take care of yourself, Rose. Let us know if there's anything we can do."

"I will. Thanks."

He left her by the fire to join his wife and children in the dining room. Rose quickly got Ranger onto his feet, acknowledging with a little jolt of surprise as they headed out that she felt better for having seen her brother. She didn't lack for offers of company, friendship, solidarity and even protection, but she was looking forward to being back on her hill, alone, with her dog.

She drove out to Four Corners and turned up Cameron Mountain Road. Her small house was tucked onto a hillside, with expansive views of the surrounding mountains and valley. Anyone could stand at the top of her driveway with a pair of binoculars and see people getting in and out of cars in the Black Falls Lodge parking lot.

Which was what Lowell Whittaker had done in November.

He'd waited, watching for Melanie Kendall, one of his hired killers, to get into her car. When she did, he'd set off the crude pipe bomb he'd assembled and placed under the driver's seat. She'd screwed up an assignment and the penalty was death.

Rose had been out of town at the time. When Hannah and Sean had uncovered Lowell's role in the violence in Black Falls, they learned that he himself had killed Melanie Kendall.

But what if he'd had help?

As Rose pulled into her steep driveway, she noticed Nick's rented car parked close to a snowback and eased in next to it, sighing at Ranger. "We have company."

She noted smoke curling out of the chimney and figured Nick, being a bold type, had built a fire in her woodstove and made himself comfortable. Maybe he was taking a nap. He'd be jet-lagged, after all, and he hadn't had a good first day in Black Falls.

She and Ranger took the stone steps to the back door. She kicked off her boots in the tiled mudroom, grabbed a rag from a peg and wiped off his wet, muddy paws, then went through the cozy kitchen into the adjoining living room.

Nick was stretched out on the couch with his ankles crossed. He hadn't taken off his boots.

"Locks, Rose," he said, sitting up. "Locks."

Ranger seemed unoffended by Nick's presence and collapsed on his bed by the woodstove, a brisk fire burning behind the glass doors. Rose stayed on her feet. "I have locks."

"Doesn't matter if you don't use them."

"How much difference do you think locked doors would make if someone wanted to get in here?" She gestured out at her view of the mountains, shades of white, blue and gray in the afternoon sun. "I have no neighbors. There's no one else close enough to hear someone break a window."

He rolled up onto his feet, his dark gray sweater—probably

cashmere—falling neatly over his flat abdomen. "You're obviously not afraid living up here by yourself."

"Why should I be afraid? If you want to check the cellar and closets for intruders, go right ahead."

"Maybe I already have." He pointed to her small flat-screen television. "No cable?"

"I have DVDs, and I love to read."

"I've been through your DVDs. You have the entire collection of the new BBC Jane Austen videos and all four *Die Hard* movies. You do mystify, Rose Cameron."

She smiled. "Good."

He glanced out at the mountains. "Nightfall comes early up here in the winter. Do you have an extra bedroom or do I get the couch?"

"You get to go back to the lodge."

His eyes skimmed over her, as if he were gauging just what tone he should take with her. "Then you're staying at the lodge tonight, too?"

"I didn't say that—"

"I'll sleep in my car at the bottom of your driveway if I have to, Rose. You found a dead man this morning. Either he wanted you to find him or someone else did."

"Or his death was a terrible accident." She spun over to her woodbox and saw that he'd refilled it. "Or you were meant to find him. Have you considered that, Nick? I hadn't run into so much as a dead chipmunk at the Whittaker place. Then you show up in town, and look what happens."

"Then maybe I should stay here so you and Ranger can protect me."

"Give it up."

She felt as if she were talking to a sexy stranger, not a man she'd slept with.

Nick walked over to the front windows. "Sean mentioned that he, A.J. and Elijah read you the riot act about spending so much time alone."

"I've traveled a lot this past year with my work, but I haven't gone anywhere this winter."

She knew she'd taken on more than she'd needed to—that she'd been running away from her past with Derek Cutshaw, her grief over her father's death, even the scare over nearly losing her brother Elijah in combat. Since Lowell Whittaker's arrest in January, she'd made a conscious effort to refocus on her work with the lodge and reconnect with her hometown and even her family.

Nick continued to stare out at the mountains. "Tell me about you and Derek Cutshaw."

His question caught her off guard. She felt her entire body stiffen and shook her head. "This isn't happening."

He glanced back at her and shrugged. "Okay. I'll get one of your brothers to ask you."

"You're missing an important point here, Nick. My brothers and I may fight among ourselves, but we're loyal to each other. You're the outsider."

"Cutshaw was, too."

"You can go now," she said coolly. "Ranger and I are fine here on our own."

Nick walked over to Ranger and crouched down to pet him. "I had a golden retriever as a kid. Nothing cuter as puppies. How old was Ranger when you got him?"

"Twelve weeks."

"Here locally?"

"Woodstock. From friends. They'd already named him Ranger, which has earned me some ribbing in the search-and-rescue world since it's almost a cliché."

"Did you know he'd be a search-and-rescue dog?"

"That was the plan."

As Nick stood up, Rose noticed he moved smoothly, with no hint of fatigue or stiffness, and reminded herself that he was held to a high standard of fitness as a smoke jumper.

Not a man to underestimate.

"I'm not distracted, Nick," she said, as much for herself as for him. "You can afford to buy half of Black Falls, so you can afford another night at the lodge."

"Fair enough." His eyes, even darker in the afternoon shadows, lingered on her for a few seconds longer than she found comfortable. "I'll go if you agree to have dinner with me at the lodge. You can come early. Really early."

"That's blackmail. You'll go even if I don't have dinner with you."

He reached for his jacket on the couch. "Get some rest, clean up and meet me there. If you don't show up," he said, heading for the front door, "I'll come find you."

"We're not talking about anything serious over dinner."

"Sounds good."

She sighed. "Has anyone ever told you that you're completely relentless?"

He winked at her. "All the time."

Only after he'd left did Rose acknowledge that she

wouldn't be spending the evening alone, wrapped up in an afghan, watching Jane Austen DVDs. She'd meant to keep her distance from Nick, but he'd just let himself into her house, lit a fire in her woodstove and invited her to dinner.

And she'd caved, completely.

Nick Martini was a mission-oriented man. He liked to get what he wanted. In this case, he wanted her not to be up on her hill by herself for any length of time. She didn't know if he were concerned for her safety or her emotional state after this morning's tragedy, or if he just wanted to pry information out of her.

Maybe all of the above.

"No wonder he's rich," she muttered to Ranger. "Who wouldn't cave?"

Ranger stretched, yawned and went back to sleep. Rose plopped down on the couch, still warm from Nick, and admitted to herself that she'd also, at least to a degree, let him win this round.

The truth was she didn't want to be alone right now.

She glanced at the open door to her bedroom and couldn't remember if she'd shut it before she'd left for the Whittaker place in the predawn dark. She wondered if Nick *had* checked her closets and cellar for intruders. Had he gone through her small office in back? Had he looked for information about her and Derek?

About *him?*

She got up again and headed into her bedroom to shower and change, glad, at least, that she wasn't the type to keep a diary.

Five

Nick tried to get up to his room without running into a Cameron or pink-cheeked guests enjoying a getaway in the mountains, but he didn't succeed on either score. An older couple holding hands passed him in the parking lot, and A.J. intercepted him in the lobby and steered him to a booth in the lodge's cozy wood-paneled bar.

Nick ordered whiskey. A.J. stuck with water and leaned back against the dark wood, in no way relaxed.

So, Nick, thought, it was going to be that kind of chat.

His whiskey arrived. He took a sip, eyeing the man across from him. He figured A.J. was as kick-ass in his own way as Special Forces soldier Elijah or smoke jumper Sean.

"First time in Vermont?" A.J. asked.

"It is."

"You could have come last week when Sean was out here."

He could have, Nick thought, but he hadn't made up his mind yet about venturing East. More to the point, he'd known he wouldn't want Sean with him when he saw Rose.

Bad enough to have to deal with big brother A.J. "I had business to take care of."

A.J. waited a moment, then said, "What made you decide to come now?"

A state homicide detective and a state arson investigator had asked Nick the same question. "The timing was right," he said, repeating what he'd told the detectives. "I figured now that things had settled down out here—"

"They haven't settled down."

Nick drank more of his whiskey, really wishing he hadn't run into A.J. "No, they haven't." He set his glass down. "Sean and Hannah returned with company."

"Beth Harper, Scott Thorne, Beth's brother, Zack," A.J. said, as if to point out to Nick that he knew what was going on. "I heard Scott left early."

"He and Zack Harper both responded to the fire this morning. You all have had a hell of a year, which I guess made me even more curious to get out here."

A.J. didn't look satisfied. "There's more to it than that. So long as you've told the police everything, you don't need to tell me." His tone suggested otherwise, but he didn't push the point. "I didn't realize you knew Rose that well."

"She's been to California a number of times."

Nick didn't want to lie or get into details about his relationship with Rose. Black Falls was a small town, and she was an intensely private woman who didn't like making mistakes.

Then there was A. J. Cameron, who could have house-keeping short-sheet his California guest's bed or poison his clam chowder.

"I'm glad Rose wasn't alone this morning," A.J. said, then abruptly got to his feet and left Nick to his whiskey.

Nick figured it was as close to a vote of confidence as he'd get from the eldest Cameron.

He settled back in the quiet booth, feeling jet lag and the events of the day gnaw at him. In Beverly Hills, he'd be by the pool or running on the beach, or working. The Vermont winter was beautiful, or at least it was today. He liked to ski and snowshoe, and he knew how not to die in a tent in a blizzard—but he also liked to return to Southern California sun and palm trees.

He'd gone under the North Pole in a submarine. He wondered if that'd count with the rugged Camerons.

He allowed himself one more sip of whiskey and went up to his room. He had a voice mail from Sean asking for an update and texted him back: It's 24 degrees. Balmy. Say hi to Hannah for me.

Sean would get it: things were under control in Black Falls.

Sleeping with the sister of his business partner and friend had been one of his stupider moves, but Nick didn't regret it.

He just wished he hadn't done it.

He stripped and took a shower, ending it with a shot of ice-cold water that he hoped would clear his head. He put on clean clothes that didn't smell like smoke, grabbed his jacket and headed down to the lobby and back out again. The older couple he'd seen earlier had moved to soft chairs in front of the fire. He imagined himself in another thirty years. Would he be resting by a fire, enjoying a few days at a mountain lodge with the woman he loved? Or would he be working long hours in his high-rise office, making new deals?

Scrooge, Nick thought, gritting his teeth.

Hell. In another thirty years, he could be Ebenezer Scrooge.

He put on his gloves and walked up the country road in front of the lodge, in the opposite direction of Four Corners and Rose's house. The temperature was dropping as nightfall descended, the sky turning the color of slate, the mountains a deep purple in the distance. He pictured Rose that morning when she'd seen him. Her tight expression. Her self-control, even as her emotions churned under the surface.

She was hiding something, at least from him. No question in his mind.

He reached a marker for a steep, narrow trail up to the waterfall for which Black Falls was named. He noted rock outcroppings amid towering evergreens, bare maples, oaks and white birches—and the quiet. The stillness as night descended in the mountains. No houses were visible from where he stood on the edge of the road. No cars passed. No people.

Rose had grown up on this ridge. She'd lived in Black Falls her entire life.

It was different from Beverly Hills, for sure.

Nick headed back along the road to the lodge. Rose hadn't arrived for dinner yet. He stopped in the bar and found Lauren Cameron, who, unlike her husband, had a glass of red wine. She motioned for Nick to join her at her booth. She was a beautiful woman, her long, shining blond hair pulled back. She wore a black sweater, jeans and black boots, her only jewelry a simple watch and wedding ring.

"Let me buy you a drink," she said.

"Thanks," Nick said as he sat across from her, "but I'm still working off the whiskey I had earlier with A.J. It's a good day to keep a clear head."

"Yes, it is." She finished off her wine. "I'm not from Black Falls, either. I moved to Vermont to reinvent myself after a very short, very bad marriage. It took me a while to get used to the rhythm of life here, but I love it now."

"Where are you from?"

"Suburban New York. There's plenty to do in Black Falls and the surrounding area. It's just different."

Nick smiled. "Way different from Beverly Hills."

"You mean you don't have a life-size stuffed moose in your condo?" She laughed softly, nodding to a giant stuffed moose standing in the corner of the bar. "It used to be in the lobby. I had it moved in here. Fits, doesn't it?"

"I'm just glad it's not real."

Her eyes sparked with humor. "You and me both. I should go." She eased to her feet, pausing to look down at Nick. "Rose isn't fragile. We all know that. She's as tough as her brothers, but she's the youngest and the only girl. I think sometimes she believes she can't make the same mistakes they did."

Nick leaned against the back of the bench. "Was her father hard on her?"

Lauren stood up straight, her manner elegant, restrained. "Drew was a good man, but he lived in a black-and-white world. Good, bad. Do, don't. Own up to your mistakes. Move on." Her eyes glistened suddenly with unshed tears. "He saw more shades of gray in life at the end. I think Rose knew that."

"You've all had a rough year."

"I have my little ones. They keep me from dwelling on the past for too long. Rose was close to her mother. She died a few months after A.J. and I were married." Lauren sniffled, getting control of herself again. "She helped soften some of the hard edges around here."

"I met her once when she and Drew came out to California."

"Of course. I hadn't thought of that. It's so strange. You've never been to Black Falls, but we all know you."

"The lodge is everything Sean said it was."

She smiled. "I hope that's a good thing. Well, I've had my time to myself. A glass of wine, a few pages of a book by the fire—I'm ready to brave a two-year-old and four-year-old again."

She obviously relished getting back to her family. Nick watched her retreat across the bar and figured Lauren Cameron's diplomatic manner had to be an asset at Black Falls Lodge. He could see why she was beloved by her brothers-in-law, and undoubtedly Rose, too.

Deciding he hadn't drunk that much of his first whiskey, he went ahead and ordered another as he contemplated what to do if Rose didn't show up. He probably shouldn't drive out to her house to fetch her: alcohol, dark, unfamiliar winding roads, no streetlights. No traffic, either, but if he ended up in a ditch, he was a dead man in this cold.

He could walk but the same issues applied: alcohol, dark, unfamiliar territory, cold.

He took his whiskey to the dining room, where other guests had already gathered at tables covered in white linen, decorated with votive candles. A waiter led him to a small table by another fireplace.

In another two minutes, Rose rushed in, sexy as hell in boots, jeans and a thick sweater some grandma must have knitted. Her hair was damp, obviously from a recent shower. Nick shifted in his chair. That morning in Beverly Hills last June, even after they'd both realized they'd made a mistake, they'd made love a second time in his walk-in shower.

He shot to his feet at the vivid memory and greeted her. "Would you like to sit by the fire, or are you warm enough in that sweater?"

She pulled out a chair across from him, away from the fire. "Here's fine, thanks."

He nodded to her sweater as he returned to his seat. "Looks hand-knitted. Your grandma?"

"I never knew my grandmothers. My parents married relatively late." She fingered the sweater. "I knitted it myself last winter."

"Ah. Good job."

She laughed. "You are such a liar, Nick. It's a terrible job. Dropped stitches, uneven stitches—"

"Color's nice."

"Maybe in this light. I think it's a sickly green. The yarn was on sale. I can see why, can't you? I was experimenting."

He studied her across the table, her eyes almost navy in the candlelight, her skin translucent but still pale. He'd liked hearing her laughter. "So you wore the sweater to remind me you're a frugal Yankee mountain woman who doesn't care how she looks?"

"It's warm and it was handy. I don't need to remind you of anything."

"I'm drinking Jack Daniel's if you'd care to join me."

Instead she ordered a martini. "I don't even like martinis," she said when the waiter withdrew. Her laughter had vanished, her expression challenging now, about one click from outright suspicious.

Nick gritted his teeth. "Why don't we pretend we just met? Rose Cameron, right? Well, hello, Rose, it's good to meet you. I'm Nick Martini. Your brother Sean and I are business partners and wildland firefighters out in California."

She was having none of it. "You and I have too much history, Nick. We can't pretend anything. We can't start over." Her drink arrived and she held it in one hand as she nodded toward the crackling fire. "I could toss my martini into the fire, but not tonight. It's the wrong symbolism."

"Rose—"

She didn't let him finish. "Scott Thorne stopped by before I came over here." She took a sip of her martini but continued to hold on to the glass. "They're looking for one of Derek's friends, Robert Feehan. Robert was with Derek the night at O'Rourke's last year. He's a private ski instructor, too. The police have talked to Brett Griffin, who was also at O'Rourke's, but he was less vocal than Robert, or *especially* Derek, and has distanced himself from both of them."

"Are they concerned about Feehan?"

"Scott didn't say. Robert and Derek were sharing a house for the season. The police talked to another of their housemates, who said Derek had told him he'd be gone for the night and back sometime today. He didn't say why, or where he was going." Rose stared into her drink a moment, then added, "For whatever reason, Derek decided to camp in that shed last night. He must have wanted to be there when I arrived at sunrise."

"Had he ever met you out there before?" Nick asked.

"No."

"Anywhere?"

She didn't answer and tried more of her martini, making a face this time. "Needs a little lemonade or something."

"Horrors," Nick said with a mock shudder. But he didn't let her off the hook. "Did you tell the police about your history with Derek?"

"You're assuming we had a history."

"Yeah. I'm assuming."

"It doesn't matter. I hadn't had anything to do with

him in months. What about you, Nick?" she asked coolly. "Last June we got in over our heads with each other after we tried and failed to save Jasper Vanderhorn. He was after an arsonist. Obsessed. Investigators haven't produced a reason for that hot spot flaring up and trapping him, have they?"

"Rose, don't."

"Jasper burned to death, and now here we are. You and me, again, with a man dead..." She set her glass down and looked at him, her gaze unflinching. "You shouldn't have come to Vermont."

"If I hadn't, you'd have been alone this morning."

"If you hadn't, maybe Derek would still be alive. Maybe this arsonist followed you out here and killed Derek to get under your skin, or he's in Vermont and found out you were on your way. You're a smoke jumper, Nick. You jump out of planes to fight fires. You'd drive a firebug crazy. If Jasper was closing in—"

"Jasper didn't have a suspect."

"It doesn't mean he wasn't closing in on one. He was working his own personal theory. You're here to see for yourself if his death has anything to do with Lowell Whittaker and his network of killers."

Nick nodded to the handwritten menu. "What do you want for dinner?"

"Nothing."

"Not me. I'm starving. If you drink that entire martini on an empty stomach, you're not going to be fit to drive home. It's okay, though. There's a pullout sofa in my room."

She pushed her drink aside. "You're right. No more martini."

He got her play on words now. "Lemonade. Right. Clever, Rose." He glanced at his menu, but he'd already made up his mind. "I'm going with the Vermont turkey."

She finally relented and ordered a salad and butternut squash soup with nutmeg.

"Tell me about winter fest," Nick said quietly.

"Nick—"

"Will there be sleigh rides?"

She ignored his slight sarcasm. "Sleigh rides, maple sugaring, guided snowshoe hikes, backcountry ski treks, a bonfire. We're auctioning off a quilt that Myrtle, Dominique, Beth and I stitched from old fabric pieces Hannah discovered in the trunk in her cellar. It'll be the centerpiece of a silent auction to benefit the local volunteer mountain rescue organization."

"I didn't know you could quilt."

"I imagine there are a lot of things you don't know about me," she said. "Winter fest will run all weekend. It's as much for the town as for the guests. Vice President Neal and his family want to come if they can. They were all here two weeks ago."

"So I heard," Nick said.

"They were quite taken with the old sugar shack. They cross-country skied out to it. It's just in the woods across the meadow. It was built around 1900, but it's in great shape. Lauren and I are trying to get it up and running and trees tapped in time for this year's sugaring season."

"Starts soon, doesn't it?"

"As soon as the temperature warms up a bit. We need freezing nights and above-freezing days."

Nick smiled at the prospect of maple sugaring. "Sounds romantic."

She smiled back at him. "It's fun work. I've been trying to do more here at the lodge, but Lauren's in charge of winter fest. I just do what she says."

"The Secret Service doesn't object to the Neals coming?"

"Not enough to stop them, at least not right now."

"Do you believe that all of Lowell Whittaker's contract killers have been accounted for?"

Rose's smile vanished, her eyes distant, cool again. "You get talking about sleigh rides and such, then spring that on me. You're testing my reaction. Nice, Nick."

He shrugged. "What's the answer?"

"The answer is no. No, I don't believe all of Lowell's killers are either dead or in custody. I don't think anyone does. It would be reckless to assume otherwise."

A.J. joined them, giving no indication he noticed the tension between his sister and guest. "I know better than to ask how you are—you'll just say you're fine, no matter what." He pulled out a chair and sat down, but clearly had no intention of lingering. "You can't stay up in that house tonight by yourself. Listen to me, Rose. You can't."

"I feel safe there."

"I'll come up—"

"You can't leave your family, A.J. You know I won't let you do that."

"We'll all come. The kids would love it."

Rose shook her head. "I don't feel unsafe, A.J. If Derek was murdered, his killer had every opportunity to attack me, too."

"Maybe Nick here scared off the killer," her brother said.

Nick picked up his whiskey but didn't drink any. "I don't think anyone was lurking in the woods when I arrived, but it's possible."

A.J. glanced at him but made no comment.

Rose sighed and took a healthy swallow of her martini. "The police will have checked for prints in the snow, tire tracks. If they believe Derek's death wasn't an accident or suicide and I'm in danger, they'll tell me. I don't take undue risks, but I'm not one to panic, either. But tonight," she added, "for your sake, A.J., Ranger and I will stay here at the lodge." She gave her eldest brother a faint smile. "I anticipated this and brought my things."

"You always were the smart one," A.J. said with a grin.

Rose waited for him to leave before she picked up her drink glass. "This means I can have another martini, this time with pomegranate juice." She gave Nick an enigmatic smile. "I like my martinis a little on the sweet side."

The radiator in Nick's room clanked as if just to remind him he was out of his element, on Cameron turf. He didn't have a radiator at home in Beverly Hills.

After dinner, Rose had ventured off to another part of the lodge with Ranger, his dog dishes and a backpack.

Nick kicked off his shoes and called Sean. "Where are you?"

"Out by the pool. It's sunny and warm today."

"Go to hell."

"Okay," Sean said. "I'm in my car, stuck in traffic, looking at smog on the horizon."

Nick grinned. "That's better. I had dinner with your sister. She's had to deal with dead bodies in her work. That part she can handle, but this time she knew the victim."

"Training Ranger is repetitive and requires a lot of discipline. She loves it, but the Whittaker place was probably a welcome change of scenery. She's always felt safe in Black Falls."

"Feeling safe's an attitude. Anything can happen anytime, anywhere. How well did you know this guy Derek?"

"Not well."

Curt answer. Nick looked out the window with the full moon casting shadows on the snow. He could make out groomed cross-country ski tracks. Black Falls Lodge seemed less dark and isolated tonight. Maybe he was seeing the nuances Lauren had implied he would if he looked. Or maybe he was experiencing the effects of jet lag, whiskey and Rose Cameron.

"The bar fight last March," he said. "What kinds of insults did Cutshaw and his friends hurl at Hannah?"

"The personal kind," Sean said. "Her mother waited tables at O'Rourke's before her death seven years ago, and Hannah hasn't had it easy, working herself through college, raising her two younger brothers on her own."

"So the insults were all about her?"

"As far as I know."

That left a fair amount of wiggle room, Nick thought.

Sean added, "Hannah hasn't seen Derek since he, Robert Feehan and Brett Griffin stopped by the café last March to apologize for their behavior."

"Telling me to back off, Sean?"

His friend sighed heavily, less defensive. "Derek said some fairly nasty things before Bowie O'Rourke intervened and prevented him from saying more."

"He wasn't just talking about Hannah, was he?"

Sean clearly didn't want to answer, but he said, "That's my guess."

Nick contemplated the moonlit landscape. "Hannah knows," he said finally, certain he was right.

"She and Rose have been friends for a long time. Hannah was in Black Falls all last year after Pop's death while I was out here in California." Sean let it go at that. "She's here now. I'll talk to her."

"If anything went on between Derek Cutshaw and Rose, this Bowie character knows, too."

"Bowie was willing to get into a fight and end up on probation to shut Derek up."

"I'll keep that in mind," Nick said.

The comment went right over Sean's head. "Bowie wasn't just defending Hannah's honor, or Rose's if you're right. He has a hot temper. He likes a good fight."

"Used to be a bar was the perfect place for a good fight."

"Now you sound like my father," Sean said, almost amused.

"What about the two guys with Cutshaw that night?"

"Robert Feehan said a few things. Brett Griffin was mostly quiet. They're not local guys. I didn't have anything to do with them after the fight. I doubt A.J. did, either. Elijah was on leave. He headed back the next day."

"Your father?"

"He died a few weeks later. We never talked about the insults. You can ask A.J. He might know."

"You ask him."

"You managed to piss him off already?"

"Scared to," Nick said with a short laugh. He stepped back from the window, feeling his fatigue for the first time since he'd looked at the clock at four-thirty that morning. "Feehan and Cutshaw rented a house for the ski season up by Killington. Griffin's in town—right up the road."

"You've been doing your homework."

Nick figured there was no point beating around the bush. "You and your brothers are in close touch. Maybe think about including Rose, too. Even with you three, she still seems isolated."

"Her choice," Sean said.

"Doesn't matter. Sean, a fire killed this guy today."

"Lowell Whittaker could have turned a kerosene lamp into one of his homemade bombs."

"And investigators missed it?"

"They might not have thought twice about seeing an old lamp in a shed."

"Where did Whittaker learn how to make bombs?"

Sean didn't respond. Lowell Whittaker had placed a crude pipe bomb in Hannah Shay's heap of a car. She narrowly escaped when it exploded, then warned Bowie O'Rourke, who was with Vivian Whittaker at the farmhouse, that they were next.

There was also the bomb Whittaker had used to kill Melanie Kendall, one of his hired assassins in November, as well as the unexplained fire at Myrtle Smith's house in Washington.

Nick sank onto the edge of his four-poster bed, the charm of the room bypassing him. "If Jasper was right, his firebug is still out there. What if he decided to get paid for his work and hooked up with Whittaker?"

"So that's why you're in Vermont," Sean said quietly. "I should have known. It doesn't mean this match-happy idiot killed Derek Cutshaw."

"I show up and someone dies in a fire? That's too much of a coincidence for me."

Nick had observed his friend under stress countless times on the fire line. Sean was levelheaded, committed, careful—not a reckless, glory-seeking yahoo. That didn't work in the wildland fires they fought or the business they were in. It got people killed. Nick was more likely to leap without looking, but he'd learned to rely on his training and experience and to calculate and mitigate his risk-taking nature.

Eliminating risks altogether wasn't possible.

If he thought his presence wasn't a coincidence, the police would be thinking the same thing. Nick had answered their questions and provided them with contact information. They could find him if they wanted to talk to him again.

"Yeah," Sean said finally. "For me, too. I'll talk to Hannah."

He disconnected, and Nick tossed his phone onto the side table.

The radiator again clanked loudly as heat surged into the room.

It'd be a long night. He checked the room service menu. He could order hot cocoa for two and go find Rose's room.

He raked a hand through his hair.

"No, you moron," he muttered. "Are you out of your damn mind?"

No hot cocoa for two, and definitely no finding Rose's room.

Instead Nick stripped to his shorts, dropped onto the sunflower carpet and burned off his energy and frustration with a hundred push-ups and a hundred sit-ups.

Six

Washington, D.C.

Ryan "Grit" Taylor had dreamed about tupelo honey, which he didn't think was crazy or anything, since that was his family's business. Still, it had been a long time since he'd dreamed about honey, or growing up on the Florida Panhandle. He sat up in his bed in Myrtle Smith's first-floor guest room at her home just off Embassy Row in Washington, D.C.

Less than a year ago, he'd been a Navy SEAL searching for enemy weapon caches in Afghanistan. Now he was waking up under a fluffy peach-colored blanket and watching sunlight stream through lacy shear panels on a tall window overlooking a dormant flower garden.

Myrtle's house was more traditional and girly than Grit would have expected. She'd probably threaten something untoward if she knew what he was thinking, but he hadn't seen her in a few weeks. She was still up in

Vermont, bitching about the cold and snow and baking cookies and scones and such. The front of her house—especially her office—had burned in a suspicious fire in November, but the back was in good shape.

Grit went through his routine to put on his prosthesis, a new one, his left leg having adapted and adjusted to the mechanics of prosthetic use. The procedure was automatic now, at least most days. He seldom experienced phantom pain anymore, either. The nerves in his residual limb were learning a new way to communicate to his brain.

Not that he'd forgotten he'd had his left leg amputated below the knee in a remote Afghan mountain pass, after he'd been shot in an ambush.

A Special Forces master sergeant who'd been with him that day was camped out down the hall in Myrtle's second guest room. Elijah Cameron had taken a near-fatal gunshot wound to the femoral artery and nearly bled out. Only his own quick action to tie a belt around his thigh, creating a tourniquet, had saved him. He was now fully recovered.

Grit didn't know why things had worked out the way they did.

He put on his service uniform and headed to the kitchen. Elijah was at the little round table with his size-twelve feet up on the rattan-seated chair across from him as he cradled a flowered mug of coffee. He nodded out the French doors at the patio. "Do you think we ought to fill Myrtle's bird feeders?"

"They're the wrong kind. She's only feeding squirrels with those things." Grit got down another flowered mug and poured himself coffee. The kitchen had dark cherry cabinets and a collection of delicate china tea-cups and saucers—more flowers—displayed on a shelf. "A badass Washington reporter like Myrtle and look at this place. Reminds me of my grandmother's house by the Apalachicola River. Myrtle even knows what tupelo honey is."

"So do I," Elijah said.

"No, you don't."

"I do. You told me after we were shot up. In the heli-copter. White tupelo trees. Bees. Only honey that doesn't crystallize."

"No kidding. I said all that? You remember?"

Elijah shrugged. "It was something else to think about."

Besides dying. Besides the dead.

Grit sat with his coffee. "Moose's widow sent me a picture of the baby. You get one?"

"Yeah." Elijah kept staring at the half-dozen empty feeders. "Cute kid. Ryan Cameron Ferrerra. I didn't even know Moose that well. I couldn't keep him alive. I get why his wife named a baby after you. Not after me."

"We were with him when the Grim Reaper came for him."

Elijah nodded. "We were."

"I remember the two of you talking about why he was called Moose but grew up in Arizona and had never seen a moose, and you this Vermont mountain man."

Grit glanced out the window, no sign of spring yet out in Myrtle's backyard. He half expected Michael "Moose" Ferrerra to be on the patio. Moose had liked to joke about wanting to go back to Southern California and grill hot dogs on his patio. Instead he'd died in Afghanistan, doing the job he'd trained to do, made the commitment to do.

Half to himself, Grit said, "Doesn't seem like almost a year."

"Nope," Elijah said, "seems like ten years."

Grit almost laughed as he turned back to his friend. "What're you up to today?"

"Painting Myrtle's woodwork."

"She won't say so, but she's afraid to come back here. She almost got her butt burned up in her own damn house. If I hadn't come along and saved her, who knows."

"That's not her version," Elijah said.

"She's a reporter. You trust her version?"

"She says she'd have saved herself."

"Ha." But if that was what she needed to believe, Grit didn't care. "It'd help if we knew who set the fire. You know my theory. Myrtle was onto Whittaker's network. He ordered her house torched but he didn't strike the match himself."

"It was an electrical fire. No match."

"I was speaking metaphorically."

Elijah grinned. "'Metaphorically'?"

Grit nodded out the window. "Look, pansies. See them? They must have reseeded. We didn't plant them. I like pansies. They're like little smiling faces."

"Grit, you worry me."

"Projection. You worry yourself. What's on your mind? Jo?"

"Jo's fine. She won't stay here and won't let me stay

with her until she gets herself straightened out with her job."

"You two—"

"She's at work now. What about you? You going in?"

"The Pentagon and Admiral Jenkins await. You want me to corral some general, get you a job?"

Elijah dropped his feet to the floor. "No need. I've been called in to do some intel work and analysis."

"Ah. Involve toting a gun?"

"A.J.'s talked about having me back at the lodge."

It wasn't a direct answer, but Elijah would know that. Grit let it go. "With Jo down here working for the Secret Service?"

"She doesn't have to stay in Washington." A twitch of a smile from Elijah. "She and Myrtle could open a quilt shop in Black Falls."

It was a ray of humor from Elijah, anyway. Grit wasn't a contemplative sort. "The dead guy in Vermont's on your mind. He would be even if your sister and this Nick Martini hadn't found him. It was a kerosene lamp fire. Do those happen much up there?"

"We have electricity in Vermont, Grit."

"Was it Lowell Whittaker's lamp?"

"I don't know." That thought clearly didn't sit well with Elijah. "Lowell might not be stupid, but I can see him putting the wrong fuel in the lamp. This guy sees it and figures he doesn't need to waste his flashlight batteries."

"Strike a match, and *poof.*"

Elijah stood up. He was tall, but Jo Harper liked to say

she could take him in a fair fight. Grit wasn't sure how she defined fair. She was another native Vermonter, in love with Elijah since high school—but he was the bad boy and she was the police chief's daughter. Grit had spent enough time in Vermont in recent months to work out who was who in little Black Falls.

"At least it wasn't the woodstove," Grit said. "I hate woodstoves."

"What's to hate?"

"Wood boxes, smoke, ashes. Every time I ran out of wood in my cabin up there, it was icy and snowy out."

"It's winter, Grit. What did you expect?" Elijah walked over to the sink and rinsed out his mug. "Rose didn't need this."

Grit turned from the pansies and bird feeders. "She picks through rubble for survivors of disasters. She finds lost little kids. She can handle herself."

Elijah gave Grit a hard-assed Cameron look. "You aren't thinking about asking her out, are you?"

"No. She's like a sister to me."

"She *is* my sister."

"That's why you don't see her as one of you."

Elijah frowned. "Grit, that makes no sense."

"It makes perfect sense. What's with this Nick Martini character?"

"I've met him a few times out in California, but I don't know him well. Sean trusts him."

"Vivian Whittaker trusted her husband, and turned out he was running a network of paid assassins out of their study for fun and profit. You'll talk to Sean between coats of paint?"

"Yeah."

Grit started for the utility room, which led to Myrtle's tidy garage. "Say hi to Jo for me. You know, three's a crowd. If I stayed at her apartment in Georgetown and she stayed here—"

"Won't work that way."

Grit didn't pursue the subject, because he had a feeling if he did, Elijah would shoot him—not to kill, just to wing him and shut him up.

Or maybe to kill him, after all. Elijah and Jo had reunited under stressful conditions, and fast. They had stuff to work out. Not the big stuff. The little stuff that could eat away at a relationship.

Not, Grit thought, that he knew from experience. He'd never found anyone he'd been tempted to marry. He wasn't sure now he ever would, not specifically because he was missing his lower left leg—it had more to do with the ambush, watching a friend die. He'd watched himself become more and more distanced from everyone he knew. He realized what was happening, but as can-do as he was, he couldn't seem to do anything about it.

He went out to the garage and got into Myrtle's second car, a 1989 Buick that she'd inherited from some dead uncle in South Carolina. The interior smelled faintly of cigars.

Grit was almost at Massachusetts Avenue when his cell phone jingled next to him on the passenger's seat. He picked up.

"Where are you?"

He recognized the voice of Charlie Neal, the sixteen-year-old son of the vice president of the United States.

"Stop sign," Grit said. "I'm driving. I threw caution to the wind and answered the phone. Aren't you in school?"

"On my way. I have a calculus test today. So boring."

"You aren't taking one for your coconspirator cousin Conor, are you?"

"Conor took a test for me. I didn't take one for him. He did terrible."

The two look-alike cousins had done prince-and-the-pauper switches so that Charlie could get out from under his Secret Service detail. They both were in trouble with their parents, the Secret Service, Elijah Cameron and Grit Taylor.

Grit pulled over into the shade. He wasn't that used to driving again, and he'd learned to give any conversation with Charlie and his 180-IQ his full attention. "What do you want, Charlie?"

"Our arsonist is back."

Grit wasn't that surprised by Charlie's comment. Cars zipped past him on the residential street that ran perpendicular to the one he was on. The Buick was warm, the morning temperature almost springlike, but he didn't roll down his window. The car wasn't bugged—he'd checked. The Secret Service was onto his friendship with Charlie Neal. Jo Harper didn't like it, but Charlie's dad, the vice president, had decided Grit was someone the incorrigible teenager would listen to.

A positive influence, Grit thought. Him.

Preston Neal probably hadn't thought Grit and Charlie would be talking pyromaniacs again. Charlie had figured out a network of paid killers was at work back in

November, before anyone else. He didn't need such nice-ties as evidence. He remained convinced a serial arsonist had been one of Lowell Whittaker's contract killers and was still on the loose.

"Whose phone are you on?" Grit asked him.

"A friend's."

Defensive, vague. Grit knew better than to try to get specifics out of him. Charlie would be ten questions ahead by now. Being direct with the kid was his only chance. "The Secret Service know?"

"I have to be in class in one minute forty-eight seconds."

"Any candidates for who this firebug is?" Grit asked.

"I have a list of names."

Charlie would. Grit regretted his question. "'Firebug' can mean anything."

"Serial arsonist, then."

"Go take your calculus test."

"I told you my sister Marissa has an ex-boyfriend in L.A., right? An actor. He writes screenplays, too. He dumped Marissa when Dad was tapped as veep."

Marissa Neal was the eldest of Charlie's four sisters and a history teacher at his northern Virginia private high school. She was also beautiful, and she didn't think Grit was such a positive influence on her brother.

"The only connection—and I use the word loosely—between your sister and this guy is an ex-boyfriend in California?"

Charlie was undeterred. "Jasper Vanderhorn was a California arson investigator."

"Do you know how many millions of people there are in California?"

"He was based in Los Angeles County. The ex-boyfriend's in Beverly Hills. Well, maybe not quite. On the border. Close."

"You're a genius, Charlie. Do the math on the odds—"

"Nick Martini is a smoke jumper, and he was with Rose Cameron when she found the victim of yesterday morning's fire in Black Falls."

"Charlie."

"I asked Jo about it. She wasn't that nice."

"Good."

"You're missing the nuances."

Grit felt the sun hot on the back of his neck. "I'm not good with nuances."

"The ex-boyfriend and Marissa broke up eighteen months ago. Last June, Jasper Vanderhorn, the arson investigator, died in a suspicious wildland canyon fire north of Los Angeles. Sean Cameron and Nick Martini tried to get to him but they were too late. At the same time, Rose Cameron was nearby, searching for an eleven-year-old boy who'd wandered off when his family had to evacuate."

"So? I'm not connecting the dots here, Charlie."

Charlie ignored him. "Jo was assigned to protect Marissa then."

"Special Agent Harper," Grit said, not letting it go this time.

"Right. Special Agent Harper. Then last October, Marissa was almost killed when a gas stove blew up at a place she rented with friends in the Shenandoah

Mountains. Jo—Agent Harper—saved her." When Grit didn't respond, Charlie took a breath. "Then in November, we had the fire at Myrtle's."

"Miss Smith or Ms. Smith."

"She said I could call her Myrtle."

Grit was silent.

"Miss Smith could have been killed. The same day as that fire, we had the improvised explosive device in Vermont that killed Melanie Kendall. Then in January, we had the two IEDs that almost killed Hannah Shay, Sean Cameron and Bowie O'Rourke—and Vivian Whittaker, too, but I'm not sure I want to count her. Awful woman."

Grit tried not to let himself get sidetracked by Charlie's pinball-machine of a mind. "We don't know who set Myrtle's house on fire, but the bombs were Lowell Whittaker's doing."

"With the help of one of his hired killers, who happens also to be a serious pyromaniac," Charlie said with absolute certainty. "I have a list of other fires around the country he could have started."

"Could be a she."

"Eighty percent of arsonists are men."

Grit knew better than to doubt, never mind argue with, Charlie Neal's information. "I know you're working hard on this, Charlie. Your sister's fire was an accident."

"What if it just looked like an accident?"

"Your one minute forty-eight seconds are up. Good luck on the calculus test."

"I'll get a ninety-six. I've already decided where I'll

shave off the points. It's obnoxious to get a hundred all the time. I stopped doing extra credit in fifth grade."

"There's no hiding you're smart, Charlie."

The kid was already gone. Grit finally rolled down his window. He thought he could smell lilacs in the air, but it was still too early for lilacs. He turned onto Massachusetts Avenue, again thinking about tupelo honey. His folks had told him he could come home if he decided to quit the navy. *"There's always a place here for you here,"* his mother had said.

Good to know, given what he was thinking.

Charlie texted him a name: Trent Stevens, Beverly Hills.

Marissa Neal's actor ex-boyfriend.

Grit tossed his phone back onto the seat next to him. Charlie Neal was playing with a fire of his own.

By the time he arrived at the Pentagon, Grit had formulated the bones of a plan. Admiral Jenkins had been after him to go to San Diego to meet with some experts or some such out there—Grit hadn't paid attention and didn't care about the particulars. Charlie wanted him in L.A. to check out the actor.

Grit figured he'd found a way to make everyone happy.

Seven

---❧◗❧◗❧◗❧---

Black Falls, Vermont

Rose stayed in a small room on the second floor of the main part of the lodge, its dormer windows looking out on Cameron Mountain. It was one of her favorite rooms. She and her mother had picked out the cheerful blue-and-white fabrics and colorful autumn prints.

She'd slept fitfully, waking up sweating, heart racing, from nightmares she couldn't remember but knew had been bad. At first light, she grabbed Ranger and went for a run, sticking to Ridge Road. At Four Corners, she waved to the McBanes, the elderly couple who lived in the old tavern directly across from the cemetery. They were sanding their walk and filling their bird feeders. Sean had quietly bought the place, making them life tenants.

Rose continued a half mile past the partially collapsed barn on the opposite corner before turning back, Ranger trotting comfortably at her side. A few guests were up at the lodge, but she didn't see Nick as she helped herself to a muffin and coffee and slipped up to her room for a hot shower. She changed into warm, dry clothes, brushed Ranger and headed back down to the lobby. She and Lauren had agreed to meet at the old sugar shack in an hour.

Both Scott Thorne and Zack Harper were in the lobby. Rose didn't detect any awkwardness between the two men given Scott's sudden breakup with Beth. Rose suspected the trauma of the past year had taken a toll on both of them, but neither would admit it. They were professionals. They weren't supposed to fall apart. At least, according to Hannah, it had been an amicable split. Beth and Scott, who hadn't grown up in Black Falls, had always done well as friends.

"Hey, Rose," Zack said, cider doughnut in hand. He looked so much like his two older sisters, but his eyes were a darker turquoise, his hair a darker copper. He was one of a handful of full-time firefighters in the town's otherwise volunteer department. "Quiet morning."

"I ran five miles first thing. I can feel it in my legs."

"Running off your stress?" Scott asked.

Rose doubted he was teasing her. She smiled. "Running to run."

Nick came in from the dining room, moving easily, as if he'd slept well and didn't have a care in the world. He had on a thick, soft-looking sweater, canvas pants and boots. "While you were running," he said, "I was helping myself to the breakfast buffet. They're serious about breakfast here."

Rose was aware of Scott and Zack observing her with obvious interest and hoped her face hadn't turned red, despite the rush of heat she felt at Nick's presence. "What would you have had at home?"

"Nothing."

"That's not good for you."

Nick grinned at her. "Pancakes, sausage, butter and maple syrup are?"

"You can have whole-grain pancakes, turkey sausage and not overdo the butter and syrup. Nothing, though… you need to jump-start your engine in the morning."

"I do. I have coffee when I get to work."

"You're on California time. It's still early there." Ranger, who had been sitting beside her, lay down and put his head on her feet, as if he understood how ridiculously self-conscious she was all of a sudden. She turned to Scott. "Are you here on official business?"

"Just stopping by," he said, not giving a direct answer.

"I've been thinking about yesterday," she said. "It had to be a hot, sudden fire for Derek to have been killed. He must not have had any serious chance to put out the flames. How does a kerosene lamp basically turn itself into a bomb?"

"Different possibilities," Scott said.

Zack dusted cinnamon sugar off his hands. "We're not getting into them with you, Rose."

"White gas would do it," Nick said, leaning against the back of a chair in front of the stone fireplace. "It's highly refined petroleum that burns very fast and very hot. It's great in camp stoves for just that reason. Kerosene burns at a slow, steady rate, even under pressure. Put white gas under pressure in an old lamp and light it, and you've got what we saw yesterday."

Zack didn't look annoyed at Nick's explanation, but Scott did. Rose felt Ranger warm on her feet. "White gas is easy to find, easy to transport, easy to store." She reached for a cider doughnut on a sideboard. "Anyone could get their hands on it. Derek could have had it for a camp stove and just not realized it was the wrong fuel for the lamp. It's the simplest explanation, isn't it?"

"Simplest doesn't matter," Scott muttered. "Right matters."

"Did you find a camp stove in Derek's things? A container of white gas?" She didn't expect an answer and bit into her doughnut as she considered where she was going with this. "Was a kerosene lamp in the shed after Lowell's arrest and no one ever looked to see what was in it?"

"We're checking," Scott said curtly.

"Even if there was, it doesn't mean Lowell filled the lamp with white gas himself, or if he did, that he meant for it to explode. The white gas just could have been a mistake. If the lamp wasn't in the shed, then either Derek brought it with him, which seems unlikely, or someone put it there. A killer would have to have known Derek would be there and would light the lamp."

"That sums it up," Zack said.

Rose kept her gaze on Scott. "Does anyone suspect Derek had anything to do with Lowell's network of killers? Could he have been targeted by one of them—one who got away?"

Scott watched her closely, expressionless. Zack cleared his throat, as if Rose had suddenly gone too far. Out of the corner of her eye, she noticed Nick calmly cross his arms over his chest and continue to take in the conversation. She had no illusions that he wasn't paying attention to every word.

"Time to pull back, Rose," Scott said finally, serious but not surly. "Let us do our jobs. You just be sure you've told us everything."

She couldn't tell if he suspected she hadn't. "What about Robert Feehan? Have you all caught up with him, yet?"

Scott sighed but answered her. "Not yet. He hasn't been in touch with you, has he?"

She shook her head. "I saw him and Brett Griffin going into O'Rourke's one night a couple of weeks ago. Otherwise I haven't seen or talked to him in months."

Scott's eyes narrowed. "Derek Cutshaw wasn't with them?"

"No."

"What were you doing in town?"

"It was cleaning night at the café. I was helping."

Rose thought she saw a flicker of pain in Scott's face but whatever it was didn't last. He would never let his relationship with Beth interfere with his work.

Zack squatted down to pat Ranger. "Hey, fella," he said, rising as he glanced at Rose. "Did you ever refer ski clients to Cutshaw, Feehan or Griffin?"

"No, never," Rose said. "Did you?"

"I'd have to know someone who couldn't ski," he said

good-naturedly. "I have to roll. Tell A.J. to put the coffee and doughnut on my tab."

"They're on me," Rose said.

A.J., Lauren and their two children entered the lodge. Her brother regarded the gathering in the lobby with obvious displeasure. Scott took the hint and followed Zack out. A.J. glanced at Rose, then silently retreated with his family into the office behind the front desk.

"I don't blame A.J. for being annoyed," Rose said as Nick stood up straight. He was intense but not, she thought, easily ruffled. "I should have moved us to a less public spot. What are you doing today?"

"I might take a cross-country skiing lesson. You?"

"You aren't taking a skiing lesson. Never mind. Right now I just want to put yesterday behind me. Black Falls is a safe, quiet little town. Lowell Whittaker bought a house here, and we all suffered the consequences of his warped thinking and violence."

Nick tilted his head back, studying her with those dark eyes. "What aren't you telling Trooper Thorne and Zack Harper?"

She pretended she hadn't heard him and fought an urge to lay her head against his thick, warm sweater and feel his arms around her. But where would that get her?

Nowhere good, she thought, and finished her doughnut. Nick watched her but said nothing as she headed outside, leaving Ranger asleep on the warm hearth.

Zack Harper was waiting for her at the edge of the parking lot. "So what are you holding back, Rose? An affair with Derek Cutshaw or with Nick Martini? You found Cutshaw yesterday. Martini was with you."

"Nick wasn't with me. He came on his own."

"Yeah, to see you. What was that all about?"

"I've answered all the questions the police asked me."

"I'm not a cop, Rose. I'm a friend."

"I know," she said quietly, then changed the subject. "Have you talked to Beth lately? How's she doing in Beverly Hills?"

Zack looked out toward the mountains, the sky cloudless, the air cold. "She called last night. She's trying to enjoy herself, but it's hard. First Scott leaves her out there, and now this thing yesterday."

"Did she and Scott have a fight?"

"All I know is that Scott planned to stay longer and didn't." Zack shrugged, his jacket open over a worn sweatshirt. "I liked Beverly Hills just fine, but it's good to be back."

"I hope you told Beth to enjoy her break and not worry about us."

"Pretty much. I suggested she and Hannah go shoe shopping on Rodeo Drive." He grinned. "Beth's even cheaper than you are."

"Ha-ha. How'd she sound?"

"You know Beth. She'll never let anyone see she's hurting."

"Did you see Nick while you were out there?"

"Yeah, briefly," Zack said. "He didn't mention he was planning to come to Vermont."

"Maybe you inspired him." Rose glanced at her watch. "Lauren and I are meeting out at the sugar shack in a little while. We're opening it up again. Doesn't that sound romantic?"

Zack grinned at her. "Sounds like work."

"It is—more than I thought it'd be. We want to get it done in time for winter fest."

"Because of Vice President Neal?"

Rose almost winced when he said the name aloud, but she knew it was just agitation and adrenaline on her part. Nothing in the investigation into Lowell Whittaker and his killers suggested the vice president or his family had ever been targeted by them. She relaxed somewhat. "Apparently the Neals love the idea of collecting maple sap and boiling it down. Opening up a historic sugarhouse will help take everyone's minds off the mess of the past year. A fresh start."

"I hope so, Rose," Zack said dubiously.

"I'm sure Jo and her Secret Service friends will go over all our buckets and pans to make sure they're safe. Bugs and bacteria are my biggest worries."

"Let me know what I can do to help get things ready."

"You could help tap trees. Anyway, I should get over there."

"Sure, Rose. Martini going with you?"

"No idea," she said. "I'm leaving Ranger by the fire."

"Golden retriever. California smoke jumper." Zack shook his head, amused. "Two different animals, Rose."

She felt another surge of heat, but he was already on his way to his truck.

Eight

⧴⋑⊙⋑⊙⋐

Five minutes later, Rose walked down Ridge Road in the opposite direction she'd taken on her run, checking for tap-worthy maple trees. Ranger loved being out on the ridge and had moved well earlier, but her aging golden retriever could miss this trek.

She turned onto a short, dead-end lane across from a trail up to the falls. It was plowed but just barely. She'd have at most a hundred yards of slogging through snow in her boots to get to the sugar shack through the woods. Lauren would head across the meadow on snowshoes, pulling the kids on a toboggan, and meet her there.

As Rose navigated icy ruts on the lane, she wondered where Nick might be, what he was up to, but knew that would only frustrate her. She'd focus on her routines and her work and let him go about his business.

She paused, noticing the sun was higher in the sky, the early promise of spring. She peered down the steep hill on the side of the lane, past a cluster of white pines, and took note of mature, healthy-looking sugar maples that would be perfect for tapping.

She heard a *whooshing* sound and spun around, just as Robert Feehan jumped out from behind a hemlock and dropped next to her. His dark hair fell into his face and curled out from under his wool knit hat, hanging almost to his shoulders. He was thin, and he looked as if he hadn't slept, with shadows under his eyes and a gray cast to his skin. He had on a black ski jacket, wind pants and heavy cold-weather boots but no gloves—they were stuffed in a jacket pocket, despite the temperature.

"Rose," he said, gulping in a breath, "I have to talk to you."

"You need to talk to the police."

"I can't. Not yet."

She didn't like his panicked tone, and took a step back toward the lane. "All right. Let's go back to the lodge."

"No, we talk here." He grabbed her wrist, clamping down hard on bare skin. "I'm not going to hurt you. I just want—"

"Let me go, Robert. Then we can talk."

He tightened his hold on her wrist and nodded down the hill. "I'm going to take you down there. Out of sight." He was agitated but seemed to have himself under control. "Then you can go."

Not a chance, Rose thought, quickly debating her options.

He yanked her into the deep snow under the tall, gnarly hemlock. Shaking visibly, he lifted her wrist and pressed her forearm against her chest, pushing her into the prickly boughs of the hemlock. "What happened? Why is Derek dead?"

"There was a fire—"

"I know there was a fire. That's not what I'm talking about."

"I don't know any more than you do."

"The police think I was involved, don't they?" He sniffled but didn't ease his hold on her. "This damn town's been nothing but bad luck for me."

"Robert," Rose said, forcing herself not to tense under his grip and waste energy, "you have to let go of me. Don't make things worse for yourself. I know you're upset. I know you and Derek were friends."

"He cared about you. He never would have hurt you."

Rose didn't argue with him. "We hadn't had anything to do with each other in a long time."

Robert's grip on her softened. "Rose, did someone kill him? Was he murdered?"

"A state trooper was just at the lodge. He can't be that far—"

"I saw his cruiser go up the road. I waited for it to go by again." He kept his voice low, but he practically spit his words. "I'm an outsider around here. I don't know anyone. It'd be easy for someone to set me up, blame me—come after me."

"Brett Griffin's in the same position you are. He talked to the police."

"Brett's not sharing a house with Derek. He's kept both of us at a distance since last year." Robert glanced up at the lane, then back again at Rose. "What if someone did kill Derek? What if I'm next?"

"All the more reason to talk to the police."

"They can't help me. What's with you and this guy from California?"

His question took her by surprise. "Nick? What do you know about him?"

"Nothing. Derek was all freaked out about him."

"When?"

"Last night. He stopped at the house and got his camping gear and took off. What's this Nick character doing in Vermont?"

"He's my brother Sean's business partner. Why would his presence freak out Derek?"

"He didn't say," Robert said, suddenly loosening his grip on her. "I have to go."

Rose started to pull her wrist free, but Robert shoved her backward into the hemlock and bolted up the hill. She twisted away from the tree and its sharp, dried-up lower limbs, and sprawled into the snow, breaking her fall as best she could with an outstretched arm.

She rolled onto her hands and knees.

"Rose!"

It was Nick, swooping down the hill toward her. Robert must have spotted him through the woods. She scrambled to her feet, but Nick caught her by the elbows and stood her up. "I'm going after him," she said.

"Hold on," Nick said, his dark eyes on her, intense. "Are you hurt?"

"I'm fine." She shuddered at the shock of cold as snow melted on her face, into the heels of her hands, into her ankles—down her back. "Robert Feehan just shoved me and took off through the woods, toward the road. He must have seen or heard you."

"I saw him. I didn't realize what was going on."

"I'm going after him," Rose said again, pulling herself out from Nick's hold.

He shook his head. "No, you're not."

Rose realized her hands were shaking from cold, anger, fear—and Nick. His presence, his touch, his hard gaze. She pushed past him in the deep snow. "Lauren's on the way to the sugar shack. You should go there. I'll meet you—"

"Not a chance, Rose."

She didn't respond and followed Robert's footprints past a pine tree. She heard Nick sigh and cut up the hill, intercepting her just as she reached the dead-end lane. He was in boots, too, not on skis or snowshoes, and wore his lightweight jacket from yesterday. Again no hat, but he didn't seem cold.

"Robert Feehan is Derek Cutshaw's friend," she said without looking at Nick. "The one the police are looking for. He wanted to talk to me."

"Did he attack you?"

"*Attack* is too strong a word. He wanted to talk to me alone. I told you—he didn't hurt me. I just got snow down my back."

"Now there's an image," Nick said, his voice husky, but his humor didn't reach his eyes. "Do you want to call 911, or one of your friends in law enforcement personally?"

"Robert was agitated—"

"He knows the police want to talk to him and took off when he saw me. What does that tell you?"

"Why didn't you go after him?"

Nick's dark eyes narrowed. "I wasn't about to leave you alone."

It was what she'd have done in his place. Rose wiped melted snow from her cheek. "Robert didn't have to run." She exhaled, feeling calmer. "I'll try Scott first. I have his cell number and he was just at the lodge."

"Can you get a call out?"

"I don't know. Cell service is spotty. Robert lost a friend yesterday. He's upset, understandably. He said Derek knew you were in Vermont and was freaked out." She pulled off her gloves and withdrew her cell phone from her jacket pocket, her fingers stiff, red with the cold. She found Scott's number, not looking at Nick as she dialed. "I don't know if the call will go through. The signal's pretty weak."

Scott answered on the first ring. "What's up, Rose?"

"Robert Feehan just paid me a visit," she said, then briefly told him what had transpired between them.

He listened without interruption. "Feehan pushed you?"

"Yes, but it was no big deal. I'm not hurt, just cold and irritated."

"Where are you now?"

"Nick Martini and I are on our way to meet Lauren at the sugar shack."

"Good. Wait for me there."

Rose disconnected and slipped her phone back into

her pocket. She turned to Nick. "Did you see Lauren and the kids before you left?"

"They were just starting out across the meadow."

"They should be there now. I don't want Robert backtracking through the woods and harassing them."

She climbed over a snow bank at the end of the lane. Nick stayed with her, and she led him to a narrow path, the snow disturbed only by the occasional deer and wild turkey tracks. Just past a curve, she saw the old sugar shack through leafless, graceful deciduous trees.

She found herself smelling for smoke, but the air was clear, clean and cold.

Nick moved ahead of her as they came to the small field where the sugar shack, constructed of rough-cut lumber, grayed now with age, was situated above a stream, just through the woods on the edge of the expansive, open meadow behind the lodge. A few days ago, she and Lauren had shoveled out the area in front of the entrance, exposing an outside stone fireplace.

Rose heard the happy squeal of her niece and nephew through the trees and felt her knees weaken in relief, telling her just how keyed up she was.

Nick opened the barn-style door.

"You can go on about your business," Rose told him. "We'll be fine. I'll tell Scott—"

"You're my business." Nick peeked inside the rectangular-shaped shack and asked, his tone deceptively casual, "Does Feehan know what happened between you and Derek Cutshaw?"

She stiffened. "I'm not talking about this with you."

He glanced back at her. "I just saved you from being thrown down a frozen hill."

"You did not. Robert wanted to avoid you. He panicked."

"Right," Nick said skeptically. "Ever take private ski lessons from him or his friends?"

"No. I know how to ski."

"Feehan's good?"

"I would think so if he's giving private lessons."

"But you don't know," Nick said. "Do you know why Cutshaw would be upset because I was in town?"

She shook her head. Her sister-in-law, laughing, ducked around a scraggly white pine, with little Jim and Baylee, in puffy snowsuits and mittens, clinging to the edges of their toboggan.

Lauren pulled the sled up to the entrance and moaned, grinning at the same time. "These kids are getting too heavy for me to haul this far!" She kicked off her snowshoes, then swooped down, scooped them up and leaned them against the door frame. She clapped her gloved hands at Jim and Baylee, who hadn't moved off the toboggan. "Up you go. Say hi to Aunt Rose."

They jumped up, and ran to Rose. She hugged them, but they couldn't wait to play in the snow.

Lauren listened quietly as Rose explained that Scott Thorne was en route and what had happened. Her sister-in-law swallowed visibly but maintained her composure. "Is Nick staying until Scott gets here?"

"I imagine so. Lauren, I'm sorry. If I'd had any clue—"

"It's not your fault, Rose. Show Nick around. I'll hang

out here with the kids. I have the radio. I'll let A.J. know what's going on."

Rose started to argue but instead stepped into the shack. She and Lauren had already replaced broken panes in the windows and cleaned them, and they now let in the late-morning sun.

Nick stood next to the old evaporating pan in the middle of the floor. "Looks like something from a post-card out here," he said.

"This is part of the original farm." She pulled off her hat and gloves, wet from when she'd landed in the snow. "We've ordered a new evaporator. It should be here any day. This one's ready for a museum. I'm surprised it's still here, but I guess who would want it?"

"Will the new one also be wood-fired?"

She nodded. "We're bringing in a couple of cords of wood and stacking it on the back wall. It'll stay dry there. We'll collect sap from trees close by and boil it down to syrup. It's about a forty-to-one ratio—forty gallons of sap to make one gallon of syrup."

"That's a lot of sap."

"A lot of boiling, too. The evaporation pan speeds up the process. It creates lots of steam." She pointed up at a vent in the ceiling. "Hence the vent."

"Clever."

"We'll collect most of the sap in buckets. Guests can participate if they want to. We'll bottle the syrup in mason jars and sell it at the lodge. Any profit will go to our local mountain rescue team."

"A nice little cottage industry."

"I hope so. There's an outdoor fireplace, so we can do

some boiling outside. That's really more for atmosphere. The fireplace is made from local stone. I love that, don't you?"

His eyes were on her as he smiled. "A lot of rock in Vermont."

Rose laughed. "Something to keep in mind when you try to argue with one of us." Suddenly warm, she unzipped her jacket. "Nick, if there's someplace you need to be—"

"There isn't."

"It's supposed to get above freezing today. Of course, you're spoiled from living in Southern California and might not realize what an event that is. When are you going back?"

"Sometime. Not today. You forget I haven't always lived in a high-rise condo. Some days…" But he didn't finish his thought and nodded to the open door. "Go on and do what you came here to do. Pick out maple trees, whatever. I'll be right here."

"Scott will want to talk to you."

"No problem."

Rose felt the snow melting in her hair, dripping onto her forehead. Nick struck her as a rich Californian who didn't belong in the middle of the Vermont woods, but maybe it was just her. She'd first met him five years ago, when she was starting out in search management and he and Sean had just formed Cameron & Martini and were struggling to make it work.

Nick had been fearless, confident and sexy, but it hadn't occurred to her to sleep with him.

He'd had his share of close calls fighting wildland

fires. She'd run her fingertips over burn scars when they'd made love in June. She'd realized he could be vulnerable, could suffer and bleed. He'd continued to do the work he loved even after he'd taken a hit.

She resisted saying anything else and headed back outside. Jim and Baylee were helping their mother dig snow out of the fireplace. "We have a lot of work to do," Lauren said, her cheeks pink with cold and exertion, "but I think we'll make it before we seriously start collecting sap."

"We should have some warm days coming up to drill tap holes."

Lauren smiled through her obvious uneasiness. "Excellent."

She was clearly holding her breath, hoping Derek's death had been a terrible accident and Robert had simply panicked given the violence of the past few months.

The lodge didn't need another Cameron in the middle of more violence.

Rose heard someone coming through the woods, but it was just Scott Thorne, arriving along the same path she and Nick had taken from the lane. He wore his state trooper's parka over his uniform, his expression tight and serious as he approached the old fireplace. "No sign of Feehan," he said.

Lauren herded the kids into the sugar shack with her. Rose, feeling the cold again, rezipped her jacket and told Scott about her encounter with Robert Feehan. Nick joined them outside and related what little he'd witnessed.

Scott glanced up at the cloudless sky once they

finished. "All right," he breathed, then sighed at Rose. "If you see Feehan, call 911. Don't approach him." He shifted to Nick, whose eyes were unreadable. "You, either."

"Scott," Rose said, "do you have any reason to believe Robert's a danger to anyone?"

"You mean other than you?"

"I told you—"

"Just do as I ask, Rose," he said. "No argument, okay? For once?"

She smiled. "Sure, Scott."

He trudged through the snow back to the path. Rose watched him disappear around a curve before turning to Nick. "You look cold," she said.

"That's because it's twenty-six degrees out."

"It's a beautiful winter day. Lauren and I will be fine. Don't let us keep you."

"If I got lost, would you come find me?"

"You won't get lost."

"Bet you're a good skier. I'm okay with snowboarding and alpine skiing, but Nordic skiing—that's work."

"You're enjoying this, aren't you? You think we're quaint."

"Quaint?" He sputtered into incredulous laughter. "No, not quaint. I'd put A.J. up against any Los Angeles businessman I've ever dealt with. Three Sisters Café would clean up on Wilshire Boulevard." He placed a foot on the icy, rough edge of the stone fireplace. "And you, Rose. I know you've been offered jobs in Southern California."

"Only two jobs, both in emergency management."

"But you don't want to leave Vermont," he said quietly.

She shivered from a sudden light breeze, but her mind was on the other side of the continent, on a hot, dry, windy day in June. Without looking at Nick, she said, "We did what we could to save Jasper. We all did. If his death is related to Lowell Whittaker's network of killers and Derek somehow found out and that's why he freaked out when you showed up—"

"We don't know that Feehan was telling the truth."

Rose pulled her hat out of her pocket and put it back on, yanking it down over her ears. "I don't know. I wish I did."

Nick frowned at her. "Your knee hurts, doesn't it?"

She hadn't noticed but realized her right knee did, in fact, ache. "Some. I must have twisted it when Robert shoved me."

"You should ice it."

"Thanks, Dr. Martini, I will."

"I have EMT training."

But he didn't press the issue as Lauren emerged from the sugar shack. "A.J.'s meeting us with the car out on the road," she said. "He's got the lodge on alert for Robert Feehan. No sign of him as yet."

She tucked her snowshoes under one arm and got the kids back on the toboggan, which Nick pulled as they hiked back to the dead-end lane. Rose spotted Brett Griffin out on Ridge Road with her brother and went ahead of Nick, Lauren and the kids. A.J. gave her a quick glance as he ran down the lane to his family.

Brett was decked out in winter gear, his camera

hanging from a cord on his neck. "I just told A.J. that Robert Feehan flagged me down a few minutes ago."

"Where?" Rose asked.

"Up the road, not far from the place I'm staying. He jumped out of the woods. Scared the hell out of me. He asked about you. He said he wanted to talk to you. I know he's upset about Derek, but he really wasn't himself. I told him he might want to calm down before he saw you."

Rose grimaced. "Too late."

"Ah. He found you already. I wondered. I gather it didn't go well."

"As you saw yourself, he's on edge. Do you have any idea where he might be now?"

"No, sorry. He ran up the road. I didn't follow him. I think he might have had a car up there. I heard an engine start."

"He didn't drive back by you?"

Brett shook his head. "He must have gone in the other direction. I don't have a cell phone—I borrowed A.J.'s and called 911. I know the police want to talk to him about Derek's death."

"Robert could be anywhere."

"I wish I could have delayed him but I had no idea what was going on." Brett tilted his head back and sighed. "You don't look so good, Rose. Did Robert hurt you?"

"No, but he was out of control."

"Yeah. It's crazy. I think he wishes now he hadn't gotten mixed with up Derek, too, but Derek had his good qualities. He thought he could do anything."

"He could put on the charm," Rose said tightly, "but he could turn it off in a heartbeat. Brett, you're house-sitting just up the road. Could Robert have come out here this morning to talk to you, too?"

"I suppose so." Brett fingered a button on his camera. "I got the feeling he was hiding in the woods and jumped out on impulse when he saw me. I wish I could be more help. Robert didn't say so in as many words, but he obviously thinks Derek went to the Whittaker place to kill himself."

Rose's stomach twisted, but she said nothing.

"So that you would find him," Brett added.

"Did he say why he thought Derek might be suicidal?"

Brett shook his head. "He really wasn't making much sense."

"If Robert knows anything," she said evenly, "he should tell the police."

"Yeah, I know."

She followed his gaze down the road as Nick walked out from the lane carrying the empty toboggan. A.J. was behind him with a child on each arm, Lauren next to him.

"I hope Derek didn't commit suicide," Brett said. "I hope he just wanted to talk to you, and the fire was an accident—just one of those dumb things. From everything I hear, Lowell Whittaker's the type to leave flammable stuff around."

Would he put a volatile, highly flammable liquid into a kerosene lamp and just leave it for anyone to light? Rose shuddered at the thought. "Given what else he's done, I suppose anything's possible."

"He puts a whole new spin on the term 'gentleman

farmer.'" Brett gestured toward Nick as he loaded the toboggan into the back of A.J.'s SUV. "Who's that? Got a new boyfriend, Rose?"

Rose squinted at Brett in the strong midday sun. "That's Nick Martini, my brother Sean's business partner."

"What's he doing out here? Is Sean with him?"

"Sean's not with him, no," she said carefully.

"Wait, is this the guy who was with you yesterday when you found Derek?"

"Nick was there, but we weren't together."

Brett blew out a breath, shaking his head. "What a mess. Well, I should go. I told the police I'd meet them up where I saw Robert. I'll leave you to your family."

Rose watched him cross the road and head past the trail up to the falls. She was still looking in his direction when she felt Nick next to her. "I'm walking back to the lodge," she said. "You can ride with A.J., Lauren and the kids—"

"I'll walk with you."

She didn't argue with him. A.J. muttered something to her about hoping she knew what she was doing and headed off with Lauren and their now tired children.

"I think I'm getting used to the cold weather," Nick said as he started up the road. "Feels good in its own way."

"The low humidity today helps," Rose said.

She walked with him up the quiet road, telling him about Brett's encounter with Robert. Nick stopped abruptly and took her by the arm, not ungently. "Do you ever ask yourself if you're too brave by half?"

"I'm not reckless, Nick." She faced him as he continued to hold on to her. "Black Falls and my family have had their problems this past year, but I've never felt unsafe here."

"Problems? A woman was blown up in the lodge parking lot—"

"A killer, killed by the man who hired her to murder people, including my father. Yesterday…" She pulled her arm free of Nick's grasp, aware of her reaction to him, the same mix of physical and emotional sparks that had landed him in bed with her eight months ago. "We don't know what happened to Derek."

"A kerosene lamp exploded and burned him to death."

The raw words rocked her back onto her heels.

Nick didn't relent. "You're an amazing woman, Rose, as well as brave, but you're fighting demons. You won't let anyone help you. Your brothers, your friends—me."

"I don't even know you, Nick."

He took her scarf, hanging loosely down her front, and tied it warmly under her chin. She felt the brush of his bare hands on her skin. "Maybe that's why I'm here," he said. "So you can get to know me."

Her breath caught but she shook her head. "You're here because of Jasper. If he hadn't died last June…" She didn't finish, shaking off any thought of the tragic death of the arson investigator. "What if Lowell Whittaker filled the kerosene lamp with Coleman fuel with the plan of killing his wife? I could see Vivian walking into the shed, lighting the lamp—"

"I never wanted to hurt you," Nick said next to her.

She pretended not to hear him. "Fire scenes are difficult forensically. We might never know how the Coleman fuel—assuming that's what caused the fire—got into the lamp."

"Rose. Stop ignoring me."

She plunged down the road, feeling the scarf rub against her chin, but stopped after a few yards, turning back to him. "You didn't hurt me, Nick," she said. "We had a good time together that night. Let's not beat ourselves up over it."

"Easy to say." He walked up the road to her. "You were still dealing with your father's death and Elijah's near-death. You'd done some difficult searches. You almost didn't get to the missing boy in time. The search for him put you dangerously close to the flare-up that killed Jasper."

"You're right about all that, Nick. I still have no regrets."

"If I took advantage of you—"

"You didn't. You'd just lost a friend yourself." She raised her hand and skimmed her knuckles across his cheek. "I hope I didn't take advantage of you."

Nick winked at her, his serious mood over, or pushed down deep. "Sweetheart," he said with a grin, "you can take advantage of me like that anytime."

She groaned, shaking her head. "You started this conversation. I'm not letting you off the hook with a joke and off we go. You're Sean's best friend. We were both still reeling from some tough stuff that'd happened to us. There's no way you and I could have made anything real happen."

His dark eyes flashed. "What happened between us was very real."

"We had a moment in time that came and went. We were there for each other. That's how I think of what happened."

"Were you also on the rebound from Derek Cutshaw?"

She bristled involuntarily, his question catching her off guard—as he'd intended, she realized. She kept her tone steady. "No, I wasn't."

"Fair enough." Nick took off a glove and with one finger pushed strands of hair off her face, then let his fingertip trail across her cheek to her lower lip. "Anything you need or want, I'm here in the sticks with nothing to do."

Without answering, she continued down the road at a brisk pace.

"Come sit by the lodge fire with me," Nick said, easily keeping up with her. "We can play Scrabble. Join Ranger."

"I have work to do. You must, too."

"Yeah, sure. Calls to make, asses to kick." Clearly he didn't believe her. When they reached the lodge, he said, "I'll be upstairs. Lunch?"

She nodded in spite of herself. "I'll meet you in the dining room."

As he trotted up the stairs, she noticed the shape of his hips, the energy with which he moved and the same sheer, unbridled masculinity she'd experienced during their night together.

She found Ranger right where she left him, enjoying the fireplace in the lobby. "Not a word, puppy dog. Not a word."

Nine

Nick bought a decent winter hat and rented cross-country skis at the lodge shop, a short walk down from the main building, and headed for the groomed tracks in the meadow. Rose hadn't joined him for lunch. He couldn't say he blamed her. She'd disappeared with Ranger down a hall past the front desk, presumably to discuss winter fest plans with her sister-in-law. After seeing the old sugar shack, he'd decided he wouldn't mind checking out winter fest. He'd pictured galvanized buckets hanging from maple trees, steam rising out of a bubbling pot, snow and bonfires.

Could be fun.

First they had to find Robert Feehan. Accosting Rose and avoiding questioning by the police weren't helping him. He'd already bolted when Nick spotted him. He'd focused on getting to Rose, making sure she wasn't hurt. He hadn't gotten a good look at Feehan, but Scott Thorne had shown him a photo.

Not a glimmer of recognition, Nick thought as he put on his skis. He doubted he'd run into Feehan in California or anywhere else.

The air was brisk but not frigid, with little wind. Nick couldn't ski worth a damn, but he did all right on groomed and backcountry trails. All right enough, anyway. He wasn't skiing for the fun of it.

He needed to think.

He had the mcadow to himself. No other lodge guests were on the trails. He skied hard, pushing himself. He remembered Rose last June during the frantic search for the missing eleven-year-old boy, and then for Jasper Vanderhorn. She'd been dedicated, tireless, determined and professional.

And also eaten alive by her own limitations.

Nick had thought he understood then, but he did even more so now that he'd been to Black Falls. She hadn't been able to save her father. She'd been helpless when her brother Elijah was shot in Afghanistan. According to Sean, Rose had buried herself in her work that spring. When she arrived in Los Angeles in June, Nick had considered her off-limits, but that was nothing new. She was mountain man Sean Cameron's little sister. A Vermonter. A search-and-rescue type. Nick had dated real estate agents, decorators, actresses and producers, but he'd been too devoted to his work with Cameron & Martini and as a smoke jumper to have a serious relationship.

In the aftermath of his long, hot days on the fire line and Jasper's tragic death, there was Rose with those incisive blue eyes. That tight, fit body.

Sexy. Very sexy.

And there'd been vulnerability, need, heat—and a night of nonstop sex.

By daylight Nick had come to his senses. He had seized the moment with her in an attempt to distract himself from his own anger and grief. They'd both encountered death in their work, but Jasper's death was different. He'd been an intense, dedicated arson investigator, and everyone knew he'd been targeted that day—murdered.

Nick could rationalize his behavior, but only to a point. Rose had needed him to keep his distance, and he hadn't.

Now he wondered if she'd also been struggling to put whatever had happened between her and Derek Cutshaw behind her.

Nick paused at the top of a curving downhill stretch, with woods to the left and a snow-and-ice-encased rock outcropping to the right. He noted a spot in a drift off the trail where someone had obviously taken a tumble.

Great, he thought without enthusiasm.

Then again, if he went headfirst into the snow, Rose could rescue him.

He smiled at the thought and plunged down the hill, navigating an icy patch with ease. He only just made the curve without going down. He paused at the bottom of the slope, in the shadows of a tall oak under a clear blue sky. He'd hoped that eight months apart from Rose would lessen his attraction to her, but no such luck.

Then he'd hoped coming to Vermont, seeing her on her home turf, would do the trick.

No luck there, either.

He followed the groomed tracks along the edge of the

woods and cut back across the middle of the meadow toward the lodge.

In January, when Sean and Hannah had confronted Lowell Whittaker and nearly became his latest victims, Nick had worried about the impact of their close call on Rose. When he met Hannah in Los Angeles, she made it clear she suspected something had gone on between him and her friend. He'd admitted to nothing. He'd promised Rose to keep their night together a secret.

A bundled-up couple he'd seen at breakfast passed him, going in the opposite direction, laughing as they moved haltingly on their skis. Nick stopped on top of an open knoll. He could see a trail that wound down the steep hillside to the lake where Elijah Cameron had built a house.

The Camerons were a tight-knit lot. No question. A.J., Elijah and even Sean wouldn't be pleased, Nick thought, that he'd hopped into the sack with their little sister at a vulnerable moment for her.

He'd never convince them he'd been vulnerable, too.

Not that he'd ever convince himself.

If nothing else, staying at Black Falls Lodge had crystallized the differences between Rose and him.

Nick headed back to the lodge and returned the skis before going up to his room. He took a shower, changed clothes, checked his email and made a few calls. When he ventured back to the lobby, there were no guests by the fire.

No aging golden retriever, either.

He settled onto a comfy sofa facing the massive stone fireplace and let himself become transfixed by the flames, let them take him back to the moment he and Sean had realized a hot spot had flared up and Jasper was trapped.

The hot spot had had help flaring up. It hadn't been an accident.

But suspicions weren't evidence.

A. J. Cameron dropped into the chair next to him and stretched out his legs, his boots scuffed, worn. "How was the skiing?"

"Good. You don't stay cold cross-country skiing."

"I know what you mean. Lauren and I are twisting Rose's arm to have dinner at our house tonight. She's been spending a lot of time alone lately, and with what happened yesterday and this morning..." A.J. cast his steely eyes on Nick. "She needs to be with family."

"Makes sense."

"You're welcome to join us."

Nick took it as a grudging invitation. "Thanks, but another time."

A.J. leaned back in his chair, but there was nothing casual about his mood. "Sean says you're solid but you can be thickheaded."

"That sounds like Sean, and Hannah tells me he's the charming Cameron."

A.J. didn't respond with even a hint of humor. "Rose doesn't want to stay here again tonight. I think it's partly because of you. If she told you to get lost, you'd leave her alone, right?"

Nick listened to the fire hissing as a hunk of bark burst into flames. "I can take no for an answer if that's what you're getting at."

"If she asked you to go back to Beverly Hills?"

"She hasn't. I don't know what's on your mind, A.J., but I can see it'd take a strong man to fall for Rose with her three big brothers ready to pounce."

"Consider the situation," A.J. said grimly.

"There's always a situation to consider, isn't there?"

A.J. got heavily to his feet. "Not one involving a man burned to death."

Two men burned to death, Nick thought—Jasper Vanderhorn and now Derek Cutshaw.

The firstborn Cameron seemed genuinely concerned for his sister's well-being. Nick tried to lighten the dark mood. "What's for dinner? You aren't going out to shoot a moose, are you?"

A.J. glanced down at him. "Derek Cutshaw isn't dead because of you, is he?"

"I hope he's not dead because of anyone. I hope his death was an accident." Nick could feel the heat of the fire. "Did Rose agree to meet you for dinner?"

"I'm picking her up myself," A.J. said.

Nick stood up. "Maybe I'll head into the village and check out the Black Falls nightlife."

A.J. grinned slightly. "That won't take long."

Nick parked in front of the Black Falls library across from the town common. It was open, lit up against the dark night.

Looked cozy.

He took a sanded, shoveled walkway through the middle of the picturesque common and crossed Main Street to Three Sisters Café. It was closed, but lights were on and he could see Myrtle Smith and Dominique Belair with a patchwork quilt spread out over a couple of tables they'd pushed together. They had needles and thread in hand and were doing what appeared to be a few last-minute stitches.

Nick didn't think he'd ever actually seen anyone quilt anything.

He wondered if Rose could quilt any better than she could knit.

He left the two women to their sewing and continued down Main Street. The temperature had dropped fast with nightfall. The village was dark and quiet, but O'Rourke's appeared to be filled with people. He could hear raucous laughter inside as he mounted the sanded concrete steps.

A three-person band was setting up opposite the bar and nearly every table was filled with Vermonters and tourists enjoying their drinks and the hearty food.

Nick sat on a high stool at the bar. Liam O'Rourke took his order. "Sean's told me about you," Liam said. "You two have been friends for a long time."

"Ever been to Beverly Hills?" Nick asked him.

"I like winter."

"You could come in summer."

"Too hot."

"That's Arizona. Most of the time Beverly Hills is relatively mild."

"Then why the fires?"

"It's dry."

"Fire season's over out there?"

"Fires can happen anytime, but the peak season is

September and October. We're relatively wet and cool right now. That helps keep fires down." That was the short answer. Nick doubted Liam wanted the long answer. "It's good you like Vermont. Is your cousin Bowie here?"

"I don't have patience with troublemakers."

"You mean Bowie or me?"

"I mean anyone who makes trouble."

Did that include Hannah Shay? Derek Cutshaw and his friends? Rose?

"Have you seen Robert Feehan today?" Nick asked as Liam set a frosted beer glass in front of him on the worn bar.

"Not in a week or more. Same as what I said yesterday when you were here with Rose." *In case you're testing me,* Liam's tone said. "I told the police the same thing, so don't think you're being subtle."

"I'm not the subtle type." Nick glanced at a narrow, vertical menu. "I'll have the beef stew."

"Salad?"

"No, thanks." He grinned. "Stew's got carrots and onions."

Liam didn't seem amused.

Another big guy who looked a lot like Liam entered O'Rourke's. The stonemason, Nick thought. Bowie O'Rourke, currently on probation after taking on Derek Cutshaw right here in his surly cousin's bar.

Liam made what passed for introductions, handed his cousin a Coke and moved down to the end of the bar. Bowie stood next to Nick. "How's Hannah doing in California?"

"Loves it," Nick said.

"Is Sean spoiling her?"

"Trying, but she's stubborn and self-sufficient."

"Her brothers? They like it there?"

Nick knew Devin Shay, the older of Hannah's two younger brothers, better than he did Toby. "They like California even more than Hannah, at least for now. Devin's working for Sean and starting on the road to becoming a smoke jumper. Toby's mountain biking to his heart's content. He likes being an exchange student. I think he'll end up finishing his senior year there."

"Hannah still studying for the bar?"

"Every day by the pool, but I don't know if she's signed up to take it yet." Nick sipped some of his beer. "She seemed happy to have Beth come for a visit."

Bowie nodded, not touching his Coke. "Hannah's like a sister to me," the stonemason said, making it sound like a warning. "We grew up in a hollow out past the Whittaker place."

"So I hear. What about Rose Cameron? Is she like a sister to you, too?"

Bowie glanced sideways at him. "What difference does it make to you?"

Nick took no offense. "I've been trying to figure out why Derek Cutshaw might have gone to the Whittaker place when he did. I've picked up an undercurrent around here. I think he had something going on with Rose, and you knew. You weren't just keeping him from spouting off about Hannah last year in that fight, were you?"

"Rose wasn't even in Black Falls then."

"Hannah's one of her closest friends, and she was here. So were all three of Rose's brothers. If Cutshaw was out of control and lied or exaggerated about her in front of everyone—or even told the truth, shared a secret—"

"Now you're the one going too far," Bowie said darkly.

"I don't care about any history between Cutshaw and Rose. If you intervened to keep him from embarrassing her, then good for you. It's a small town. She's entrusted with people's lives. She didn't need some drunken idiot carrying on about her. I only care that she's safe."

Bowie relaxed slightly. "Derek was an SOB, especially when he'd been drinking. He was manipulative, controlling and self-absorbed. Everything had to be his way."

"Was he potentially suicidal?"

"No."

"You didn't hesitate."

"Correct, I didn't."

Nick drank more of his beer. "Cutshaw was from somewhere out West?"

Bowie nodded. "Colorado, I think. I don't really know. Not California, if that's what you're wondering."

"What about Robert Feehan?"

"I don't have a clue. From what I've heard, Feehan and Brett Griffin hung out with Derek because he was always up for anything—skiing, partying, driving up to Burlington or down to Boston at the drop of a pin. Feehan stuck with Derek after the fight here. Griffin got out."

"You seem to have good insights into people."

"I don't know about that." Bowie shrugged, glancing at the band as they finished setting up. "I've just had to figure things out to survive. I haven't kept track of Derek and his friends since last year. I can't afford to mix it up with anyone again. I'm on probation as it is. I stay busy with work."

"Do you come in here often?"

"Yeah, but I don't drink or get into it with anyone. I'm working on my house out on the river." He frowned at Nick. "What are you doing, playing arson investigator?"

"I'm just a friend."

"Rose has helped a lot of people with her work. People are alive now who'd be dead without her. If she needs anything, I won't be the only one who's there for her."

"Anyone good enough for her?"

Bowie didn't hesitate. "Probably not."

Nick thought he could get along with Bowie O'Rourke.

"I didn't kill Derek if that's on your mind. I didn't wish him well, but I didn't kill him. I heard about Feehan this morning. I haven't seen either one. We don't operate in the same circles. I expect you already know that." Bowie tapped a thick finger on the bar. "You're looking for trouble. I know the signs. Pull back."

"Thanks for the advice."

Bowie seemed to give up on the idea of eating anything and left with a curt farewell to his cousin. Nick didn't have high hopes for his beef stew but it was fine— rich, thick, just what he needed after cross-country skiing and raising the hackles on the Black Falls natives.

He finished his stew and left as the band started on their first set. Even in the village, the stars and half-moon stood out against the black night sky. When he arrived back at the lodge he passed a young couple and their curly-haired daughter, who couldn't be more than ten, playing Scrabble in front of the fire.

The kid was about to nail her folks with a seven-letter word.

Nick headed upstairs. His room was toasty warm. He stood at the window, the drapes open to a view of the moonlit meadow, and called Sean. "Derek Cutshaw and Rose—what does Hannah know?"

"None of the details," Sean said, obviously not completely taken aback by the question. "She doesn't want to talk about Rose behind her back."

"These aren't ordinary circumstances, Sean. Rose is a perfectionist. She doesn't like to make mistakes."

"I have a feeling Derek Cutshaw was a big mistake."

Nick backed away from the cold air seeping through the window. "Bowie O'Rourke knows something, but whatever it is, he's keeping it to himself."

"Rose wouldn't keep anything germane from the police." Sean sighed. "Hell, Nick. She would hate owning up to falling for some weasel like Cutshaw to A.J., Elijah and me. It's her own pride. We wouldn't do anything. We've made enough mistakes of our own."

"None of you Camerons likes to make mistakes," Nick said, leaving it at that as he hung up. He wouldn't lie, but he had no intention of discussing his night with Rose last June with Sean or anyone else.

Nick thought of her alone in her isolated little mountain house. He agreed with A.J. that she wouldn't stay at the lodge again tonight if she could get out of it. A.J. and Lauren lived on Ridge Road, a few miles from her.

She had friends she could call if she wanted company or protection.

Nick grabbed his coat anyway and headed back down to the lobby. The Scrabble players were still in front of the roaring fire. The kid was killing her folks, who seemed surprised she could spell that well. Lively piano music emanated from the bar, laughter from the dining room. Nick could have had a warm, enjoyable evening on his own, but he slipped outside.

His car had cooled off. He'd left his gloves in his room, and the steering wheel was irritatingly cold. He cranked up the heat as he drove along the dark road and turned onto Cameron Mountain Road up to Rose's house.

There were no other cars in the driveway. He assumed she was still at dinner with her family and parked in front of her garage. She hadn't left on any outdoor lights.

Nick wasn't even sure the place had outdoor lights.

As he got out of his car, he noticed the glow of a green tennis ball in a snowbank. Ranger's doing, undoubtedly. Nick smiled, thinking of Rose out here playing fetch with her golden retriever, and started up the stone steps to the front door, which surely she had locked.

He'd check, anyway.

He heard a sound in the evergreen shrubs by the door and reacted instantly, dropping back down a step, but he already knew he was too late. A man sprang out of the darkness, wielding a snow shovel. Nick raised his arm in an effort to minimize the blow, the shovel glancing off the side of his head. He landed a fast, hard, low kick, striking his attacker below the knee, catching the soft tissue just above a thick boot, forcing him to drop the shovel.

The man groaned and leaped down the steps, bolting onto the driveway.

Nick felt blood trickling into his mouth, tasted it. He jumped off the steps but saw headlights through the trees and heard an engine. He grabbed the shovel, reaching the bottom of the steep driveway just in time to see the rear lights of the car disappear on the narrow, twisting road.

He swore and turned back up to the house. The driveway seemed icier and more treacherous than on the way down. His head throbbed as he mounted the stone steps and checked the front door.

Yes, indeed, Rose had locked it this time.

He descended the steps once more and got back in his car, turned on the engine for the heat and dialed Sean in California. He didn't give his friend a chance to speak. "What's A.J.'s number? Never mind. Call him." Nick wiped blood off the side of his face. "Tell him not to let Rose come home alone. I'm at her house. I don't want her on the road by herself."

"Nick, what the hell—"

"I just surprised some jackass breaking into her house. We scuffled. He took off. He had a car parked out of sight. I'm calling the police next."

"Got it."

"Do you know where Rose keeps her spare key?"

"She usually doesn't lock up."

"I know."

"The gutter by the back door," Sean said. "Stay in touch."

Nick got out of the warm car. He hadn't switched on the headlights, and his eyes had adjusted to the dark. He found the key stuck in the base of an icy gutter, above another bright green tennis ball. He let himself in through the back door, flipping on lights, checking for any sign the intruder had gotten inside.

He dialed 911 as he moved into the kitchen. He dug a dish towel out of a drawer and pressed it to his bloody head. He got ice from a small freezer and explained the situation to the dispatcher, who clearly knew Rose.

The dispatcher instructed him to stay in a safe place.

Yeah, good idea.

Nick put ice on his scrape and sat on a chair in front of the cold woodstove. It was a cute house. Little. Nice location, except some SOB could walk in and toss the place without worrying about nosy neighbors. Rose didn't have an alarm system. His condo had twenty-four-hour security, cameras, proper locks, alarms.

Rose felt safe here because this was her hometown, and because until Lowell Whittaker had picked Black Falls for his country home, she *had* been safe here.

The ice was damn cold. Nick pulled it off his head and considered standing up, but what if he passed out? What kind of rugged smoke jumper would he be to the Vermonters about to descend? He'd fit Rose's stereotype of some rich Southern Californian who couldn't make it in the mountains of northern New England.

He heard her at the back door. "Nick? Nick, where are you?"

And A.J. "Hold on, Rose."

She ignored her brother and ran into the living room, immediately checking the bloody scrape just above Nick's right cheekbone, her hands soft, warm. "You're bleeding. Damn it, Nick, what happened?"

"I got hit in the head with a shovel. It's nothing to worry about."

"Who was it? Did you see—"

"I didn't get a good description. He was six feet tall, lean, white. Black gloves. Black hat and ski coat." Nick concentrated on Rose's face, her blue eyes as she stood back from him. She wore a sleek dark burgundy sweater and slim jeans, her tawny hair shining as she studied him. He forced himself to stay on task. "He had a ski tag on his jacket."

"Robert Feehan," she said without hesitation.

Nick wasn't surprised. A.J. eased in next to her, looking grim as the first of the police arrived.

Ten

Rose did her best to keep her emotions in check with Scott Thorne and the two police officers from town who responded to Nick's call. Her house hadn't been tossed. The man who'd jumped Nick, presumably Robert Feehan, hadn't gotten inside.

As Scott and the two officers left through her front door, she could feel their mounting urgency to find Robert and talk to him. If he simply was in a panic, terrified because of Derek's death, then why? If he believed he was in danger, all the more reason to turn himself in to police and tell them what he knew.

Nick had refused even the idea of an ambulance, never mind a trip to the E.R. Rose wasn't worried about him. He was an EMT. He knew he hadn't been seriously injured. He'd started to build a fire, but A.J. had gruffly asked him to stay on the couch and was tackling the woodstove himself.

Her brother and her former lover were a strong

presence in her little house, she thought as she went back to the kitchen. She pulled more ice out of the freezer and wrapped it in a fresh, soft towel.

"Maybe Robert thought you were breaking in," she said, returning to the living room.

Nick took the ice-filled cloth from her. "Why would he think that?"

"He's scared, on edge, because of Derek." She stood back from Nick and added, "Because of you and why you're here. Maybe he's afraid you're Jasper's firestarter, or one of Lowell's killers."

A.J. glanced back from the woodstove but said nothing. Nick placed the ice to his bloody scrape for half a second, then set it on the coffee table. "I don't need more ice, but thanks." His voice was even, unemotional. "How would either Cutshaw or Feehan have known about Jasper?"

"I didn't tell them if that's what you're asking," Rose said, not defensively.

"Just wondering if you have a theory. I didn't see his car on the road when I turned up your driveway."

"Scott says he must have parked in the small turn-around just past my driveway. You can't see it coming up the road. I use it when I can't get up the hill because of freezing rain, sleet or whatever."

Nick settled back against the soft cushions of her couch. "Feehan knew I wasn't an intruder," he said. "He didn't want to have to explain what he was doing here. I surprised him, and he smacked me with a shovel and took off."

Rose sat on a chair at the end of the couch. Ranger

had taken the men in the house in stride and was curled up on his bed by the woodstove. Nick didn't look that bad for someone who'd just been ambushed on icy steps. She frowned at him. "You're lucky you weren't hurt worse."

"It wasn't luck," he said lightly. "Feehan just wasn't as good as I am."

"Ah. I see. So you don't have a concussion or need stitches right now because of skill."

"You got it. If he wasn't here for trouble, why didn't he go up your driveway?"

"A lot of people don't like going up my driveway in winter."

"The guy teaches people how to downhill ski. He must be used to driving up mountains in snowy weather." Nick studied her a moment, his injury having no apparent effect on his ability to focus. "Why are you defending him?"

"I'm not. I'm trying to figure out what just happened. I have to keep an open mind."

A.J. adjusted the dampers on the woodstove. "You can't stay here alone, Rose."

She bristled. "The police are looking for Robert. He won't be back."

"Non sequitur," her brother said.

She shifted to Nick and attempted a smile. "A.J. gets even gruffer and bossier when he's worried."

"He's had a lot to worry about lately," Nick said quietly.

Rose jumped to her feet, ignoring both men as she

sighed down at Ranger. "Well, fella, looks as if we're back at the lodge again tonight."

Nick rose smoothly, steady on his feet, and stood next to her. "You can stay here. I don't need to make the drive back to the lodge. I'll camp on the couch out here by the fire."

A.J. turned from the woodstove. "Is this okay with you, Rose? You know you're welcome to stay with Lauren and me at the house."

"I'm used to being on my own," she said. "It's probably a good idea for Nick to have someone within yelling distance, in case he's hurt worse than he thinks."

Neither A.J. nor Nick argued with her rationalization, which she didn't quite know how to interpret.

"I'll have your stuff sent over," A.J. said to Nick.

Nick thanked him and returned to the couch, and Rose followed her brother out through the back. The night air was frigid, but A.J. didn't seem to notice as he paused on the steps. "Having Nick Martini here is maybe half a notch better in my mind than you being here alone."

"He's not going to hurt me, A.J."

"That's not what I'm saying. What if Feehan's right and Cutshaw's death and Martini's arrival in Vermont aren't a coincidence?"

"We don't even know for sure if Derek was murdered—"

"Yeah, right," her brother said skeptically. "Why would Cutshaw have cared about Nick being in Vermont?"

"I don't know that Robert was telling the truth, or what Derek was thinking."

"Who else knew Nick was on his way to Vermont?"

"Sean did." Rose shivered in the cold night air. "Do you suspect him?"

"I don't suspect anyone. I'm asking questions." A.J.'s gaze narrowed on her. "So are you."

"Nick's asking the same questions," Rose said.

"Yeah. I know. Call me if you need anything."

She crossed her arms on her chest to stay warm. "This all will end, A.J. We can't beat ourselves up because we didn't figure out about Lowell Whittaker and his killers sooner. They wanted us to believe that Pop's death was an accident."

"Elijah knew it wasn't."

"In his gut, but it didn't do any good until he had more to go on. He wasn't here when it happened. He could put fresh eyes on the situation. He was almost killed the same week Pop died. He was tuned in, maybe."

A.J. looked out at Cameron Mountain rising behind her house, silhouetted against the night sky. "I've never wanted to live anywhere but here. I want my kids to grow up in Black Falls. I want them and Lauren to be happy and feel safe."

"They will, A.J. Black Falls hasn't changed."

Her brother turned back to her. "Have you, Rose?"

She hesitated, then said, "It's been a rough year."

"You can talk to us, Rose. Sean, Elijah, me," A.J. said. "Any one of us or all of us together. You know that, right?"

"Always."

"You know it, but you don't think you need to talk to anyone." He let out a heavy breath. "Keep me posted. Be careful."

"I'm sorry about this, A.J."

"It's not your fault."

She didn't respond, but she couldn't help wondering if somehow it *was* her fault. She watched her oldest brother head down the steps and get in his car, his movements brusque, his concern—his fear—palpable. He'd been quiet during dinner. Even Lauren had been unable to get him to laugh and join in on their talk about winter fest, the sugar shack, the Neals' return to Black Falls and when Jo Harper and Elijah would get married.

Suddenly aching with the cold, Rose quickly ducked back through the mudroom to the kitchen.

Nick was at the sink, rinsing a bloodstained dish towel. "If the blood doesn't come out, I'll buy you a new towel."

"I don't care about that," she said, kicking off her boots.

He grinned back at her. "Mountain woman Rose."

"I can still take you to the E.R."

"Nah. I'm fine." He left the towel in the sink. "I'm glad you weren't the one who surprised him."

"Me, too, unless he just wanted to talk to me."

"Yeah. Talk. He grabbed you this morning, pinned you against a tree and shoved you in the snow."

"He could have done worse, or tried. I'd have defended myself. I know the woods up here better than he does."

Nick shook his head. "Not buying it."

She came closer to him and took a look at his injury, noticing the dark stubble of beard on his jaw, two small scars, his tanned skin. She tried to focus on where he'd made contact with the shovel. "It's a pretty good scrape," she said, "but there's not much swelling. Damn, Nick. You really were lucky."

"Good," he amended with a wink. "I was good. I landed a solid kick—"

"It wasn't hard enough," she said, amused. "He still was able to run."

Nick put a palm to his heart in mock hurt. "Cut to the quick."

Rose laughed and pulled open the refrigerator door. "Can I get you anything? Something to drink? I have orange, grapefruit, tomato, pomegranate juice."

"So you weren't kidding about pomegranate juice in your martini. You like that stuff?"

"Yes, especially in a martini."

"Ha-ha. I'll just stick with water. I should call Sean back and fill him in."

"I'll call him."

She shut the refrigerator and went into her small back office. She'd arranged her desk to take advantage of the view of a giant, old sugar maple in her side yard. Ranger wandered in and sat at her feet, as if he were mystified as to why Nick hadn't left yet. She dialed Sean from her landline. Of her three brothers, he was closest in age to her but had left for Southern California ten years ago. She'd been out there more than a dozen times and understood its appeal. Her father never had, but he'd always kept Sean close in his heart and hadn't treated him any differently from his other children.

Not until last month, when she'd watched him fall in love with Hannah, who'd never lived anywhere but Black Falls, had Rose realized that he'd come to feel as if he stood apart from their family and his hometown. But he didn't stand apart and never had. She, Elijah and A.J. knew that, even if Sean didn't.

Elijah had left Vermont at nineteen, but for different reasons. He'd spent long months in war zones, risking his life. He'd butted heads with his father forever, but on some level they'd understood each other. Elijah had always wanted to come home to Black Falls. He'd never felt alienated from his family or his hometown.

Of course, Rose thought, she and her brothers had never discussed any of this among themselves.

Sean picked up immediately, clearly relieved as she updated him. "If Nick just got hit on the head, all's well. He's got a hard head." But her brother's gallows humor didn't last. "Do you have any idea what Feehan would want with you?"

"No, I don't," she said, aware of Nick leaning against the doorjamb.

"Does Feehan know about whatever went on between you and Cutshaw?" Sean asked her.

She took a sharp breath. "Sean—"

"Elijah and I guessed in January that something happened between you two. Rose, come on. Relax. No one expects you not to have lived. Why should you be perfect?"

"Maybe after this past year we're not as hard on ourselves as we once were."

"Or on each other."

She noticed Nick's eyes were half-closed as he watched her from the door. She wondered what secrets she was betraying simply by how she stood, how she looked at him.

She smiled into the phone to help keep any self-consciousness out of her tone. "How's Hannah?"

"Worried," Sean said. "She's got on her prosecutor's face."

Rose doubted her friend would ever become a Vermont prosecutor. It was the path taken, then changed by circumstance—namely, falling in love with Sean. "I'd like to talk to her."

While she waited for Hannah to come on the line, Nick withdrew back into the kitchen, giving her privacy. Ranger glanced at her, then, his tail wagging, followed Nick as if they were now best friends.

"Rose," Hannah said. "What on earth is going on?"

"You don't have to keep secrets from Sean," Rose blurted. "Tell him what you know about Derek."

"He's already guessed most of it, and I don't know much. If you'll recall, you didn't go into detail." Her friend sighed. "You're a very private person, Rose."

"It's one reason you and I get along so well."

"Beth and I can come back—"

"No, enjoy the bougainvillea and the pool. Beth needs a break, and you and Sean have waited a long time for each other."

Hannah hesitated, then said, "Beth's hurting over Scott, but she's doing her stiff-upper-lip thing. We're having a good time. Devin and Toby are coming by to see her. You should see Devin—he's getting downright buff. He's determined to become a smoke jumper. It's a long route but wherever it takes him, it'll be better than where he's been. He has his own apartment now. Toby's doing well with his host family. He's in mountain-biking heaven. I think he'll stay and graduate out here."

"Going out to California's been good for all of you," Rose said.

Hannah had become her brothers' legal guardian after their mother died when they were ten and eleven and Hannah just twenty-one. Their father had been dead for years. She remembered their lives in the isolated hollow, just downriver from Bowie O'Rourke, better than Devin and Toby did.

"During the bar fight last year," Rose said thoughtfully, "did you get the feeling Derek was deliberately trying to provoke Bowie?"

"Maybe. Bowie didn't care. He wanted to shut Derek up."

"How did Bowie take it when Lowell Whittaker tried to frame him for the pipe bombs?"

"Bowie just wants to get on with his life, Rose."

"That's what I thought." She remained on her feet, restless. "Thanks. I didn't mean to imply I suspect him of anything."

"I'm sorry if I sound defensive."

"Do you know what precipitated Nick coming out here?"

"No, but I can guess."

"What? The investigation into Jasper Vanderhorn's death? Did something come up after you and Sean got back last week and Nick decided to head to Vermont?"

"Not that I know of," Hannah said. "Rose, I think Nick's in Vermont because of you."

She looked out the window but saw only her reflection against the black night. "Did he tell you that?"

"He didn't have to."

"Does Sean have any idea?"

"Not a clue."

Rose could sense her friend's smile but wasn't smiling herself. "Please don't do anything that would jeopardize their friendship on my account."

"That's not your problem. You have to figure out what you want. *Who* you want. Nick and Sean live in a big world. Private planes, money."

And women, Rose thought, but now she made herself smile. "Does that mean the prospect of bicoastal living in Vermont and California doesn't scare Sean?"

Hannah laughed softly. "Not in the least."

"What about you, Hannah? Does it scare you?"

"It did for about five minutes. Sean and I can make this work," her friend said. "I've never been so happy. I hope you can be happy, too, Rose. No one deserves it more."

"Don't worry about me."

"Easier said than done. But you should go. You must be exhausted."

"Thanks. Say goodbye to Sean for me."

Nick had stretched out on the couch, leaning back against pillows he'd arranged behind him. "This'll work. Hurts less to sit up, and I've got a strategic view of the door should anyone else pay you a visit."

"You're not armed."

"I could go find your snow shovel," he said lightly,

then nodded to a pair of her shoes by the fire. "Or I could throw one of your shoes. What are those things?"

"Waterproof running shoes. They're good in the snow." She felt hot, but was amused. "I can wear starlet high heels, you know. Christian Louboutin, Manolo Blahnik, Jimmy Choo. I can't buy them in Black Falls, but I get to Boston on a regular basis. I know what they are."

"Can you walk in four-inch heels?"

"Not on my driveway in the snow, but I could manage quite nicely at a Beverly Hills cocktail party. In fact, I have. Sean took me once."

Nick was clearly unimpressed, as well as skeptical. "You've never worn four-inch heels in your life."

She grinned. "All right, two inches."

"Where would you wear heels around here?"

"More places than you obviously think. For instance, there's a dance at the lodge during winter fest."

"Hell, shoot me now."

"Why, Nick Martini, what a snob you are." Rose lifted a log out of the woodbox. "I don't care if you're a hotshot smoke jumper, you're actually more Beverly Hills these days. I can see you waltzing into some cocktail party with a babe on each arm."

He settled deeper into the pillows. "I might have a few pictures of me just like that."

She set the log on its end on the stone hearth and lifted the lid on the top of the stove. "If I'm just one of the guys—some mountain woman in sensible shoes—why did you sleep with me?"

"We needed each other that night."

He spoke softly, his tone even and unemotional, as if he were stating a simple, indisputable fact. Rose dropped the log on the fire, almost choking it out, and reached for the poker. "I know why I needed you," she said, shifting the log, rekindling the flames. "Why did you need me?"

"You just asked and answered your own question." His voice was steady, and she could feel his eyes on her. "I needed you because you needed me."

She shut the lid on the fire and returned the poker to its rack. "That's it, huh?"

"That's it."

She dusted bits of wood off her hands and turned around, feeling an immediate jolt at the unbridled sexiness of the man on her couch. His dark eyes, his flat stomach and long, muscular legs. She felt the heat of the fire behind her and decided it wasn't helping. Moving away from the woodstove, she pushed back a faint sense of irritation at herself that she was still attracted to him.

She sat in her favorite knitting-and-DVD-watching chair. "Then why are you here now?"

He grinned at her. "Because my head hurts."

"In Vermont, Nick. Why are you in Vermont?"

He glanced at the fire blazing behind the glass doors of the woodstove. "Unfinished business."

The dim light from a floor lamp by the couch caught the raw scrape on the side of his head. As tough and accustomed to pain as he was, he nonetheless looked a little ragged and hurt, and he had to have a screaming headache. Rose knew she'd gone too far as it was. Did she really want to go further and press him about what he meant by "unfinished business"?

She launched herself to her feet and marched down to her bedroom, flipped on the overhead and pulled open her closet. She dug out a pair of dressy black heels. She'd worn them to an event Sean had dragged her to in Beverly Hills last summer. Did they just prove Nick's point? They were heels, but they weren't four-inch or expensive.

She shoved them back into her closet. "What am I doing?"

But she dug out a pair of nude-colored sling-backs with two-inch heels. She'd worn them to A.J. and Lauren's wedding five years ago. They weren't even close to sexy. They were...utilitarian.

She caught a glimpse of herself in the full-length mirror on the inside of her closet door. She'd changed into jeans and a dark burgundy sweater for dinner with her brother and sister-in-law. She hadn't fooled with her hair—it looked okay, maybe a little wild. Of course she'd worn boots. It was winter.

Definitely not starlet material.

It wasn't as if no one in Black Falls was. Lauren was elegant and beautiful, always perfectly, if simply, dressed for her days at the lodge. She had a natural sense of style. Hannah was pretty with her delicate features. Jo Harper, Elijah's love, the Secret Service agent, had amazing turquoise eyes and that great copper hair.

Rose had never paid much attention to her appearance—well, she had. She just hadn't done much about it. Spas, manicures, pedicures, hair treatments. They all took time and money she didn't have. She'd been known to have her hair flop into her face, get irritated, grab scissors and hack off a hunk over the sink. One of her best friends from high school owned the one salon in town and would lament Rose's self-cuts and recommend regular hair appointments. But how could she with her schedule?

Nick Martini had slept with her because she was there, and now he wanted to absolve himself of any guilt that would intrude on his friendship and business with Sean. That was all there was to it, and it wasn't such a bad thing. She had to be smart and not set herself up for an emotional fall.

Or another night of hot sex with a man who'd walk away from her in the morning. They'd just had another adrenaline dump, and here they were—attracted to each other, restless, alone.

Who was she kidding?

Nick was a type A, mission-oriented man. He wasn't in Black Falls because of her. He was in Vermont because he wanted answers. The possibility that Jasper's death was linked to Lowell Whittaker was Nick's only "unfinished business."

Rose returned to the living room. Nick had pulled a knitted afghan over him. "Your handiwork?"

"Penny Hodges. She owns the only flower shop in town. She and my mother were friends. My dad used to say they spoiled Elijah."

"Did they?"

"You've met Elijah," she said, dropping back onto her chair, the fire bright orange inside the glass door. "He's impossible to spoil."

Nick crossed his ankles under the afghan. He'd taken off his boots, set them next to her snow sneakers. "You flew to Germany after he was wounded."

Rose pushed back a wave of memories of those hard days of fear and grief last April. "He was recovering at Landstuhl. I could get there faster than Sean or A.J."

"Sean said Elijah was shot in the femoral artery. If you don't bleed to death in the first few minutes, you can make a full recovery."

"Which he did."

"You told him about your father's death."

"Yes."

She could see Elijah in his hospital bed, her tough, impossible-to-hurt soldier brother bandaged and in pain. The doctors and nurses had been as helpful to her as they could be, but she'd insisted on being the one to tell him that their father had died of exposure on the mountain he loved.

"A.J. had to tell Sean and me," she said.

She saw that Nick's eyes were shut. He wasn't asleep, but, she thought, he didn't need to sit there and listen to her. She felt the strains of the past two days catching up with her. "You can keep the fire going overnight or just let it go out. Up to you."

She thought he was at least half-asleep, but he eased out from under the afghan and got up, standing close to her. He took her hand into his kissed her softly on the cheek. "Sleep, Rose," he said. "We'll talk tomorrow."

She squeezed his hand. "I can do heels and sequins, you know."

"Baby, you're sexy in those wool socks of yours."

She laughed. "I think you might have a concussion after all."

"Not a chance." He slipped his arms around her waist and kissed her on the lips this time, again softly, as if he wanted to prove he could restrain himself after their mad, wild encounter last June. "No concussion."

She let herself lean into him, put her arms around him and feel his warmth, his strength—and her undeniable, uncontrollable physical reaction to him. She forced herself to pull back and stand up straight. She smiled. "Go on and get back under your afghan," she said. "You're in no shape to figure out what's going on between us. I'm not sure I am, either."

"Rose—"

She saw car headlights on her driveway and dropped her hands from Nick's hard middle. "That must be your stuff from the lodge." How fortuitous, she thought.

While Nick went outside, Rose fetched sheets and a proper pillow and blanket from the linen closet. She dumped them on the couch as he returned with a small suitcase and set it on the floor.

She watched him put another log on the fire. As a smoke jumper, he had a different relationship with fire than most people. He reached for the poker and she made her exit. She locked the front and back doors and ducked into her bedroom.

She pulled off her clothes, still able to feel Nick's solid chest and abdomen, taste his lips on hers. She sank into her bed, her sheets cold.

Ranger looked at her from the threshold, then

lay down just out in the hall. Rose smiled. Her own d'Artagnan—her own Musketeer.

Who needed a multimillionaire smoke jumper?

Eleven

Washington, D.C.

Grit Taylor thought he was free and clear of the U.S. Secret Service when he got through security at Reagan National Airport and arrived at the gate for his late-evening flight to Los Angeles.

Except Jo Harper was there.

No Elijah. Just Jo standing by a floor-to-ceiling window with her Special Agent badge and look.

Grit sat on a vinyl chair with his carry-on bag. He was in his dress blues. On his way through the airport, people had thanked him for his service. He'd responded the same every time: "It's a privilege to serve."

Jo just glared at him. "What're you doing, Grit?"

"Getting ready to board a flight to California."

"I like how you say 'California.' You're obfuscating the issue."

He grinned at her. "Obfuscate, Jo?"

"You know what it means." She dropped her arms to her sides. She was pretty with her dark copper hair and turquoise eyes, but she was all federal agent right now. "You're flying to Los Angeles. You're supposed to be flying to San Diego."

"Cheaper to fly to L.A. I'm saving the taxpayers." It was the truth, he thought, as far as it went.

Jo continued to glare at him.

"You do that to Elijah?" Grit stretched out his legs, not really noticing his prosthetic. "What does he do, throw you over his shoulder and—"

"Has Charlie Neal been in touch with you?"

Grit wasn't surprised by her question. He'd anticipated it the moment he'd spotted her at his gate. "I'm his new role model."

"He's called you on the sly with one of his theories, hasn't he?"

"Why, is he missing?"

"I'm asking the questions."

"Sit down, Agent Harper. We're good. All's well. No worries. Charlie likes to share theories with me. I listen. Sometimes I indulge him. I have a number of reasons to go to California, including navy business. They all coalesced and now I'm going. Coalesced," he added, "is one of those words like obfuscate. It sounds like what it means."

"Onomatopoeia." She seemed more relaxed and sat down, if on the edge of the seat. "Charlie's going to get me fired yet."

"That's not what he's after."

"The fire in the Shenandoah Mountains in October..."

She paused, clearly not eager to discuss the matter with Grit. "It wasn't bad but we got it out fast. If it'd spread, it could have killed Marissa. But we went over everything. We brought in all the pros. The ATF. The best people, Grit. *Nothing* points to a deliberate fire."

"What about the ex-boyfriend in California?"

Jo showed no reaction to his question. "Trent Stevens is an actor and an aspiring screenwriter and director. He didn't want the distraction of dating the daughter of a vice president. He thought it would affect his brand, as well as his work." Jo was silent a moment. "Trent's very serious about his work."

"You keep tabs on him since the breakup?"

"You know I'm not going to answer that."

Grit shrugged. "Have you ever been to Sean Cameron's place in Beverly Hills?"

"I stopped in once when I was out there on assignment."

"Checking out Marissa's ex-boyfriend?"

"You're relentless, Grit. Did you interrogate Taliban and Al-Qaeda fighters?"

"That's classified."

She gave him a grudging smile. "Have a safe flight. Don't encourage Charlie. Say hi to Sean and Hannah. My sister Beth's out there, too. Say hi to her."

"Should I tell them when the wedding is?"

She unconsciously fingered the engagement ring on her finger that Elijah had bought for her at nineteen. She narrowed her turquoise eyes on Grit. "You do know how to cut to the heart of things."

"You can move into Myrtle's place while I'm in California."

"If that's one of the things that had to 'coalesce'..."

"Three's a crowd. I was in one of your cabins at the lake, right under your noses. Now I'm in D.C., down the hall. It's awkward."

"I have my own apartment, Grit. It's not awkward."

"Myrtle's stuck in Vermont. I think she's suffering from Stockholm syndrome or something up there. We might have to mount a rescue mission."

"Maybe she likes Vermont."

"This is what I'm saying. She's identifying with her captors."

Jo scowled and shot to her feet, then glared at him again. "Is *obtuse* one of those words that sounds like what it means? Because you're being obtuse, Grit."

He crossed his real ankle over his prosthetic ankle and wondered if anyone in the waiting area had guessed he was an injured SEAL, but he realized he didn't care one way or the other. He grinned up at Jo. "We all want to hear wedding bells."

"You'll hear them for Hannah and Sean sooner than you will Elijah and me. Elijah's waited for fifteen years. What's another year or two?"

She didn't wait for Grit to respond—she obviously didn't want him to—and left. Once she was out of sight, he called Elijah: "I think you should buy Myrtle's house and turn the back bedroom into a nursery. A zoo theme would be cute."

Elijah ignored him. "Nick Martini was attacked at

Rose's house. He took a snow shovel to the side of the head but he's fine."

"Ouch. That's what he gets for going out there in the dead of winter. Who attacked him?"

"Robert Feehan, most likely. Whoever it was got away. The police have been looking for him since Derek Cutshaw's death yesterday. He jumped Rose that morning."

"She didn't get a shovel to the head?"

"He said he wanted to talk to her. Nick showed up, and Feehan took off."

"Lots of places to hide up there in the snow. All right. Thanks for the intel." Grit got up. "When I'm in San Diego, I'll stop at the zoo and buy a stuffed giraffe for the nursery."

But Elijah was gone. Grit heard his seating area called. It was almost a six-hour flight across the continent.

Anything could happen while he was in the air.

Twelve

Beverly Hills, California

Beth Harper took a late-night swim in Sean Cameron's heated pool. The temperature in Beverly Hills was cool by Southern California standards, but by Vermont standards—even in the summer, never mind late February—it was just fine.

She climbed out of the clear azure water and quickly dried off with a large beach towel and pulled on a soft terry-cloth robe. She was alone on the expansive patio, red bougainvillea trailing down a privacy wall.

She didn't mind. Alone, she thought, was good.

She went through French doors into the quiet, spare house, heading into the guest room where she was staying. She thought she just might chuck going back to Vermont and apply for a paramedic's job here.

Except Vermont wasn't the problem.

She changed into a T-shirt and flannel boxers and

climbed onto her bed, sitting against the pillows with her knees tucked up under her chin. Late nights were the toughest. That's when she'd obsess about Scott stiffly packing his things and clearing out, the cab he'd called already waiting in the driveway. No warning. No discussion. He'd had enough of Beverly Hills and was going home.

What he'd meant was that he'd had enough of her.

They hadn't talked since. A state detective had called to ask her about Derek Cutshaw's death and Robert Feehan's possible whereabouts, but nothing from Trooper Thorne.

"Bastard," Beth muttered, sniffling back tears as she reached for her cell phone and dialed her sister in D.C.

"Beth, are you okay? What's happened? Did Grit—"

"Everything's fine. Sorry. I forgot about the time change. It's late there."

"It's late in Beverly Hills, too." Jo breathed out in relief. "You scared the hell out of me."

Maybe, Beth thought, but Jo didn't scare easily. "Elijah called a couple hours ago and asked Sean to fetch Grit at the airport. He's there now."

No response from Jo. After several beats, she said, "Just as well Grit's not there on his own. Elijah won't admit it, but Grit's potentially out of control. He's had a long recovery from his leg amputation, and he's a Navy SEAL—he's not used to being idle. I'd hoped this new job at the Pentagon would help."

"I'm sure it will," Beth said.

"Anything weird happens, you call me."

"Are you asking me to be a federal informant?"

"I'm not speaking officially. Elijah and Grit are friends. I've become fond of Grit myself. He's...different." Jo changed the subject. "How're you doing out there? Getting in much shopping?"

"Lots of window-shopping." Beth smiled, trying to ease her tension—and her sister's. "I bought socks and underwear on Rodeo Drive."

Jo laughed. "Even that must have set you back. I wish I could be there with you and Hannah."

"I've been thinking about heading home. Jo, you've heard—"

"Yeah. Poor Rose. I'm glad you didn't have to respond to that fire yourself. You could use a break."

"We all could," Beth said.

Jo didn't take the bait. "Did you call just to talk, or is there something on your mind?"

"Why is Grit in California?"

"Navy business, he says."

"You think Charlie Neal's been in touch with him again, don't you?" Beth knew her sister wouldn't give a direct answer and didn't wait for one. "Charlie will be with his family for winter fest at Black Falls Lodge. I guess you know that, though."

"I plan to be there myself." She added, "For fun."

"Are you keeping on top of yesterday's fire? Could Derek have been involved in Lowell's network? Do you think Robert's just frightened—"

"Anything's possible."

Beth heard Sean arriving back at the house and hung up with Jo, then slipped into her robe and headed down the hall to the kitchen, all stainless steel and spotless chrome. It had a masculine feel despite the presence of Hannah's raspberry-colored sweater on the back of a chair and Beth's handbag on the kitchen floor.

Sean, tall and good-looking, walked in from the garage with Grit, black-haired, dark, wiry and relaxed, both men exuding masculinity and restraint.

"Hi, Grit," Beth said cheerfully. "How was your flight?"

"Good. The plane landed."

Beth noticed he moved a little unevenly as he set his bag on a stool at the breakfast bar. She suspected his injured leg had given him trouble on the long flight. It had to be his first since his medical evacuation to Bethesda last April.

He showed no sign of being in pain, or even noticing his difficulties. He glanced around the expensive house. "Not bad, Sean," Grit said. "Life could be worse."

"Help yourself to anything you need," Sean said.

"Who am I to argue with a Cameron?"

"You wouldn't win, anyway," Beth said.

Grit directed his black eyes to her. "Good point. How'd you all find out about my flight? I figure Jo told Sean, or she told Elijah, who told Sean—or maybe told A.J. or their sister—or Jo told you, *her* sister." He shrugged. "Lots of ways news travels among the Black Falls crowd."

Sean paid no attention. "We've got a houseful," he said. "I hope you don't mind the small bedroom in back."

"I thought I'd be on a chair at the airport bar until morning." Grit remained standing. "Any news from the Green Mountain state?"

"I assume you know about the attack on Rose this morning and on Nick tonight," Beth said.

"Sean filled me in. No stitches. No concussion. No deaths. I'm not minimizing, but I wouldn't want to go up against his sister. Everyone in town loves her. Martini's capable, too, right?"

"He's good," Sean said.

"Submariner." Grit gave a mock shudder. "Submarines aren't my favorite place to be."

Beth had a feeling Grit had been on his share of submarines and had done fine. He was a man who took life as it came. She couldn't say the same for herself. She was always trying to push life into what she wanted it to be. Was that why Scott hadn't stayed with her?

She shook off the thought. "I just hope this mess isn't all starting again."

"Not starting again," Grit said. "Continuing. Those your brother's boxers?"

She rolled her eyes. "They're mine. They're comfortable. Flannel." She drew her robe shut, knotted the tie. "I'm not discussing my damn boxers with you, Grit."

"You're more like Jo than you think," he said, matter-of-fact, and looked back at Sean. "Want to join me in a glass of whiskey and walk through this thing?"

"It's five o'clock in the morning your time," Sean said.

"Okay. So I'll have two glasses of whiskey."

Hannah entered the kitchen. She was dressed in a flowing coral nightgown and robe that Beth knew she hadn't brought with her from Vermont. She eased onto the stool next to the one where Grit had left his bag and stared at her hands.

Sean seemed to struggle not to say anything, but Beth didn't have that problem. "You seem preoccupied, Hannah. What's on your mind?"

She looked up. "Rose is so proud. Bowie knows that, too. If our keeping her secret has endangered her—"

"Cutshaw's the one who's dead." Grit stood back, obviously gauging the reaction in the room. "Ah. I see my comment isn't going over well."

"Your bedside manner sucks," Beth said.

"Pot, kettle," Grit said, unperturbed. "You really are a lot like Jo, never mind that you stayed in Black Falls and she left the first chance she got." He turned back to Hannah. "So, what happened? Did Cutshaw sexually assault Rose?"

Hannah went pale and didn't answer. Sean tensed visibly as he got out a bottle of whiskey and glasses and set them on the counter. Beth forced herself to keep her mouth shut. She'd had inklings of something between Rose and Derek, but only inklings—not enough to raise the subject with Rose, who was even more private than Hannah.

Hannah twisted her hands together. "Rose said that what went on between her and Derek...that his behavior wasn't criminal."

Sean ripped open the whiskey but didn't respond.

Clearly uncomfortable speaking about her friend, Hannah nonetheless continued. "Rose said Derek was a mistake that she wanted to keep to herself. I wouldn't be talking about it now except she said to." She raised her pale blue eyes to Sean. "I don't think she wanted to have to tell you and your brothers herself."

"When did you find out?" Grit asked.

"In January, after Lowell's arrest." Hannah reached down the counter for the glass of whiskey Sean had poured for her. She pulled it toward her but didn't drink any. "I figured it out. Rose didn't tell me. She never would have said a word if I hadn't confronted her. As it is, she didn't tell me much."

Beth picked up an empty glass and held it out to Sean. "Just a splash."

He complied, but she could see his jaw was clamped tightly shut, presumably with thoughts of his sister, and probably Nick, too. Beth took a too-big swallow of the whiskey. It was smooth, smoky and expensive.

Grit looked over the rim of his glass at her. "How much of this mess with Rose and Cutshaw did you know or guess?"

"Next to none of it," she said truthfully. "Derek always struck me as a bastard, but I didn't know him that well— just to say hi to. I didn't want anything to do with him after the fight at O'Rourke's."

"Rose never mentioned him?" Sean asked, his voice low, tense.

Beth shook her head. "She never said a word to me. She'd been burning the candle at both ends. Maybe she was vulnerable to a guy like Derek. Good-looking, great skier, partier. He didn't care about anything more serious than snow conditions and having a good time. There's nothing wrong with that, but he was also a self-absorbed ass."

Hannah stared into her drink. "I don't see him camping out in a cold, uncomfortable shed in the middle of winter. He must have had a compelling reason."

Sean remained quiet, sipping his whiskey. Grit tried his and nodded with satisfaction. "Good stuff. How long were Rose and this Cutshaw character together?"

"I don't know that she'd describe them as ever having been 'together,'" Hannah said.

"Think they could have been meeting at the shed, seeing each other on the sly—"

"No." Hannah's tone was curt to the point of unfriendly. "Why are you here, Grit?"

He shrugged, no sign that Hannah's irritation with him affected him at all. "Navy business."

Yeah, right, Beth thought, but she could tell no one else in the room believed him, either.

"What about Rose and Nick Martini?" Grit asked.

That was too much for Sean. He sprang to his feet and collected Beth's empty glass and his own and brought them to the counter.

Beth realized she was gaping at her friend. Hannah, who had barely touched her drink, was even paler now. Her expression said it all. "Hannah—you're kidding." Beth couldn't contain her shock. "You mean there's something between Rose and Nick?"

"I don't know anything. Nothing. I just…" She looked at Sean. "It's none of our business. They're adults."

Sean obviously had to pry his teeth apart to talk. "I'd trust Nick with my life. I *have* trusted him with my life."

"That doesn't mean you'd trust him with your sister," Grit said.

Sean didn't respond.

"Would you trust anyone?" the Navy SEAL asked.

"Not the point," Sean muttered, and moved down the hall.

Hannah exhaled and picked up her whiskey. "Don't let him fool you. He's guessed about Nick and Rose. He's just in denial. Rose would only tell me that Nick was a sexier mistake than Derek." She winced. "It'd just kill her if she knew we were here discussing her love life over whiskey."

Beth pushed to her feet. "Not her love life. That's the problem. Maybe she's the smart one. Have a fling and walk away. Not everyone has a soul mate out there." She retied her robe. "Back to bed with me."

She marched down the hall, shutting her bedroom door hard behind her. She wasn't the crying type but she found her eyes brimming with tears. She blamed the late hour, the news from home, the whiskey, but she knew it was Scott.

She glanced at her cell phone. He worked odd hours as a trooper. He could be up for all she knew.

"He can call me," she muttered, brushed the tears out of her eyes and climbed into bed.

Grit finished his whiskey alone in the kitchen. The house was quiet. While he had regarded all the women of Black Falls as sisters since first venturing to Vermont in November, he did entertain a moment's surprise at his reaction to Beth Harper as she'd tightened her robe over plaid boxer shorts and a tight little T-shirt.

All that up and down the mountains of northern New England had kept her in shape.

But she was clearly worried about what was going on in Black Falls.

He headed to his assigned bedroom in the back. It wasn't that small. It had its own bathroom. He was used to rats and cockroaches at the apartment he'd given up in D.C. before moving to Myrtle's place. Before that...

Before that, he'd been someone else.

His leg ached when he took off his prosthesis. The long flight had taken its toll, and probably the whiskey, too. He distracted himself by thinking about firebugs and Beth Harper in her flannel boxers.

Just because he'd thought of her as a sister before didn't mean anything. She wasn't his sister.

No, she was the sister of Elijah's fiancée and on the rebound from her state trooper.

Out of reach. Out of bounds.

Didn't mean she didn't have great legs.

"Give it up," Grit whispered to himself, and emptied his mind. Time for sleep. He had work to do after daylight.

Thirteen

Black Falls, Vermont

Rose stood at the top of her driveway in the soft, gray morning light and watched Ranger run into the snow after a tennis ball. She noticed he looked stiff in his hindquarters. He was a good dog, eager and fit, but, inarguably, he was slowing down. She couldn't face his approaching infirmities now, and whatever his future as a search dog, he still had plenty of life left in him.

A dusting of snow overnight had freshened up the landscape. While Ranger searched for the ball, she shoveled some sand onto the more treacherous sections of her front walk.

Nick came out of the house, his coat open, his hair tousled. Rose hoped he couldn't see her reaction to him—not that it would be a surprise. He knew. She'd made it plain in June that she found him physically irresistible.

He headed down the steps, not looking as if he'd been

attacked twelve hours earlier or had slept on a couch. "Damn," he said with an exaggerated shiver, "spring didn't come overnight, did it? It's still winter."

"The sunrise is earlier. It was a gorgeous one this morning. The entire sky turned shades of pink and lavender."

"You have a beautiful spot here."

"I do. I feel very fortunate." She emptied her shovel onto a slick spot at the bottom of the steps. "How are you this morning?"

Nick grinned. "I feel like I got hit in the head with a shovel last night."

She saw that the bloody parts of his scrape had scabbed over and were healing nicely. "I'm glad you weren't badly hurt. You kept whoever it was—"

"Feehan."

"You kept him from doing serious damage to you."

Nick hunched his shoulders against a sudden breeze. "If he'd landed a clean hit, he had time to stuff my body in a snowbank and wait for you to come back from your brother's place."

Rose leaned the offending shovel against the garage. "The odds were against him. That's why he ran. He knew he couldn't win."

"I made coffee," Nick said, not arguing with her. "I figure we can go to the lodge for goat cheese omelets."

She didn't know if he was being sarcastic. "They're good. Goat cheese, fresh chives—"

"I'm sold."

"You're just cold."

"That, too." Ranger leaped out of the snowbank and

catapulted to Nick with a bright green tennis ball in his mouth. He laughed. "If there's a ball within a mile, a golden retriever will find it. I had a golden as a kid. Bo. He was great company when my dad was at sea."

"Most of the time Ranger's all the company I need."

"I'm not going there," Nick said, taking the slobbery ball and tossing it into the snow. Ranger leaped after it, more agile now that he'd warmed up.

For a few seconds, Rose let herself imagine that this sexy, confident, successful man had come to Vermont just to see her, with no other agenda. Would she want such a man in her life? Her life would change, that was for sure.

Her golden retriever returned with the tennis ball. She took it from him, lavishing praise as she glanced at Nick. "I want to go back out to the Whittaker place later this morning," she said.

He gave a curt nod. "I do, too. We can go together."

Ranger led the way up the front steps, the wind blowing hard now, the sunlight gleaming on his golden coat. Rose paused and smiled back at Nick. "The air feels good, doesn't it?"

"No."

"At least you don't have to worry about a wildfire sparking out here in the snow. That fire last June—I just happened to be in Los Angeles working with firefighters on canine searches. I could just as easily have been here."

"But you weren't," Nick said.

"You never said anything to Sean about us, did you?"

"I kept my promise to you."

"Ah. A gentleman."

Nick stood next to her at the front door. "If I'd been a gentleman, I'd have taken you back to his place that night."

She turned and looked out at the mountains in the distance, felt Cameron Mountain looming behind her. She was quiet for a moment. Finally she said, "Derek didn't like to take no for an answer."

"Rose," Nick said, his voice dark.

"I made him take no with me. Not soon enough, but I did it. He was a mistake. A short-lived, stupid mistake. He was a mean drunk, and he wasn't nice when I refused him. We'd been seeing each other, quietly. Never here." She kept her tone even, as if she were giving a post-search report. "We went skiing, had dinner together a few times. I thought he was...I don't know. Interesting. Action-oriented. He wasn't one of the usual suspects involved in my search-and-rescue work."

"A fresh face," Nick said.

She nodded, determined to get this over with. "He was fascinated by what I do, or pretended to be. He loved Vermont. I was in the mood for a little romance in my life."

"That's not how it worked out."

"It never does work out that way, does it?"

"Flowers, chocolates. Romance isn't that hard." Nick patted Ranger and shrugged. "It might get tough if I had to write a poem."

She smiled at him. "I'll settle for flowers and chocolate."

"Cutshaw?"

"He was about conquering and control. He assumed I'd go along with him without question, but I said no. He didn't like it. He was nasty. Threatening, belittling, abusive. He didn't physically hurt me. He wouldn't have dared."

"Verbal abuse can flatten people."

"Yes, it can. He was very manipulative. Moody and mercurial. I never knew if I would get the Bad Derek or the Good Derek. I didn't put up with it for long, but I put up with it for too long. I was in a tough place and I wanted to believe in the Good Derek." She was aware of Nick's eyes on her, but she concentrated on the view of the mountains she loved. "I don't like talking about this."

"Understood."

"Derek went from calling me at inappropriate times to being openly hostile after I told him I didn't want a relationship with him. He never left a trail, and I wasn't sure who'd believe me that he was as awful as he was." She shifted her gaze to the evergreen shrubs, the trampled snow from last night. "Vivian Whittaker was psychologically abusive toward her husband. I'm not saying that's why he did what he did."

"You got away from Cutshaw. Lowell stayed with his wife."

"Derek and I saw each other for less than six weeks. He thought he was doing me a favor by being interested in me at all. He was used to women falling all over him. He couldn't believe I would walk away." She turned back to Nick. "He made sure I knew he didn't think I was anything special."

Nick tucked a few windblown strands of hair off her face, out of her eyes. "You're beautiful, Rose, and you're sexy as hell."

"Sure, Nick. I'm out here in one of my father's old flannel shirts."

He grinned at her. "With your blue eyes standing out against the snow and your cheeks pink with the wind and the cold."

She groaned. "Sure, Nick."

"Cutshaw was a fool if he treated you as anything but a strong, desirable woman." Pain flashed in his eyes. "Me, too."

"You're nothing like he was." She tugged open the storm door. "I told you about Derek because of what's happened in the past forty-eight hours. The rest doesn't matter."

"It does matter."

She felt her throat tighten. "You're good-looking, rich, rugged. You can have any woman—"

"No, I can't. No one can, and who'd want to? Come on. Give me a break. Some guys would say one woman's plenty."

"Some women would say no man is fine."

"From what I remember, that wouldn't be you."

She couldn't help but smile. "Bastard."

He slipped an arm around her middle and drew her close to him. "I'm sorry Derek Cutshaw was such a son of a bitch, but he's in the past. He was in the past when you and I got together."

"Got together, Nick?"

"Yeah." He kissed her on the top of the head and tightened his hold on her. "Very together."

"We had a one-night stand." She didn't wait for him to respond and pulled away from him as she entered the house. "We can grab something to eat at the café on our way out to the Whittaker place."

He waited a half beat before responding. "All right. Sounds good."

"Sorry if I was prickly."

"That was nothing. You forget I've been friends with a Cameron for ten years. I figure you held back. I'm lucky."

Rose laughed as she dug the tennis ball out of her pocket and set it in the closet along with a dozen others. "You wanted to make me laugh, didn't you?"

"Always." But Nick was serious now. "Don't be so hard on yourself. You got away from Cutshaw. That's what counts."

"I thought of myself as so strong…"

"A hit to your ego like that undermines your confidence. Only thing to do is to get back up and carry on." His voice was quiet, his eyes on her. "Being strong doesn't mean you never get hurt."

"Or do something stupid."

He smiled. "That, too."

She took one of Ranger's leashes from the closet. "Nick, what if Derek somehow knew about us and went into a jealous rage and arranged to kill himself so that I'd find his body?"

"From everything I've heard, he wasn't even remotely suicidal."

"I keep asking myself why was he out there. What did he want with me?" She started back to the door but stopped abruptly. "Why now, Nick? Why are you here now? Is there anything you haven't told me?"

"The timing was right. That's all. Nothing more."

"Right for what?"

"To make sure you were okay, and to see if there was any indication Jasper was killed by Lowell's network. Informally," Nick added. "I'm not part of any investigation."

Rose yanked open the front door again. "We can take my Jeep out to the river."

Nick touched her upper arm, stopping her. "Rose," he said, "I haven't told anyone about us because I promised I wouldn't. That doesn't mean I regret making love to you. I don't."

She held on to the doorknob, letting cold air seep into her house. "Hannah suspects."

"Hannah *knows*. She's good at reading people, especially her friends," Nick said, obviously liking her. "A prosecutor in the making."

"I told her she didn't have to keep any secrets from Sean."

"Yeah, I know. I had a text message from him waiting for me this morning."

"What did it say?"

"My sister?" Nick winked at her. "Sums it up, doesn't it?"

Rose pulled the door open wider. "I guess it does.

I probably should be more embarrassed than I am. I'd hoped he didn't have to find out."

"Hell, so did I, but not for my sake. Sean and I have covered a lot of ground together."

"I can assure him you didn't take advantage of me."

Nick shook his head. "He won't ask. He was just telling me he knows. The rest is none of his business. He understands that."

"Then Hannah told him about Derek, too." Rose groaned. "I said she could, but I hate this. Derek was already at the Whittaker place when you arrived. Could he have known or guessed you were on your way and just got there first? Maybe he wasn't there to see me at all."

"I didn't know until I woke up at four-thirty that I'd head out there. I was lucky A.J. gave me directions. Derek was dead by then." Sunlight angled through the door, shining on his striking hair, his dark eyes. "We're speculating."

"Which can lead to trouble—just as it does in a search." She motioned for Ranger to come to her and clipped the leash onto his collar. "I'm neutral about you, Nick."

"Neutral? What's that mean? You didn't want to crawl under my hand-knitted afghan last night, or you didn't even think about it?"

She'd thought about it. She'd wanted to. Had he thought about knocking on her bedroom door?

She said nothing and headed back outside with Ranger.

"So neutral means you're resisting being attracted to me," Nick said as he trotted down the steps behind her.

She glanced back at him. "Could I say the same about you?"

"I'm not neutral, and I'm not resisting."

"Then you're—"

"Restraining myself. You're under duress. We already did that. It didn't work out so well."

"We were both under duress in June." She stopped at the bottom of the steps, choking on her words, then forced herself to continue. "If one of Lowell's killers created that hot spot and lured Jasper Vanderhorn into it—"

"Don't jump ahead."

"Nick, *could* Jasper's serial arsonist be in Black Falls?"

"Jasper's serial arsonist might not even exist. He never could prove his theory. One thing at a time, Rose," Nick said quietly, winking at her as he opened the back of her Jeep for Ranger. "Let's go to Three Sisters Café and see what's cooking."

Ninety minutes later, Rose let Ranger out of the back of her Jeep. He leaped onto the snow-packed driveway of the sprawling Whittaker estate, which, she thought, had to occupy one of the most scenic stretches of the shallow, twisting branch of the Black River.

Nick went ahead of her onto the shoveled walk. She tried to relax, but sitting next to him on the drive into the village, then across from him at the café and again on the drive out to the river had nearly done her in.

He was the sexiest man she'd ever met.

Telling him about Derek—giving Hannah permission

to tell Sean and Beth—had been difficult but also a relief. Her past with Derek had turned into a secret that rapidly had taken on a life of its own. Derek's lies and exaggerations and the fight at O'Rourke's had only made matters worse.

For months, Rose had wondered if she'd have fallen into bed with Nick if not for her brief, awful relationship with Derek Cutshaw.

Ranger looked up at her, as if he remembered that their last visit here hadn't gone well. The wind whipped the dusting of snow into the cold, clear air.

Nick eased close to her, putting a hand on her hip. "Hold on."

"I see," she said, noticing a man coming down the walk from the boarded-up farmhouse, then recognized Brett Griffin.

Brett waved as he approached them, his camera hanging from his neck. "I heard the investigators were done here and thought I'd stop by and see for myself." He gestured down the slope toward the stone guesthouse. "I parked in the turnaround and walked up the road. It's windy as all get-out. Took me by surprise."

"Did you come alone?" Rose asked.

He nodded. "The police came to see me last night to ask about Robert. I heard he tried to break into your house."

"That might be a bit of an exaggeration, but it doesn't matter. He should stop sneaking around and talk to the police."

"I think so, too. I told him as much yesterday morning. Whatever he's hiding, it can't be as bad as having the police think he was involved in Derek's death. That's what's going on, isn't it?"

"I wish I knew," Rose said. Another strong gust of wind blew up from the river. She felt a spray of snow in her face and could see Nick, who remained at her side, was hit with it, too, but he didn't seem to notice.

Brett looked up toward the boarded-up farmhouse, his face pale even in the wind. He seemed to force himself out of his thoughts. "I ran into Bowie O'Rourke at the guesthouse when I got here. He was checking on the work he did for the Whittakers in January. You two aren't meeting him, I take it?"

Rose shook her head. "No, we're not. Is he still there?"

"I don't know. Bowie and I don't exactly get along. We only exchanged a few words." Brett raised his camera and eased the strap over his head. He had on layers that were well suited to the conditions, and he could easily spend the day in the cold. "I thought I'd take some pictures of the river while I was here. It's therapeutic."

"Did Feehan mention coming out here?" Nick asked.

"Not to me. I've tried his cell phone a few times but it goes right to voice mail. He hasn't called back." Brett grimaced as he squinted past Nick toward the shed. "I don't know why Derek or Robert would want to come here. They had nothing to do with the Whittakers."

"Was there any tension between them?" Rose asked. "They were housemates. It'd be understandable if they got on each other's nerves."

"To the point of Robert setting Derek on fire?"

Brett turned ashen, obviously taken aback. "Damn, Rose. No."

"That's not what I meant."

He started up the walk, leaving footprints in the light snow, but stopped after a few steps and looked back at Rose. He seemed pained, but also resigned, as if he'd come to terms with what they were thinking about the man he'd once called a friend. "There was tension between Derek and everyone. He and I got along okay because I didn't cross him. That's why I finally backed off. I didn't need all that drama. The guy had no sense of his own limits. No boundaries. He was a great skier, though. Confident. I'm not nearly as good as he was. Robert's better than I am, too." Brett nodded to Nick. "Did he give you that scrape on your face?"

"Yes, he did," Nick said.

"This is crazy," Brett said half under his breath. "I don't even know why I'm here. Just couldn't stop myself, I guess."

Rose watched him continue tentatively up to the farmhouse, as if every step were torture. Nick edged closer to her. "More company," he said, pointing down to the driveway.

She noticed Zack Harper's pickup truck pull behind her Jeep. Ranger bounded to her left side, and she stroked his broad back, settling him down and combating her own uneasiness.

Zack clearly wasn't expecting to find anyone there. "What're you all doing," he said as he ambled up to them, "setting up for a winter picnic?"

Rose grimaced at his sharp tone. "Just wanted to have

another look now that the police are done here. What about you, Zack?"

"The same." He glanced down the snow-covered slope. His jacket was open, and he wasn't wearing gloves, a hat or a scarf. He seemed unaffected by the cold and the wind. "Bowie and Dominique left, huh? I saw them down by the guesthouse when I drove by about an hour ago."

"Dom Belair?" Rose couldn't contain her surprise. "She was with Bowie?"

"She was in her own car. Bowie had his van."

Rose frowned. "I didn't realize she even knew her way out here."

"I didn't stop," Zack said. "I had a call to make down in the hollow. I was on my way back to town when I saw your Jeep."

"Brett Griffin's here, too," Rose said.

"Yeah, I saw his car." Zack turned to Nick. "Want to take a look at the fire damage with me?"

"Sure," Nick said.

Rose let Ranger poke around in the snow and went with Zack and Nick to the farmhouse. Brett seemed frozen in place by Lowell's woodpile and said nothing to the two firefighters as they headed onto the narrow path behind the shed.

"You okay?" Rose asked Brett.

He sucked in a breath. "Those two will look at the scene differently than either one of us. I understand that Nick and your brother Sean are elite smoke jumpers. Do you think Zack feels inadequate?"

"Zack? Not a chance." Rose smiled. "He's a Harper, for one thing."

She noticed Brett had pulled off his gloves. He fiddled with a knob on his camera and chuckled. "There's that. I heard all four Neal sisters have a crush on Zack."

"They wouldn't be the first. It'll be interesting to see if they all turn up for winter fest." Rose realized there was still a faint smell of smoke in the air. "Unless Derek's death isn't resolved by then."

"Why should that make any difference? The Neals live in Washington. Imagine all the ongoing death investigations there. They're under Secret Service protection. They'll be fine wherever they are."

"Good point. Brett, did you see Dominique when you arrived?"

He shook his head. "Just Bowie, unless they came together—"

"She came in her car."

"I didn't see it when I arrived." Brett abandoned his adjustments to his camera. "Coming out here's harder than I imagined it'd be. I thought I wanted to see for myself where Derek died. Now I don't know if I can look."

"You don't have to look," Rose said sympathetically.

He raised his gaze to her. "It really was bad, wasn't it?"

"Yes, it was. I'm sorry."

"Have you talked to Elijah and Jo yet? I don't know them myself. I saw Elijah at O'Rourke's last year when Derek got drunk and said those things to Hannah. We didn't chitchat, obviously. He's very controlled, isn't he?"

"When he needs to be, I guess."

"Spoken like a true baby sister," Brett said with a strained laugh. "I've heard that Jo and Trooper Thorne don't get along."

"That's too strong."

"She's a federal agent, and he's a state trooper. It's not surprising there's a bit of a rivalry between them, is it?"

"There's no rivalry on Jo's end, and I doubt there's one on Scott's. It's nothing they couldn't work out if he and Beth decide to stay together." Rose straightened sharply. "Brett? Are you and Beth—"

"No, no. I'm just an observer. There's nothing between us—on her side or mine." He seemed taken aback by any suggestion he might have a romantic interest in Beth Harper. "I don't mean to pry. It's the classic curse of the outsider in a small town."

"I guess I wouldn't know about that, since I've lived here all my life." Rose nodded to his camera. "You're also a photographer. An observer. I'd love to see some of your photos one day."

"That'd be great." Watching Ranger wander over to the shed, Brett quickly snapped his picture, then lowered his camera. "Trooper Thorne's on the state police search-and-rescue team. Are you and he rivals?"

Rose got Ranger back to her side. "I don't think of what I do in those terms. I doubt he does, either."

"Sorry. I'm saying all the wrong things." Brett edged onto the narrow path that led to the back of the shed. "I'm just blurting out whatever pops into my head. Being here…" He sucked in a breath. "I think I can do it. I think I can look. I'd hate myself for being a coward if I didn't."

"I'll go with you."

"All right, but you don't have to. Zack and Nick have experience with fires. They'll be objective. They'll help if I can't handle being there."

"There's not much fire damage to the shed, Brett."

He looked grim. "So Derek took the brunt of the flames."

"If Coleman fuel was in that lamp, it's highly combustible. The flash and fire—"

"He didn't stand a chance if he was standing close, didn't know."

Rose remembered every detail of walking into the shed. The smell, the cold, the stillness. Seeing Derek's coat on the back of the chair. The shed wasn't heated but he'd had on layers. He could have been warm from hiking up from his car.

She signaled Ranger to follow her as she and Brett went around to the ell. Even with the fresh snow, the area in front of the door was still visibly trampled from the investigators. The smell of charred wood was stronger here, but the shed blocked the worst of the wind. The rough wood door was propped open with a brick.

Brett hesitated, gripping his camera, and jumped, visibly startled, when Zack exited the shed.

"It won't be easy to figure out exactly what happened here," Zack said.

Nick was right behind him. "It often is with a fire. Arson's one of the hardest crimes to prove, solve and prosecute."

"Too many of these bastards get away with setting their little fires," Zack said, his disdain clear. "You can't generalize about arsonists. Each one's an individual. They have their own methods, their own reasons, if you want to call them that, for doing what they do."

Brett's breathing was rapid, shallow. "Do you know for sure this even was arson?"

Zack's turquoise eyes seemed lighter in the brightening sunshine. "You'd have to talk to the lead investigators."

"First they have to rule out a natural or accidental cause," Nick said. "In this case, that's going to be difficult because of the circumstances. Coleman fuel is easily accessed and commonly used. If it works under pressure in a little camp stove, why not in a kerosene lamp? I can see someone thinking like that, just making a stupid mistake."

Brett shook his head. "Not Derek."

"It could have been one of the Whittakers, even one of their guests." Zack bent down and rubbed Ranger's front. "That was a rough morning for you, wasn't it, buddy? You come out here to play fetch and get put to work." He stood up again and looked at Rose. "I promised Beth I'd fill in for her tonight at the café. It's cleaning night." He grinned. "Feel free to take my place."

Rose knew his good humor was as close as she'd get to an apology from him for his earlier surliness. "I've done cleaning night with you, Zack. Mostly you just eat leftover brownies."

"Dom's brownies are the best," he said. "See you all later."

He took the path around to the front of the shed. Rose

sighed at his retreating figure. "Zack hasn't changed since fifth grade."

Brett had stepped just inside the shed, his gaze fixed on the spot where his friend had died. He backed out suddenly, stumbling, dropping his camera in the snow. "I knew this'd be hard, but—" He broke off, looking agonized, and scooped up his camera. "Why didn't the whole damn place didn't catch fire?"

Nick answered, his tone neutral, professional. "It looks as if your friend Derek put out the flames when he hit the floor."

"He probably wasn't killed instantly, then."

"Probably not, no," Nick said. "If this was arson, his killer undoubtedly intended for the shed to burn down. There'd be even less evidence for investigators to go on."

Brett held his camera in a bare hand, staring at it as if its familiarity gave him comfort. "I can't imagine what it was like to find him. I've never seen a dead body. I've dealt with a few injuries skiing and giving lessons, but nothing like what Derek must have suffered."

"I know it's difficult," Rose said quietly.

"If you'll excuse me, I have to get out of here." He cleared his throat. "I'm glad you two were here. I thought I wanted to do this alone, but I see now I was wrong."

"I can drive you down to your car."

He shook his head. "It's not far. The walk will do me good."

Nick waited until he was out of earshot around the other side of the shed before he spoke. "Griffin seems to get along with you. Does he know about you and Cutshaw?"

"There was no me and..." Rose stopped herself, hearing the defensiveness in her tone. "Some. Not as much as Robert."

"Either one of them date local women?"

"Not that I know of. I thought from something Brett said that he might be interested in Beth but he said no. I don't know him or Robert that well."

Nick picked up the brick that had been propping open the shed door and set it inside, then shut the door. "You'd all let a newcomer like Brett in?"

"It's not a question of 'newcomer,'" Rose said. "Most of the people I know in town take newcomers one at a time, if that's where you're going with this. Derek, Robert and even Brett hurt their chances by what they did last year at O'Rourke's, but nobody would hold it against them forever."

"Bowie and his cousin Liam would," Nick said without hesitation. "So would Sean. What about you?"

"I told you. I wasn't there." She looked through the woods, down at the frozen river, and noticed deer tracks disappearing down the hill. "Derek found me up at the falls on Cameron Mountain about this time last year. I was training Ranger. It wasn't as cold and as windy as it is today. It was one of those mild late February days that make you think spring is closer than it is."

She could feel Nick behind her. "What happened?"

"He was in a rage because I'd told him I didn't want to see him again. Saying we broke up is too strong, at least in my mind. I always knew we weren't meant to be together forever." She shivered, then turned to Nick. "Anyway, Derek stomped and swore at me and got nasty and pathetic. Then he left."

"Did he hurt you?"

"He tried to grab my arm. I backed off and tripped, and Ranger jumped between us."

Nick came up next to her. "Good for Ranger."

"When I picked myself up out of the snow, Derek was gone. I wasn't hurt. I didn't tell anyone."

"Did he stalk you? Threaten you?"

She shook her head. "He more or less left me alone after that," she said.

"What does 'more or less' mean?"

"It means he didn't do anything that would have made me go to the police."

"Or tell your family and friends," Nick said.

She didn't answer.

He didn't back off. "Bowie knew?"

Snow blew off the shed roof into her face. "He ran into Derek when he was still raging about my having stood up to him at the falls. Derek bragged about things that never happened between us. He wanted to get under Bowie's skin because he knew we were friends."

"So Bowie was ready for a fight that night at O'Rourke's."

"He thinks his presence provoked Derek to start in on Hannah in the first place. Derek was spoiling for a fight." Rose signaled Ranger to come to her side. "It's complicated."

"Not that complicated," Nick said. "It's a small town. Your brothers were there. Cutshaw wanted to hurt you.

You're a trusted canine search-and-rescue expert. All he had to do was lie or exaggerate, and you'd be hurt."

"What happened between Derek and me was bad enough without him making up stuff." She glanced back at the ell of the shed where he'd died, smelled the burned wood. "I told the police everything."

"Was Cutshaw interested in search-and-rescue work?"

"He wanted to get into mountain rescue, but he wanted it for his ego, which is exactly the wrong reason."

Nick studied her a moment. "Did your father know what went on between you two?"

"I don't know. He asked me if I was okay not long after Derek came after me at the falls. It wasn't like Pop. I said yes, and that was the end of it."

Her throat tight with emotion, Rose signaled to Ranger to heel and headed briskly with him around to the front of the shed.

Nick kept up with them and eased in next to her behind the farmhouse. He nodded to the boarded-up back door. "Did Sean run in through the back when he saved Bowie from the fire?"

"Yes." Rose crossed her arms against the cold. "Bowie grabbed Vivian Whittaker after Lowell set off a bomb on the second floor and ran downstairs with her. She thanked him by tripping him and leaving him to burn to death. Who'd ever know? She wanted him to take the fall for Lowell."

"Sean got Bowie out of there," Nick said, pensive. "That's not as easy to do as it looks in the movies. It's an older house. Always a nightmare for firefighters."

"It was built by a wealthy New York couple who loved Black Falls and were nothing like the Whittakers. It's always been owned by people from out-of-state. Not many people here could afford it."

"The Camerons?"

"Not unless we turned it into something that could produce an income. It'd be a risky investment."

"A challenge."

Rose smiled, her tension lessening. "Maybe that's why you're a multimillionaire. Do you love any of the buildings you and Sean have bought?"

"We don't invest in a property we don't love. We've refurbished some historic beauties. We're looking into a grande dame of an old hotel in Beverly Hills right now. Hannah loves it."

"I'm glad to hear that."

"But it's still business," Nick said.

"It has to be. You and Sean had a fire in a building last winter. I hadn't thought about that. Did Jasper investigate?'

"Not at the time. Afterward."

"Because of his serial arsonist?"

A strong gust of wind howled and whistled in the trees. "It's cold," Nick said, heading back onto the walk. "Let's go."

They returned to her Jeep. Ranger hopped in the back, agile and eager, no sign of stiffness.

A mile down the riverside road, Nick settled back in his seat. "What's on your mind, Rose?"

"Nothing."

"Uh-huh," he said skeptically.

She gripped the wheel. "I was thinking about driving up to Killington to check out the house Robert and Derek rented together."

"Bad idea."

She sighed, the emotion of being back at the scene of Derek's death—reliving the weeks they'd seen each other—still weighing on her. "I have some work to do at my house. I'll drop you off at the lodge."

"I can keep myself busy at your place. I'll chop wood."

"When's the last time you chopped wood?"

He grinned at her. "You just forgot I'm a rugged smoke jumper, didn't you? I can wield an ax. You insist on always imagining me in a tux at a five-star Beverly Hills hotel."

"Wrong, Nick."

"Ah. So you also imagine me in the shower."

She felt a jolt of pure sexual awareness. The shower. Great. Just what she needed. If she hadn't been imagining him naked thirty seconds ago, she was now, which, she suspected, had been his goal.

Was he imagining *her* naked in the shower?

She ground the gears turning onto the main road into the village and tried not to look at him. So much for being a private person. Now Nick knew about Derek, and Sean, Hannah and everyone else knew about Nick. She had no secrets left.

Maybe it was just as well, she thought. Maybe now she could put the pain and mistakes of the past year behind her.

She glanced at Nick, saw the scrape and bruise on

the side of his head and realized that nothing would be behind her, nothing would be over, until he had his answers. Until he was satisfied that Jasper Vanderhorn's serial arsonist—his killer—wasn't in Vermont.

Fourteen

Beverly Hills, California

Grit woke up and checked his BlackBerry. He didn't have any emails, text messages or voice mails from anyone but Admiral Jenkins, his boss, who'd left one of each at around one in the morning East Coast time. Grit eyed the email subject heading: Los Angeles?

Apparently the admiral didn't like Grit's choice of airport.

Nothing anyone could do about it now. Grit deleted all three messages.

He went through his routine to put on his prosthesis and headed down the hall to the kitchen. It was a bright, beautiful morning in Beverly Hills. No one was around. He figured Sean was off making money or putting out fires, but he noticed Hannah and Beth were out by the pool. He glanced at the clock and saw that it was just after ten. Later than he thought.

He ventured outside for coffee, fruit, cheese and cute mini-muffins at a sunny table by the pool. While he was listening to Beth describe a discussion back in Black Falls between foodie Dominique Belair and Washington reporter Myrtle Smith over the virtues of different varieties of peaches, Grit received a series of text messages—one after another—from Charlie Neal. They came through under an obvious alias, but Grit wasn't even curious how Charlie had pulled them off.

Each message included a piece of the address for his sister Marissa's actor ex-boyfriend, Trent Stevens.

Grit didn't text Charlie back.

Hannah and Beth were dressed in shorts and T-shirts, Hannah's legs slightly less pale than Beth's. Both had obviously slathered on sunscreen. Grit, who was in civilian cargo pants and a polo shirt, didn't bother. He wasn't spending the day by the pool.

"It was cool last week," Hannah said.

"It's cool this week," he said. "You two just think it's warm because you're used to it being four degrees."

"You did your SEAL training out here," Beth said, holding a bunch of grapes in her lap.

"Not in Beverly Hills."

She rolled her eyes. "I know not in Beverly Hills."

"I don't scare you, do I?"

"What?"

He grinned and helped himself to a strawberry. "Never mind. I trained down the road on Coronado. What're you two doing today?"

"Hannah's studying this morning," Beth said. "I'll

hang out here. Then we're doing a ladies' lunch at the Beverly Hills Hotel. You're welcome to join us."

"I'm not a lady."

Another roll of the eyes. Grit figured Beth Harper deserved sunlight, warmth and time away from Vermont, given the stresses of the past winter. She'd been on the search team that had hiked up the remote north side of Cameron Mountain when one of Lowell Whittaker's paid killers had pinned down Jo, Elijah, Hannah's brother Devin and another teenager—the stepdaughter of a murdered ambassador—in a tiny cabin.

By the time Beth arrived, the killer, a brutal type named Kyle Rigby, was dead. Elijah had shot him while Jo provided cover from the cabin and kept the two teenagers alive.

Trooper Thorne had been on the team that morning.

Beth was the second daughter of a Black Falls retired police chief, one of the co-owners of Three Sisters Café and, from what Grit had seen during his days in Black Falls, close to her firefighter brother and federal agent sister. But right now, Beth looked very alone to him.

Hannah gave Grit a bright smile. "What are you doing today?"

"I have a few errands to run before I head to Coronado. Should be interesting. I haven't been this far from my physical therapist since they wheeled me into Bethesda."

Beth plucked a grape off her bunch and popped it in her mouth. "You'll be fine."

"You're a hard-bitten Yankee woman, Beth Harper," Grit teased her, good-humored, as he got to his feet.

"I was being encouraging."

He laughed and headed back inside. It was a nice house. Generally it took a lot for him to notice such things. He was digging out his phone to call a cab when Beth appeared at his elbow. "Sean's loaned me a car," she said. "I can take you where you want to go."

"What about your ladies' lunch?"

"Hannah said she can use the extra study time. We'll go tomorrow."

"You could just give me the keys," Grit said.

"Nope. Can't. The idea of driving the streets of Beverly Hills with a disabled Navy SEAL scares the hell out of me."

"No, it doesn't. You're looking for distractions. In my experience, that, combined with car keys, is a recipe for problems."

"Add jet lag and unfamiliar roads and it all cancels out," Beth said. "I'll have to concentrate."

Who was he to argue with such logic?

Grit followed Beth to the garage and took the passenger seat of an expensive sedan while she got behind the wheel and snapped on her seat belt. He thought about getting her to talk about Rose Cameron, but she hadn't been kidding about the jet lag and unfamiliar roads. Even after a week in Southern California, she said, she wasn't used to the three-hour time difference. He had a feeling she just didn't want to admit she'd been sleeping badly since Trooper Thorne had gone back to Vermont early.

"Didn't you think Beverly Hills would be flatter?" she asked as she careened around a sharp, downhill curve.

"No. It's got 'hills' in the name."

"There are hills and there are hills. Where are we going?"

Grit checked the directions Charlie had obsessively provided. "Two lefts and a right."

They came to a square, three-story stucco apartment building off Wilshire. Beth pulled into a small parking area out back. Grit got out. His left leg was doing better after his flight but still ached. He had instructions from PT on what to do about any kind of discomfort, rash or swelling that flared up.

"You can wait here," he said to Beth.

"I get bored fast." She pushed open her door and got out. "Who are we going to see—some SEAL buddy of yours?"

He glanced back at her. He really should have told her to keep her lunch date with Hannah. She didn't need to be with him. "An actor," he said. "A friend of a friend."

She looked skeptical. From what he'd seen of her, she had good instincts about people, undoubtedly including him. Her big sister, Jo, was the same, although Charlie had gotten the better of her with his prank last fall.

Then again, Charlie got the better of most people.

Grit went ahead of Beth to a rear apartment on the corner of the first floor. A little hybrid car was in what appeared to be the apartment's designated parking space. On the cracked concrete landing, a basket with dried-up red flowers poking out of it hung from a hook.

"Is that a flower that needs a lot of water?" he asked Beth.

"How would I know? I'm a paramedic."

"That doesn't mean you don't know flowers."

"They're red," she said. "They look like they need more water than they've been getting."

He glanced back at her. "You're not going to be much help, are you?"

She didn't answer. He stepped onto the landing and reached to press the rusted doorbell, but Beth grabbed his arm.

He knew why. He'd smelled it, too. It wasn't strong, but he recognized the sickly, tangy-sweet smell of rotting human flesh.

"Call 911," Beth said. "Someone's dead in there."

"You call." Grit turned to her, serious now. "Okay? Do it now."

He tried the doorknob. The door was unlocked. He heard Beth's sharp breath behind him but ignored her and went in.

A woman lay sprawled on her back on the kitchen floor. She was young, about five-four, with wide hips and a flat stomach and long, straight hair as black as Grit's.

She'd been dead for some time, at least a couple of days.

"Looks like she was electrocuted," Beth said, tight. "See her hands? Burned."

Grit pointed at a stainless-steel electric kettle turned over on the tile floor by the counter. Bare wires poked out of the bottom of the pot. "Well, well. Some son of a bitch stripped the wires, set them between the heating element and the pot.... She grabs the pot for a nice cup of tea and she's toast."

"Literally." Beth was grim as she nodded to a sponge

mop standing in a bucket of water. "She'd been cleaning the floors, too. Water and electricity don't mix."

Not an accident, Grit thought.

Beth called 911, identified herself and calmly, professionally described the emergency, but when Grit started into the adjoining living room, she waved frantically at him. He ignored her. They'd already contaminated the crime scene, and how did they know there wasn't another victim—someone who might be alive and need their help?

No one was in the living room. Grit ducked down a short hall and checked the one bedroom and bathroom, then returned to the living room and checked the door there, which led to a hall and the building's front entrance.

There were no other victims and no obvious signs of an intruder.

The apartment wasn't neat. It was decorated with white shag carpets and bright, cheap artwork, with a state-of-the-art media setup.

The dead woman hadn't gotten far with her cleaning. Grit considered that she might not be an outside housekeeper. Maybe she was bunking in with Trent and it had just been her turn with the mop.

So where was he?

A corkboard above the dining table was covered with photos of a very good-looking, fair-haired man in his earlier thirties. Grit helped himself to one and tucked it in his back pocket as he dialed Jo Harper on his cell phone.

She didn't bother with a hello. "How's California?" she asked him.

"Well, it's like this, Jo. I'm in a small, stuffy apartment in Beverly Hills. The tenant's not here but a dead woman is."

He heard her breathe in through clenched teeth. "Damn, Grit. You weren't supposed to go out there and find a body."

He decided to get it over with: "Beth's with me."

"My sister? *Beth?* Why? Is she okay? Where is she?"

"She's in the kitchen calling 911. She's a pro. She's my driver."

"Grit, what the hell were you thinking?"

"She was bored. I can drive okay with the leg, but I don't have a car." He returned to the kitchen. Beth was still speaking with the dispatcher. Grit glanced again at the dead woman. Were her family and friends looking for her? Did they have any idea she was here?

"Grit," Jo said.

"Your people are going to get involved, aren't they?"

"Describe the woman."

"Long, straight black hair. Pretty. Light brown skin. Probably about thirty."

"I don't recognize the description."

"So she wasn't in Trent Stevens's life when Marissa Neal came under the care of the Secret Service?"

No response from Agent Harper.

"The woman was mopping the kitchen floor when she was electrocuted," Grit said. "A lot of aspiring actors do odd jobs to make ends meet while auditioning. House-cleaning, for instance."

"Not your problem, Grit," Jo said sharply. "Don't touch anything. You and Beth are observing crime scene protocols, aren't you?"

Grit could feel the photo in his pocket. "Sure. As best we can."

"Did you break in?"

"Door was unlocked."

"That's not good enough."

"There was a plant that needed water and the distinct smell of death. We felt compelled to see if anyone was in distress and needed our assistance."

"Dead people aren't in distress. They're dead."

"Could have been someone else alive in here." Grit scratched the side of his mouth. "I'm going to have a lot of explaining to do."

"I'm about to. Damn it, Grit." Jo sighed, but she seemed less irritated. "My boss was just starting to like you. How was this woman electrocuted?"

"Someone rigged the electric kettle. Once she grabbed it to make herself a cup of tea, she was done. She probably never knew what happened. She's here in the kitchen, mop and bucket right beside her."

"Any guess how long she's been dead? Ask Beth."

Grit didn't need to. "At least two days. Maybe longer. We're in the right place, Jo. There are photos of the actor everywhere."

"Everywhere? Grit, what the hell? Did you search the place?"

"As I said, I was concerned there might be someone in distress. Your sister's a paramedic. If someone was injured on the bathroom floor, she could help."

"Trying out that line on me before the homicide detectives get there? Grit, a killer could have been hiding in the closet."

"Even better," he said.

"My sister isn't a SEAL."

"She was never in danger. I'm right here with her. I'd have protected her, but I didn't have to."

"Did she see you help yourself to a photo of the tenant?"

"What makes you think I did that?"

"Elijah would. You would, and did."

"He's good-looking. The tenant. We're not saying his name in case your boss or any bad guys have tapped this place or your phone, right?"

"Describe him."

Grit eased the three-by-three photo out of his pocket and held it in his palm. "It bothers me that I'm predictable."

"You couldn't care less, Grit, and you know it. What does he look like? I want to be sure it's the same guy."

"Blond hair, green eyes—hazel, maybe. Slight cleft chin. Straight nose. He's wearing a suit. Tie and everything. Your guy?"

"Probably, yes," Jo said. "Do you recognize him? Have you run into him in the past few months? In Black Falls, here in D.C. Anywhere?"

"No. He's good-looking but he's sort of an everyman." But Grit knew what Jo was asking. "If I'd seen him in D.C. or Vermont, or anywhere near my genius teenage protégé, I'd remember."

"Beth?"

He glanced at Beth, who was off the phone now. She had the back door open and was pale but composed as she stared out at the wilted flowers. "I don't think so," Grit said. "She's more out there than you, Jo. She's not used to keeping secrets. She didn't recognize the dead woman or this guy. This guy's got his own pictures are all over the refrigerator, too."

"Actors," Jo said, as if that explained Trent Stevens's apparent self-absorption. "Your young friend in D.C. is going to run with this."

"Maybe you should let him."

"If he finds a way to be in touch, you let me know. Understood?"

"You or the Secret Service?"

"We're one and the same."

"I'll let you know." Grit slipped the photo back in his pocket. "Jo, whatever's going on, you need to find this guy. He could be dangerous, or in danger himself."

"We'll take care of what we need to on our end."

Meaning he should butt out and let the Secret Service do their job. They'd keep the vice president's family safe. "Do you want me to put your sister on?"

"I want you to get her out of there and sit her by Sean's pool with a mojito. Tell her to have one for me. And you," Jo said. "No more bodies."

"Aye-aye, Special Agent Harper."

She ignored him and disconnected. He heard a buzz in his ear, and for a split second thought she'd found a way to zap him from D.C., then realized it was another call coming in.

He checked the screen. Elijah. Great.

Grit took the call. "You didn't find a body on Myrtle's patio, did you?"

"No. What are you talking about?"

His friend didn't know yet about the dead woman.

"Never mind," Grit said. "What's up?"

A half beat's pause. "Something's happened, hasn't it? That explains it. Charlie just called. He said to tell you he's checking for aliases. That you'd know what he meant."

"What did you tell him?"

"Study his calculus."

"That's the problem. He doesn't need to study. He knows the answer before the question's asked." Grit watched Beth stiffen by the door and then heard sirens. "I have to go. Talk to your fiancée."

"Jo? What's she got to do with—"

Grit pretended not to hear and clicked off his phone and slid it back in his pocket. He felt a sharp arrow of pain in his left foot, but not even for a split second did he think he still had a left foot.

By then, the police were descending.

Ninety minutes after Beth had walked into the small apartment, she and Grit were standing in the parking lot in the Southern California sun. She had a tight grip on her emotions. Either Grit did, too, or he wasn't all that bothered by the scene they'd come upon, which she didn't believe. He just had the ability to take one thing at a time.

She could see the muscles in her wrists and forearms tighten as she crossed her arms over her chest and eyed the array of law enforcement vehicles that had gathered at the scene.

The police she'd expected. The FBI and Secret Service agents had unnerved her.

The victim was identified as Portia Martinez. She'd worked part-time as a sound technician and cleaned houses for actor friends for extra cash. She didn't live in the apartment. She and the tenant, Trent Stevens, apparently were friends. Stevens didn't look as if he had the money for a housekeeper, but, on the other hand, he didn't look as if he were someone who'd clean his own house. He'd get someone else to do it and exchange favors or run up his credit cards.

Beth glanced back at a stern FBI agent standing under the wilted flower basket. "We're cleared to go, you know."

Grit put a hand out to her. "I'll drive."

She started to protest but dropped the keys into his palm. She wasn't in the mood to argue.

An unmarked black SUV backed out of the way so they could leave. Grit got behind the wheel. Beth, feeling surly, slid into the passenger seat. "Have you even driven a car since you got your leg blown off?"

Grit seemed to take no offense at her rudeness. "I drove around Vermont, seeing the mountain vistas."

"Vermont isn't Los Angeles."

"No, it's not."

He remembered the way back to Sean's house, which was good because Beth didn't. She sat looking out her window as Beverly Hills slid past her.

When they pulled into Sean's driveway, she turned to Grit. "I'm sorry about the crack about your leg."

"What crack? It was blown off. No one came and stole it while I was sleeping."

She scowled at him. "Are you ever serious?"

"I was serious just now."

He parked, and Beth flung herself out of the car. Hannah and Sean came out to the driveway. They'd already heard the difficult news and were expecting them.

Grit got out of the car and tossed Beth the keys but was focused on Sean. "I want to see where Jasper Vanderhorn was killed. I want you to tell me about that day."

Sean nodded. "Now?"

"Yeah. Now."

"All right. Let's go."

Beth headed inside, slamming the door behind her. She went straight out to the pool and stared at the clear, turquoise water. She'd reached for her cell phone a dozen times to call Scott. He'd want to know about the dead woman, if only from a professional point of view. From a personal one, Portia Martinez's murder would just be another sign to Scott that he'd fallen for the wrong woman.

Beth was too close to the violence of the past year.

"You served the Whittakers *muffins*," he'd yelled at her, utterly irrational.

Muffins? As if she'd had any choice. As if she'd known Lowell Whittaker was a killer and his wife an abusive lunatic who'd leave Bowie O'Rourke, an innocent man, to burn up in a fire so that she could avoid the embarrassment of having her husband's murderous activities come to light.

Beth had irritably countered that Three Sisters Café had also served the two paid assassins who'd left Drew Cameron to die in a snowstorm, run down an ambassador, poisoned a Russian diplomat and nearly killed two teenagers.

That was when Scott had packed up and gone back to Vermont.

Hannah opened a French door and came out onto the patio. "Beth?"

"I'm good. Please don't worry." Her eyes brimmed with tears. She felt terrible, and alone. "I'm ruining your time with Sean. Grit never should have come. He said so himself."

"Don't start with that. He and Sean have gone out to the canyon where that arson investigator was killed. His death's been weighing on Sean's mind. Nick's, too." Hannah stood next to Beth at the edge of the pool. "It's good that you and Grit found that woman, Beth. Her family and friends must have been looking for her and had no idea she was there."

"Assuming they even realized she was missing. Sometimes people don't, not for a while. If she was new in town, if she…"

"It must have been awful," Hannah said.

"It wasn't great."

"What can I do?"

Beth turned to her friend. "Tell me if I should call Scott."

"Beth—"

"I know you can't," she whispered. "I know it wouldn't help if you could."

"I'm sure of one thing. Scott wouldn't want you to be afraid and hurt right now."

"No," Beth said, "my dear, uptight Trooper Thorne would want me hiding under a rock for the rest of my life, so I wouldn't do anything or have anything happen to me that might interfere with his next promotion. I don't even blame him."

"We've all had a run of bad luck."

"Not bad luck, Hannah. We've been targeted by a bunch of murdering sons of bitches. I'd like to haul Lowell Whittaker out of his jail cell and make him tell us who electrocuted that poor woman."

"He might not know. So much of his work was done anonymously. His killers weren't even aware he was the one arranging their hits. It's possible he didn't know the identities of all of them, either."

Beth raised her eyebrows at her friend. "I see your prosecutor's mind hasn't been baked by the California sun."

Hannah gave a small smile. "I'll make us sandwiches. We can sit by the pool, and you can tell me everything. In the meantime, call Scott, will you?"

"Hey, I thought you weren't going to interfere."

Hannah was already through the door, and Beth pulled out her cell phone and flipped it open, debating what to do—and there was a text message, already, from Scott: Call me. Tell me you're okay.

The feds would have been in touch with him, maybe even her sister.

Beth stared at the message, seeing Scott right here by Sean's pool just a few days ago, pacing, tense, unable to articulate what he was feeling. She hadn't done any better. Neither of them was particularly introspective, but the past few months of their lives demanded at least some insight and understanding.

She dialed his number but got his voice mail. "I'm okay," she said. "Thank you for calling. I—" She almost said she loved him, but stopped short. "Call me anytime. I'm here."

When Hannah returned with the sandwiches, Beth opened an umbrella at one of the tables at the edge of the pool and sat down, keeping her phone close in case Scott—or anyone else—called.

Fifteen

⸻❧⸻

Black Falls, Vermont

Rose fingered squares of the soft, old fabric left over from the quilt that she'd helped stitch over the past month. She was at a riverside table at the café, which had just closed for the night. She remembered how she and Hannah had discovered the fabric, which seemed to be from the 1940s, neatly stacked inside the nineteenth-century trunk up they'd hauled up from the cellar. Hannah had given the trunk to Dominique to refurbish for the house she was renovating in the village.

Nick was down in the cellar now. He'd already checked out the struggling gallery next door, with its offerings from New England artists. Rose knew he was giving her a chance to regroup. There'd been no news of Robert Feehan. For all anyone knew, last night had been an outburst—a frightened, nervous man caught off guard and overreacting.

The square Rose held in her hand now was obviously from a man's blue oxford-cloth shirt, much worn in its day before being cut up. Some of the pieces hadn't survived decades in the trunk, but enough had for a simple, authentic, beautiful quilt. Rose welcomed the distraction after talking with Beth Harper in Beverly Hills, the impact of her discovery of the murdered woman evident in the strain in her voice.

"I'm glad Hannah didn't find a murder victim in January," Beth had said. "That's one thing, anyway, don't you think, Rose? You and I have more experience with injuries and death because of our work."

Rose hadn't known how to answer. Hannah had almost become a murder victim herself. Was that any better? But Rose understood that Beth had been grasping for something positive to hang on to—some reason she'd been with Grit Taylor that morning and found a woman dead.

Was Portia Martinez's murder connected to Derek's death and Nick's presence in Vermont?

How?

Rose knew she'd be better off contemplating leftover quilting pieces than speculating.

Myrtle Smith came out from behind the glass case and joined Rose at her table. "Are you thinking about starting your own quilt?"

"Maybe. I don't know. There's enough fabric here for a pillow or a wall hanging, anyway." Rose set her square back on the table. "My mother loved to quilt."

"Mine, too." Myrtle plucked a blue calico square from the pile and held it to the fading afternoon light in the window. "I swear this could be from one of her dresses. My mother, my sister and I would sit under a pecan tree in summer, with a pitcher of tea and a plate of pimento cheese sandwiches. Granny would be there when she wasn't coughing up a lung in the back room. She lived with us until she died."

Rose smiled. "I can just see you. Where are your sister and mother now?"

"Still in South Carolina. Mother's in assisted living. Gorgeous place."

"Do they still quilt?"

"I doubt it. Mother has arthritis in her hands, and my sister's a high school principal with four kids—two in high school, two in college. Husband's a doctor. They're on the go all the time."

"But you're the one who left home," Rose said.

"I am. No husband, no kids. No house these days, either. Well, it's still there but I'm not. Grit and Elijah are minding things for me. A SEAL and a Special Forces soldier." Her lavender eyes sparked with unexpected humor. "Couple of macho guys, the two of them."

"I don't think of Elijah that way."

"Of course not. He's your brother. Maybe he and Grit will change the *chi* in the house. I tried burning sandalwood incense. That's supposed to help, but it just reminded me of the fire. I'd have burned up if Grit hadn't rescued me. I don't like to admit that. I was in shock. Stunned. Frozen in place." Myrtle carefully placed the calico square back on the pile. "Classic, huh? I never thought I'd be like that, completely useless."

"You don't know what you'd have done if Grit hadn't

come along," Rose said. "There's no reason to be embarrassed about getting rescued by a Navy SEAL. You're a reporter. Grit would probably freeze in place if he had to interview someone."

"I don't think Grit freezes in place for any reason."

"He's a Southerner, too."

"I don't get the impression he ever wants to go back."

"Do you?"

Myrtle seemed startled by the question, although Rose couldn't imagine she hadn't considered it before now. "Washington's far enough south for me."

"It's home," Rose said.

"I didn't say it's home. I said it's south enough. You've never lived anywhere else but here. If you did, wouldn't Black Falls still be home?"

"I guess it would be, but I'm almost thirty. How old were you when you left South Carolina?"

"Twenty-one. I've been based in Washington for thirty years, but I've traveled a lot, spent long stints overseas. A tumbleweed." She seemed to make an effort to pull herself out of the past. "I told the police to find out if Derek Cutshaw and Robert Feehan were in Washington around the time of the fire at my house."

Rose felt a sense of dread deep in the pit of her stomach. "What do you think is going on, Myrtle?"

"No idea. I just keeping asking questions. I know I won't relax until I find out who set my house on fire."

"It's a leap to get to Derek or Robert as the arsonist."

"It was a leap to get to Lowell as the mastermind

of a network of killers." Myrtle sighed and looked out the window, the snow and ice on the river cast in late-afternoon shadows. "I've been trying to think back to that week in November. Grit was in town. We ran into each other outside the hotel where the ambassador was killed in the hit-and-run—on orders from Lowell Whittaker, we now know. The same two who killed your father did that hit."

"We know Melanie Kendall and Kyle Rigby didn't set the fire at your house," Rose said. "Is there any concrete evidence that could point to Derek or Robert?"

"Not that I know of. Have you talked to Beth since she and Grit found the woman in Beverly Hills?"

"Dom and I both have."

"Dom's a mess. This is all finally getting to her. She's been so cool, cooking, keeping the café running while you all hunt killers." Myrtle picked up the oxford-shirt square that Rose had abandoned but immediately placed it back on the table. "I hope that didn't sound callous. Gallows humor is sometimes my way of coping. Scott Thorne stopped by just before you got here. He's hurting. I can see it, but he won't say anything."

"Neither will Beth," Rose said.

"Ah, yes. So true. I don't have to be born and raised in Black Falls to see that. Do you know what happened between the two of them? They seemed to be getting along great. Then all of a sudden, he comes back from Beverly Hills without her."

Rose shook her head. "I don't know what happened. Maybe Scott doesn't have a lot of room in his life for someone else with a demanding job."

"Not to mention someone whose sister is a Secret Service agent," Myrtle said.

"I suspect Jo's been an issue, too, if not the main one. Scott's solid and decent, but he's insecure."

"Who isn't these days? Does he want a woman who'll worship him?"

"I don't think that's what he'd say, but Beth—"

"The Harpers all say what's on their minds. Dominique's convinced Beth and Scott have been on the skids for longer than most of us realize. They got together after your dad died. In my opinion, they talk shop too much. Their work's become the focus of their relationship. It's all they have in common."

"Jo's a federal agent and Elijah's a soldier."

"Totally different worlds. They've also known each other since you all were kids. Didn't she cut the rope on his tire swing? When they're together, you can see they're for real. Scott doesn't have that depth of history with Beth."

Rose thought about Nick. They had no history. She'd seen him maybe a dozen times on her trips to California. She'd always envisioned herself with someone from Vermont, or at least from New England. But a former submariner? A smoke jumper? Her brother's best friend and business partner?

Myrtle waved a hand, her nails bright red. "Scott and Beth can figure out their own relationship. I'm lucky I know where I'm sleeping tonight. By the way, I talked to the owners of the gallery across the hall. They'd love to get out of their lease and move to a smaller place down the street. I've been trying to convince the 'sisters' into expanding and starting a dinner service."

"So I've heard," Rose said, welcoming the change in topic. "Dominique's for it."

"She's not sure Hannah will want to stay involved in the café."

"Sean still owns the building."

"He'll approve of my plan," Myrtle said confidently. "He's a businessman. I more or less ran it past him in January and again last week. O'Rourke's would benefit from bringing more people into town at night. The lodge, too. People like a lively village."

"You have big heart," Rose said with a smile.

"More likely I'm meddling in matters that don't concern me. Where's Nick Martini off to? Didn't he come in with you?"

"He's in the cellar last I checked."

"Your Nick's another macho, testosterone type." Myrtle grabbed the corner of a square of faded fabric at the bottom of the pile. "Gingham. My goodness. I haven't thought about gingham in years. So, Rose. Any idea why Grit Taylor is in California?"

It wasn't an idle question, Rose thought. Idle questions weren't in Myrtle Smith's nature. "Beth says he's there on navy business. He arrived late last night."

"What kind of navy business brought him to that apartment this morning?"

"I haven't talked to him. Beth said he had Sean take him to the spot where an arson investigator died in a fire last summer." Rose added quietly, "His name was Jasper Vanderhorn."

"Charlie Neal," Myrtle whispered, then waved her fingers again at Rose. "Forget I said that." She patted the pile of fabric squares. "I'd love to know the history of these pieces, wouldn't you? They look as if they're all from men's old shirts, ladies' dresses. Well. They won't have belonged to anyone I know."

Nick entered the café through the center hall door. He tucked his cell phone into a jacket pocket, and Rose envisioned him making deals while he paced. He clearly wasn't used to small-town life and her fits-and-starts work schedule. He was used to being on the go all the time. She could work for long stretches, at home or in the field, but she appreciated her downtime—her solitude, she thought.

He walked over to the window by her table and looked down at the river. He obviously had no interest in quilting, and Rose doubted he was particularly curious about the building since it wasn't a Cameron & Martini property.

Myrtle stood up. She had on one of the café's evergreen canvas aprons over a white shirt, slim, pricey jeans and impractical boots. "You're a suspicious sort, aren't you, Mr. Martini? I'll bet we're all under your scrutiny. I wouldn't be surprised if you suspect me of setting fire to my own house."

"Has it been ruled arson?" he asked.

"Suspicious in origin," Myrtle said curtly.

Nick glanced out at the river, more shadow on the ice formations now than sun. "It must bother you that the police have no idea who started that fire."

Myrtle grunted. "This all bothers me."

He was silent a moment before finally turning to Rose. "I'll be outside."

Myrtle waited for him to cross the hardwood floor and go out the main door before she spoke. "He's stir-crazy. I get that. Think he'll stay here through your winter fest? Get him to demonstrate swinging an ax."

"Ha, right," Rose said, although she could picture it.

"He is a bit of a rogue, isn't he? I imagine he can be ruthless, too. Is he reckless?"

"Sean wouldn't continue to fight fires with him if he were."

Myrtle nodded, thoughtful.

Dominique burst out from the kitchen, still in her hat and coat, her face red from the cold. "Ever have one of those days you just want to bury yourself in work?" She pulled off her hat, her dark hair filled with static. "I stopped by my house for a few minutes. I don't know what possessed me to choose the bathroom tile I did. I'm installing it myself. It's a total pain and looks so... wrong."

"Sounds like a case of cabin fever to me," Rose said with a smile. "Don't change a thing until the maple sap is running full force. It's a rule I swear by."

Dominique laughed. "It's a good one." She unbuttoned her coat. "I'm going to make something with lemons. Cheerful, yellow lemons. Pie, pudding, cupcakes, chicken, salmon. Something."

"You miss having Beth and Hannah here," Myrtle said, retying her apron. "Nothing bothers Beth. She's like a mood stabilizer, unless she's fighting with Trooper Thorne. Then it's not so pretty."

Rose debated how to raise the subject of Dominique's presence at the Whittaker guesthouse that morning and decided the only choice was to be direct. "Dom, Zack Harper says he saw your car and Bowie's van at the Whittaker place this morning."

"Zack must have happened along at just the right moment." Dominique walked over to a window, adjusted a lock that probably hadn't been touched since cold weather had settled in for the winter. "I saw Bowie and stopped to say hi. I didn't stay long."

"What were you doing out there?" Myrtle asked.

"Curiosity." Dominique stood back from the window, her dark eyes impossible to read. "Aren't we all curious about what happened there? It's a beautiful spot. I hope one day it'll be filled with life instead of memories of violence and death."

Myrtle scooped up a paper napkin that had fallen onto the floor. "I imagine the Whittakers or someone acting on their behalf will put it up for sale as soon as possible."

Dominique moved to another window, adjusted another lock for no apparent reason except to have something to do. "The police came by here first thing this morning and asked me if I'd seen or heard from Robert Feehan. I hate the idea that the violence isn't over—that there's still someone out there...." She finally shrugged off her charcoal wool coat and draped it over one arm. "Business was slow. I knew Myrtle could handle things. I so seldom get involved in anything in town. I cook. I work on my house."

"Dom," Rose said, "I'm not criticizing you for going out there."

"I know. I'm sorry." She gave a feeble smile. "I just know how a little thing like being seen with Bowie O'Rourke at an isolated guesthouse can get blown into something it wasn't. Never mind. I'm not making any sense. By the way, he said he'd be stopping back there this afternoon. He wants to get the last of his stuff cleared out."

Before Rose could respond, Dominique bolted back across the café and swung behind the glass counter and into the kitchen.

"Maybe she has a soufflé in the oven," Myrtle said drily. "Everyone adores Dom, but she is something of a mystery, isn't she? Any chance she and Bowie are seeing each other?"

"I guess there's a chance, but I'd be surprised if they were." Rose got to her feet and grabbed her jacket off the back of her chair. "Even if Bowie didn't tell me—and I think he would—he'd have told Hannah."

"Not if Dom wanted to hide their relationship. I swear there are more secrets in this one little town than in all of Washington, D.C." Myrtle nodded out to the street. "Mr. Southern California is pacing. He's too rugged to admit he's cold. He'll just say he's impatient."

"I have to put away the fabric."

"I'll get it. You go on."

Rose thanked her and went out into the center hall, Ranger already up and eager to get moving. He led the way down the steps to the sidewalk. Nick had stopped pacing and was leaning against her Jeep, his jacket open, his arms crossed on his chest. Rose sucked in a sharp breath at the sight of him, the sun glinting on his hair, the

casual, sexy way he stood. All day, she'd kept remembering him making love to her. It might have been yesterday
instead of eight months ago.

"Myrtle can run you up to the lodge," she said as she
opened up the back for Ranger. "I have something I want
to do."

"You're going back out to the Whittaker place to check
on Bowie. I'm going with you." Nick eased up next to her
and reached into her jacket pocket, pulling out her keys.
"My turn to drive. It'll be fun navigating all the potholes
and curves around here."

"What if I want a private moment with Bowie?"

"You can have one. I'll make myself scarce."

"Oh, sure. Make yourself scarce where? Behind a
snowbank?" Ranger hopped up into the back of the Jeep.
"All right, Nick. Go right ahead. Drive."

Nick had no trouble with her Jeep or the roads, not
that Rose had expected he would. When they reached the
Whittaker estate, he continued down to the guesthouse
turnaround and pulled in next to Bowie's van.

Rose released Ranger from the back and let him run
off into the snow, down to a small, frozen pond. "This
is such a beautiful place," she said as Nick joined her. "I
hope the Whittakers weren't here long enough to ruin it
for someone else."

"People will remember the good more than the
bad."

"I hope so."

"You all rose to the occasion and rooted them out."

They went around to the other side of the van. Bowie

had the side door open and was rummaging in a wooden box on the floor. He stood up, watching Poe charge down to the pond with Ranger. "Maybe Ranger will rub off on him. Better than the other way around, I guess. What's up?"

"Dom said you'd be out here," Rose said.

He glanced at Nick, then at Rose again. "I haven't seen Feehan, if that's what this is about. I'm not getting sucked into this business. I want to get my stuff and be gone."

Nick watched the two dogs roughhouse with each other, but Rose knew his attention was focused on her and Bowie. She wasn't even sure why she'd come out there. Maybe Bowie had a point. Maybe she was worried he'd get sucked into whatever was going on. "Actually," she said. "I've been meaning to ask you if you'd like to help with winter fest at the lodge."

Bowie's eyebrows went up. "Quick thinking, Rose. All right. What could I do?"

"You could help with sugaring. We have trees to tap and more to do on the shack. There's an old stone fireplace you could look at for us."

He slid the van door shut. "Yeah, sure, put me to work."

"You're serious?"

"I'm serious. I can do sleigh rides, too."

Rose smiled. "I thought you'd find a way to be out of town that weekend."

"That was the old Bowie." He grinned back at her. "The new Bowie is downright sociable."

"Does that mean we'll see you at the dance at the lodge?"

"In a suit with shiny shoes?" He laughed. "Well, you never know."

"I've seen Dominique's dress. It's gorgeous. She has a great sense of style."

Nick headed onto the walk to the stone guesthouse. Poe charged for him. "Poe!" Bowie yelled. "Get your four-legged self over here!"

His dog abandoned Nick and came running. Rose made a hand signal for Ranger to come, too. He responded immediately. Bowie just shook his head in amazement, opened up the van's front passenger door and got Poe inside.

Bowie sighed and nodded toward Nick. "What's with you and this guy?"

"Nothing." As if that explained everything. "I assume you have a key to the guesthouse?"

"Yeah. I'm leaving it for the lawyers after I clear out trash and a few tools and supplies I left behind."

She followed him onto the walk and mounted the steps to the guesthouse porch. The strong winds had blown snow into the corners. Shades were pulled on the front windows.

Nick had the storm door open and tried the solid main door, which wasn't locked, either. He glanced back at Bowie. "You didn't lock up after you left this morning?"

"I never went in," Bowie said, moving to one side of Nick. "Dom distracted me when she stopped by. I only had a few minutes. I had to get out to the lake. I figured I'd come back this afternoon."

"What about Dom?" Rose asked. "Did she go in?"

"No. We both were here and gone within fifteen minutes."

"Wait out here," Nick said, entering the guesthouse.

He stiffened, stopping abruptly in the entry. Bowie grimaced. "Something's wrong," he said.

Rose slipped past him into the entry. Nick grabbed her and pulled her close to him. The guesthouse had been divided into two side-by-side apartments, the door to the one on the right half-open. She could see a sleeping bag unfurled on the hardwood floor. Arranged next to it were packets of freeze-dried camp food, a water bottle and a small camp stove.

Next to it was a metal canister of liquid fuel for the stove.

White gas.

"My stuff's all in the other apartment this morning," Bowie said, stepping inside the guesthouse. "I didn't do any work in here."

Rose eased back from Nick's embrace and turned to Bowie. "There was snow overnight," she said. "Did you see footprints when you and Dom were here this morning?"

"I don't remember. I was focused on making a quick stop and getting to work." Bowie pointed at an old, dusty glass kerosene lamp on the floor just inside the apartment. "Some sick son of a bitch set Derek on fire."

Nick directed his hard gaze at the stonemason. "If you know anything else, now's the time."

"Rumors. That's it." Bowie rubbed the back of his thick neck. "I've heard talk that Derek and Robert have been providing illegal prescription drugs to some of their ski students. Pain pills, mostly."

Rose bit back her shock. "Bowie, you're not—"

"No. I'm not involved. I told the police everything I know."

Nick pulled her even closer, his dark eyes intense. "We need to get them back out here."

Sixteen

Wind howled down from Cameron Mountain, as if Drew Cameron himself were up there, trying to warn his only daughter—about dangers, Nick wondered, or about him? It was dark by the time they arrived back at the lodge. Small white lights draping the evergreens along the walk twinkled, casting long shadows as he and Rose headed to the main entrance.

"Do you trust Bowie?" Nick asked quietly.

Rose seem startled by his question. "Yes, I trust him. Did you think I didn't?"

"I hadn't thought about it one way or the other."

"Do you trust him?"

"I don't know him. I have no reason to trust or not trust him." Nick paused at the door and looked out at the sky, clear and black against the stars and moon. The air didn't seem as cold as last night. "Bowie and Hannah grew up together in difficult circumstances. Have you always been close to them?"

"Hannah and I have been friends since junior high. She's not that easy to get to know. Then she was so busy with school, work and raising Devin and Toby. She's very smart and driven. She and Sean have that in common."

"And Bowie?"

"He was like another big brother when we were kids. I guess he still is in a way."

"Then you and he—"

"No, never," Rose said, not letting Nick finish. She reached past him and pulled open the lodge's heavy door.

He didn't take the hint. "Have you left any broken hearts here in Black Falls?"

She pretended not to hear him and went into the warm lobby. A half-dozen guests were gathered in front of the roaring fire, reading books, playing Scrabble, drinking hot cocoa.

Lauren Cameron rushed out from behind the front desk. Nick left Rose to explain their discovery at the Whittaker guesthouse and headed upstairs to his room. Half his things were still at Rose's house. He had a feeling she wouldn't want him sleeping there again tonight. Or she would, but wouldn't admit it, which amounted to the same thing.

Not that he had any intention of letting her stay at her house by herself.

He was restless, not even remotely tired when he entered his room. He hadn't talked to Sean since he'd called on his way with Grit Taylor to the canyon where Jasper had died. Nick gritted his teeth and dialed his friend's number.

The heat was clanking and hissing, the room too hot.

As soon as Sean picked up, Nick said, "I've been out to the river three times now, and I'm still trying to picture what happened in January. Hannah really flung herself into the snow a split second before the bomb went off in the backseat of her car?"

"That's what happened," Sean said, tight.

"What a spitfire. She's lucky. If the bomb didn't kill her, the snow, cold, rocks and tree roots could have."

"Nick," Sean said, "what's going on?"

Nick stood by the double windows and filled him in on the scene at the Whittaker guesthouse, then said, "It's possible Feehan camped out there last night and took off first thing this morning, before any of us arrived."

"And he killed Cutshaw over drugs?"

"No one's going that far. Not yet."

"His story about Cutshaw taking off when he found out you were in town could all be BS meant to mislead the police."

Nick had considered that possibility, too. "How's Hannah holding up?"

"She's worried about Rose more than ever. Beth is, too."

"And you," Nick said. "Would you be less worried if I came back to L.A.?"

"I'd be less worried if Rose wasn't so—" Sean broke off with a small grunt. "I don't need to tell you."

"Rose is as hardheaded and independent as the rest of you. What's going on there? Where's Grit Taylor now?"

"Staring at the pool trying to figuring things out. He's Elijah's friend. He's self-confident, and he doesn't quit. He didn't like finding that woman today. Jo's not happy with the situation, either."

"Are she and Elijah on their way out there?"

"I won't know until they show up in my living room. Everyone's being tight-lipped."

"You can use my place for spillover company if it gets crowded. That'd give Jo a handy excuse to have a look around and make sure I've been straight with everyone."

"She doesn't need an excuse. She'll get a warrant."

She would, too, Nick thought.

"Is anything Jasper told you making sense now, or setting off alarms?" Sean asked.

Nick moved back from the windows and sat on the edge of the bed, the comforter folded up at the foot. "No, but something about my trip out here's triggered what's been happening. Any news on the actor?"

"He hasn't turned up. I emailed you a photo of him. He hasn't had much of an acting career. Apparently he's working on several screenplays."

"What did Marissa Neal see in him?"

"I'm not in the loop with the Secret Service," Sean said stiffly, "but as far as I can tell he was something of a departure from the straight-and-narrow for her. High energy, big dreams, big ego. Good-looking, too."

Nick knew the type. After he disconnected, he checked his email, but he didn't recognize Trent Stevens from the photo Sean sent. He took his BlackBerry and headed back to the lobby. A woman at the front desk informed him Rose was in the ballroom.

Ballroom?

He got directions and went down a hall and around a corner to a large room that jutted out of the main building, windows on three sides with what in daylight would be breathtaking views of the meadow and the surrounding mountains.

Rose, A.J., Zack Harper and Myrtle Smith were gathered at a long table.

Lauren was on her feet, her daughter on one hip as she welcomed Nick. "Help yourself," she said, nodding to the end of the table, which was spread with glasses and bottles of wine.

Nick thanked her and splashed wine into a glass. A.J. and Zack's concern for Rose was evident, but they were circumspect with him, as if the white gas and old kerosene lamp at the guesthouse had confirmed he'd brought an ill wind and bad luck to town.

Maybe he had.

He showed Lauren the picture of the missing actor, without saying who it was.

"A.J. and I see a lot of people in our work," she said. "I don't remember this man."

Her husband joined them and glanced at the actor's smiling face. A.J. didn't recognize Stevens, either. "We have the Secret Service breathing down our necks as it is with the Neals coming for winter fest." His expression turned flinty. "Unless they cancel, given this latest violence."

Nick slipped his phone back into his pocket. "I hope the police will have some definitive answers by then."

The flintiness didn't let up. "You attend fancy parties in Beverly Hills. Could you have run into this actor at one of them?"

"Possibly, but I don't have any specific recollection of ever having met him. I'm not great with faces. Sometimes Hollywood types come to us for information on smoke jumping and wildland fires." Nick sipped his wine and observed Rose, her eyes a deep blue in the ballroom's soft light as she, Myrtle and Lauren went over logistics for the silent auction. He turned back to A.J. "I wish I could be more help."

"I spoke to Sean. He and Grit Taylor went up to the site where the arson investigator was killed. His death is the reason you came out here, isn't it?" A.J. didn't give Nick a chance to answer. "Could Robert Feehan be this serial arsonist you're after?"

"I'm not with law enforcement, A.J.," Nick said. "I'm not here on any kind of official business. If my presence is putting anyone in danger, I'll clear out. I won't stay."

The eldest Cameron seemed satisfied. "Fair enough. If Feehan's mixed up with illegal prescription drugs, that could explain why he's avoiding the police."

"He could also be afraid he's next on the killer's list."

A.J. sighed heavily. "If he's innocent, running only makes his situation worse. He needs to talk to the police and get it over with."

The two little Camerons were now racing around in circles in the wide, open space. Lauren kept a watchful eye on them. A.J. went to them, handing his wife a glass of wine. Nick watched the young family, pushing back a wave of regret and guilt that he knew would get him nowhere. He had anticipated a certain amount of awkwardness on his trip to Black Falls, given his situation with Rose, but he hadn't expected to run into violence. He'd figured he'd talk to the lead investigators into Lowell Whittaker's network about Jasper's death, check out the Whittaker estate and Cameron Mountain.

Instead not only had he run into violence, he could very easily have caused it just by coming here.

Zack Harper scooped up a glass of wine as if he didn't have a care in the world. "Looks as if your theory about Coleman fuel in a kerosene lamp's right on target. Some poor unknowing bastard wanders by with a match and that's it." He drank some of his wine. "Not pretty. Feehan must have figured the Whittaker guesthouse was the last place anyone would look for him."

"Assuming what we found wasn't planted there," Rose said, holding a glass of wine in one hand as she joined them.

"Is that what you think?" Zack asked.

"I'm just trying to keep an open mind."

"You don't have to. You're not investigating the case."

Brett Griffin entered the ballroom, still wearing his parka. He looked tentative, his fair cheeks and nose red from the cold. "The woman at the front desk said you all were down here. I just finished talking to the police. I was taking night shots up at Four Corners." He didn't seem to be addressing anyone in particular. "I'd heard rumors about drugs but I had nothing to go on. No evidence to take to the police. I didn't want to get anyone into trouble over rumors."

Zack drank some of his wine. "Think that's what all this is about? A fight between friends over drugs?"

Clearly it wasn't what Zack believed. Nick glanced at Rose, but she just kept a tight grip on her wineglass and said nothing.

Brett shifted to her. "There's one more thing I wanted to mention. I didn't want to get into it before—but now..." Red spots blossomed high on his cheeks. "Derek told me he blamed you for how he lost control last year at O'Rourke's. The fight hurt his reputation. He felt bad Bowie got arrested. I didn't want to say anything before now because it just didn't seem to matter. There was no point."

"Are you suggesting he wanted to get back at me for what happened?" Rose asked quietly.

Brett glanced around the ballroom as if he were looking for someone to help him.

"Brett," Rose said, prodding him.

"If Derek felt under pressure—threatened for some reason—I think he'd have tried to strike back at you if he could."

Rose maintained a neutral expression. "Yesterday morning Robert said Derek didn't want to hurt me. He said Derek was upset because Nick was here."

Brett's cheeks reddened even more. "He would say that, don't you think? He'd want to divert attention from himself. Never mind. I'm not making any sense."

Nick noticed perspiration on Brett's forehead but he

kept his coat on. "Does Feehan have the knowledge and capability to pull off the fire that killed Cutshaw?" Nick asked.

"I don't know," Brett said in a low voice.

"What about Cutshaw?"

Brett turned ashen and didn't answer.

Zack Harper shrugged and polished off the last of his wine, setting the glass on the table. "How much knowledge does it take to set yourself or someone else on fire?"

Rose turned to Brett, and Nick noticed she was slightly pale herself. "Do you have any idea where Robert could be now?" she asked.

Brett wiped his sweaty brow with the heel of his hand and shook his head. "I told the state detective who interviewed me that I'd let them know if Robert contacts me, or if I remember anything else—friends, favorite spots."

Rose stayed focused on him. "How well did you all know the Whittakers?"

"I didn't know them at all. I'm not sure about Derek or Robert."

"I suppose it's possible Robert stayed at the guesthouse but the Whittakers left the old kerosene lamp there, and he just used it. Did any of you have a key?"

"I didn't," Brett said.

"The apartment where we found the camping gear is the one Kyle Rigby used in November. Could Rigby have given Robert or Derek a key?"

"I don't remember ever running into Rigby," Brett said, frowning. "The police asked me about him. Robert,

Derek and I talked about what happened in November. Of course we did. I don't think they knew Rigby, either."

"What about contacts in California?" Nick asked.

Brett seemed surprised by the question. "We all know people in California. We've all taught skiing out West. I've taken up enough of your time. You all have a good night. I'm sorry about all this. I wish I'd known what was going on and had found out a way to stop it from happening."

Nick set his wineglass on a tray as Brett Griffin and Zack Harper left together. Rose rejoined Myrtle at the table and consulted drafting paper they had unfurled with drawings for how to set up the ballroom for the winter fest auction and dance. Nick had no doubt Myrtle had listened in on as much of the conversation as she could.

Lauren Cameron smiled faintly next to him and nodded to her husband across the room, their children chasing him, giggling as he let them catch him. "A.J. hates for any of us to be out of his sight."

"Understandably," Nick said.

"Maybe so," she said, "but I refuse to live in fear. I did that before I moved up here. A.J.'s actually the one who helped me get past my fear. I was escaping a difficult relationship. I thought I had it well behind me, but it had an insidious effect on my ability to trust myself. Here I was, a strong woman..." She didn't finish. "Matters of the heart sometimes require the greatest strength of all."

"You fell for a bastard?"

A twitch of humor played at the corners of her mouth. "I did, yes."

"And we're talking about Rose here, too, aren't we?"

"Could be," she said diplomatically.

"Wasn't your fault. Sometimes you can't see a bastard coming. The really good ones know how to charm you, reel you in. You just have to fight your way out of the net and move on."

"You're not terribly controlling, are you?"

"Only person I can or want to control is myself."

"Rose is strong, but she's also very proud," Lauren said, her eyes warm with emotion. "Her missteps seem magnified with three older brothers. I had no idea about her and Derek. A.J. didn't, either. Nick...are we safe? You'd tell us if you had reason to believe we weren't, wouldn't you?"

He wanted to reassure her, but wasn't sure he could. "Law enforcement knows everything I know."

She acknowledged his words with a quick intake of breath, then a nod as she continued. "Beth was with Grit this morning." Lauren seemed to struggle to find the right words. "I saw Scott earlier. He was as stoic as ever, but Beth discovering that poor woman with Grit can't have gone over well with him."

A.J. had scooped up both children and perched one on each arm. Lauren mumbled something to Nick and returned to her family. A.J.'s expression softened as she approached him. He looked less flinty, less fearful and angry.

Nick saw Rose noticing, too. Her eyes connected with his, and she quickly grabbed her coat and moved out into the hall.

Her brother's gaze lifted over the towheaded curls of

his daughter, and Nick saw that the eldest Cameron was ready to go after her. Nick left A.J. with his wife and children and followed Rose.

He caught up with her in the parking lot. "I figure you didn't wait just so you could get me out here in the cold without a coat."

"Why would I wait for you? I'm going home." She nodded toward the lodge. "Go back and enjoy the fire. I'm sure I'll see you tomorrow. You deserve a bed tonight."

"So I do."

She obviously realized her mistake and got out her keys. "I'm not a target if Derek and Robert were fighting over drugs. I'll lock my doors. Ranger will alert me if anyone tries to get in."

"And what will you do, hide under the bed? You're alone up there."

"What difference does that make? Robert's had his chance if he wanted to hurt me. Maybe he just wanted to hurt Derek and now that he's succeeded, he's on the run."

"Rose."

She sighed and shook her head at him. "Remind me never to sit across a conference table from you. All right. Thank you for your concern for my safety." She seemed to make an effort to smile. "Go get your coat. Take your car. That way Ranger and I don't have to come back here."

"You're in denial about what's going on."

"I'm not in denial."

Nick didn't argue. He returned to his room and

grabbed his coat. He could be on a plane in the morning and in his condo by tomorrow night.

He headed back outside to his cold car.

A state cruiser was in Rose's driveway when Nick pulled in behind her Jeep. She had Ranger at her side and was talking with Scott Thorne at the bottom of the front steps. The trooper glanced at Nick but was grim, distracted. "I tried calling Beth," Thorne said. "Have you talked to her, Rose? I just want to know she's all right."

"I spoke to her, Sean and Hannah earlier this afternoon," Rose said. "Beth's okay."

"Grit Taylor's still there?"

"Yes, as far as I know."

Thorne kept his attention on Rose. "I wish Beth had gone shopping with Hannah instead. She went out there to enjoy the so-called good life. Beverly Hills is fine for a visit, but I have no desire to live there. I don't know much for sure, but I know I'll never be rich, or live in Southern California."

Nick wasn't offended. He'd said the same thing when he'd enlisted in the navy a year out of high school.

"Do you think that's what Beth wants?" Rose asked.

Thorne shrugged. "Doesn't matter." He sighed, clearly uncomfortable with his reasons for being there. "I should go."

"Beth's coming back." Rose gently rubbed Ranger behind an ear. "Black Falls is home for her. Beverly Hills isn't what's come between you two, anyway. You think you both work in the same sandbox. Jo being back in town just brought it all home to you, but she's a federal agent—Beth's a paramedic. Her work's not the same as yours."

"Thanks for the analysis," Thorne said through gritted teeth.

Rose wasn't intimidated. "You'd prefer if Beth were a kindergarten teacher, or just worked at the café full-time."

"Good night, Rose."

Thorne nodded curtly at Nick, returned to his cruiser and drove off.

Rose sputtered at the retreating cruiser, then spun around and marched up the steps. Ranger waited for Nick and walked up with him. Once inside, the golden retriever yawned and flopped onto his bed by the woodstove.

Rose peeled off her coat, hat and gloves and kicked off her boots. "I should wipe Ranger's paws and brush him, but I'll do it in the morning."

Nick kept his coat on, remained standing as she started a fire in the woodstove, her movements sure, automatic. As she added kindling, got it going, then laid on some small sticks, he could see her alone on her hilltop on quiet winter evenings.

"You're self-sufficient," he said. "You don't need anyone, do you?"

"I manage." She turned to him, her cheeks flushed from building the fire. "Any plans to quit as a smoke jumper?"

"Not yet. I only work seasonally or when needed. I'll keep it up as long as it makes sense to."

"You'll know when it doesn't make sense when—what, you fall out of a plane or catch your hair on fire?"

"Already caught myself on fire."

She blanched. "I'm sorry. I didn't mean—"

"It's okay. It was a while ago. I did something stupid and paid for it with a few skin grafts. It could have been worse." He smiled. "I haven't fallen out of a plane yet."

"Do people think you're reckless?"

Jasper had asked Nick the same question. "My fellow smoke jumpers don't think so," he said, repeating the answer he'd given Jasper. "If they did, I wouldn't last as one."

"Sean's not reckless," Rose said.

The scars on Nick's right arm and side suddenly felt as if they were still burning. "Sean's as good as they come. I screwed up as a young smoke jumper and I paid for my mistake with a lot of pain and some permanent scars. Fortunately I was the only one who got hurt or was ever in danger that time."

She knelt down in front of her dog and stroked his golden fur. "Ranger can't tell me when it's time for him to retire. I have to tell him."

"You two have made a good team."

"He has a hard job, but he's done it well."

"You both have," Nick said.

Ranger yawned and stretched, and Rose stood, looking down at him. "I'm as careful and as responsible as I can be, but sometimes I wonder if I asked him to do too much."

"Think he'd be happier if Bowie O'Rourke had adopted him?"

"Maybe."

"You've had a long day. You're beating yourself up for no good reason."

She grabbed a log out of the woodbox, added it to the fire. She shut the lid on the woodstove and stared at the flames through the glass. "I have a hundred 'what-ifs' floating in my brain, Nick. Derek and I got together and broke up all before my father was killed. What if Derek was involved with this serial arsonist after all? What if everything that's happened this past year ultimately leads back to him—to me? To something I did or didn't do? What if I'm responsible for bringing this violence to Black Falls?" She turned to Nick, her eyes a blue-black in the shadows. "What if Lowell Whittaker chose Black Falls for his country home because of me, my work, Derek?"

"You didn't kill anyone or hurt anyone," Nick said.

"When did Jasper get on the trail of his guy?"

"Rose."

She hesitated, then said softly, "I know I'm leaping ahead of the facts. Nick, what if my distractions helped lead to Jasper's death? I was out there in the canyon—I was searching for the boy who'd wandered off. What if I missed something that could have saved Jasper?"

"It wasn't your job to save him. You know that. You're not a firefighter, and Jasper was a man with a mission."

"And now you are," Rose said.

Nick forced a quick smile. "I'm always a man with a mission."

She gave him only the slightest smile.

He unzipped his coat, the house quickly warming up with the fire. "Jasper was pursuing a firebug theory that every other professional considered far-fetched. He was trying to connect suspicious wildland fires, structural fires and explosions to the same arsonist. Different types of fires like that are rarely connected. He was convinced a serial arsonist was at work setting fires for his own pleasure and drama as well as hiring himself out as a contract killer."

"To Lowell."

"Possibly. Jasper died before anyone knew Lowell's network existed."

"What if he got too close to Lowell?" Rose was very pale now. "My father did, and Lowell had him killed. Did Jasper give you anything, Nick, anything at all?"

He stared at the flames through the woodstove's glass doors. When he looked at Rose, she'd shifted just enough that fiery colors reflected in her eyes. "You and I were both in tough spots emotionally in June. We didn't save Jasper. It was a bad fire. Everything was out of control."

"It's okay, Nick," she said. "I'm not holding you to any romantic entanglements. I didn't then, I haven't in the past eight months. I'm not now."

"No regrets, then?"

"None."

"Good." He grinned at her. "But that's what I am? A romantic entanglement?"

She almost smiled in return. "Go back to the lodge," she said. "Relax, have a nice dinner and sleep well. I'll be here. I'm fine."

He stepped closer to her and noticed her lick her plump lower lip. He remembered the taste of her mouth that hot, frantic night. He'd let his emotions get away from him. He'd been raging, out of control. He'd wanted Rose Cameron more than he'd ever wanted any woman.

Sean's sister. The forbidden woman.

Except it was all so much more complicated than that.

"Rose." Nick said her name quietly, gently, and touched his thumb to the corner of her mouth. "I didn't mean to hurt you then and I don't want to hurt you now. But I do want to kiss you."

"You're asking my permission?"

"I don't want there to be any misunderstanding."

She placed her hands on his shoulders and pressed her lips to his in a perfunctory kiss.

Almost as if she were kissing a friend.

She stood back and smiled. "There. All done."

Nick tilted his head back and studied her a moment. "Was that enough for you?"

"For me? You're the one who wanted to kiss me and asked permission."

"You make it sound as if you needed a permission slip to be excused from gym class."

"Well?"

"We moved too fast before."

"We're not moving at all now, are we? Nick, I'm okay. You don't owe me. You don't have to pretend I ever meant anything to you on a romantic level. Nothing will change now that Sean knows about our fling. I didn't want him to find out, but he'll never ask me for details."

"That doesn't mean he won't ask me."

"I'm not going to come between you and your friendship with Sean. You two have known each other longer than I've known you. I never should have allowed myself to get involved, even for one night, with my brother's best friend. We're all adults, but that notion is still tough, at least for a Cameron."

"Back up," Nick said. "Fling?"

"That's what it was."

"Then that talk before about possibly having been attracted to me for a long time—"

"Just talk."

"Ah. Just talk. Well, then this is just a kiss."

His mouth found hers. He was deliberate, giving her a chance to decide how she was going to react. He felt her take a step back, but she couldn't go too far with the woodstove right there. She stumbled slightly, grabbed him by the hips, steadying herself. Nick wasn't distracted. He relished the taste of her, the feel of her. She was strong and soft in all the right places.

"Is this what you mean by romantic entanglement?" he asked, amused, even as he kissed her again, forcing himself to resist doing more—carrying her off to bed, for instance.

She tightened her grip on him, and he wondered if she was doing the same—resisting, holding back.

Finally he released her and stood back.

She took a shallow breath. "I guess you had to get that out of your system. Maybe we both did. It's good. The romantic entanglement stuff is behind us. Now we can be..." She considered a moment. "Friends and colleagues."

"Ah. That's what I was thinking. Couldn't you tell?

Is that what you want, Rose, for us to be friends and colleagues?"

"It's what has to be."

"Not what I asked."

"I wanted that kiss," she whispered.

"Which kiss? The chaste one you gave me or the one I gave you?"

"Chaste?" She laughed, her eyes sparking. "That's not a word I expected from Nick Martini, submariner, smoke jumper and multimillionaire, ass-kicking businessman."

"What word would you use?"

"Careful. Repressed." She pushed both hands through her tangled hair. "I'm not good with emotion."

"You wanted more than a kiss," he said, then added, "You do now. So do I."

Color rose in her cheeks.

He decided he'd made his point. "It's not a good idea for you to stay here, Rose."

She nodded. "I know. I'll get my things. If you can grab Ranger's food and dishes, I'll pack."

Nick was already on the way to the kitchen.

She took her Jeep. Nick understood. She wasn't going to be stranded. She was independent, and she was afraid. Having her own transportation gave her confidence. He was unsettled himself as he walked into the lodge under the starlit sky, the unfamiliar landscape spread out around him. He could do snow and cold and all that, but Black Falls was a small New England town and new turf. He knew the players only from stories from Sean and trips west by various friends and family members.

He'd met Rose several times but hadn't considered sleeping with her until fate had thrown them together in June.

At least in the lodge there was no question of sharing a bed or even a room.

Maybe that was why she'd agreed to spend another night there.

As soon as he arrived at the lodge, Nick went up to his room and checked the phone messages, but there was nothing new on Portia Martinez or the missing actor.

He met Rose in the dining room. She wasn't wearing a badly hand-knitted sweater tonight. Instead she wore a black knit dress with her hair up. She even wore makeup, her eyes smoky, her lips glossy and very pink.

She could fit in anywhere—on a mountaintop, a wilderness rescue or at a Beverly Hills party.

"We're expecting snow tonight," she said as she sat across from him. "Just a few inches."

"Great," Nick replied with a wry smile.

She ordered handmade wild mushroom ravioli and a salad. He ordered the same. The discovery in the guesthouse and the murder in California weren't far from his mind, nor, he thought, hers, but both had experience compartmentalizing such things and pretending otherwise.

Seventeen

Beverly Hills, California

Grit stood by Sean Cameron's glistening pool and remembered his first days of SEAL training, with the Pacific Ocean glistening before him. He hadn't considered he might fail. He'd entered the weeks of difficult training not with cockiness but with absolute certainty. He'd known he'd be a SEAL.

That was over a decade ago. He'd had two whole legs back then, and he'd only imagined what combat was like.

Hell, he'd only imagined what life outside the Florida Panhandle was like.

Now he'd experienced both combat and life outside of his hometown and the Taylor world of tupelo honey. He wondered if he was certain about anything anymore.

He settled for appreciating the sunshine and his pleasant surroundings.

He was back to thinking of Beth Harper as a sister again. She and Hannah were doing laps in the azure water, their way, he suspected, of combating their fears and frustrations.

Beth came up for air and hugged the side of the pool. She was in a tank suit two tones darker than her eyes. Grit figured Thorne was an idiot for getting into a snit and leaving her in California. "What did you and Trooper Thorne do while he was out here?" Grit asked. "You had a couple days together, right?"

She glowered at him. "Scott's not your firebug."

"That wasn't my question."

"We hung out. He was preoccupied. We argued. He went home."

"Your firefighter brother?"

She tilted her turquoise eyes up to him. "Don't even go there."

"Just curious. He was here for a few days, too. Also went home."

"As planned," Beth said. "We all hitched a ride out here on Sean's plane. Zack and Scott flew back commercial coach. That's it. No drama, no mystery."

"Your brother attracts the women, right? The Neal sisters have been to Black Falls. Maybe one or more of them has a crush on Firefighter Zack."

"What does that have to do with anything? Not that it's true."

"I get on your nerves, don't I, Beth?"

She sighed. "Isn't that your objective?"

He truly had no idea what she was talking about. "My objective?"

She scowled and kicked out her legs behind her, splashing water before going still again. "I didn't mean 'objective' in the military sense."

Grit still didn't have a clue and abandoned trying to figure out what she meant.

Beth plunged backward into the water and swam a few yards to the end of the pool. She jumped out, grabbed a big towel off a lounge chair and wrapped it around her. "You should go for a swim."

"It's not that warm out," Grit said.

"The pool's heated, and like you care given the places you've had to swim."

Pure conjecture on her part. "You've got goose bumps. You're missing Trooper Thorne, aren't you?"

"He's not missing me," she muttered, dropping onto the lounge chair.

Grit eyed her from his position at the pool's edge. Somehow she'd managed to sound objective, not whiny. "Things are happening again, Beth," he said.

She spread her towel over her legs and didn't respond. Hannah continued swimming laps on the other side of the pool. Her brother Devin had stopped by after work at Cameron & Martini and had gone for a run, determined to stick to his training program. Grit recognized the kid's enthusiasm and drive. Devin Shay was committed to becoming a smoke jumper.

He hadn't had that drive in Black Falls. He'd been haunted by the death of Drew Cameron, who had taken the orphaned teenager under his wing, and by his own brush with Lowell Whittaker's killers.

Grit was still figuring out the people of Black Falls,

Vermont. The ones who'd stayed, the ones who'd left. He was sure Sean and Hannah would end up back there, at least on a part-time basis. Grit had no illusions he could live again in his hometown. His family would welcome him back, but he wouldn't know what to do with himself.

Not that he knew what to do with himself now.

Beth grabbed a second towel off a pile next to her and arranged it over her torso. Grit smiled. "See? I said you had goose bumps."

She ignored him. "Did you see what you wanted at the canyon today with Sean?"

"That must have been a hell of a wildfire last June. High winds, low humidity, dry brush and canyons. It was a fast-moving fire. Firefighters thought they had it out but there was a hot spot. No one knew. It flared up, and the flames jumped the line, trapping Jasper Vanderhorn."

"Nick and I didn't miss anything," Sean said as he came out of the house. "None of us did. It was arson. Someone set that fire."

His and Nick Martini's quick actions had saved other people, but Vanderhorn hadn't stood a chance. Grit knew that Sean didn't want or need to hear any platitudes. "It would have taken some skill as an arsonist to target Vanderhorn that way. Why not just wire his teakettle or put a bomb under his car seat?"

"To prove he could do it. The drama." Sean watched Hannah steadily swimming her laps. He was in jeans and a polo shirt, no swimming for him. "Jasper could have made a mistake and this bastard got lucky."

"Or he's that good," Beth said.

"And you two were on the fire," Grit said. "You and Martini. A couple of hotshot smoke jumpers. That'd only raise the stakes for a committed arsonist."

Sean and Beth both gave Grit a dark look, but his observation couldn't have been anything they hadn't considered. His cell phone rang. He saw Admiral Jenkins's number on the screen and decided to answer. "Yes, sir, Taylor here."

"Where's 'here'?"

"Southern California."

"You found a body this morning."

Grit didn't respond because no question had been asked of him.

"The Secret Service has already been in my office," Jenkins said.

"Jo Harper?"

"Her boss, Mark Francona. I told you to be careful out there."

"I'm trying not to fall into the pool at the moment. No one's shooting at me."

"I'm not worried if someone does." Jenkins paused, as if debating whether to say the rest of what was on his mind. Finally he added, "I'm worried people who aren't as straightforward as you are will end up throwing you under the bus."

In his weeks at the Pentagon, Grit had learned that Jenkins wasn't big on people who weren't straightforward. He was professional and did his job well, but he'd rather be thrown into a viper pit than attend a D.C. political cocktail party. He wouldn't care that the Neals were a regular family except for Preston Neal being vice president. Jenkins would only care that Grit was in position to be the fall guy if there was any political blowback from Porita Martinez's death.

"Coronado," Jenkins said. "Tomorrow. Be there, Petty Officer Taylor. Do your job."

"Yes, sir."

Thirty seconds later, another call came in. A private number. Grit figured it was Charlie Neal and answered.

"I don't have much time," Charlie said without preamble. "I'll go fast. Don't interrupt. I talked to my sister. Her ex-boyfriend likes to immerse himself in research, whether it's for a part or a screenplay he's working on. He's also good at disguising himself, going into character. I'm looking at all the parts he's played, and my sister's trying to remember what his screenplays are about. Maybe there's something there. She doesn't remember if they were ever at any events with Sean Cameron or Nick Martini."

"What about Jasper Vanderhorn?"

"I asked her about him back in November when his name first surfaced in my investigation—the investigation. She'd read about the fire. That's it. I'm doing all the cross-referencing I can."

"Just on the internet, right? Nothing top secret."

"I can't access top secret sites. Well, I probably could, but—"

"Don't."

"Right. I won't. How's Beverly Hills?"

"Beverly Hills is fine," Grit said. "This morning was difficult."

He watched Hannah pop out of the pool and adjust her swimsuit, her skin still pale after months of winter in Vermont. She smiled at Sean. She wasn't demonstrative but she wasn't shy, either, about being totally in love. They both sat at a table by Beth's lounge chair.

"My sister met Portia once," Charlie said. "She told the Secret Service. It's sad, what happened to her. I wish I could have figured this out before she died. I hope I can before anyone else dies."

"Charlie, it's not your job to figure out anything. If someone's killing people, that's the person responsible for any deaths. No one else."

"What about you?"

"I went out to where Jasper Vanderhorn died."

"What's it like?"

"The land's being reborn."

Charlie was silent a moment. "Don't think because I'm smart that I have no feelings."

"I don't think that. I think you want to matter, and I think you're afraid this firebug is coming after your family."

"What if he's a Secret Service agent?"

Grit gripped the phone tighter. "Charlie."

"I can speculate all I want. It's not Robert Feehan, unless he's operating under an alias."

"How do you know about Feehan?"

Charlie didn't seem to hear him. "He's on the run but he's innocent. He didn't kill Derek Cutshaw."

"Charlie."

"Internet. That's how I found out."

"I can't stop you from theorizing, but don't do more than that."

"I'm not. How could I? The Secret Service is all over me. You'd think I was vice president, not my dad. I ran for class president in ninth grade. You know how many votes I got?"

Grit wanted to throw his phone in the pool. "No, Charlie, how many?"

"Two. My cousin Conor and me. Nobody likes me."

"Why do you think that?"

"Two votes, Grit. Two. That's why."

"What would happen if you ran now?"

"I doubt even Conor would vote for me."

"That's because you've gotten him in trouble with the Secret Service."

"And the school," Charlie said.

"Charlie, just because your classmates didn't want you as their president doesn't mean they don't like you."

"Yeah, whatever. Think about it, Grit. Portia Martinez was murdered in Beverly Hills probably the day before Derek Cutshaw was murdered in Vermont."

"Maybe Robert Feehan is the firebug, using an alias."

"I can't find any connection between him and Marissa," Charlie said, loosening up on using names. "Trent isn't a bad guy. He's just a self-absorbed prick."

"Language."

"Jackass? Son of a bitch? Lout?"

Grit gave up. "Any idea where Trent could be now?"

"No. On your end?"

"No. Is he immersing himself in Vermont for some

screenplay or acting role? Never mind. I'm starting to think like you. If you make any connections using that 180 IQ of yours, call me. Don't do anything else. Got that?"

"Got it. There's something here, isn't there?"

"I don't know. I just know I found a dead woman today."

"Marissa...Grit, she'd fall for you if she got to know you."

"Who wouldn't?"

"I'm serious," Charlie said.

"Hell, so am I. Hang in there, kid. You can't have everything. You have to live in the world as it is, not as you want it to be."

"Are we talking about your leg?"

Grit gripped the phone. "No, we're talking about you."

"Oh." Charlie seemed oblivious. "Okay. I'll talk to you later."

He was gone. Grit sighed. In some ways, Charlie Neal was thirty. In other ways, he was twelve. Rarely was he a regular sixteen-year-old. He had a good family, tight-knit and strong, but they were in the limelight, which was difficult enough without adding a genius IQ and four older sisters to the mix. Marissa was attractive and intelligent, but she wasn't getting involved with a disabled SEAL from the Florida Panhandle.

Grit looked over at Beth Harper, still under her towels. "Getting back in the pool?"

"Not right away."

"Have you talked to Special Agent Harper?"

"Yes."

"Want to tell me what she said?"

Beth pulled the towels off her upper body and her long, strong legs. "She said you're trouble."

"Ah."

"I came out here to relax. Everything was supposed to be over. Then you show up."

"That woman was dead before my flight was even in the air."

"But we found her, not the neighbors, not her family, not her friends."

"Just as well, don't you think? Someone had to find her, and we've both seen dead bodies before. You're just out of your element and you're here to swim and buy shoes."

"I'm not buying shoes." She sighed at the slowly darkening sky. "I'm taking my emotions out on you. I'm scared, Grit. If one of these killers slipped through the cracks or some other killer's attracted to Black Falls because of Lowell Whittaker and what he's done..."

"Don't do that to yourself. We have to deal with the facts as they are."

She shivered as a breeze hit her wet swimsuit. Grit figured she thought of him as a brother. He wasn't sure he liked that. It was one thing to think of her as a sister, another for her not to even consider that he might be checking her out.

It was Thorne, Grit decided. Beth was preoccupied with their romantic issues, on top of the murder scene they'd walked into and the goings-on in her hometown.

"Have you always been a one-thing-at-a-time, let's-not-jump-ahead type?" she asked. "Or did your injury force you to take things a day at a time?"

"I move forward. I don't dwell on what I can't control. It gets me nowhere. You're the same, or you couldn't do the work you do."

"I'm resentful because I don't want any more violence," Beth said.

"Trooper Thorne resentful, too?"

"I wouldn't know. Are you trying to counsel me, Grit? Because you don't have to. I'm fine. If Scott wants to check in with me, he knows how to reach me."

"Think you'll quit as a paramedic?"

"And do what?"

"Help Myrtle Smith open a dinner service at the café."

Beth's laughter seemed to catch her by surprise as much as it did Grit. "We'd kill each other within two weeks," she said. "Myrtle's not staying in Black Falls no matter what she's telling herself right now, and I'm not cut out to run a restaurant. I like the mix of what I do at the café and as a medic. I often know the people I respond to, but I'm not burned out."

"If you'd been in Black Falls, you could have ended up checking out Derek Cutshaw."

"Possibly. Anyway, this isn't about me." She directed her attention to Sean at the table next to her. "Do you trust Nick Martini with your sister?"

"Nick's solid."

"Rose has—"

"Rose is solid, too," Sean said. "Whatever they have to work out between them is none of my business."

"Ha," Beth said.

"Do you think Martini told you the whole story about why he picked now to go to Vermont?" Grit asked, not for the first time.

Sean leaned back, his gaze on the clear, heated water of his pool. "There was no precipitating incident that I knew of, not a recent one, anyway."

"It's Jasper Vanderhorn, isn't it?"

"It's a lot of things." Sean got up abruptly. "Let's have dinner and give what happened today a chance to simmer."

Hannah paced at the side of the pool. She was reserved but visibly shaken by recent events. Beth was surly, but their emotions felt the same. Grit wished he hadn't come to see them. He had to be on Coronado tomorrow morning. He could leave now, but Sean had offered him the small guest room for the night. He probably wanted Grit and Beth both to clear out so that he and Hannah could have time together.

But they would, Grit thought. They'd have a lifetime together.

"I'm not hungry," Beth said. "I'm going for another swim."

Sean grimaced but made no comment. Grit saw a little of Elijah in him. From what he'd observed over the past few months, Rose was the same—which boded well for her. The Camerons were pure granite.

But they'd bleed if cut, Grit thought. Everyone did.

Beth swam until she thought she'd drown if she took another stroke, then bundled up in a dry towel and headed for a long, hot shower in her private bathroom.

She wanted to be back in Vermont, cleaning the café with her friends on a dark, cold winter night. She'd checked the weather. It was snowing in Black Falls.

"Damn you, Scott," she muttered, slipping into a soft, fluffy robe and pacing in her spacious room. "Why don't you call?"

She finally dialed Jo's cell phone. "There's no emergency," Beth said as her sister picked up.

"Good. I can't talk right now," Jo said. "Give me an hour, okay?"

Beth disconnected, feeling agitated, ready to put on a dry swimsuit and go back outside for more laps. The temperature was dropping, but she didn't care. She just couldn't stand being still, obsessing, waiting.

She hit Scott's number on her cell phone but didn't let it dial. Where would he be now? What would he be doing? What did he know about Portia Martinez?

She could call her father, the Black Falls retired police chief. The Harpers were solid, predictable types. Wasn't that what Scott wanted?

It was what he was. Was it what *she* wanted?

Finally she let Scott's number ring. She realized her hand was shaking and her eyes were filling up with tears. There'd go her reputation with Grit Taylor as a rock-ribbed New Englander, an experienced paramedic who'd seen it all.

The call went right to Scott's voice mail.

Beth didn't leave a message.

Eighteen

Black Falls, Vermont

Rose ducked into the woods on the edge of the meadow behind the lodge, moving well on her snowshoes, avoiding the cross-country ski trails. Ranger, accustomed to searching out ahead of her, was up by a large boulder. He, too, steered clear of the groomed tracks.

Nick was a few yards behind her. He was smooth and strong on snowshoes he'd borrowed from A.J. Several inches of snow had fallen late last night and into the morning. The sky was beginning to clear, a few streaks of blue breaking through the white, the late-morning sun beaming through in a thin ray of light. There'd been a brief alert overnight for a pair of hikers lost on state land, but they'd turned up unharmed.

Ranger paused just past the boulder, his golden coat standing out against the white landscape. Rose caught up with him, then looped behind a hemlock, its branches laden with snow, onto a shortcut to the sugar shack.

Nick eased in next to her. She smiled at him. "It's a beautiful day. I'd love to head down to the lake after we're done at the sugar shack. The trail's steep. It's a little tricky even on snowshoes."

"You can manage?" he asked her.

"Of course, but I've done the trail practically since I could walk."

"No worries, sweetheart," he said. "I'll be fine."

She grinned. "All right, we'll do it."

Rose took the lead again in the soft, undisturbed snow. She had strapped her ready pack to her back, standard whenever she was out in the woods. If either of them fell, she had basic supplies for repairs and first aid, as well as food and water.

Last night after dinner, Nick had gone straight up to his room at the lodge. Rose had stopped in the bar for a drink with a few friends. She hadn't wanted to go to her room too early. She'd needed time to put their kiss out of her mind, to cool her reaction to him and to convince herself they'd had to get that out of their system and it wouldn't happen again.

Nick hadn't surfaced again until after she'd had breakfast and met with Lauren to work on winter fest. Rose had struggled to focus. She'd slept badly, preoccupied with Nick and whether Derek's death and Robert's whereabouts could be connected to the murder of the woman in Beverly Hills.

She glanced back at him gliding through the snow and felt the sparks between them all over again. Nothing had cooled. He was strong, athletic and very sexy. She could still feel his kiss and her response to him.

Utter madness, and she wasn't the mad type.

Everything about Nick Martin was wrong for her.

The path curved along the edge of a finger ridge. Rose noticed prints in the snow a few yards down through the trees. Boots, she decided. Not skis or snowshoes. Given the fresh snow, the prints had to be relatively recent.

Ranger paused, his head in the air. He'd obviously picked up a scent and looked back at her, expectantly. She motioned for him to stay.

Nick came up beside her. She pointed out the tracks. "For all we know," she said, "they're from a guest on the trail of an owl."

"Stay close to me."

He adjusted his ski poles and pushed through the snow. Ranger stayed at Rose's side on her command. This wasn't a search, at least not yet. Nick moved deliberately, his strides controlled, neither aggressive nor tentative as the prints led into the woods toward the lake. The ground was uneven under the deep snow, the going difficult, requiring concentration and skill.

Finally they picked up a trail with enough switchbacks to keep the trek from getting too steep. Ranger grew excited, agitated and barked, looking up at Rose, eager for the command to track. "Ranger, heel," she reminded him.

Rose spotted an orange dome tent, designed for winter conditions, pitched on a level spot amid white pines, just above a stream encased in snow and thick, opaque white ice.

A black scarf lay in the trampled snow in front of the tent.

Nick put a hand on her hip. "Hold on," he said.

She noticed now. The air smelled of gasoline.

A small canister of what appeared to be Coleman fuel was turned over, its contents spilled out into the snow.

Nick dropped his hand from Rose's side and checked the tent, its flaps up, its opening unzipped. He peered inside, then looked at Rose as she eased her pack off her shoulders. "Is anyone in there?" she asked.

He shook his head. "It's empty."

"It's Robert Feehan's tent, isn't it?"

"I don't know. Do you have a radio? I imagine there's no cell service out here."

She nodded and dug her handheld radio out of her pack. She contacted the lodge and alerted A.J. to the presence of the campsite and described its location.

"You're with Nick?" her brother asked.

"Yes. It's just the two of us. No one else is here."

"All right. I'll get there as soon as I can—"

"No, A.J., you need to stay there. You know you do. Call the police. I'll radio you the second I know more." Even as she spoke, the smell of smoke mixed with the gas in the still, cold air. "A.J.—" She caught her breath. "A.J., there's a fire."

Nick pointed through the trees, past the stream. "There."

"It's at the lake," Rose told her brother, then gave him what information she could and switched off the radio. Thick, gray smoke was drifting up above the trees now.

Nick clearly was anxious to get moving. "How far to the lake?"

"Five minutes if we move fast."

"Let's go." He shifted his gaze to her as a slight breeze stirred in the evergreens. "Stay close to me."

"I've been on this trail a million times, and someone could need our help."

"Rose—"

"It's okay, Nick. This is what I do."

He nodded. "All right. Lead the way."

Rose returned to the trail, heading down a sharp curve in the deep snow. Ranger bounded just ahead of her. She was less aware of Nick behind her but wasn't concerned he couldn't manage the conditions.

Smoke became more noticeable, thicker in the air as it rose in the trees on the hill above the lake. Rose reminded herself that the cabins were unoccupied and Jo and Elijah were out of town.

Bowie.

She almost stumbled. Was he working at the lake?

Someone else could have seen the smoke by now and called 911. Fire trucks could already be en route.

Nick moved next to her as they reached one of the most run-down of Jo Harper's dozen cabins on the edge of the lake.

Ranger barked, on full alert. Rose saw what had him upset. The small cabin that Grit Taylor had occupied before his return to Washington was on fire, fully engulfed in flames.

No one inside could have survived.

Rose told Ranger to sit. She couldn't let him plunge

into a dangerous situation. "We need to make sure no one's in any of the cabins," she said to Nick, forcing herself to remain calm, professional.

"I'll do that," Nick said.

She knew she didn't need to tell Nick Martini what to do in a fire. He kicked off his snowshoes and was on his way. She removed her own snowshoes and peered down the hill, trying to see if Bowie's van was on the access road.

A scream—a woman, terrified—rose up from a cabin closer to the frozen lake.

Jo? Was she here after all?

"Ranger, stay," Rose said, then ran through the snow behind Nick.

He charged to the cabin's only door, but it was padlocked from the outside. He grabbed a splitter from a woodpile and smashed through the door. He raced inside. In two beats, he came out again, with Dominique Belair over one shoulder.

He shoved her into Rose's arms. "This place could be rigged," he said. "It could go up in flames. Move back. *Now.*"

Rose didn't hesitate and half carried Dominique, sobbing, gulping in air, down to the road. Dominique sank onto a snow-covered rock between the road and the lake. She was shaking with fear, shivering with the cold. She had on a winter jacket over leggings and running shoes, but she wasn't wearing a hat or gloves.

Rose didn't see Bowie's van anywhere on the road.

She squatted down in front of her friend. "Are you hurt?"

Dominique shook her head. "I'm okay," she said, her voice hoarse. "Thank you."

"Dom, what happened? What are you doing here?"

"I came for a run. I arrived about twenty minutes ago. I saw a man." She was panting, as if she couldn't get a decent breath. "I just got a glimpse of him. I thought it was Bowie, because he's been working out here."

"His van isn't here." Unless it was up at Elijah's, Rose thought with a jolt of panic. "Did you see him, Dom? Is he in one of the cabins?"

She looked up at Rose in terror. "I don't know."

Rose saw Nick charging for a second cabin that had started on fire. He crashed his splitter into the door.

"The man had on a black ski mask and parka." Dominique's lower lip trembled, but she was regaining her natural composure. "I didn't notice until I got closer that he was too thin to be Bowie. He grabbed me. He threw me into the cabin. I fell. I hit the wall."

"Were you knocked unconscious?" Rose asked.

Dominique shook her head. "I just had the wind knocked out of me. I was so stunned. Oh, Rose. I couldn't get out. He locked me in. I smelled smoke." She shivered, her teeth chattering. "I thought I was going to die."

Nick burst into the cabin and immediately backed out again, dragging a man into the snow. Even from where she stood with Dominique, Rose could see the man was badly burned and not readily identifiable.

He was clearly dead. There was nothing anyone could do.

Her heart almost stopped. It couldn't be Bowie, she told herself. She saw bits of a black ski mask, a black parka, just as Dom had described. And the victim was lean. Too lean to be an O'Rourke.

Rose remembered that Robert Feehan had been wearing a black parka when he'd grabbed her out by the sugar shack.

Was Bowie in the cabin that was fully engulfed, orange flames shooting through the roof now?

"Dom," Rose said, "did you see Bowie at all?"

"No. I left Myrtle in charge at the café and came out here for a run. Just a short one along the lake. Bowie said he'd be here. I thought I'd be safe. I saw someone up by the cabins. I called...." Dominique started shivering uncontrollably again. "I had no idea."

"Was he alone?"

"I didn't see anyone else. He didn't say anything. He just threw me into the cabin and locked me in. He seemed to be in a hurry." Her voice faltered. "I was terrified. Then I smelled smoke."

"You need to stay warm." Rose rummaged in her pack for a bottle of water. "Here, try to drink some."

Dominique took the bottle. "I'm okay. I just can't stop shaking."

Rose pulled an extra pair of gloves from her pack and handed them to Dominique as she strained to see if Bowie's van was up at Elijah's house. He could be working at a different site, or he could have already come and gone and Dominique had missed him.

Nick covered the body with a tarp from the woodpile and started checking the rest of the cabins before flying embers or a bomb could ignite more of them. He'd gone in and out of two, finding no other victims, when the first fire trucks, ambulance and police cruiser arrived.

Zack Harper was in the lead truck. He glanced at Rose and Dominique but said nothing as he and the other firefighters quickly got to work.

The ambulance crew ran toward Dominique. Rose left her friend in their care and got Ranger's attention, signaled for him to come to her. When he was at her side, she went with him up the slippery road to Elijah's house.

"Don't go in," Nick said, materializing next to her. He must have come through the trees that divided Jo's property from Elijah's. "This place could be rigged with some kind of explosive device."

She looked up at her brother's deck. The steps hadn't been shoveled. There were no prints in the snow. "The man is Robert Feehan, isn't it?"

"I'm sure it is," Nick replied. "It looks as if he couldn't get out of the cabin fast enough and got caught in his own scheme."

"Or that's what we're supposed to believe."

"Exactly."

"I should call Elijah and let him know what's going on. He can tell Jo."

Nick didn't argue. She walked down to the lake for better cell reception but it took several tries to get through to Elijah in Washington. When she did, she tried to be as clear and succinct as possible in informing him about the fires.

"I'm on the next flight up there," Elijah said grimly. "Was this show meant for you and Martini?"

"I don't know." Rose ran the toe of her boot over snow that clung to a low rock. "Either Robert accidentally got himself killed setting these fires or that's what we're supposed to think."

"Could he have known you two were out snowshoeing and rushed his plan?"

"It's possible. It must be his campsite we found. Maybe he was past caring about his own safety and got reckless."

Her middle brother was clearly tense. "Your voice is shaking."

"I'm cold."

"Once you're sure my place is safe, go inside. Get warm."

She almost smiled. "Yes, Sergeant Cameron."

He sighed. "You know what to do. I forget. Be careful. I'll get there as soon as I can."

"What about Jo?"

"I don't know if Jo will be with me. She's got her own problems."

The death of Portia Martinez and the whereabouts of Marissa Neal's former boyfriend, Rose thought, but Elijah had disconnected.

She saw that Nick had returned to the cabins. He would want to talk to the firefighters about exactly how the fires had started.

Two state detectives intercepted her as she started back to Elijah's house. They asked her if she wanted to talk to them inside where it was warm, but she answered their questions in the driveway. Once she finished, they headed back to the cabins.

Scott Thorne walked slowly up the icy road to her. "Hey, Rose." His emotions were under tight control. "I'm glad you're okay. We checked out here last night and didn't see anyone."

"Robert could have been keeping an eye out for you."

"We didn't see a trail, a light or footprints, but the snow was steady by then," he said curtly. "Visibility was lousy. Jo's cabins are a wreck, but this isn't how anyone wanted to get rid of them. How many burned?"

"Just the two. Grit's and the one next to it. The one Dominique was locked inside wasn't rigged. Robert, or whoever did this, might have planned to get to it next and wanted her to know what was in store for her."

"Elijah's house?"

"It's okay," Rose said. "Elijah and Jo haven't been here in several weeks. Neither has Grit. Robert had to know that."

"Bowie's been working out here," Scott said.

"It doesn't look as if he's been by yet today." Rose noticed a few white clouds on the horizon across the lake, even as the sky cleared directly above her. "I used to think Derek and Robert were just a couple of fun-loving ski bums who wouldn't hurt anyone. I learned about Derek's darker side a year ago, but Robert…"

"None of us knew them that well."

"Any idea how he started the fires?"

"Martini says he thinks there was some kind of accelerant used."

"White gas? There was a canister at the campsite Nick and I found up behind the cabins."

"The investigation's only just started, Rose," Scott said. "Be patient, okay?"

She noticed Nick coming up the road, moving smoothly. The physical demands seemed to have had no effect on him. "How did Robert get caught in a fire of his own making?" she asked Scott. "Did he trip?"

"It's tempting to speculate," he said, "but you know better."

Nick joined them, standing close enough to Rose that his arm brushed hers, but his eyes were on Scott. "Did Feehan have an alibi for the death of Portia Martinez in California?"

Scott shook his head. "Not going there, Nick."

He didn't give up. "Do you know for sure he was in Vermont when she was killed? Did he know this missing actor?"

"Feehan worked with a number of private students at various ski areas and didn't keep good records," Scott said. "It'll take some time to sort everything out and work a timeline."

"What about Marissa Neal?" Nick asked.

Scott clearly didn't like Nick's questions. "Not going there, either." He shifted back to Rose, his expression blank, impassive. "Call me if you think of anything else."

She watched him bypass an unsanded section of glare ice as he walked back to the cabins.

Nick pulled off a glove and zipped up her jacket. "Don't let adrenaline fool you," he said, his hand lingering at her collar. "It's cold out here. You'll cool off fast now that you're still." He smiled slightly. "Which I realize you know."

"It's easy to forget the basics when you're emotionally involved. I don't know why Dom's cabin wasn't set on fire." She swallowed, her throat dry, tight. "Maybe because Robert didn't get to it."

She called Ranger and they went up the snow-covered stairs to Elijah's deck. He had someone plow and shovel while he was away, but the three inches of snow that had fallen overnight could wait. She heard Nick on the stairs behind her and slipped inside through the slider. Snow fell off her boots onto the hardwood floor of the comfortable main room, but her brother wouldn't care.

While Ranger sniffed out the place, Rose pulled off her hat and gloves and looked out the wall of sliding doors at the view of the lake. Nick entered the house through the slider next to her. She could feel his intensity, smelled the fire on him as he took in her brother's house.

"Elijah loves this place," she said. "He left home at nineteen. I was fourteen. I wrote to him almost every day that first year. I'd made it my goal. Three hundred sixty-five letters to my soldier brother."

"Did he write back to you?"

"Some, but I didn't expect an answer to every letter. Even if he hadn't been a soldier, that would have been unrealistic. The long silences didn't come until later, when he became a Green Beret." The sky had cleared and was a bright winter blue against the white and gray landscape.

"He bought this land three years ago and worked on this place whenever he was home."

"He did a good job."

"Pop would come down and help. He knew Elijah always wanted to return home to Black Falls. I think Pop left Jo the lakefront property because he believed she and Elijah were meant to be together. He discovered them in one of the cabins. Running off with Elijah was the only time Jo veered off the path she'd set for herself and did something crazy. Elijah says he'd have ended up in jail if he hadn't gone into the army when he did."

"But your father felt guilty," Nick said.

"Not in the beginning. He came to believe he'd interfered with something that was meant to be. I think leaving Jo the cabins was a way for him to make amends. She wouldn't have been here in November if he hadn't. Who knows if or when she and Elijah would have gotten back together again." Rose glanced at Nick, realized his gaze was on her, not the view. "Do you have a place you want to be? A place you think of as home?"

He shrugged as if he had never really considered such a question. "My father was career navy. We bounced around when I was growing up. I'm used to making a home where I am." Humor played at the corners of his mouth. "I didn't grow up in a small New England town where my family had lived for generations."

"Not all Camerons stayed. For instance, some took off for Ohio after a brutal winter in the early nineteenth century." Rose wasn't letting him off the hook. "If you closed your eyes, clicked your heels together three times and whispered, 'There's no place like home,' where would home be?"

"It's not a place. It's an attitude. It's the people who'd be with me."

His tone made her breath catch, but she saw more police cars arrive on the narrow lake road. "I should go check on Dominique. Nick, I was so scared. First Dom. Then…I thought it was Bowie in the burning cabin."

"I know, sweetheart." He slipped an arm around her. "I know."

She leaned her head against him, his muscles taut, still tensed from wielding the splitter, carrying out first Dominique and then Robert. "I can't imagine what Robert was thinking. None of this makes any sense. What about you? Are you okay?"

"No worries." He drew her closer still and brushed his lips over the top of her head. She hadn't even realized she'd pulled off her hat. "I'll snowshoe back up to the lodge. I want to take another look at the campsite. The police are there now."

"Dominique can't be up to driving. I'll take her back to town in her car. Someone there can give me a ride back to the lodge. Would you mind taking Ranger with you?"

"Sure. Ranger and I have bonded."

"Say his name, then give a one-word command. Stick to basics." Rose smiled. "Be the alpha dog. He'll behave."

"I love being the alpha dog."

The humor helped her to absorb the events of the morning. "Nick…"

He slipped her hat out of her pocket and tucked it onto her head. "Soon, Rose," he said softly. "We'll figure all this out soon."

Nineteen

Dominique put on an evergreen-colored canvas apron in the café kitchen. She'd wanted to go right back to work. Rose hadn't argued and watched her friend hop onto a stool at the butcher-block worktable. Dominique was visibly trembling, still ashen from her ordeal at the lake.

Rose stood across the worktable from her. "Dom, what's going on?"

"We'll have a late lunch spurt because of the fire. It'll bring people out." She placed her hands on the clean wood and splayed her fingers, as if she weren't sure what to do with herself. "I just have to think a minute."

"The police want to talk to Bowie."

She nodded. "Of course. It only makes sense."

"Were you meeting him? Is that why you chose the lake for your run?"

Dominique looked up, her dark eyes clear, shining. "I wouldn't say I was meeting him. I knew he'd be there. Excuse me, Rose. I really have to get busy."

"Sure."

As Rose started out of the kitchen, Dominique jumped off the stool and gave her a hug. "Thank you," she whispered. "Thank Nick Martini for me, too."

"Dom..."

She stood back, smiling, trembling even more. "Cooking's my refuge."

She returned to the worktable, and Rose went out through the swinging door to the dining room, where, in fact, business was picking up. Myrtle was behind the glass case, filling an order for fruit salad and house-made yogurt. "Dom's back?"

"Yes," Rose said. "Thankfully she wasn't seriously injured. She's more shaken up than anything."

"She'll make soup. It'll be good for her."

Rose noticed a coffee spill on the counter and grabbed a cloth and wiped it up. "Myrtle, did Dom tell you why she was going out to the lake?"

"She said she was going for a run." Myrtle handed the fruit and yogurt to a teenager from town, took her money and turned back to Rose with a sigh. "If Andrei could see me now."

Andrei Petrov was the Russian diplomat whose death Myrtle had looked into, bringing her to Lowell Whittaker's attention. The result was the fire at her house—and, ultimately, her presence at Three Sisters Café on Main Street in Black Falls.

Myrtle fussed with the tie on her apron as she continued. "You'd think a serial arsonist who sets fires for his own pleasure *and* contracts out as a paid killer wouldn't end up burning himself to death in a falling-down Vermont cabin." She straightened, her lavender eyes clear, incisive. "I suppose it could have been suicide, but he didn't exactly go out in a blaze of glory, did he?"

"Good points." Rose helped herself to an apple from a plate on the counter. "Any idea what Dom's hiding?"

"She might not be hiding anything. She just might be keeping her business to herself. She's pleasant to everyone, but she's reserved. She doesn't blab about her private life."

"Myrtle, are Dom and Bowie seeing each other?"

"I don't know," Myrtle said as a couple from town walked up to the glass case.

Rose ate her apple as she walked down to O'Rourke's. She found Liam out back, taking off his winter gear. "I was out snowshoeing," he said. "If it's above zero, I like to get out before work. Just has to be above zero. I heard sirens and called a friend. I heard what happened."

She leaned in the doorway, every inch of the tidy back room lined with shelves and hooks for supplies, tools and Liam's personal outdoor gear. "Where were you snowshoeing?" she asked him.

"Cameron Mountain." He leaned his snowshoes and poles against the wall. "I ran into Lauren, as a matter of fact. She was on the way to the sugar shack. She seemed preoccupied."

"Was anyone with her?"

He pulled off his coat and shook his head. "She was meeting the guys delivering the new evaporator for the shack. I can't believe you all are getting into sugaring."

"It's more for fun than profit."

"Impractical," Liam said.

Probably true. Rose thought. "Did you see any smoke from the fires at the lake?"

"Yeah, I didn't know what was going on. I drove straight back here." He frowned at her, his face still red from the cold and exertion. "You interrogating me, Rose?"

"Dominique was attacked, Liam."

He went very still. "Dom? Is she okay?"

Rose quickly explained what had transpired earlier at the lake. "Dom says she was meeting Bowie. He wasn't there."

"I haven't seen him today."

"Robert was camping up in the woods. You didn't run into him?"

"No. I didn't snowshoe in that direction."

"When the Neals were in town—"

"Damn, Rose, you think I had anything to do with the Neals when they were here?"

She reined in a burst of impatience. "Did anyone ever brag about seeing them? You know, tales told to the bartender?"

"No one said anything to me about the Neals, beyond talk about Charlie Neal's prank on Jo Harper last fall that got her back up here. Everyone thought that was hysterical."

Which would mortify Jo. "What about me?" Rose asked quietly.

"You mean has anyone been crying in their beer to me over you? There was gossip about you, but you're a Cameron. There's always gossip about you all. You're out there, Rose. You do search and rescues all over the country."

"My work's not glamorous, Liam," she said, feeling defensive. "I'm doing more and more training and consulting these days. I don't want to give up the volunteer work, but Ranger's getting on in years. I haven't decided yet if I want to train another dog for myself. I think he prefers wilderness work. Disaster work is hard on both of us."

"It'd be hard on anyone." Liam seemed to relax slightly and hung his jacket on a metal hook. "A lazy life with a bone by the woodstove is in Ranger's future. Was he a help this morning?"

"He's always a help."

Rose stood up straight. "I wish someone had whispered a secret in my ear that would explain everything and stop more violence and tragedy."

"Did you think Derek was getting his act together?"

"I'm not sure he was capable of reforming," Liam said, changing out of his winter boots to regular shoes. "I don't know what to say, Rose. Getting pounded by Bowie may have helped Derek get some perspective. He hadn't been in trouble since then that I know of."

Rose thanked him and went out the back door and around to Main Street, debating a moment before heading to the café. She entered the building through the center-hall door and peeked into the dining room, where Myrtle Smith was still alone behind the glass case, dealing with the lunch crowd and looking restless. Rose continued down the hall to the ladies' room.

Her reflection made her grimace. She peered into a

mirror that Hannah and Beth had found at a yard sale and saw that she had smudges of soot on her face. Her skin was windburned but pallid, with dark shadows under her eyes that showed the strain of the morning.

Figured no one had told her she was a mess.

She cleaned up and slipped into the kitchen. Dominique was alone, her cheeks flushed as she pulled a pan of steaming roasted vegetables from the oven.

Rose tried to stay out of the way. "How are you doing?"

"How am I doing?" Dominique slammed the pan onto a cooling rack on the counter. "A man is dead, Rose. I'm lucky I'm not dead."

"Dom, you and Robert weren't—"

"We weren't anything. He'd come in here. I'd see him. Same with Derek. Not often." She tossed her pot holders onto a pile by the stove. "I told the police."

"Were you friends?"

"Friends? What's a friend? Lowell and Vivian Whittaker used to come in here, too. They acted as if we were their friends. We were all taken in." Dominique washed her hands in the stainless-steel sink. "I'm sorry. I don't mean to be rude."

"Something's going on with you, Dom," Rose said quietly. "Whatever it is was there even before you went out to the lake this morning."

Dominique briskly dried her hands with a soft cloth. "Nothing's going on. Forget it. I have work to do. Please excuse me."

"Dom—"

"I was in the wrong place at the wrong time this

morning. I surprised Robert. He panicked." She snatched up a long-handled spoon and stirred the vegetables. In summer, she'd use fresh local produce when she could. "If he and Derek were preying on vulnerable young people, selling them prescription drugs..."

"Were you trying to expose them?"

"I'm not a police officer. I'd heard rumors. Bowie had, too. I told the police everything I know, which, fortunately or unfortunately, is very little."

Dominique set the spoon on the counter and returned to the worktable, making it clear she didn't want to talk, but Rose continued to press her. "You were at the Whittaker place yesterday and the cabins this morning—"

"I know where I was," Dominique said irritably.

"Why were you there, Dom? I've never known you to run out at the lake."

"I signed up for a half marathon in June. Jo and Beth Harper run there. Beth showed me their route." She stared down at her hands on the butcher-block table. "And because I wanted to talk to Bowie. I wanted to see if we could figure out where Robert was."

"Why?"

"I wanted to convince Robert to talk to the police before he ended up like Derek."

"Then you don't think he killed Derek and accidentally killed himself?"

Dominique, calmer, shook her head.

"Robert could have fooled everyone," Rose said. "He could have pretended to be a carefree ski instructor when, in fact, he was one of Lowell Whittaker's killers. He could have realized he was caught and went out the way he wanted to."

"I don't know whether it's more frightening to think that Robert was one of Lowell's killers, or that he wasn't. If he wasn't, there's someone else still out there."

Rose leaned back against the counter. "You tend to stick close to home."

"I've been working on my house."

"You hardly ever go out, Dom."

She raised her brown eyes. "Are you suggesting I'm hiding something?"

"Asking."

She twisted her hands together. "Nothing that matters."

"Whatever you're hiding, Dom, people are going to find out. It's hard enough to keep secrets around here when things are normal."

Dominique shut her eyes briefly, then spoke without looking at Rose. "I was married for about five minutes four years ago." She paused, rubbing her fingertips over the butcher-block tabletop. "He had money. *Has.* He's not from around here. Cleveland. He's an alpine skier, though. He loves Vermont. He took lessons from Derek. I did, too."

"Dom, as far as secrets go…"

"I got involved in prescription drug abuse," she said quietly. "I'm clean now. I have been for four years. Belair's my maiden name. I found myself in cooking—and here," she added, her voice cracking, "with you all."

Rose steadied herself against Dominique's admission. "Bowie knows?"

She gave a small laugh. "Bowie knows everything that happens around here, I swear."

"True," Rose said, still not satisfied. "Where's your ex-husband now?"

"Still in Cleveland. He's remarried. He's not a bad guy, we just weren't right for each other. We were both spoiled."

Rose saw it now. "You come from money."

Dominique's eyes lowered. "I'm what you all would call a 'trust fund baby.' I didn't want anyone to know. I wanted to be known for myself, for who I am."

"Don't we all, Dom? Give us a little credit."

"I do now. It just became easier to keep not saying anything."

Rose felt her energy sagging. "I can't argue with that," she said softly. "The police know?"

"Everything, yes."

"Bowie?"

"He guessed," Dominique said.

"He's good at keeping other people's secrets."

"Maybe we ask too much of him, or he asks too much of himself." She stood back from the worktable. "I really do have things I need to do."

Rose smiled. "Cook to your heart's content, Dom."

When she reached Main Street, Rose noticed the air was warmer, above freezing. Nick would be back at the lodge by now.

No sooner did she have the thought than he called. "Do you want me to pick you up?"

She spotted Bowie's beat-up van down the street.

"Thanks, but I'll get a ride. Be back soon. What are you doing?"

"Thinking and making calls. I brushed Ranger. He didn't like it."

"He never does." Rose didn't ask any follow-up questions and disconnected, walking down to Bowie's van. He was climbing in. "What're you doing in town?" she asked him.

"Stopped to see Liam to see what he knew about the fire. He said I just missed you."

"Have you talked to the police?"

"Oh, yes."

"Then you know Dominique was attacked?"

"I stopped by to check on her, but she was busy. I talked to her for two seconds, probably while you were with Liam. She's pretty shaken up." Bowie narrowed his eyes on Rose for half a beat. "You are, too."

"I don't deny it. Can you give me a ride up to the lodge?"

He nodded. "Where's Ranger?"

"Nick hiked back up to the lodge. Ranger went with him."

Rose shoved stuff off the van's front passenger seat and got in. The interior smelled like mud and cold, wet stone—at least not like gas, she thought.

They passed the police station. "Every cop in town must be out at the lake," Bowie said.

"Probably so." She stared out the side window at the familiar landscape of her hometown. Snow had melted into her wool socks. She'd unzipped her coat, but she was still too warm. "When you were in that fight at

O'Rourke's, did you ever imagine Derek and Robert would be dead in less than a year?"

"I wasn't thinking about the future. I was locked in to the idea that I needed to punch Derek in the head."

She couldn't help but smile at Bowie's irreverent tone.

But his eyes were serious when he glanced over at her. "That fight's in the past, Rose. It's not why Derek and Robert are dead."

"You protected me last year."

"You can look at it that way, but I wasn't really thinking. I was mad. Derek was out of control. I reacted."

"I keep wondering if I'd confronted my problems, maybe things would have gone differently this year."

"Don't go there. We are where we are. Whether or not it's where we would be if we hadn't dealt with these bastards doesn't much matter."

They drove up the mountain in silence. As they came to the lodge, Rose said, "I miss Hannah."

"Yeah, me, too."

"I miss her, but I'm glad she's with Sean and not here now, for this."

"You're her friend. I talked to her earlier. She wants to be here for you. Beth, too."

"You told them to stay in California, didn't you?"

"Yeah. Do your work, Rose. Let the police do theirs. You're a can-do type, just like your brothers, but sometimes you have to know your limits. We all do."

"It's easier on a search than with something like this. It all feels so out of control, with no rules."

"There are rules. Rule one—you don't get to kill some-one. Rose, you okay with this guy?"

"I can handle him."

"Could he have set the fires? It only takes a cell phone to detonate a simple homemade bomb."

"It wasn't Nick, Bowie. Absolutely not."

Bowie grinned at her. "See? There's an attraction there." He pulled into the lodge parking lot and glanced in back at Poe. "Look at him. Not a peep out of him. Ranger's influence."

"Ranger's not perfect, you know," Rose said. "Poe looks tired. Did you have him out running this morning?"

"He charged around while I was working. He's in good shape. He's just lazy. The vet said he needed to lose weight, so I've been getting him out more. It's good for me, too."

"Dominique said she was meeting you at the lake this morning. What happened? Where were you?"

"Late," he said, his voice heavy with regret.

"Why?"

He threw the van into Park and looked over at her. "I made a stop to give an estimate. It took longer than I ex-pected. The police have all the details. You want them, too, Rose?"

"I'm not doubting you. Don't get defensive. I just wanted to know."

"Maybe you want to know too much. Maybe you should get on a damn plane and go train dogs in Alaska or something. I worry about you, Rose."

She let his worry roll over her. "Thanks for your

concern. Bowie, are you and Dominique seeing each other?"

"She and Poe are both trying to get in shape. She wants to run a half marathon this summer. Nothing more than that."

"I grew up here. I can be private all I want and it won't do me any good. Everybody's always sticking their noses in my business."

He grinned at her. "Like you'd have it any other way."

"You're a good friend to have, Bowie. Thanks for the ride."

"Anytime."

"Want to come in?"

He shook his head. "I have work to do. Call or come find me if you need a friend."

Rose promised she would and thanked him as she got out of the van.

She spotted A.J. down by the shop and walked in that direction. He was pacing, clearly agitated, and she assumed it was because of the scene at the lake. He shoved a hand through his hair. "I can still smell smoke," he said. "Damn."

"I'm sorry, A.J."

"Yeah. Me, too. I've been trying to sort everything out in my own mind. I don't see how a couple of ski-bum drug dealers had anything to do with the death of that woman in California and this missing actor."

"We can come up with a thousand different scenarios if we want to." Rose recognized a middle-aged couple ski from the lodge on the groomed trails in the meadow.

"Most guests won't associate what happened at the lake with the lodge. It's far enough away—"

"They could see the smoke from the dining room."

"A fire in the middle of winter, down in the valley. It's understandable they'd look."

"A fatal fire on top of another fatal fire just the other day." Her brother stared at a display of winter sports gear in the shop window. "I'd hoped winter fest would be a fresh start for everyone in town."

"It still can be," Rose said. "There's time to figure out what's going on and put an end to it."

"That's what we keep saying. It's what we said in November when Jo and Elijah confronted those two killers. It's what we said in January when Hannah and Sean figured out Lowell Whittaker was behind this network of assassins."

"The lodge is busiest in the warm-weather months. By then, most people aren't going to remember if this all happened in another town, or even know that it happened at all. We're in the middle of it. We'll know. I've been to the scene of so many disasters—"

"This isn't a natural disaster."

Rose sighed. "I'm not helping, am I? Okay. I'm going to find Ranger."

A.J. shifted back to her. "Lauren panicked when she heard sirens and saw smoke. I don't know how much more of this she can take."

"She's strong, A.J. So are you."

"She's scared." He let out a breath, shook his head. "Never mind. We'll get through it. You just concentrate on staying safe yourself. When you radioed this morning and I saw the smoke..." He stood up straight and managed a small smile. "I was glad Nick was with you."

She grinned at him. "Ha, the faith my brothers have in me." She touched his arm. "We're going to be okay, A.J. You know that, right? Whatever happens."

"Yeah," he said, and followed several guests into the shop.

As she headed back up to the main lodge, Ranger bounded toward her with the energy of a puppy. Nick's influence, she decided, her heart jumping when she saw him ambling toward her.

She believed what she'd said to A.J. They'd be okay. What other choice was there?

Twenty

Beverly Hills, California

Grit could tell the Black Falls women were restless, frustrated that they were on the other side of the continent while so much went on at home. Sean was more accustomed to not being in the eye of his hometown storms but the events of the day had clearly disturbed him, too.

The fire at Jo Harper's cabins on the lake—Robert Feehan's death, Dominique Belair's near death—bothered everyone.

The cabin Grit had stayed in had burned, but he wasn't nostalgic. He figured the accursed woodstove had probably made it through just fine.

Devin and Toby Shay arrived at Sean's house, and Grit was of a mind to leave them and Beth there while he and Sean drove out to the Cameron & Martini building that had burned a year ago.

Beth had other ideas. Testy and silent, she climbed,

uninvited, into the back of Sean's car and put on her seat belt.

Sean glanced at Grit, as if seeking his wisdom on what to do. Grit shrugged. "How far is this place?"

"Twenty minutes, longer if traffic's bad."

As far as Grit could see, traffic was always bad. He figured he could handle thirty minutes with Beth biting her nails in back. Let Sean be the one to kick her out. "Drive on."

Sean gritted his teeth and steered his expensive sedan out of the driveway.

Grit turned to Beth in the backseat. "Have you talked to Trooper Thorne?" She just stared out her window. He tried again. "Your brother? Your sister? Rose? Dominique?"

"I don't want to talk."

That could work, Grit decided, and turned back around. Seventeen minutes later, they pulled into a small parking area by a three-story Art Deco building that Cameron & Martini had saved from the wrecking ball, refurbished and still owned.

There'd been a fire during renovations. Nick Martini's quick actions had almost certainly saved the building.

Sean led Grit and Beth into a cool, elegant lobby, no indication that there'd been a fire or that the place had ever needed renovating. Sean said, "The fire was last January, months before Jasper Vanderhorn was killed."

"Your sister was just getting involved with Cutshaw then," Grit said.

Beth stiffened visibly, but Sean was calm. "I don't see how the two could be connected."

"Me, either." Grit looked up at the Art Deco ceiling. "Vanderhorn investigated this fire?"

Sean shook his head. "Not officially. He looked into it on his own after the fact."

"He was trying to connect this fire to his serial arsonist?"

"I suspect so, yes," Sean said, diplomatically.

Grit noted the list of businesses with offices in the building but none struck him as being related to Hollywood and their missing actor. Advertising, digital media, financial planning. He turned back to Sean. "How'd the fire start?"

"Electrical short," Sean said. "The work crews missed it."

"No arrests?"

"No. There's no proof it was arson."

"But you think it was," Grit said.

Sean shrugged without answering.

Beth wandered over to the elevator but was obviously listening in.

Grit continued. "The police will be looking into whether Robert Feehan was or could have been in Los Angeles then. Cutshaw, too. Maybe they worked together and just had a falling-out."

Sean considered Grit's comment. "Why target Nick and me? The Whittakers were already in Black Falls, but my father wasn't suspicious of Lowell yet. No one was."

Something Drew Cameron's four offspring now had to live with, Grit thought. He said matter-of-factly, "Lowell didn't like you. You're everything he isn't. His crazy bitch wife threw you in his face. Why *not* target you and your smoke jumping buddy?"

"Nick was only here by accident. I wasn't here at all. The fire couldn't have been meant to kill us." Sean looked around the lobby, as if imagining the flames a year ago. "Most arsonists work alone."

"Okay," Grit said. "So it's Feehan, and Cutshaw wasn't involved. Feehan finds out a Cameron is a rich Californian and locates one of your enemies or one of Martini's enemies to pay to mess things up for you. Was construction delayed?"

"For a few weeks."

"Maybe that was enough. Maybe this fire was about profit. How'd Martini find out about it?"

"Nick was out that night and got a call from the security guard that there was a fire. He arrived before the fire crews."

"Could he be the arsonist himself?"

Sean cast Grit a cool look. "No."

"Is that friendship or your head talking?"

"Both."

Beth stalked over to them. Her turquoise eyes showed the strain she was feeling, but she still glared at Grit. "What happened to your navy business?"

"Tomorrow," he said.

They headed back out, the air warm, the light now a filtered brownish color. This time Grit took the backseat. Beth got in front without a word.

Sean was pensive as they drove to his house.

"I have to go home," Beth said, watching Beverly Hills slide past her.

Sean nodded. "I've been thinking the same thing. We'll all go."

Once at Sean's, he and Beth went inside to make plans. Grit stayed out in the driveway and took a call from Charlie Neal.

"Anything new?" Charlie asked, but didn't wait for an answer. "Never mind. I'd have heard. I've been looking into Portia Martinez—all on the internet, so don't worry. She grew up in Fresno. Her parents are schoolteachers. Totally ordinary and normal. She wanted to work in Hollywood from the age of four."

"The police must know this, Charlie."

"They must, but here's what I'm thinking. What if Portia somehow got wind of this firebug and his plot to kill my sister?"

"Jasper Vanderhorn's the only one who had this theory about a serial arsonist. How would she have found out? And your sister's fire was months ago, and it was an accident. If Ms. Martinez knew anything about it, she'd have reported what she knew to the police or the Secret Service, don't you think?"

"She might have only just found out, and there could be a new plot. It's unfinished business. Killing Marissa, I mean."

Grit sighed. He was getting used to Charlie's labyrinthine way of thinking. "You think Jasper Vanderhorn was onto the plot and that's why he was killed?"

"Maybe Portia was his confidential informant."

"There any evidence of that?"

"How would I know? I'm in high school in northern Virginia."

"You're maddening."

"I am?"

"Yeah. You're a big pain in the ass, Charlie."

"Good." He sounded relieved. "How's the leg?"

"Which one? All's well." Grit watched a car edge past the house on the quiet street. "Go back to class."

"Jo and Elijah are upset about the fire this morning—Agent Harper and Sergeant Cameron, I mean."

Grit had wondered if Charlie would get to that part. "You've talked to them?"

"I saw Jo and called Elijah. They didn't want to talk to me."

"You weren't surprised, were you?"

"No, but it's okay. They told me to butt out, which I expected, but I got my point across. What do you think the fire on Jo's property means? Is the firebug mad at her for foiling his attack on Marissa last fall?"

"Evidence, Charlie. Speculation just gets you tangled up."

"That's what Elijah said."

"I'm sure he did."

"Two fires, Grit—Petty Officer Taylor," Charlie said. "That's evidence."

Beth was in the shade by the front door when Grit disconnected. He'd seen her come out but hadn't done anything about it. She shook her head at him. "Jo would skewer you."

"For what?"

"For talking to Charlie Neal. That little devil caused Jo big problems and almost got her fired, and now he's going to get you arrested."

"Jo might not have hooked up with Elijah again if Charlie hadn't shot her in the butt with those Airsoft pellets."

"They'd have found a way back to each other."

Grit noticed a flicker of what he interpreted as sadness and regret in Beth's eyes. "You're a romantic."

"Not me." She almost smiled as she stepped out of the shade. "I'm a hardheaded, repressed New Englander."

"That doesn't mean you're not a romantic. It'll be a while before you get over Trooper Thorne, won't it?"

"I'm not talking about my love life with you, Grit. What about yours?"

"Too busy learning to walk again."

"It's been almost a year."

"You'd expect more of me?"

"A strapping Navy SEAL? It was just your lower leg you lost."

Her bluntness was refreshing. "Man, you're tough."

She didn't seem at all embarrassed or chagrined. "Tell me about Charlie."

After Grit went back inside, Beth stifled her guilt at having been surly with him and dialed Scott's cell number. He'd left her a message to call him. She had no idea what to expect. She only knew that she wanted to talk to him in private, not where Hannah, Sean or Grit could scrutinize her for her reaction.

She stood in the warm sun and steadied herself when she heard Scott pick up. "It's me," she said.

"Hey, Beth." He sounded tense but not angry, and not, she thought, unpleased to hear her voice. "You okay?"

"I am, yes. You?"

"Just doing my job."

"You called me—"

"I called to find out how you are. I meant that's how I am—I'm just doing my job." He sighed. "Don't complicate everything."

Beth smiled in spite of her tension. That was Scott: literal, no-nonsense, a man of clarity and purpose. "I talked to Rose," she said. "Dominique's been concealing an ex-husband and a trust fund. How long have you known?"

"Awhile."

But he couldn't and wouldn't tell her. She appreciated that about him. He wouldn't torture himself. He'd just put the information under "secret work stuff" in his mind and not go there when they were together. "Jo knows?"

"Ask her."

Beth took that as a yes. "So how the hell rich is Dom?"

"She's from a Midwest manufacturing family. Old money."

"And here she is, living in a little fixer-upper in a small Vermont town and baking scones and grilling salmon for a living."

"She just does her own thing, which you, she and Hannah all share."

"Scott—"

"When are you coming back?"

"As soon as I can figure out how to get there."

"Plane," he said.

For Scott Thorne, that was a major display of humor.

Beth felt tears hot in her eyes, the anger draining out of her. She tried to laugh. "I kind of miss winter."

"No, you don't. You miss being in the middle of things." He paused and sucked in a breath. "I miss having you in the middle of things. Going out to the lake this morning…knowing you wouldn't be there to help…" His voice was lower, almost tentative. "It wasn't what I thought it'd be."

She knew he'd said all he meant to and if she pushed for more, she'd only make him uncomfortable. If she'd learned anything in the past twenty-four hours, it was to hold her damn tongue once in a while.

"You law enforcement types don't think Dom could be your firebug, do you?" she asked him. "Because that'd be nuts—"

"Go swimming."

She could hear the relief in his voice. She smiled into the sun. "I love you, Scott."

"Yeah," he said, and it was enough.

Beth quickly shut her phone and headed back inside.

Twenty-One

Black Falls, Vermont

Nick was on Rose's couch, welcoming the quiet and coziness of her little house after the long, tense day. She lay stretched out in front of her woodstove, with Ranger asleep, one ear flopped off the side of his bed. It was dark, the promise of warmer temperatures in the forecast for tomorrow.

He could see the white on Ranger's undercoat. "Will you train another search dog after Ranger retires?" he asked.

"Not right away," Rose said. "Maybe not ever. Ranger has time. Another year, I think."

"You're both on the road a lot."

"Especially this past year."

"How much was volunteer and how much was for pay?"

"My search-and-rescue work is on a volunteer basis.

I'm a member of a team that responds to disaster calls around the country, but most of our work's in New England. I've been doing more and more consulting in search management. That pays, but I still need to do projects at the lodge to make ends meet."

Nick watched her run her palm over Ranger's golden coat.

She added, "I can't take on the intense commitment to train another dog anytime soon."

"You and Ranger are still a team."

"We have more work to do together. We could drop back to local wilderness searches. The disaster work's intense and demanding for both of us." She glanced up at Nick, the effects of the fire on the lake that morning— the needless death of a man she knew—less evident in her eyes, her mouth. "Enough about me."

"You're driven," Nick said.

"This from Nick Martini," Rose said, amused, and sat up, stretching out her legs in front of her. She'd changed into slim pants and a soft sweater and was barefoot. She seemed aware he was watching her every movement. "Sean's driven, too, but he's more subtle about it. Not you. Submarines, smoke jumping, making money—you dive into whatever you're doing with absolute commitment. What's your family like?"

He smiled slightly. "Intense but likable."

Rose laughed. "You're intense. 'Likable' remains to be seen. I know your father's retired. For how long?"

"Five years. He misses the sea, even if he was under it most of his career. He has a number of different irons in the fire as a military consultant. My mother's a geologist.

She teaches at a local college. I have a sister, too. Diana. She's career navy."

"You enlisted. How'd that go over?"

He grinned. "It went over."

"You were impatient. You still are. It can be a virtue. You didn't hesitate today. You did well."

Again his gaze settled on her. "So did you."

"I'm not an adrenaline junkie," she said, not defensively. "Maybe at first I had visions of drama and heroism and adventure, but canine search and rescue requires teamwork and a tremendous amount of dedication, training and practice, practice, practice. People who go into it for the glory usually don't last."

"It's similar with smoke jumping." Her toes almost touched his boots. "Training weeds out most of the people who are there for the wrong reasons. It weeds out those who have the right attitude, too, but just can't do the job, for whatever reason."

"I remember what Sean went through. It's a grueling process." Rose glanced at the fire blazing behind the glass doors of the woodstove. "Some firebugs are frustrated glory hogs."

Nick didn't respond. He knew her statement wasn't a non sequitur.

She turned back to him. "They set fires out of an inflated sense of vanity. They like watching the fire itself, but they also like to watch the crews charge in to put it out—the feeling of power it gives them." The fire glowed in her tawny-colored hair. "I don't know what kind we're dealing with. A glory hog mixed with a cold-blooded killer?"

"Not a good mix," Nick said.

"No."

He shifted the subject. "Ranger loves it here, doesn't he?"

She smiled, slipping on her socks and boots. "You can tell, can't you?"

"He'll have a long, good retirement."

They left him by the fire and headed out. They'd been invited to dinner at A.J. and Lauren's house.

Summoned was more like it, Nick thought, but he understood. A.J. was worried about his sister, and not for no reason.

Rose didn't protest when Nick suggested they take his car. He appreciated the short, easy drive to a white clapboard farmhouse on Ridge Road, just past Harper Four Corners. The driveway was crowded with cars. It had been a bad day in Black Falls, and Lauren and A.J. had also invited Dominique Belair, Myrtle Smith, the O'Rourke cousins, Zack Harper and Scott Thorne.

The little Camerons were already in bed. The house was simply decorated with a lot of bright, cheerful colors. Children's finger paintings hung on the refrigerator. Guests were helping themselves to a simple buffet of cold meats and cheeses, salads, rolls and cookies.

The O'Rourkes and Dominique, clearly exhausted, didn't stay long. Zack pulled Nick aside in the dining room and talked fires. The youngest Harper was a heartbreaker, but he wasn't going anywhere. Black Falls was home. They discussed the emerging timeline of Robert Feehan and Derek Cutshaw's actions over the past few days in particular. Zack commented that Feehan could have locked Dominique in the cabin and set the other two on fire and still have made it back to his campsite without burning up himself.

"I don't think he meant to get killed," Zack said. "It wasn't suicide."

"What was he doing at the lake?" Rose asked, sitting next to Zack at the pine table. "His tent was cozy, well hidden. Why not stay up there?"

Zack leaned back in his chair. "He could have been meeting someone, and Dom surprised him."

Rose wasn't satisfied. "Why the ski mask?"

"Maybe he was cold. Maybe he didn't want a casual observer to recognize him. He knew the police wanted to talk to him."

"Doesn't make sense," Rose said. "Dom was a casual observer, and she got locked in a cabin. Why didn't Robert just take off for Miami or someplace? Why stay here in town?"

A.J. and Lauren stood arm in arm in the doorway of the dining room. "He had unfinished business," A.J. said.

Rose frowned. "What, lighting Jo's cabins on fire?"

"Who knows?" A.J. shrugged, but he was anything but casual or relaxed. "We all want this to end here. It'd be easier if Feehan and Cutshaw were having a personal feud over their drug dealing that had nothing to do with Lowell Whittaker and his killers."

"And no one else was involved," Lauren added.

Myrtle came in with a plate heaped with salad and nothing else. She sat next to Nick. "Could either one of them have set my house on fire and taught Lowell how to build a pipe bomb and detonate it with a cell phone?"

Silence descended over the gathering. Nick bit into a slice of cucumber. "From all I've heard, Lowell Whittaker hired very competent people."

"That's right," Myrtle said, "and this guy Feehan just burned himself up in a run-down cabin."

"Maybe he knew he was caught and chose how to go out," Zack said. "Maybe it wasn't a calculated move and he just acted on impulse."

"Let me repeat," Scott Thorne said from the arched doorway to the living room. "The investigation's only just started. We should resist speculating when we don't have all the facts."

Myrtle waved her red nails at him in dismissal. "I like how you say 'we,' Trooper Thorne. You mean the rest of us. I'm just saying if these two bastards were in D.C. in the hours before my house caught fire, it's a cinch. If not, we still don't have all of Lowell's contract killers."

Scott eyed her. "We might never be able to prove who started the fire in your house."

"I refuse to accept that," she countered.

Nick leaned back, appreciating Myrtle's determination. "You don't want to go back to your house until you know what happened," he said.

She raised her lavender eyes. "Unlike some of us, fires scare the hell out of me."

Lauren, looking drawn and tired, changed the subject to plans for winter fest and an uptick in bookings at the lodge for that weekend. Nick sat back, observing the interplay among people who'd known one another all their lives and newcomers to Black Falls. He'd been Sean's friend for ten years but understood him better now. Sean was a part of this. He thought he'd left, but he still had a place here with his family, his hometown. It wouldn't have mattered if he had never bought property in Black Falls.

Nick ate another cucumber, not really hungry.

What if one of these people was a killer?

What if he ended up being the one to point that out?

Everything would change. Better that two ski bums had unraveled over drugs and one had set the other on fire and then killed himself, whether on purpose or by accident.

Better, even, that Robert Feehan was a skilled arsonist who'd worked for Lowell Whittaker and now was dead and out of the picture.

Nick didn't think either was the case, and he doubted Rose or anyone else in the room did, either.

Rose was quiet on the drive back to her house. Nick could guess why. "You don't want me near you tonight," he said as he turned off the engine.

"Are you reading my mind or warning me?" She didn't wait for an answer. "I can't keep worrying that some masked man might come through my window. Derek and Robert were around long before this week, and now neither one is a threat."

"They're not why you want to kick me out."

"I'm not kicking you out. You're staying at the lodge. I live here. If you were my guest, that'd be different. Besides, my couch is lumpy and short."

"I managed fine."

"I haven't vacuumed in days. The dog hair's piling up."

"Keep talking. Maybe you'll convince yourself."

She sat next to him in the dark. The car hadn't had a chance to warm up on the short drive back from her brother's house. "You think this is about you?"

"No," Nick said. "It's about you. You're not sure you want a man in your life right now. You like living alone on your hill with a dog."

"Dogs are easier than men."

But he was serious and so was she. She was distancing herself, and he thought she knew it. She stared at her house, dark but for a light in the entry.

"I have to regroup," she said.

"At least let me check inside first," Nick said.

She nodded. "Sure."

He followed her up the front steps, noting the shape of her hips, remembering her legs wrapped around him as she'd pulled him deeper into her, clawed at him in the throes of her climax.

Not good, he thought. He should do some distancing of his own.

Ranger barely stirred from his bed by the fire when Rose entered the house. He certainly wasn't alarmed at Nick's presence.

She went to the stove, grabbed the poker and stirred the fire. "Nick." Her voice was hoarse, soft. "I'm used to being around intense, masculine men, but you—damn. Now it does feel as if I'm kicking you out."

He slipped an arm around her and turned her to him.

"I'll take the poker," he said with a smile, setting it on the hearth. He kissed her on the forehead. "It's been a long day. Neither of us wants a repeat of last June. That worked out great on some levels but not others."

"I'm as attracted to you as I was then. I can't help myself."

He grinned. "I'll take that as a compliment." He tucked his finger under her chin and kissed her lightly on the lips. "Sleep well." He winked at her. "Lock your doors."

Headlights shone down on the driveway. Rose frowned and went to the window. "It's Jo and Elijah." She glanced back at Nick. "You knew. That's why you're being so cooperative."

Nick was amused. "A.J. might have said something to me."

"Coconspirators," she muttered.

She opened the front door for her brother and his fiancée. Elijah struck Nick as being more like Rose than either A.J. or Sean, but the Camerons were all down-to-earth hard-asses who loved the mountains and their small hometown.

Jo looked every inch the Secret Service agent she was. She and Elijah were grim and circumspect. "We thought we'd stay here tonight," Jo said to Rose. "It still smells like smoke down at the lake."

Elijah patted Ranger and looked at his only sister. "I'll sleep out here on the couch. Jo can take the futon in your office."

Nick smiled to himself. No way were Jo and Elijah sharing a bedroom under Rose's nose. It was a question of sensibility and nothing else—Nick was sure of that much.

Elijah went with him down to the driveway. "You want to give me your gut on what's going on?" he asked, his tone a sharp reminder of his experience as a Special Forces soldier.

He was falling in love with Rose? Nick smiled to himself, imagining where that would get him. He pulled open his car door, the lights of the lodge visible in the distance. "Jasper Vanderhorn was on the right trail. He wasn't crazy, and he wasn't wrong."

"You think whoever he was after hooked up with Lowell Whittaker."

"A paid assassin who is also a firebug," Nick said. "Not a good combination."

Elijah was silent a moment, thoughtful. "All right. See you in the morning." His eyes narrowed on Nick. "Jo and I will take good care of Rose."

"Just don't tell her that," Nick said with a small grin, and climbed into his car.

Twenty-Two

Jo and Elijah were up early. Rose didn't have to tiptoe past her brother. He hadn't lasted on the couch and had moved to the floor. She had no doubt he'd slept fine. He was a Special Forces soldier and could sleep anywhere. Jo ducked in the shower while Rose made coffee. "You two—"

"We're not talking about Jo and me," Elijah said.

Rose smiled, filling the pot with water. "Yes, sir."

"I'm not a 'sir.'" Her brother moved out of her way as she turned from the sink. "Rose, what's with Nick Martini? He's a rich smoke jumper. What the hell's he doing here? With you?"

"We're not talking about Nick and me," she said lightly, throwing his own words back at him.

Elijah scowled at her.

She dumped the water in the coffeemaker. "He and Sean have been friends for ten years. Sean trusts him."

"With you?"

"Just because I messed up with Derek doesn't mean I can't be trusted to make up my own mind about men."

"Who are you trying to convince?"

"No one. I imagine Nick will be heading back to California soon, so you can forget what you're thinking." She opened a cupboard, remembered she was out of coffee, and shut the cupboard again, abandoning her task. "I don't have anything for breakfast. I meant to go grocery shopping yesterday."

"A.J. can feed us at the lodge."

Jo joined them in the kitchen, showered and dressed. From the way she and Elijah looked at each other, Rose had no doubt they were fine as a couple. They'd come together again in November in a mad rush of adrenaline, but they'd known each other all their lives. They'd loved each other, run away with each other, as teenagers.

Unlike her and Nick, Rose thought.

Elijah drove by himself to the lodge. Rose went in her Jeep, with Jo up front and Ranger in back.

"I'm sorry about your cabins," Rose said.

Jo shrugged. "Now I can't keep pretending I can renovate them. The two best ones burned."

"Have you decided what to do with the land yet?"

"Give Elijah some waterfront," she said with a smile. But she was clearly in a serious mood.

"You're here on official business," Rose said, pulling into the lodge. "You're working."

Jo smiled. "I'm here for buckwheat pancakes."

Nick was in the dining room, seated at a table by the fireplace, not looking at all like a guest enjoying a few days at a Vermont mountain resort.

Elijah and A.J. fell in on either side of Rose. "Not that there's anything between Nick and me," she said, "but has it ever occurred to you two that you scare guys out of my life? Now that you're back in town for the most part, Elijah, it's worse. All I need is for Sean to move back to Vermont. The three of you, glowering every time a guy looks at me."

Elijah was mystified. "Are you blaming your messed-up love life on us? Hell, Rose, you scare guys off all by yourself. You don't need us."

Jo groaned. "They don't get it, Rose. They never will. It's a good thing you're a Cameron yourself."

They invited Nick over to their larger table. Lauren arrived, subdued but resilient. A.J. looked agonized as he watched her go about her normal routines. Rose knew he hated his helplessness. Everything he and Lauren had worked for, the life they'd created together, had now been touched by violence and more fear. Luckily, the guests seemed to regard yesterday as a local matter that had no impact on their Vermont getaway. A local matter that was over.

Rose got up and joined her sister-in-law by the windows that looked out on the meadow and the surrounding mountains. Lauren glanced back at the table. "Is it over, Rose, finally?"

"We all want it to be over."

"But you don't believe it is. I don't, either."

Rose was spared having to respond when Myrtle arrived to help sort items that were coming in for the silent auction. Lauren withdrew to set up in the ballroom.

Myrtle helped herself to coffee and a muffin and came

over to the windows. "Bowie's helping Dominique with the morning rush. I think he's just worried about her after yesterday." She sighed at the view, the meadow quiet now, not a soul visible between where she stood and the edge of the woods. "Scott Thorne stopped by the café first thing this morning and tried to tell me it feels like spring today. This is not spring."

"Welcome to northern New England," Rose said with a laugh.

"I have a feeling it won't feel like spring when it *is* spring. I think Scott misses Beth. You can see it in his eyes, but he won't talk about it."

Scott's reticence, Rose thought, was something she could understand. "Some great items are coming in for the auction. The quilt came out even better than I thought it would. It's beautiful."

"Every stitch reminds me of home. I tell myself it's soul work, but it's more like torture." Myrtle glanced back at the dining room. "Where's your dog?"

"Asleep by the fire. He's tired today."

"I had a cat, but I haven't gotten another. It's just as well. A cat would have been in my office when the fire started. I'd have stayed behind looking for her. We'd both have burned up. Grit Taylor saved me. I tell him I'd have saved myself, but I don't know. I don't like being saved. I mean, the guy's sexy as hell—a Navy SEAL, never mind the leg—and there he was, carrying me out of a burning house. All that damsel-in-distress stuff isn't for me."

"You legitimately needed help," Rose said.

"Maybe, but I think my work's made me believe that

most people end up in trouble because they screw up. That's harsh, don't you think?"

"My job is search and rescue. I leave judging to others."

"Doesn't it annoy you when some idiot bungee jumps off a bridge into a ravine, doesn't calculate the pendulum effect of his little bungee cord, slams into a rock wall and you have to go rescue him?"

"That's a technical rescue. It's not what I do."

"A lost hiker, then. Some idiot in the wrong clothes, with no compass, no plan, out alone. I'll bet you've rescued a ton of hikers like that."

"Yes, I have, but you can also do everything right— do your best—and you still can end up in trouble."

"I had no idea Andrei—Andrei Petrov, my Russian friend who was killed by Lowell Whittaker's assassins." Myrtle paused, her lavender eyes distant as she stared out at the meadow. "I had no idea he was a target until he died on the bathroom floor after those idiots poisoned his toothpaste. But I knew I was onto them when they targeted me. I'd been researching similar unexplained deaths. My notes were in my office. That's what burned."

"You did the best you could," Rose said.

"Did I?" Myrtle turned from the window and fixed her gaze on Nick, Jo and Elijah at their table. "What if Grit Taylor had been killed that day? What if some firefighter had had to scrape my remains off the walls and then live with that image?"

"Myrtle, what if the police never know for sure who set your house on fire?"

She smiled knowingly. "Ask Nick Martini the same question. Ask yourself."

She didn't wait for an answer. "I'm off to help Lauren. I hope you have a chance to enjoy the springlike air."

After breakfast, Rose went down to the maintenance shed with Jo and Elijah and collected drills, mallets, taps and measuring sticks and threw them in the back of her Jeep. They wanted to capitalize on the above-freezing temperatures and tap trees for maple sugaring. Rose knew, too, that it was a chance for her brother and future sister-in-law to take another look out by the sugar shack. They would snowshoe across the meadow while she drove the equipment.

As she stuck her key in the ignition, Nick jumped into the passenger seat and grinned at her. "Tapping trees for maple sugaring?"

"You'll love it."

She headed down Ridge Road to the dead-end lane. Jo and Elijah met them and they went in search of appropriate sugar maples to tap. Rose had to admit Nick didn't seem intimidated at all by Elijah, or Jo, for that matter. In fact, the opposite. He was natural, at ease with them and his surroundings. As they plunged through the snow to a trio of old maples, Rose noticed he didn't make an effort to distance himself from her. He also didn't do anything provocative, like put an arm around her or wink at her.

Not that he had a chance.

Jo dived in with questions. "Tell me about Jasper Vanderhorn," she said as she adjusted the strap on one of her snowshoes. "How convinced was he that he was after a serial arsonist? How'd you two meet?"

Nick rubbed the rough bark of an old maple with a gloved hand. "This guy must have been here when Lincoln was president," he said. "I ran into Jasper a few times smoke jumping, but I got to know him better when he looked into a fire at one of our buildings."

"What was he like?" Jo asked.

Rose made her way to the middle of the three maples, which she remembered tapping with her father as a child. Elijah looked up at its bare limbs, and she wondered if he were remembering, too.

Nick continued. "Jasper was quiet, measured, systematic."

Jo pulled a metal tap from her pocket. "Obsessed?"

"He was trying to connect the dots on a number of different fires. He believed a clever killer was at work, not some yahoo."

Elijah eyed Nick, but it was Jo who spoke. "Some of his fellow arson investigators thought he was a little wacky, creating a mythical bogeyman instead of following the evidence. There's a reason half of all arson cases are never solved. It's tricky. He didn't have what he needed to make his case that there even was a firebug at work, never mind who it might be."

"He'd been a firefighter," Nick said calmly. "He'd caught arsonists before. He said this one was different. He was working on a profile."

"Did he share any details with you?" Jo asked.

"Someone very skilled, not impulsive or purely opportunistic—not just about wildland fires and massive conflagrations, or structural fires, or murder. Someone who did it all."

"A hybrid," Elijah said.

"Man, woman?" Jo asked.

"He didn't know. He was convinced he was after a cold-blooded killer who wouldn't stop until he was captured or dead. Jasper wasn't given to hyperbole. That doesn't mean he was right."

Rose realized she had gone still. Elijah had, too, and she was aware of him watching her, gauging her reaction to Nick, to what he was saying.

Jo closed her fingers around the metal tap. "Do you think Vanderhorn was targeted by this guy? Was he the victim of premeditated murder?"

Nick gave her an unflinching look. "Yes."

"This all has to be hard for you." Jo's tone softened slightly. "You were friends, and you knew he believed he was after what amounted to a serial killer. But you couldn't protect him. You couldn't save him."

"We tried. Sean and I both did. We weren't the only ones, either." Nick glanced at Rose, his expression giving nothing away, then added, "It was a bad day."

Jo turned to Rose. "You were in L.A. then. What all were you up to?"

She'd been anticipating the question. "I was training firefighters in advanced dog handling techniques. I'd been there several days."

"Were you staying with Sean?" Jo asked.

"Yes." She carefully avoided meeting Nick's eye, knowing Jo as well as Elijah would notice. "I had Ranger with me. I volunteered to help search for a boy who'd gone missing during a mandatory evacuation because of the wildfire."

Jo leveled her gaze back on Nick. "You and Sean were in big trouble out there, weren't you?"

"It was a close call, but we were prepared to handle the conditions." Nick shrugged. "We had backup."

"Vanderhorn wasn't prepared?"

"He shouldn't have been there."

"Why was he?"

Nick paused before he answered. "I think he was lured."

"It had to be tough," Jo said. "Knowing a friend was trapped. Finding him."

Rose thought of Nick that night as he'd pushed back his emotions and focused just on her, or at least on making love to her. He hadn't wanted to talk, or to think. Looking at him now, she could see he wasn't the same man he'd been then. He was under tight control, and he was thinking, putting the pieces of the past months together. He didn't respond to Jo's comment and moved around to the other side of the old maple.

Elijah positioned his drill at a spot for a tap. "Vanderhorn was off duty?"

"Yes," Nick said, stepping into snow that had drifted against the base of the maple. "He went out to the canyon on his own. He shouldn't have, but he wasn't reckless. The fire should have been out."

Jo tossed Elijah another metal tap before turning back to Nick. "Is it possible Vanderhorn wasn't lured out to that canyon but instead let his obsession get away from him and put you, Sean and others in danger as well as himself?"

Nick met her gaze straight on. "Yes, that's possible."

"What about Sean?" Elijah asked.

"Sean didn't know Jasper that well."

Jo leaned against the tree, watching Elijah drill the tap hole. "Do any of you have a candidate for this killer?" she asked Nick. "Could it be one of your own?"

"Another smoke jumper? No."

"What about Feehan?"

"Jasper didn't go over names with me."

"Feehan look familiar to you? Could you two have run into each other in California?"

Nick shook his head. "I don't recall ever having met him, but I meet a lot of people."

"Trent Stevens?" Jo asked.

"Sean and I have actors and screenwriters come to us for help with research on a fairly regular basis. Stevens could have been one. I don't remember him specifically. He might not have used his real name."

"Grit Taylor and my sister discovered a dead woman in his apartment," Jo said. "Did Vanderhorn say anything that in retrospect might tie his investigation to Portia Martinez?"

"Not to me, no," Nick said without hesitation.

"We want to find him," Jo said, stating the obvious.

"Is there any chance that Derek Cutshaw or Robert Feehan knew him?"

She didn't answer.

Rose helped Elijah finish placing taps in their tree and moved to the next one. Jo showed Nick where to drill on their maple, the placement and number of taps determined by the size of the tree. When they finished, they headed up the hill to the sugar shack. Rose and Nick, who were in boots and not on snowshoes, fell in behind Jo and Elijah.

The air was warm, more like late March than late February, but Rose doubted Nick even noticed. He moved silently next to her, preoccupied, she thought, with his conversation with Jo. When they came to the sugar shack, Jo and Elijah took off their snowshoes and went inside to check out the new evaporating pan.

Brett Griffin walked up from the stream below the small clearing. "I was taking pictures of this place. Classic. I want one of a galvanized bucket hanging from a maple tree." He was on snowshoes, without poles, his camera around his neck. "The light's perfect right now—moody but serene."

Rose stood next to Nick by the fireplace. "Are you spending all your time taking pictures these days?" she asked.

"As much as I can, but I still teach skiing." Brett seemed slightly out of breath as he raised his camera. "I've had the police all over me now that Robert's dead, too. I don't blame them, but it's good to be out in the woods, away from all that."

"It's hard to think of Robert as an accomplished arsonist," Rose said.

Brett snapped a picture of the sugar shack. "How accomplished was he considering the way he died? Maybe there is no arsonist and Robert made all this happen to cover up his involvement in drugs, or for his own amusement. Maybe he mixed truth and fiction to suit his purposes and instigated fights, took advantage of the situation."

Rose hadn't heard Brett speak so articulately about what had happened, but he seemed almost embarrassed and quickly focused his camera on the fireplace and took another picture.

Nick scooped up a handful of wet snow and patted it into a small snowball. "Do you think you'll stay in Black Falls?" he asked.

"Not past spring," Brett said, calmer. "Once the snow melts and the daffodils pop up, I'm on to Colorado to teach wilderness skills and work on another photography project there."

"A fresh start," Rose said.

He gave her a feeble smile. "Yeah, I guess. I wish I'd done more to figure out what was going on with Derek and Robert. That's going to be hard to put behind me. I can't tell if the police think Robert was actually one of Lowell Whittaker's paid killers."

She couldn't, either. "If he was, did Lowell choose Black Falls because of Robert—or vice versa?"

"The police aren't going into that kind of detail with me. It's unnerving to think Robert was a paid killer." He averted his eyes. "At least he and Derek can't hurt anyone else. Then again, they can't provide answers, either."

"It's been a difficult few days," Rose said quietly.

"Yes, it has." Brett suddenly seemed overwhelmed with emotion. "I'll leave you all to your get-together."

"Good luck with the photos. I hope you got some great ones."

"Yeah, thanks."

He moved well on his snowshoes, heading back through the woods to the path out to the lane and Ridge Road. When he was out of sight, Rose smiled at Nick. "Going to start a snowball fight?"

He tossed his snowball into the fireplace and grinned back at her. "I'd be outnumbered."

"It is a gorgeous day, though, isn't it?"

"Any nicer and you'll be having a mud fest instead of a winter fest."

She laughed, but she could see Nick was tense. Jo had to have stirred up difficult memories. "Mud season hasn't even started."

"Ah. Mud season."

"You'll be long gone back to Beverly Hills by then."

His eyes settled on her, but he said, "Tell me more about maple sugaring."

Twenty-Three

─⟨୧⟩⟨୧⟩─

San Diego, California

Grit pulled in front of a cream-colored stucco house in an attractive, upscale San Diego neighborhood. Unless he'd screwed up the directions, he was at the house where Tony and Regina Martini, Nick Martini's folks, lived, with a partial view of San Diego Bay. A sticker on a nice car parked in front of a two-car garage indicated they were members of the San Diego Zoo.

He followed a curving brick walk to the arched front door. He'd left Beverly Hills before light, borrowing one of Sean's cars and managing not to have Beth with him. He got to Coronado in time for a long, highly classified meeting that wasn't as boring as he'd feared. Admiral Jenkins was proving to be an interesting naval officer with far-reaching tentacles, and he obviously wanted Grit back fighting the enemy in whatever capacity he could.

After the meeting, Grit had grabbed a sandwich

on the fly and punched the Martinis' address into Sean's GPS.

Captain Martini opened the door and gave Grit, who was in his service uniform, thirty seconds to explain what he wanted, then led him back to a softly lit tiled sunroom overlooking a backyard of carefully maintained citrus and avocado trees.

"Have a seat," Captain Martini said, remaining on his feet. He was wearing neatly pressed, expensive golf clothes. "What do you want to know about Nick?"

Grit didn't sit down. "I'm friends with Elijah Cameron, Sean's brother. I was in town on navy business and figured I'd stop by. You know Nick's in Vermont, right?"

"Skip the small talk, Petty Officer Taylor. Get to the point."

"Yes, sir. Did Nick always want to be a smoke jumper, or did he want to be a multimillionaire businessman—"

"He's my son. Whatever he decided to do was okay with me."

"Enlist? You didn't want him to be an officer?"

The captain had no visible reaction to Grit's intrusive questions. "Petty Officer Taylor, why are you here?"

Grit didn't have a clear answer. Atmosphere? Background? Instinct? He wasn't sure about Sean's best friend and business partner?

He shrugged. "Admiral Jenkins sends his best."

The older man's eyes narrowed. "You know him?"

"I work for him now." As Grit had expected, that went over well. "Nick and Sean met and became friends as smoke jumpers. Was Nick still in the navy then?"

"Early on. We're proud of all his accomplishments."

"Was he into fires on the sub?"

"He was a weapons specialist."

"He set fires as a kid? I did. I just wanted to see what would happen if I lit a trail of gunpowder. Nothing good, I can tell you. It worked better in the old Westerns."

"I'm sure you want to get back to L.A. before the traffic gets even worse."

That was it. Captain Martini pointed out his favorite avocado tree and walked Grit back outside. Grit wasn't surprised he hadn't gotten much out of the retired senior officer and absorbed as much of his surroundings as possible. Even if Nick had never lived in this house, it would reflect his family and their feelings about their world, him—which seemed pretty good from what Grit could see. He wondered if Nick had bought the house for his folks and decided that would be an impolite question.

"Thank you for your time, sir," he said.

"Good luck with your rehab."

The captain went back inside. As Grit opened his car door, a woman in a little red sports car pulled in next to Grit's borrowed car. She was in civilian attire, and she had dark hair and eyes and looked a lot like the man he'd just left. "I think I just saw your kindergarten picture. Nick's sister, right? Diana Martini? I'm Ryan Taylor. Grit. I'm friends with the Camerons."

"I know all about you, Petty Officer Taylor. I'm Lieutenant Martini."

"No kidding? They let navy officers drive red cars?"

She almost cracked a smile. "Nick's not here, but I assume you know that. No games, okay?"

"Has anyone else been by looking for him?"

"When?"

He appreciated her need for precision. "In the past year or so."

"Think I'm going to remember?"

"Yes, Lieutenant, I do. You remember."

"Why would I tell you anything about my brother?"

She had a point there. "Are you friends with Sean Cameron?"

"Of course. My entire family knows Sean. That's how I found out about you, Petty Officer."

Grit let her suspicion, if not outright animosity, roll over him. "Ever date Sean?"

Her eyes were half-closed now. "That wouldn't be a good idea."

"Anymore than for Nick to get involved with Sean's sister?"

"I have to run."

Ta-da. "You know Rose Cameron."

"I only have a few minutes to say hi to my folks—"

"Are you stationed in San Diego?"

"Yes, as a matter of fact."

"Did Rose stop by to check on Nick while she was out here last June? Did you approve of them seeing each other?"

"I'm not discussing my brother with you."

"What about Jasper Vanderhorn?"

She stopped abruptly, her expression under tight control. "You should go."

"Lieutenant, if you don't tell me, I'll tell Sean Cameron. He'll tell the task force that's looking into multiple

explosions, fires and murders. Someone will come out
to your nice, tidy office on the base—"

"I'm on a ship."

"Even better."

She sighed. "I met Mr. Vanderhorn once. Here. My
folks weren't home."

"Did he suspect Nick was his firebug?"

"We didn't discuss Nick or arson, but of course not.
What a ridiculous thing to say, or even to ask. Why are you
asking? You're a SEAL. You're not law enforcement."

Grit pretended he hadn't just been asked a question by
a superior. "When did Vanderhorn come down here?"

"About a week before he died."

So, June of last year. Same time Nick was lusting after
Rose Cameron. "Do you know Trent Stevens?"

"Who?"

"Portia Martinez?"

"No. Go, okay? Say hi to Sean for me. He's very
charming. I must remember that not all his friends
are."

Grit laughed. Diana Martini darted inside.

Interesting. When it came to Cameron & Martini,
the sisters—Diana and Rose—were mustn't-touch and,
Jasper Vanderhorn had looked into Nick Martini's background, despite their friendship.

Grit called Elijah on the way back to Beverly Hills.
"I'll be quick. I think it's illegal to talk on a cell phone in
California while driving. Did Sean and Nick sign a contract or take a blood oath not to sleep with each other's
sisters?"

"Why?"

"You notice anything going on between Nick and Rose?"

Elijah sighed. "They're fighting it."

"Ask Jo if the task force has looked into Nick's travels and considered if he could be an arsonist, one of Lowell's killers for hire."

"Grit."

"All this California sun is getting to me. You're Special Forces. You wouldn't understand the appeal of Coronado."

"Are you nostalgic, Grit?" Elijah didn't wait for an answer. "If my sister is in danger from Nick Martini—if there's even a shred of a possibility—I want to know."

"Heroes with scars worry me."

"That describes you and me, too, Grit."

"I worry me. You don't worry me now that you've got Jo."

"We're both solid. Nick is, too. None of us has targeted innocent people."

"Derek Cutshaw and Rob Feehan weren't innocent."

Good point, Grit thought, and disconnected.

He was back in Sean's driveway when Charlie Neal called with a similar theory about Jasper Vanderhorn suspecting Nick Martini, but Charlie didn't really believe it, either. "We're running down blind alleys and into brick walls," the vice president's son said.

Grit didn't even bother correcting Charlie's use of *we*. Let the kid be a part of something.

"How are your sisters?" Grit asked.

"We're all going to Black Falls for the winter fest weekend at the lodge. Marissa in particular can't wait to be back there. She's signing up for cross-country ski lessons and a sleigh ride. I hope the sap will be running so I can make maple syrup. Did you know it takes about forty gallons of sap to make one gallon of syrup?"

"That's a lot of sap."

"Real maple syrup and tupelo honey have a lot in common." Charlie hesitated. "Marissa won't tell me anything. I think the Secret Service got to her. You're not reporting back to them every time I call, are you?"

"That's not my job."

"Because my calls are innocent. Totally. I'm not making any progress. I can tell Marissa's upset. I think she still has feelings for Stevens. Did you notice? Could you tell?"

"I met her for about seventeen seconds three months ago."

"Are you getting transferred to San Diego?"

Grit was almost used to the pinball machine that was Charlie Neal's mind. "No."

"But you like it there."

"What difference does that make? Anything else you want to tell me?"

"I wish I could do more to help."

"You'll have your chance to do your own thing before you know it. Right now think about that maple sap."

Grit hung up and went inside. The Vermonters were pacing.

Beth shoved her hands through her hair. "I can't stand this anymore. I'm booking my flight back to Vermont. I don't care if it's twenty degrees and a hundred-fifty miles to the nearest Saks."

"Forty-two degrees today," Hannah said. "I checked."

"Spring weather," Beth said.

Which right there was why he'd never fit in there, Grit thought. He could be subtle if he had to be, but that wasn't now. "Are you worried about Rose being with Nick?"

Both women glanced at Sean. It was his question to answer. "Nick's a lot of things," Sean said, "but he's not an arsonist."

"Did Jasper Vanderhorn suspect Nick was his serial arsonist?"

"Jasper suspected his own mother by the end."

Sean didn't elaborate and walked out to the patio. Grit glanced at the two women, then followed Sean outside to see what more he could get out of him. It wouldn't be easy. The man was a Cameron.

Twenty-Four

Black Falls, Vermont

Jo Harper and two of the Cameron brothers came to dinner at Rose's house. Nick didn't know when or if she'd invited them. He watched her toss a handful of chopped fresh parsley into a soup pot, the steam rising into her face. She'd spent the afternoon holed up in her back office, leaving him by the woodstove with his laptop. Ranger would peer up at him occasionally as if he figured he had to start getting used to having him around.

Now Elijah and A.J. had the same look.

Suspicious Cameron eyes.

Rose had kicked Nick and her brothers out of her work area in the kitchen. They all had beers and stood by a small peninsula that separated the kitchen and living room. She was animated, focused, professional and determined, easily holding her own with her brothers.

Nick had sorted out the major players in her life in Black Falls. Jo pulled off her coat and draped it on a chair by the woodstove. "I've talked to some people," she said vaguely, standing next to Elijah. "Robert Feehan flew from Boston to Los Angeles last Thursday and returned on Tuesday, the day before Nick arrived in Black Falls and two days before Derek Cutshaw was killed."

Even with the steam from her bubbling soup, Rose's cheeks lost their color. "Then Robert could have killed Portia Martinez," she said.

Jo's turquoise eyes narrowed on her fiancé's only sister. "Placing Feehan in Los Angeles is an important piece of circumstantial evidence, but it's not enough." She walked over to the sink just down from Rose at the stove. "Anything I can do to help?"

Rose grinned at her. "Where were you an hour ago?" But she pointed to the peninsula and a tray of drinks and snacks. "Grab a beer or something and relax. I'm just waiting for the bread to warm up."

A.J. kept his gaze focused on his sister. He'd come alone. Lauren was still at the lodge with their children. "If Cutshaw found out Feehan was in California and started asking questions, that could explain why he was killed."

"They both knew Sean lives out there," Elijah said.

Rose snatched up a long-handled spoon and dipped it into her soup pot. "If Robert was a serial arsonist—a serial killer—then he could have been drawn to Sean because of his smoke jumping. So why not go after him? He foiled Lowell's attempt to frame Bowie and avoid arrest."

She yanked her spoon out of the soup and set it on the counter. "Why go after this woman mopping floors for Marissa Neal's ex-boyfriend?"

Jo leaned back against the peninsula, her arms crossed on her chest. "Let's focus on Robert and Derek right now. If Derek suspected Robert was a killer and the two of them were also into pushing pills, maybe he went out to the Whittaker place to talk to you and figure out what to do."

"Why would he? I hadn't seen him in so long. We didn't part on good terms."

"But you're a Cameron," Jo said.

Elijah and A.J. both grunted. Elijah said, "What's that got to do with anything?"

Jo glanced back at him. "You all have been in the thick of this mess from the start. If Robert Feehan's our guy, he was out of work as a paid arsonist because of you."

"Jo, we had nothing to do with the Neals until you came back home," A.J. said quietly.

"Fair point, A.J." Jo lowered her arms, looking tired but no less focused. "We've got a lot to untangle."

"All right," Rose said. "Let's say Derek was about to go to the police with what he knew about Robert, and Robert found out and followed him to the Whittaker place and killed him—set up the lamp, rigged it so that it would explode when Derek lit it. He could have had a backup plan in case Derek didn't do as predicted. He could have hid in the woods—" She stopped herself and switched off the heat under the soup. "It doesn't explain Nick."

Nick waited two beats before he responded. "I came out here because the timing was right for me. I'd been wondering for some time if the serial arsonist Jasper was dogging was involved with Lowell Whittaker's network. The police knew about my concern." He felt the scrutiny of the three Camerons and the Secret Service agent, but his gaze was focused entirely on Rose. "My trip wasn't a secret."

"So Feehan could have found out about it." Jo picked a cube of cheese off a plate and popped it into her mouth. "I'm hungry. Let's save all this speculating for dessert, at least."

Ranger needed to go out, and Nick seized the moment and escorted the golden retriever out the back door. Good dog that he was, Ranger dutifully headed halfway down the driveway and into the adjoining woods to do his business.

Nick hadn't put on his jacket. He could feel the temperature dropping with nightfall, but the air wasn't frigid. He dialed Sean in California. "This missing actor is connected to me. I don't know how, but he is."

"Yeah," Sean said. "Maybe to both of us."

"And Jasper."

"The police are still searching for Stevens. They must be wondering if whoever killed Portia Martinez got to him and he's dead, too. When are you coming back?"

"Soon," Nick said, although he hadn't thought about the question. What the hell was he doing? Rose had a life here. She didn't need him complicating it. "The investigation here is in capable hands. I've told law enforcement everything I know. They're going over Jasper's case files. There's nothing more I can contribute."

"Your voice is off. What's going on?"

Ranger bounded out of the dark woods, a tennis ball in his mouth. Nick smiled. "Snow and a wet dog."

"You're at Rose's, then."

"Jo and your brothers are here for dinner."

"Lucky you," Sean said.

Nick pulled the slobbery tennis ball out of the golden retriever's mouth and flung it down the driveway. Ranger leaped after it. Nick said, "I want to know why all this happened the minute I got here."

"Everyone does. That kind of coincidence—no one's buying it." Sean paused. "Rose doesn't tell anyone much about her private life. Nick, I don't get involved in your personal life, but Rose has had a tough year."

"You all have, Sean."

"She's a professional when it comes to her search-and-rescue work, but fatigue can set in with anyone. She had a lot come at her at once. We've all been preoccupied and didn't pay attention to how much she withdrew." Sean's voice was laced with regret. "She was already vulnerable before Pop died."

"She's got you all focused on her now." Nick watched Ranger return with the ball, drop it in front of him. "Sean, I'm not going to do anything to hurt Rose or your family."

"Hell, I hope not."

Nick quickly shifted the subject. "I've been thinking about the Hollywood types who came to see us to find out about smoke jumping. I've made a list of every conversation, every person who contacted me that I can think of."

"I've done the same. Grit Taylor's all over this."

"If Trent Stevens isn't dead, maybe he's playing smoke jumper."

Nick disconnected and skirted a glistening section of the driveway that was slick with black ice from snow and ice that had melted and then refrozen.

Go ahead, he thought. Fall. Get your butt all bruised and broken.

At least a trip to the E.R. would keep him from making love to Rose Cameron tonight.

Because that was what he wanted to do.

He'd spent the afternoon working—answering emails, sending instructions to his assistant, brainstorming new projects—and staring at the woodstove, trying to figure out how Derek Cutshaw and Robert Feehan had ended up dead and what his decision to come to Vermont had to do with their deaths.

All the while he'd fought the same burning desire for Rose that he'd felt last June and hadn't resisted. He might be a rogue and a snake for having done it, but he couldn't imagine not having made love to Rose then—or not having kissed her last night.

She knew her own mind. All three of her brothers had to have that through their rock heads by now.

But she'd been reeling for months, and Derek Cutshaw had done a number on her sense of confidence with men. His death had put her right back in his emotional grip.

Nick's BlackBerry notified him he had a text message. It was from his sister: SEAL stopped to see us.

Grit Taylor.

So Elijah Cameron's SEAL friend had looked into him and his family. Nick wasn't offended. Jasper Vanderhorn had done the same thing last year shortly before the fire that killed him.

Nick heard someone on the back steps. In a moment, Elijah joined him. He had on a thick sweater, no coat, hat or gloves. "We're not as trusting and as open as we were a year ago," the Special Forces soldier said.

"I get that."

Elijah didn't respond at once. There were stars out now, sparkling in breaks in the milky clouds. Finally he said, "When we were kids, we'd hike up here. Rose was upset when this house was built, but it works with the land. She bought it, made it her own. She travels a lot, but she always comes home. That's one thing we all have in common."

"You Camerons have more in common than you think some days, I imagine."

"Maybe so." Elijah picked up the tennis ball and tossed it into the snow, but Ranger wasn't as quick leaping after it. "Why are you so determined to find this arsonist?"

"Because he killed a friend of mine, and I don't like arsonists. I've dealt with them often enough. So has Sean."

"You don't think it was Feehan," Elijah said.

Nick shrugged. "We need to know more."

"Is it possible Vanderhorn was wrong and there is no serial arsonist?"

"Possible. Not likely. He went by his gut as well as evidence."

"So we might never have clear-cut answers." Elijah almost smiled. "Jo won't like that. She likes clear-cut answers."

"If Feehan didn't set those fires, then someone else did," Nick said, stating the obvious. "Feehan and Cutshaw could just have been targets of convenience."

"Eliminate a threat and provide a fall guy at the same time."

Nick had no trouble visualizing Elijah Cameron on a combat mission.

Ranger returned and headed up the dark back steps, the tennis ball still in his mouth. Nick grinned. "Guess he's done," he said, and he and Elijah followed the dog back inside Rose's little Vermont mountain house.

Rose walked Jo and her two brothers out after dinner. They were off to the lodge for drinks and more talk. Jo and Elijah would spend the night there. They hadn't bothered to argue with her about staying another night at her house.

They knew Nick would be there, she thought, and they trusted him.

She headed back inside and found him filling the woodbox. "Jasper didn't suspect you," she said without preamble. "I thought you knew."

Nick set the last of his armload of logs into the box that her father had helped her make one snowy afternoon.

Rose grabbed the afghan off the couch and folded it. "If he did suspect you, it wasn't for long, and it was because he suspected everyone. He sought me out because he'd seen the sparks between us."

"When?"

"The day before the fire. I'd stopped by Sean's office. You and Jasper were there, remember?"

Nick nodded, his eyes almost black in the dimly lit room. "Jasper had a follow-up question about the fire in our building in January."

"You took that as a sign that you were on his list of suspects."

"It crossed my mind." He stepped away from the woodbox and angled a look at her. "Sparks, though? I thought the sparks didn't start until I got you into my condo."

Heat surged to her face. "Well. I don't know. He was an arson investigator." She set the folded afghan back on the couch. "Maybe he was tuned in to those things."

She remembered that day, before Jasper's death. She'd been thinking about how good-looking Nick was in his sleek, expensive suit. He was hard-edged and self-aware, every inch a sexy rogue of a man. She'd dismissed her reaction as all mixed up because of Derek, her father's death, Elijah's near death, her nonstop work.

And because she'd thought it useless to lust after a man she could never have.

"You've been afraid Jasper died wondering if you were the one who killed him," she said. "He didn't. He knew you were his friend."

"I couldn't save him—from himself or from the fire."

"Sometimes that's how it works out."

He put a log on the fire, stirred the hot coals, adjusted the dampers. He didn't have a fireplace or a woodstove in his contemporary high-rise condo in Beverly Hills. But he had views, she thought, as incredible as hers, if different.

Finally he turned and eased his arms around her. "How do you know Jasper saw the sparks between us?"

"He said so."

"Those exact words?"

"Not exactly."

"Rose, what did Jasper say?"

She smiled. "He pulled me aside and said, 'Nick's not the playboy he pretends to be. You're not the mountain woman you pretend to be. The two of you together...'" She felt tears form in her eyes but sniffled them back. "He stopped there, and winked. Then he left. That was the last time I saw him. I'll never forget that knowing wink."

"Rose..."

She placed her hands on his sides, splayed her fingers so that she could feel more of his taut muscles. His body was warm and firm under her touch. "You weren't a mistake, Nick." She let her hands drift down to his hips and tried to ignore the instant rush of heat that spread through her. "Not then, and not now."

"We can go back to the lodge now," he said, his voice hoarse as he drew her tight against him, "and have whiskey with your brothers. Or we can—"

"Or we can not go back to the lodge," she said, smiling.

His mouth found hers, or hers found his—she didn't care. She just shut her eyes and gave herself up to the heat that burned deep into her. She felt as if she would melt.

Nick lifted her up onto his hips as if she weighed nothing. He was fully aroused, every inch of him hard and taut. She opened her eyes again. Her breath caught in her throat when she saw his dark eyes riveted on her, as if she were the only person in the universe.

"Nothing's changed." He slipped his fingers into her waistband. "I want you as much as I did in June. Even more." Slowly, he moved his hands over the bare skin of her hips. "I know what's in store for me."

He kissed her throat as he skimmed her jeans down over her hips. His hands were strong, rough against her smooth skin. He cupped her bottom, curving his fingertips lower. She felt her legs open for him and heard herself moan softly.

He lowered her onto the floor, drawing her jeans down to her knees, then off altogether. For all she knew he cast them into the fire. He tugged her socks off next, then coursed his hands up the inside of her legs, working his way higher. Naked from the waist down, she ached for his touch.

But he stopped, and in the stillness, she heard herself breathing rapidly. Her heart was racing. She shut her eyes and gave herself up to the sensations crackling over her, through her.

"Nick." Her voice sounded strangled. "What are you doing? If you're having second thoughts—"

"No second thoughts."

She felt a hot, moist touch between her legs and her eyes flew open. Her only contact with him was his tongue. He flicked and teased, probed and lapped. Without warning, he grabbed her by the hips, his grip strong, firm, and lifted her, driving his tongue deep, thrusting into her.

She shut her eyes, giving herself up to the fire raging through her.

She raked her fingers through his hair and cried out his name.

He drew back, leaving her gasping, aching.

She had no idea what was next. In another moment, she'd be a molten puddle on the floor. She heard a belt buckle, a snap. Her mind had only barely registered what was happening when he returned to her, settling between her parted thighs, his erection free, probing in the wet heat where his tongue had just teased and tormented her.

"I've thought about this moment for months. I knew I shouldn't..."

"You were wrong."

"Rose..."

He shifted, and in one swift motion, he was inside her, no hesitancy, no tentativeness. Her body responded, as if it'd been waiting, begging, for months for Nick Martini to be back inside her. She caught him by the hips and pulled him deep into her, matched his pounding rhythm.

He raised up off her, paused and searched her face in the glow of the fire. When he moved inside her, she was lost, clawing at him as the climax overtook her.

Spent, aware suddenly of the rug, the woodstove, poor Ranger dead asleep in his bed, Rose rolled onto her side, facing Nick as she smiled a little raggedly. She brushed her knuckles over his hard jawline, feeling a faint stubble of beard. "It's still relatively early," she said.

He kissed her fingertips. "So it is."

They showered together and made love again in her bed, with the curtains open to the mountains and the cold, starlit winter night.

Twenty-Five

Rose appreciated the bright, cold morning as she drove up Ridge Road and pulled over at the trail leading to the falls. She, Nick, Jo and Elijah had loaded galvanized buckets and more taps and drills into the back of her Jeep. They were all meeting on the dead-end lane in a few minutes. Temperatures had fallen precipitously overnight but would climb above freezing again by midday. Why not take advantage of the continued warm spell and tap more trees?

She had Ranger up front with her and let him out the passenger door. They would wait for Nick and hike with him up the near-vertical hill below the falls to mark a half-dozen big maples for gravity tubing. Hanging buckets and emptying them every day on foot would be too difficult. The sap would run through the tubing into large plastic containers placed discreetly at the bottom of the hill. It was a practical, efficient system, if not as picturesque or quintessentially Vermont as sap buckets.

She noticed footprints and wondered if Elijah or Jo had gone ahead of her. She heard a moan and slowed down. Ranger's head jerked up. He'd picked up a scent. Rose motioned for him to track anyone in the immediate vicinity, and he charged ahead of her, bounding up the steep hill. She followed him. She was in boots, not snowshoes, and the snow was deep, but she was still in sight of the road.

Ranger took her past a misshapen pine tree and stopped suddenly, barking eagerly.

Brett Griffin was sitting in the snow by a series of boulders. "Whoa, there." He laughed nervously at Ranger. "Easy, boy."

Rose came around a boulder. "Ranger, heel," she said, and he immediately came to her side.

"Man," Brett said. "I took a hell of a spill. There must be a spring under the snow. I hit ice and went flying."

Rose knelt down in front of him. "Are you hurt?"

"Nah. I got the wind knocked out of me. I landed on my side against this boulder. I'm lucky I didn't hit my head. I'll have a nasty bruise." He sank back against the boulder, his hat crooked on top of his head, and grinned at Ranger. "I've never owned a dog, but if I did, I'd have you help train him. He's a beauty, isn't he?"

"He is," Rose said. "What are you doing up here?"

"Taking pictures and checking the conditions. I thought I'd get some shots when you all run tubing up here. That's what you're doing, right? I was at the lodge earlier and thought that's what I heard."

"My brothers, Jo Harper and Nick Martini are on the

way. We want to have everything ready for winter fest weekend."

"The place I'm house-sitting is just up the road. I'm out in the woods all the time. I keep thinking..." Brett sat up straight, wincing in pain. "Maybe I will stick around after the daffodils start popping up."

Rose laughed. "Maybe you did hit your head."

He looked more sheepish and self-conscious than amused. She felt bad about her joke, but he rallied. "It's not anything I'll rush into. I know I'm still reacting to the fires. I saw Scott Thorne a little while ago."

"Did he want to talk to you?"

"No, no. I've cooperated fully with the police. I meant I saw him drive by. I was already up here on the hill." Brett's hands shook visibly. "I saw a deer. It startled me. I think that's why I missed noticing the ice. Usually I'm pretty careful."

Rose stood up. "Which direction was Scott headed?"

"Up this way."

Rose hadn't seen him. He hadn't stopped at the lodge as far as she knew. She frowned down at Brett, noticed that his pants were already wet with melting snow. "You don't want to sit in the cold snow for too long."

"Yeah, I know."

"You might be hurt worse than you think. Adrenaline can fool you."

"I'm okay, really. Sorry for the drama." He reached for his camera in the snow. "My pants are soaked. I know better, but I was so excited by the prospect of warm weather that I put on a pair of corduroys. Sort of mistake a rookie would make, huh? Elijah would have a fit. You aren't as tough on people."

"I don't know about that. We both focus on what we have to do."

Brett blew snow off his camera. "I don't think I could do what you do, Rose. I have basic first aid training, but I've never dealt with anything more serious than a ski student falling face-first in the snow."

"But you could," Rose said, "and you would if you had to."

"Maybe. You Camerons, though. Whenever I think about relocating here permanently, I don't know. I don't think I'd ever measure up, never mind fit in."

"Make a place for yourself and don't worry about the rest."

Ranger moved to the edge of the rocks and barked. Brett looked slightly panicked. "Careful. There's a cliff there. It's hard to see. The Neals will want to avoid this section when they're here for winter fest."

Rose knew the spot well. She felt a breeze blowing through the trees, down the mountain. "The Neals?"

"Aren't they coming to winter fest?"

"They are, but I don't know that they have plans to hike up to the falls again."

"Oh. I thought you would know."

"Do you know their plans, Brett?"

"I'm hoping to be their guide. Actually, I was up here when they hiked up to the falls a couple of weeks ago. Marissa Neal in particular loved it. It's so quiet this time of year."

"It is," Rose said, edging closer to Ranger.

Brett was shivering. Every other time she'd run into him, he'd been dressed for the conditions. It was no secret she'd been headed in this direction. Had he rushed to get here ahead of her?

"Jo Harper will be here for winter fest?" he asked.

"I would think so."

"Marissa Neal must be forever in Jo's debt for saving her from that fire when she was camping last fall. You heard about that, right?"

Rose nodded. "It wasn't widely reported, though. You must be tuned in to the Neals. Did Robert or Derek mention them?"

"Yeah, probably. I don't remember. There's been a lot of talk about them because of Jo and their trip up here." Brett dug a glove out of the snow and gave a self-deprecating laugh. "I didn't bring dry gloves. Another rookie mistake. And here I'm supposed to be a wilderness expert."

Wilderness expert? "I thought you were a ski instructor and photographer."

"I am." His eyes narrowed. "What's on your mind, Rose? You look nervous. That's not like you. I don't scare you, do I?"

She'd maneuvered herself to where he'd fallen. There was no spring under the snow. No ice. She gave Ranger a subtle hand signal, and he immediately jumped up. "Ranger's onto something," she said. It wasn't true but she wanted to get back down to the road. "I'll see what he's up to. Catch your breath."

"Aren't you going to help me?"

She moved to the edge of the cliff. "If you need help, give a shout. I'm right here."

He stared at her. She saw he didn't believe her. He and Robert were of a similar build. Had it been Brett in the ski mask, Brett who'd shoved Dominique into the cabin and left her to die? Brett who'd killed Robert—and Derek?

And Jasper Vanderhorn. Was Brett Griffin the clever, elusive arsonist the California investigator had been hunting?

"Rose."

She heard Brett's undertone of intimidation and anger.

"It's okay. I understand," he said, getting to his feet, wobbling slightly. "You're afraid given all that's happened."

She had to act. She had no choice. She could stand there and be killed or take her chances and jump. Get away from him. Ranger was already charging down through the trees toward the road. Nick would be there by now. Elijah and Jo would be right behind him.

Rose pretended to slip and threw her arms up as if trying to regain her balance. She stepped off the edge of the cliff, doing her best to control her half dive, half roll in the deep snow.

She came to a hard, sharp stop against a tree.

Under ordinary conditions, she would focus on staying warm and wait for help, not take on the elements, but Brett Griffin would come find her.

Alive, he could pretend she'd been hysterical and he was innocent.

Dead, she wasn't a problem at all.

Twenty-Six

North of Los Angeles, Southern California

Grit entered a large, square room at a remote training site for elite smoke jumpers. Sean Cameron was with him. They approached a good-looking, fair-haired man sitting alone at a cafeteria-style table.

"Trent Stevens?" Grit asked.

The man turned sharply. He looked scruffier than in the picture. "No. Don't call me that. Who the hell are you?"

"My name's Ryan Taylor."

Two minutes ago, as Grit and Sean had arrived at the training area, Charlie Neal had called with a message that his sister Marissa had finally admitted she'd sneaked off to California last fall to see her ex-boyfriend.

Trent wasn't happy about having company. "Damn. You've pulled me out of the zone. I'm immersing myself in this world."

Sean gritted his teeth visibly. This was his world. He knew the ground, the people, the stakes of the work done here. "You went to see Nick Martini last fall, didn't you? To ask him how you could go about doing research for a screenplay you're writing."

"Nick? Yeah, sure. I looked him up." As if they were best friends. "How is he?"

"Nick's fine," Sean said, barely containing his irritation.

Grit pointed to Sean and said to Trent, "This here is Sean Cameron."

"Nick's partner? No kidding. Wow." Trent laughed in amazement. "Incredible. Sorry I was abrupt. I get into what I'm doing. What can I do for you?"

"Even your family doesn't know where you are," Grit said.

Trent shrugged. "No one does. That's the whole idea. It's the only way for this to really work."

"The police don't know where you are, either," Sean said. "They've been looking for you. Don't you read the papers, listen to the news?"

"Some but—the police?" Trent frowned, sitting up straight. "What do they want with me?"

"I found your friend Portia dead the other day," Grit said.

"Portia? Dead?" Color drained from the actor's face. He seemed genuinely shocked. "What happened?"

Grit didn't spare him. "She was electrocuted while she was mopping floors at your apartment."

Trent turned ashen, clearly horrified. "She was fine last time I saw her."

"When was that?" Sean asked.

"Two weeks ago. I got into this smoke jumping thing. I've been up and down California, learning the ground, immersing myself in this life. I didn't want anyone to know the difference between a real smoke jumper and me. Portia was staying at my place. I swear, she was fine when I saw her."

Grit believed him. "Have you been in touch with her since you started playing smoke jumper?"

Trent didn't like that. "Playing? That's insulting. This is research. Actually, it's more than research."

Sean looked ready to throttle the guy. Grit said, "Since you started more-than-researching smoke jumping, then."

"No. I haven't been in touch with Portia at all. That would have taken me out of the zone." Trent shuddered. "I can't believe she's dead. Electrocuted? That's nuts."

"The Secret Service wants to talk to you, too," Sean said.

"Why? Because of Marissa Neal? I haven't seen her in months."

Grit thought Trent was on the verge of panic. "Did you talk to her about this smoke jumping thing when she slipped off to see you in October?"

"You know about that? No. I got her the hell out of my life. Think I wanted to get in trouble with the Secret Service?"

"Who else knew about her visit?"

"Portia. That's it. I swore her to secrecy."

"What about Jasper Vanderhorn?"

"The arson investigator? People talk about him with

reverence here, and frustration, because of how he died."
Trent rallied, stretching out his legs. "I'm tuned into everything I hear, see, smell, do. It's all fodder for the script I'm writing."

"Fodder," Sean said, toneless.

Trent was oblivious. "Yeah. I got the idea because of Marissa, actually. When I saw her, she was still jumpy about the fire at the camp in the Shenandoahs. You know about that, right? She was grateful to Jo Harper for saving her, but then Jo had to deal with the prank Charlie played on her. Marissa felt guilty because of what her brother did. Little jackass that he is."

Grit redirected Trent before he could go too far off course. "So Marissa Neal got you interested in fires?"

"Yeah, sort of. I broke up with her before the election. Once I got a taste of the Secret Service, I was out of there. I couldn't function. I know I broke Marissa's heart, but it's what had to be. I couldn't do it. I couldn't pretend I could, not with Secret Service agents crawling all over us. I was honest."

"What was your next step?" Sean asked. "Once you decided to learn more about fires?"

"Actually, I'd decided *before* Marissa broke free for a day. I'd read about her close call. Then I ran into a wilderness buff who works as a consultant on sets. I figured it was meant to be. Portia introduced us, actually."

Grit felt a coolness run through him. "Did this wilderness buff point you in the right direction with smoke jumping?"

"Yeah. He knew about me and Marissa. He told me about Jo Harper and how she was from this little town in

Vermont and a guy she grew up with is a smoke jumper out here." Trent's color deepened as he glanced at Sean. "I went to your offices. You weren't there. Nick was, but I didn't get to talk to him."

"Does your script have anything to do with arson?" Grit asked.

"No. It's a tragic love story. Deep."

The guy was full of himself, Grit gave him that. "What's this wilderness buff's name? Where's he from?"

"I don't know where he's from. Here, I thought. His name's Feehan. Robert Feehan."

"And he sought you out," Sean said.

Trent nodded. "That's right."

"When did you see him last?" Grit asked.

"It's been a while." The actor and would-be screenwriter didn't miss a beat. "I've been up here living the life."

Grit didn't let up. "And Portia Martinez? When did you talk to her last? Did you call her, email—"

"I called her on Monday or Tuesday. I don't remember which. She said Feehan was there and had asked about me and smoke jumping, if I'd ever talked to Sean Cameron or Nick Martini."

"What did she tell him?"

"That she didn't know where I was. Which she didn't. Portia's impulsive. I can just see her showing up here—" He stopped himself, going pale again. "I can't believe she's dead."

Grit figured Trent's grief wouldn't last long. "What else did you tell her?"

"Nothing."

"Nah, come on, Trent," Grit said. "There's more."

He squirmed in his seat. "I told her I'd heard Nick was on his way East. Other smoke jumpers mentioned it." Trent's color quickly returned and he shrugged, proud. In the know. "Everyone here's tuned in to what went on in Vermont with the bombs and fires and stuff." He glanced up at Sean. "They know what you did."

Sean had lost any patience with Trent Stevens. Grit said, "This guy probably killed Portia that night. You're lucky he didn't know where you were and come up here kill you, too."

"He's not a movie set consultant?"

Grit shook his head. "Nope. Not a movie set consultant. Would you recognize him if you saw him again?"

"Probably."

Sean produced color printouts of photos Nick had sent him of Derek Cutshaw and Robert Feehan. He handed them to Trent.

Trent laid out the photos side by side on the table and frowned. "Wow, this is weird. Neither one is Feehan. Who are these guys?"

"They both were just killed in fires in Vermont," Sean said.

"The Feehan I met is about the same age as these two." Trent suddenly seemed to be a little in shock, trying to absorb the bad turn his morning had just taken. "He's tall, thin. Quiet. Kind of tentative. I was surprised he knew as much about wilderness skills and firefighting as he did."

Sean turned to Grit. "Whoever this guy is, it's not

the Robert Feehan who died yesterday. We need to get in touch with Jo. Marissa Neal's in danger."

Grit nodded. "So is everyone else in Black Falls."

Twenty-Seven

Black Falls, Vermont

Nick stood next to Rose's Jeep and squinted up the steep hill at a trail of footprints. Then he saw a streak of gold, and Ranger leaped off a boulder to him.

"Where's Rose?" He had no idea what the dog understood and opened up the Jeep, grabbed a scarf she'd left on the front seat and let Ranger smell it. "Find Rose."

The dog ran up into the dense woods. Nick grabbed a mallet from the Jeep. It was old, chipped. It had seen a lot of use among the waste-not Camerons. He tucked it in his jacket pocket. The mallet wasn't a gun but it would do as a weapon if he needed one. He'd talked to Sean on his way out there: "Whoever passed himself off as Robert Feehan had to be close in build and have access to Feehan's ID, as well as the have the freedom to move around the country."

Nick had pulled Robert Feehan's body out of the

burning cabin. He'd been tall and lean, with long hair with a bit of a wave.

Very much like his and Derek Cutshaw's quiet friend.

"We need to find Brett Griffin," he'd told Sean.

Nick followed Rose's retriever. They were off-trail, but footprints led in several different directions. Ranger bolted away from the tracks, down a narrow ravine. The snow was deep, and evergreens predominated. Sunlight didn't hit this part of Cameron Mountain often. Nick moved through the still shadows, the golden retriever taking him over the rough ground he and Rose knew so well, as focused on finding her as Nick was.

He refused to allow his fear to get hold of him. Brett Griffin was house-sitting nearby. His photography work allowed him to go anywhere in Black Falls without anyone thinking twice about running into him. He knew Derek Cutshaw and Robert Feehan, had manipulated them and used their failings to advance his own agenda.

And Brett had killed them.

A disorganized, impulsive arsonist was hard enough to track. An intelligent, patient sociopath who chose and planned his operations with detail and care would be damn near impossible.

Ranger paused, looking back at Nick.

Snow on a sheer rock face had been disturbed, as if something had rolled down from the top of the cliff. An icicle had broken off, just its base hanging from a chunk of jutting granite.

Nick didn't breathe. "Find Rose, Ranger," he said quietly. "Find her."

The dog barked again. Nick realized he was missing something.

Then he saw it—a glove in the snow under a hemlock. He picked it up.

A woman's glove.

"Rose," he called. "Where are you?"

She came around the hemlock then, her face red from cold, snow and exertion, her hair wet, dripping as she shivered. "I'm okay," she said. "I'm not hurt—"

Nick caught her in his arms. He didn't want to let her go. Not ever.

She clung to him. "You're so warm," she whispered, but stood back from him. "We have to find Brett before he kills anyone else."

"I know," Nick said.

"He's going after Marissa Neal. I'm sure he is. He plans to do it at winter fest. Maybe he still thinks he can pull it off."

"He knows how to take over someone's identity and disappear." Nick ran the tip of his finger under a scrape on Rose's forehead. "Did he hit you?"

"No. It's nothing. I think I took out an icicle when I jumped from up there." She glanced up at the rock cliff. "I didn't have many options. Brett faked a fall to get me to come to him. He didn't admit anything. He'll say I'm being hysterical."

"Is he armed?"

"I don't think so. He didn't have a pack with him. He could have hidden one, though."

"Elijah and Jo are right behind me. They'll have talked to Sean by now. He and Grit Taylor found Trent Stevens, the missing actor."

"Alive?"

Nick nodded. Ranger barked, the ridge of hair on his spine standing up. He growled, uncharacteristically. Nick saw the branches of another hemlock stir and immediately put himself between Rose and whoever was coming around the tree.

"Nick," she said, getting Ranger back to her side.

He eased the mallet out of his pocket. "I see."

Brett Griffin emerged from behind the hemlock, stumbling—pretending to—in the snow. "Rose, thank heaven. Are you all right? What happened?"

"Keep your hands where I can see them, Griffin," Nick said, raising the mallet. He wondered what this murderous pyromaniac had on under his jacket, in his pants, his gloves, his shoes. He'd want to get them close and then make his move. "I'm a real firefighter. I'll nail you in a heartbeat if you so much as breathe wrong."

Brett seemed mystified. "What did Rose tell you? I took a tumble and she was kind enough to come help me. Then she fell and I came down here to help her."

Rose was having none of it. "You bastard, you came down here to make sure I'd bashed my head against a rock and wouldn't get in your way anymore. Were you going to set me on fire if I wasn't dead?"

Brett straightened, wincing as if he were in pain. "I think I banged my knee pretty good. Rose, yeesh. What's got into you? I thought you were dead. You're damn lucky you're not. Was it something I said?"

Nick pointed the mallet at him. "Just stay still."

"Rose is hysterical." Brett sniffled as if he were winded. "I can see now that my friendship with Robert and Derek has finally come back to haunt me. I was afraid it would. I never should have come back to Black Falls."

"You can tell your story to the police," Nick said.

"Fine, I will. I'm not even insulted. Tell them I'll meet them at my house."

Nick couldn't detect any odor of gas in the crisp air. "You're good, Griffin. Jasper said you were. He said you know how fire works."

"I have no idea who you're talking about."

"Fire moves to find oxygen. It's like it's alive, isn't it?" Out of the corner of his eye, Nick noticed that Ranger had eased off into the woods, back down toward the road, undoubtedly on Rose's command. "To control fire and make it do what you want it to do takes real skill."

"I'm a photographer," Brett said calmly. "I don't know anything about fires. I'm not even that good at lighting a woodstove."

"Jasper Vanderhorn was a friend of mine," Nick said. "He was an arson investigator. You killed him. He was closing in on you, wasn't he? He wasn't just an irritant. He was a threat."

Brett continued playing his role as the meek, injured, misunderstood photographer. "I'm going home before I come down with hypothermia." He nodded to Rose. "You should, too. We can talk after you've had a chance to calm down. I know how jumpy everyone is around here. I am, too."

"We have you, Griffin," Nick said. "We know you stole Feehan's identity."

"You're talking crazy."

"You killed Robert Feehan and Derek Cutshaw. They were fools to you, weren't they? Nuisances who interfered with your plans."

"Just because you're a rich smoke jumper doesn't mean you can bully me."

"I'm not bullying you. I'm telling you. You were in California earlier this week. You killed Portia Martinez. You knew she'd figure out you weren't who you said you were. Had she already? Did she threaten to call the police?"

Brett steadied his gaze on Nick. "I've never heard of Portia Martinez."

"You've been worried about me for a while. Once Trent told Portia I was on my way East, you knew you had to act. But you always knew you'd kill Derek and Robert."

His eyes went cold. "I have work to do. I'm glad Rose is safe. Now leave me alone. I've tried to ignore the paranoia of the people here, but I'm done."

"Uh-uh," Nick said calmly. "Stay right where you are."

Brett turned to Rose. "Tell him, Rose. Tell him you don't suspect me of anything."

"Why did you come back to Black Falls?" she asked.

"I don't know now. It was a stupid move on my part, obviously. I don't recall any of you people asking about me or my life."

"You were here originally to keep an eye on Lowell, but you came back because of the Neals," she said. "How obsessed are you with Marissa? Enough to have pictures of her in your house up the road? I hope so. They'll be all Jo needs."

His eyes settled on her. "Just stay away from me."

She didn't relent. "Were you already a serial arsonist when you hooked up with Lowell? How many fires had you set? How many people had you killed already?"

Brett laughed. "You are such fools." His eyes gleamed. "Do you think I don't have a contingency plan? There's a bomb at the café. It's just like the ones I taught Lowell to build. Not in person, of course. He has no idea who his fire and bomb expert is. You let me go about my business and I don't set off the bomb. I let you find it. Be heroes."

Nick stepped toward him. "How do you plan to set it off?"

He held up his left hand. "Dead man's switch in my glove."

Nick knew it was possible. He saw that Rose knew, too. She gulped in a breath. "Nick."

"Don't get too cocky, Griffin," Nick said and decided on his own bluff. "Elijah Cameron's at the café. He headed straight there after Grit Taylor and Sean reported in about Trent Stevens. Think a Special Forces master sergeant is going to miss your little bomb? Other people know about bombs around here. You're not that special."

He knew that would get Brett. "Trent Stevens is a self-absorbed idiot. He knows nothing about fires. He was happy to brag about Marissa Neal. Her fire was an accident. Jo Harper's heroics saved the day."

"That's how you became obsessed with Marissa Neal," Rose said.

Brett inhaled through his nose. "Don't think you've won."

"What're you going to do," Nick said, "set yourself on fire?"

Brett snapped his elbow against his side. Nick smelled gas and realized Brett had broken open some kind of container under his jacket.

He remembered Jasper's words a year ago: "This guy will want to go out in a blaze of glory. No prison for him."

Moving fast, Nick leaped to Brett just as flames erupted from inside his jacket, flashing brightly against the white and gray landscape. He locked his eyes on Nick in defiance.

Unimpressed, Nick dropped Brett with the mallet and shoved him facedown into the snow, snuffing out the fire in a matter of seconds.

There was no dead man's switch in Brett's glove.

Rose was barely breathing. "You knew he was bluffing."

Nick winked up at her. "Myrtle Smith survived one of this bastard's fires. She lives above the café. Think she doesn't sweep the place for bombs?"

"She told you?"

"Yep."

"That Myrtle," Rose said, just as Ranger reappeared along with her two brothers and Jo Harper, her gun drawn, right behind him.

Twenty-Eight

Beverly Hills, California

Three days later, Nick was stretched out on a lounge chair at Sean's pool in the Southern California sun. Grit Taylor was there. Sean and Hannah. Beth Harper, still.

Grit stood at the edge of the pool in his cargo pants and lightweight sweatshirt and glanced back at Nick. "The mountains of northern New England call, don't they? You and Rose are a smart and dedicated pair, and you're rich. You'll figure it out."

"What's rich got to do with it?" Nick asked him.

Grit shrugged. "The transcontinental thing. Vermont and California. Long way between them."

"You must have been hell on a battlefield."

"Us navy boys," Grit said with a grin.

Sean was more pensive. "Jasper didn't screw up. Neither did we. He got beat by a bad guy."

"Jasper was right about a serial arsonist," Nick said.

"Brett enjoyed setting fires, but he was never a firefighter or tried to become one. It wasn't that he could or couldn't cut it."

"Jasper never suspected you, Nick," Sean said. "Or at least not for more than three seconds."

Three seconds too many, but Nick didn't blame Jasper. He blamed Brett Griffin. "Griffin was from Chicago. Abusive father, narcissistic mother."

Grit glanced around at them. "So? No excuses."

Nick nodded. "His photography allowed him to move freely. He started passing himself off as Feehan last year. He'd already been contracting his services as part of Lowell Whittaker's network. Griffin's the only one of Lowell's killers to figure out who he was."

"Griffin knew the Whittakers had a place in Black Falls," Sean said. "He's why Lowell panicked. Lowell knew he had a committed arsonist on his hands who'd kill him if he left any loose ends. I doubt Lowell had any idea who it was."

"Griffin manipulated Derek Cutshaw and Robert Feehan." Nick pushed back images of their two burned bodies. "Scott Thorne and Jo found pictures at Griffin's house that he'd taken of Rose with me last June. We figure he used them to get under Cutshaw's skin. He and Feehan were asking too many questions, becoming a problem with their drug-dealing."

"Griffin used your arrival in Black Falls as a way to get rid of them and give you Jasper's firebug," Sean said.

Grit looked up from the pool. "Griffin had an excuse to set those fires. More fun for him."

Nick rolled to his feet, restless. "He liked being apart, watching the action."

The SEAL stared again at the clear water of the pool. "He loved the drama he created."

"He made sure that boy wandered off last year." Nick remembered the alert going out, having no idea then, that Rose would be the one who found the boy, or even would be a part of the organized search for him. "He wasn't supposed to survive. He and Rose were supposed to die in the same fire as Jasper."

"Brett liked the drama," Grit said, "and he liked showing up you smoke jumpers. You two played a key role in stopping that fire from spreading."

Beth finally spoke. "Jasper Vanderhorn died, but Brett didn't want what he saw as a partial victory. You and Rose spoiled his fun." Her turquoise eyes leveled on Nick. "When do you go back to Vermont?"

He didn't answer, just picked up his keys and left.

He drove over to his condo in a high-rise just off Wilshire Boulevard.

They'd caught Lowell's most elusive and mysterious killer. It was over.

Nick walked into his bedroom and everything there reminded him of Rose.

Hell, he thought. Nothing was over.

Grit drove with Beth Harper down to Coronado, showing her where he'd trained. "I was a different man then. A kid, really."

"You got the name Grit here?"

"Yeah."

"Who gave it to you?"

"Another SEAL. We trained together. Michael Ferrerra."

Beth's eyes were clear, and she didn't look away. "He's the SEAL who died in the firefight that almost killed you and Elijah."

"We called him Moose."

Grit took winding roads to a simple neighborhood in San Diego. Moose's widow was on the front steps of her stucco bungalow, waving a bubble wand for a baby boy, less than a year old, sitting on a blanket. The baby grinned and tried to catch the bubbles as they floated above him.

"His name's Ryan Cameron Ferrerra," Grit said as he slowed the car.

When he looked at Beth this time, she was crying.

He continued past the house and on to Beverly Hills. He and Elijah would visit Moose's widow when the time was right.

Finally he glanced over at Beth, still red-eyed from her tears. "You're finally going home, aren't you?" he asked her.

She nodded.

"Charlie Neal found out his sister Marissa has a crush on your brother Zack," Grit said.

"Are you bothered?"

"Nope."

"There's someone out there for you, Grit."

"I believe that. I didn't a while ago. I do now." He smiled at her. "Thank you."

* * *

Beth flew back to Black Falls with Sean and Hannah the next day. Grit stayed in San Diego to finish his navy business. She wasn't sure anyone would figure him out, but someone, surely, would fall in love with him. She'd never met a better man.

She entered Three Sisters Café. It was cleaning night. Bowie, Dominique, Myrtle and Rose were there. Myrtle was going home to South Carolina. Her niece was having a baby. Myrtle wanted to be there. She insisted she only stayed in Black Falls as long as she did because she liked being around other people who were home.

She was trying to talk Jo and Elijah into buying her house in D.C., furnishings and all—except her teacup collection. That would go with her to South Carolina.

Jo had finally decided that the cabins on the lake had to come down.

Not everything was meant to last forever.

Beth dipped a sponge into a bucket of hot water. Scott would sometimes join her for cleaning night.

In the past, anyway.

Liam O'Rourke walked into the café. He was hesitant at first, but then Dominique smiled as Beth had never seen her smile before and ran to him.

Rose's jaw dropped. "Bowie! You let us all think—"

"I was running interference for them. They're buying the Whit—the estate on the river, turning it back into a working farm. Cows, pigs, chickens, horses and gardens." The big stonemason grinned. "Life."

Dominique already had spoken to Beth and Hannah about starting the dinner service Myrtle had been pushing for. Maybe, Beth thought, her friend and Liam were already planning for their "farm" to provide meat and produce for Three Sisters Café and O'Rourke's.

Beth was sponging down a table by the river when the main door to the café opened again. Scott came inside, dressed in jeans and a canvas jacket. She could tell he was holding his breath. He had no idea what she'd do, which had caused tension between them. Now, she didn't care. She couldn't stand it anymore.

She threw down her sponge and started to run to him, but he got to her first and lifted her off her feet, kissing her right there in front of everyone.

Twenty-Nine

Black Falls, Vermont—early March

Rose heard laughter and smiled as she snowshoed across the meadow to the sugar shack. Winter fest weekend had begun, and a crowd had gathered over an outdoor fire in the old stone fireplace. After a cold spell and a major snowstorm, the sap had been running for the past few days. They'd collected it and now were boiling it down, most inside in the new evaporating pan but some in a big pot outside.

All just for fun on a bright, gorgeous late-winter day.

Grit Taylor had arrived back in Black Falls, at least for the moment, and was by the fire with Elijah. All the Neals were there, including Charlie, who looked smug and pleased as he watched Marissa sneak looks at Grit.

The Neal entourage of Secret Service agents kept a close eye on Charlie especially.

Sean, Hannah, A.J. and Lauren were running things inside the sugar shack, taking turns keeping an eye on Jim and Baylee.

Rose eased in next to Jo in front of the sugar shack. "It's the second-eldest sister with the crush on Zack," Jo said, sighing. "As if my life's complicated enough. Charlie was very clever in his misinformation campaign with Grit and Marissa. He made them both see what was in front of them. Where's Nick?"

Rose didn't try to contain her surprise. "Nick? Why are you asking me?"

Jo gave her a slight smile. "You've changed in the past few weeks, Rose. It's subtle, but we've all noticed. I have a feeling there's less solitude in your future."

"And you think that has something to do with Nick Martini."

"We all do. You've always been content living on your own on the mountain, doing your work, but you withdrew this past year. You needed to, I guess, to cope." Jo directed her gaze at the people laughing in the steam of the bubbling maple sap, but her attention was still on Rose. "A.J., Elijah and Sean are there for you."

"I know that," she said quietly.

Jo turned to her again. "And you're there for them. You all are still a family. You're just not demonstrative."

"Which you understand, being a Harper."

"True," Jo said with a laugh.

"None of this has anything to do with Nick."

"It has everything to do with him. You're in love with him, Rose."

She smelled sweet maple in the late-winter air and smiled. "Yes, I am."

Jo seems satisfied. "Good for you." Her expression softened. "I want you to be among the first to know. Elijah and I are getting married this spring up at the falls. Reverend McBane's agrees to perform the ceremony."

"That's terrific news, Jo," Rose said. "I can't wait."

"I can't, either. Between my friends and Elijah's, we'll fill up the lodge. It'll be good for business—"

"It'll be a lot of fun."

Jo looked pleased. "That, too."

Rose heard Hannah's laughter inside the sugar shack, then Sean's, and smiled at Jo. "I have a feeling yours won't be the only Cameron wedding this year."

Nick got a different room at Black Falls Lodge, one with a view of Cameron Mountain.

Maybe the Cameron brothers were trying to send him a message.

He gave the ghost of Drew Cameron a little salute and changed into the suit he'd brought with him from California. It was black, expensive and appropriate for Beverly Hills or the Black Falls Lodge ballroom.

He hoped it'd rock one Rose Cameron back on her heels.

When he entered the ballroom, he had no trouble spotting her in the crowd. She was standing by a window looking out at the starlit meadow behind the lodge.

He was aware of all three Cameron brothers watching him as he made his way to their sister. He liked that they were a strong family and looked after each other.

Rose was wearing a sleek dark blue dress that outlined her shape and would work just fine in Beverly Hills as well as at Black Falls Lodge. She turned, and broke into a smile as he came closer. "Nick," she said. "Couldn't resist bidding on the quilt, could you?"

Nick had noticed several Black Falls locals gathered at the quilt, hanging at the entrance to the ballroom, and overheard them swearing they recognized this or that piece of fabric from a grandmother, a grandfather, an old uncle or aunt.

He winked at Rose. "I think it'd go just fine in my condo."

Those Cameron blue eyes fastened on him. "You're not here for the quilt."

He smiled. "No, I'm not. May I have this dance?"

She lifted the hem of her dress, and he saw she was wearing black high heels. He was more interested in the shape of her ankle. She laughed, sounding just a little breathless. "If I trip in these things—"

"I'll catch you," he said, and whisked her onto the dance floor.

After two dances, Rose went off with Lauren, Beth, Hannah, Dominique and Jo to help with the silent auction. She saw Nick slip out of the ballroom. She had no idea what he was up to next but couldn't take her eyes off him.

The man was as rugged and sexy as ever, and he had her head spinning.

After the auction and everyone started to leave, her

friends and family all but threw her out and told her to go home. They'd take care of any cleaning up.

When she arrived at her house, there were no other cars in her dark driveway.

"Looks as if it'll be just Ranger and me tonight," she said to herself.

She went in through the back and noticed the warmth.

Someone had lit the woodstove.

She walked into the living room, and Nick was there, stretched out on her couch with Ranger on his bed by the woodstove.

"Locks, Rose," Nick said, shaking his head. "Locks."

He was in jeans and a soft-looking sweater, and he had her head spinning even more. But she frowned at Ranger. "Some watchdog you are."

Her golden retriever yawned at her, then rolled onto his side and went back to sleep.

Nick was on his feet. "All these months, I beat myself up for taking advantage of you last June."

"You didn't—"

"I know." He locked his eyes with hers and smiled. "I didn't take advantage of you. I fell in love with you."

"Nick."

It was all she had a chance to say as he lifted her into his arms and carried her to the bedroom. Outside her window, Cameron Mountain was outlined against the stars, and she pictured Jo and Elijah and Hannah and Sean, and herself now, with Nick, and she knew that her father was at peace.

"I belong with you," Nick said as he laid her on the bed. "That's all that matters to me."

"I love you, Nick," she whispered. "Always and forever."

* * * * *